Dirty 20

Also by Bill Schweigart

The Guilty One
The Devil's Colony
Northwoods
The Beast of Barcroft
Slipping the Cable

Dirty 20

A Novel

Bill Schweigart

HYPERION AVENUE
LOS ANGELES NEW YORK

First Edition, May 2026

10 9 8 7 6 5 4 3 2 1

FAC-004510-26057

Printed in the United States of America

Designed by LeeAnn Falciani

Illustrations © Adobe Stock

Library of Congress Control Number: 2025950077

ISBN 978-1-368-11457-8

The authorized representative in the EU for product safety and compliance is Disney Trading B.V., Asterweg 15S, 1031 HL, Amsterdam, The Netherlands

email: DCP.DL-EU.bookscontact@disney.com

www.HyperionAvenueBooks.com

Logo Applies to Text Stock Only

For Kate, Sidney, and Samaira—
living proof that magic exists

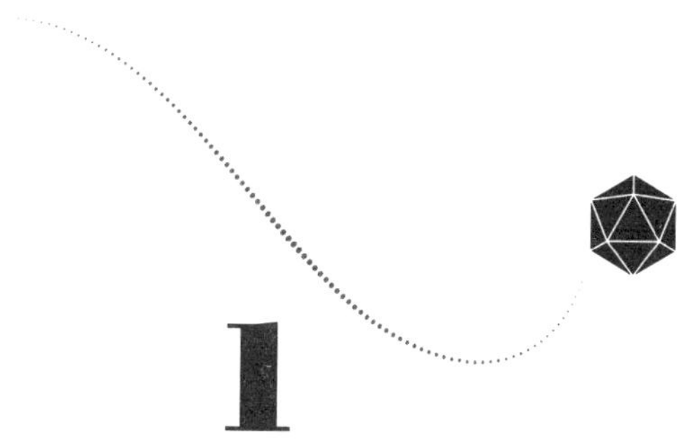

1

Tommy Fugue, son of Don Alessandro "Big Al" Fugue, stood with his accomplice before the scarred door of a loft downtown, mask in hand, psyching himself up for what came next.

Nino "Nine Ball" Dylan was a young up-and-comer, already one of Don Fugue's best soldiers at the age of twenty. He was a details guy who left nothing to chance, checking and rechecking his work . . . and then checking and rechecking again. And again. Dressed in a smart black suit, a crisp white shirt, and a black tie, Nine had his long black hair tied back in a ponytail, nary a lock out of place. He clutched a black Kabuki demon mask with silver accents. He looked slick and deadly. If anything, *he* looked like the son Don Fugue really wanted.

Tommy clutched his own samurai mask, red with horns. But looking at his partner, he suddenly wished he had put more effort into the rest of his appearance. While Nine looked like he had stepped straight out of a yakuza nightmare, or at least a cool anime, Tommy looked like he was wearing a half-assed costume. Which, he supposed, he was. White Hoka slides, checkered pajama pants, and a black hoodie. The only heart he would strike fear into would belong to a tailor.

Nine donned his mask, completing his look. Cool to ice cold.

"You look good," said Tommy.

The demon face bobbed down, then back up in scrutiny. The grinning black-and-silver mask slightly muffled the reply: "You look homeless."

"The proper term is *unhoused*."

The mask meant Tommy couldn't see—only sense—Nine rolling his eyes.

"Dress for the job you want," said the soldier.

Tommy knew his partner was just as nervous as he was. Probably more so, but the young man was conditioned not to show it. Still, his irritation was a tell.

"You're not helping, Nine."

"You want help? Stand up straight. Roll your shoulders back, stick out your chest. Chin up. You are the son of *Don Alessandro Fugue*, for fuck's sake."

Tommy pointed at Nine's mask. "Remember, anonymity is the point here."

"Then say it without saying it." He thumped Tommy on the chest. "Carry yourself like a man, okay?"

Tommy rolled his shoulders back, puffed out his chest. Jutted out his chin. Still felt ridiculous.

"Better," said Nine. "Now we are going in there and we are going to fuck them up. They are not going to know what hit them."

"Right," said Tommy.

Nine patted the small of his back reflexively, reassuring himself his piece was still there. By Tommy's count it was the third time he had done so.

"Keep that shit out of sight," he said.

The demon face stared at him, wordless.

Finally, Nine said, "You telling me my business?"

"Sorry. Nerves. No offense."

"None taken. Besides, it's not my kill. Remember what you need to do?"

"I know."

"Say it."

"Mozambique drill," said Tommy.

"That's right." Nine tapped two fingers over Tommy's heart for emphasis. "Two here." Then he tapped two fingers to Tommy's temple. "One here. Then we're ghosts. You ready?"

Tommy pulled his mask over his face and nodded. He reached up to rap on the door, but his partner seized his hand. The black demon mask shook from side to side, its silver horns slicing the air. "Amateur."

Nine turned the doorknob and shoved the scarred door open, standing still for one dramatic moment, taking in the scene with care.

Electronica, laughter, and smoke spilled out into the hallway.

"After you," said Nine, gesturing for Tommy to enter.

The loft was in the River North Art District, or RiNo, just a couple of miles north of the Denver's Auraria campus, but it felt like a world, and an age, away. The building had been converted from an old textile plant, and the unit was huge, with soaring cathedral ceilings and exposed piping. The neighborhood—surrounded by jazz clubs, brewpubs, art galleries, and working studios—was way cooler than the downtown campus. RiNo was a hive of creativity; artists, winemakers, and small batch coffee roasters abounded. Street murals decorated every facade.

It was very different from the Commerce City part of the Denver metro area where Tommy grew up. Not that he felt quite at home there, either.

Inside the airy loft, people floated by as if from a different time. Women in faux feather shawls and hooded cloaks. Men in steampunk Victorian tailcoats. Dry ice crept in from somewhere; vapor trailed everyone's movements in curlicues. Light filtered through the hazy rings in colorful bursts and patches, making the whole room a living thing.

"Whoa," said Nine. "I was expecting togas and mullet wigs and superhero onesies. This is, like, classy and shit."

Tommy looked over at his accomplice. Nine had been bracing for the worst. Even through the mask, he could see the young man's shoulders relax, relieved that this was not the foul dorm party that Tommy normally dragged him to: Spilled beer and sticky floors, skunk weed, and, inevitably, someone getting sick. Usually several someones.

"See? I told you this would be different. This isn't your plebeian costume party. This is an *art student masquerade*."

Recovering his detachment, Nine pointed to the keg in the corner. "This way, Picasso."

At the keg Nine took station at the pump, expertly filling a red cup with zero head and passing it to Tommy before pouring another for himself.

"Come on, Nine, you have to admit, this is way better than hanging out with Pop and his hangers-on in some pool hall or the back office of some restaurant."

Nine turned to Tommy.

"That's the thing, Tommy. Don Fugue could be in a strip club or the supermarket, it doesn't matter. When you have that kind of rizz, you don't need special effects, and you definitely don't need costumes. He *is* the party."

Tommy was used to people revering his father. Despite the whole crew's regular taunts, Big Al registered value in Nine's OCD, something the soldier's real family never appreciated.

Tommy clapped him on the shoulder and tried to sound cheerful. "You're going to have fun, I promise."

"Just do your thing, Tommy Gun. I'll circulate. After you take care of business, maybe I'll take you to a real party."

Tommy looked around the large, open space until he spotted the hostess, the gem at the center of it all. She looked like she'd stepped out of *The Great Gatsby*. As he shuffled toward the knot of people surrounding her, he marveled at her retro dress—iridescent sequins, whorls like a peacock, looping strands of beads. Every movement, every turn of her head, the slightest shift of weight sent a cascade of shimmers rolling across her body. She accented the dress with long evening gloves and a string of pearls. Her lips were red, her hair pulled up, the nape of her neck bare and beguiling. No matter what part of her Tommy focused on, he could only stare for a second or two at most before he had to look away, find something else to pretend to enjoy. Like staring into the sun, she was too dazzling to take in all at once.

Sanse.

The hostess turned her head toward Tommy and his resin mask and pajama pants. When he saw the question in her eyes, he quickly pulled the mask from his face.

"Oh." Sanse laughed. "It's you!"

"That dress," he said, gesturing toward her with both hands. "That's a work of art."

That's one to the chest, thought Tommy.

Tommy's plan to win Sanse over was to go to the party, say hello, be cool, make a good impression. Become friendly. Spend more time with her in class. Play it safe, get comfortable, then make the jump somewhere down the line. Essentially a ten-part plan that maybe would let him somehow back in to asking her out. But when Tommy'd mentioned Sanse, Nine had insisted on speed and ruthless efficiency. Two to the chest: Pay her two compliments that warm her heart. Then one to the head: Ask her out.

Though comparing asking Sanse out to a close-quarters shooting technique was mildly disturbing, Tommy conceded Nine's plan had merit. It saved time and kept him from overthinking things in step seven of his original plan, which invariably led to him not finishing the plan at all.

"Aw, thank you, Tommy. I made it myself."

"Really?" he said. The beadwork, the sewing, the intricacy... *What the hell is she doing in Denver?* "That's incredible."

"I'm just fucking with you," she said. "I found it in a thrift store on Larimer Street." She twirled, sending beads spinning and sequins sparkling. "Still, pretty cool, though, right?"

She was like a human disco ball, sending out shards of light that danced across the faces of everyone nearby.

"Yeah," he said. "Pretty cool."

"And who are you supposed to be?"

"Unhoused samurai."

"Dress for the job you want."

Ask her out, he thought. *Right fucking now.*

Seeing her like this, talking to her, Tommy suddenly sensed you didn't hesitate with a dazzling girl like Sanse. Nor did you play it cool. Hopeless as it may be, you reached out and tried to catch that fleeting light before it spun away.

"Sanse, I was thinking—"

Just then, someone bumped him from behind. It felt like he had been hit by a Ford F-150. Worse, it pushed him right into Sanse, and his beer onto her dress.

2

Sanse's mouth widened into a large, silent O. Then she exploded.

"Asshole!"

Tommy tried to stammer an apology. "Sanse, I'm so—"

But she was looking past him. "Todd, you *fucking clod*!"

Tommy had been so fixated on Sanse's reaction that he hadn't even seen the large block of a man standing nearby. His corn-fed cheeks were flush with drink and his face was split into a shit-eating grin.

He put a meaty paw on Tommy's shoulder. "Sorry about that. You weren't making a move on my girl, were you?"

Flapping beer off her bare arms, Sanse practically growled. "Todd, I am *not* your girl."

Todd clapped Tommy on the back, setting off another minor eruption from the dregs in his cup. "I'm just fucking with you, little guy."

Coming back to himself, Tommy looked around and saw Nine Ball knifing through the crowd. Black suit, black tie, the black-and-silver face of a demon. He imagined Nine's hidden expression mirrored the fearsome, fanged grin of the mask. He gave a small wave, imperceptible to all but the soldier, and the demon abruptly changed course and veered away.

“I’m Tommy,” he said, holding out his hand to the larger man. “You must be Todd.”

Todd gripped Tommy’s hand in his own paw. “Sanse’s told you about me?”

“No . . . but she did just say, ‘Todd, you fucking clod.’ ”

Corn-fed’s cheeks grew a little ruddier and his grip tightened. Tommy did his best not to react. He wished he hadn’t ordered Nine to stand down so quickly. But, finally, the larger man released his grip, leaving Tommy wanting to gasp.

Just then he felt someone slip something in his free hand. He looked down and saw a clean dish towel, procured from the kitchen by someone who hates a mess. By a good wingman.

“Sanse, please,” said Tommy, “allow me.”

Tommy lightly dabbed her arms, then thought better of it and handed the towel over.

“See, Todd?” said Sanse. “This is how a gentleman acts. I spent hours on this beadwork and sewing and you just doused me in Coors Light.”

“Oh shit, girl. I didn’t realize . . .”

Sanse winked at Tommy, who bit down a smile.

“Well, don’t just stand there, you dumb redwood, get me more towels!” she said with a fling of her arm.

Todd stomped off, bumping more costumed guests and spilling more beer in his broad wake. It was only after he was out of earshot that Sanse started to laugh.

It was a beautiful laugh, musical. Wet with beer, her dress twinkled all the more.

“This dress,” she said, dabbing herself with the towel. “So dumb.”

Tommy sensed he had to start over. Todd had broken his rhythm. Desperate, he blurted, “You look like a chandelier.”

She stopped wiping and looked at him sideways. "That better be a compliment."

"You're shimmering. And floating above the rest of us."

Her lips parted in surprise. It was more of a compliment than she had bargained for. And more than he'd intended to give. Time seemed to slow. The rest of the room receded. The music muffled. They were in a bubble of two—

Then his father's voice sounded from somewhere in the back of his mind. Poker lessons when he was a little kid. Five years old, when he'd rather play Go Fish.

Quit tipping your hand, kid. You're giving everything away.

"What I'm trying to say is you should take off your dress and hang it from the ceiling."

Sanse laughed again and touched his chest. It short-circuited his brain.

"You're so corny, Tommy. . . ."

He was on safe ground again. Tommy the funny guy. As much as he loved her musical laugh, he was furious with himself for it. They'd had a moment. Not a long one, but he had felt it. And he was pretty sure she had too.

Chickenshit.

Just then, her face brightened, and she lunged forward. For a rapturous moment, Tommy thought she might grab a fistful of his hoodie and pull him toward her for a hungry kiss, but she pulled a short student into their orbit instead. Hopes dashed, Tommy fought hard to keep a genial smile on his face at the interloper.

"Tommy, there's someone I wanted to introduce you to. This is Ani DeLandro."

"Anibal," said the newcomer. Standing a few inches shorter than Tommy, Anibal wore a gold medal around his neck, and a loaf of bread dangled from his hand. He looked Tommy up and

down, appraising him. It agitated Tommy, until he remembered that he was at a costume party.

"Only my mother and pretty girls are allowed to call me Ani," he said. But in the end he stuck his hand out. "No offense."

Tommy shook it. The kid had a firm grip, but blessedly not as firm as Todd's.

"None taken." Tommy gave a curt nod. "What are you supposed to be, Anibal?"

"A breadwinner."

Despite himself, Tommy laughed.

"Wait. Is that *my* bread?" asked Sanse.

Anibal shrugged. "I plead the Fifth."

"Despite his abysmally lazy costume," said Sanse, "Ani is the most amazing illustrator I've ever met. He's currently crowd-funding his own comic."

"No shit," said Tommy, impressed. Tommy loved comics. As a kid, he'd dreamed of becoming a penciler. He was a decent artist, though nothing like his mother. Once he had seen her drawings, he realized he needed to find another medium. "Like FunFunder or something? That's cool as hell."

"Is it?" asked Sanse, turning to Anibal. "Selling your soul?"

"I mean, I'm asking a good price."

Despite the interruption, Tommy found that he liked Anibal. Just being in Sanse's orbit yielded positive outcomes, like meeting her cool, comic-creating friends.

As a counterpoint, Todd the Orc returned, bumping Tommy from behind again, this time intentionally. He pushed himself into the tight circle of Tommy, Sanse, and Anibal and thrust a full roll of paper towels at Sanse.

"How gallant," she said.

Even over the music, Tommy heard Anibal's aggravated sigh.

"Catch you later," said the artist.

Tommy thrust his hand out again. "Good to meet you, man. Would love to hear more about your comic sometime."

Anibal gave him another once-over, only this time, his appraisal seemed positive. He nodded, one side of his mouth ticking upward. "Anytime, man."

Tommy turned back to Sanse. He didn't think her oversize pet would stand for Tommy re-creating their moment, let alone asking her out. Any spell created had been shattered, and if he was being honest, he had shattered it himself. He knew when to cut his losses.

"Cool party, Sanse," Tommy said. "Really. And the dress you made *from scratch* is fire. All the work you put into it really shows."

Sanse gave a side-eye to Todd, then smiled at Tommy. "Thank you for acknowledging the many hours I put into this, Tommy. And it's only 4.2 percent alcohol by volume."

Todd took a big pull from his beer.

"You look lovely," said Tommy. No one used the word *lovely* anymore. But it was occasionally thrown around in the old gangster movies and musicals that had always been playing in the house when he was growing up. The word seemed roaring twenties appropriate and not a compliment he imagined Todd capable of ever delivering.

Sanse touched her hand to her chest. At least his second compliment found its mark.

As Todd stammered another apology, Tommy nodded, donned his samurai mask, and faded into the crowd.

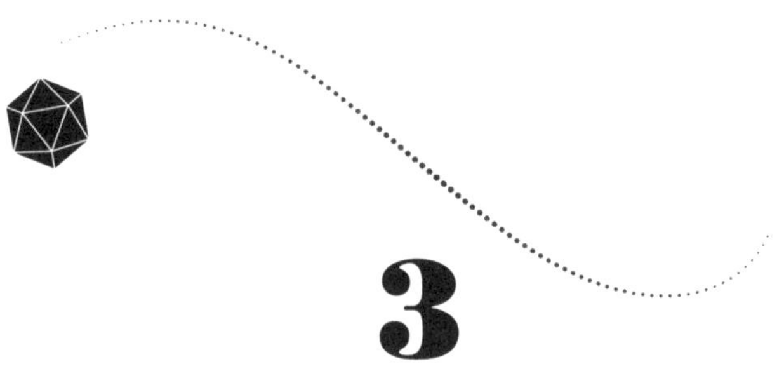

3

Thirty minutes later, Tommy and Nine Ball sat opposite each other on the patio of the RiNo CrackBurger.

Tommy salted his sorrows with fries.

Nine munched a burger. After every bite, he took a napkin from the neat pile in front of him and dabbed his mouth, the thought of an unseen dollop of ketchup too much to bear.

"Did you shoot your shot, player? *Pop. Pop,*" he said, cupping his hands together as if pointing a pistol at Tommy's chest. Then he raised his invisible weapon to Tommy's forehead. *"Pop."*

"You do get that *hitting on* a girl is not the same thing as a *hit,* right?"

"That sounds like a no. . . ."

"We had a moment," said Tommy.

"I knew you'd punk out."

"For real. We, like, locked eyes."

"Wow," said Nine, gaping at Tommy, "you made eye contact with another human being. Reminds me of my favorite movie: *When Harry Eyed Sally.*"

"I know a moment and it was a moment."

"See Anything."

"There was chemistry, I swear."

"Casa-blink-a . . . Wait, give me a minute. . . ."

"Like you'd have done any better."

"If it was me, Tommy Gun, she would've left her own party with *this kid*." He eyed his burger, then took a massive bite. "Furburger and a side of thighs . . ." Mouth impossibly full, nevertheless he laughed as soon as he said it.

Tommy laughed too. "Bullshit. You'd make her brush her teeth and take a decon shower first, you weirdo."

Nine narrowed his eyes. Immediately, Tommy realized he had overstepped and caused offense. Nine did revere order—everything tidy and in its place, at ninety-degree angles and dust free—and he had zero tolerance for chaos, but he was sensitive about his OCD.

Uncle Chongo had revealed that Nine Ball, when he was the youngest soldier, had been made to rack the balls when the captains shot pool. At the end of a game, he would hop to and corral the balls again into their triangular rack. But it wasn't enough for Nine to place them in order. He had to adjust every billiard ball, numbers centered and facing skyward, and the stripes perfectly parallel to each other. Only then, once the billiard balls were restored to order and he had touched them once more for good measure, would he carefully remove the rack as if he were defusing a bomb or playing the game Operation. When Don Fugue clocked this compulsive behavior, he called the soldier "Nine Ball." Eight Ball plus one extra touch, he cracked. A lame joke, but when Big Al made a joke, even an offhand one, everyone guffawed. The name stuck. As his own self-appointed nickname "the Al Mighty" persisted, so did "Nine Ball."

"That's ableist, Uncle Bud," Tommy had said to Chongo.

"What . . ." said Bud, taking a hit from a joint, holding it, then releasing it in a luxurious exhale, ". . . is that?"

Bud was his father's accountant, as close to an uncle as

Tommy ever had, and, for his abiding love of THC, another recipient of a nickname from the Al Mighty: Chongo.

Tommy continued, "Making fun of someone who, like, can't help it."

"Is he?" asked Chongo, waving smoke, or Tommy's notions, away. "Making fun?"

Tommy didn't know if Chongo was really asking or if this was another of his stoned-ass hypotheticals. *If a tree falls in the woods and there's no one to hear it, is it a sound? If a body falls in the woods and there's no one to witness it, is it a crime?*

"Because of his OCD."

Chongo shrugged. "Big Al busts the balls of those he loves most."

Tommy thought about this, tallying all the verbal slings and arrows his father directed his way. His every compliment backhanded and every affirmation qualified, Big Al Fugue made no secret of his disappointment in his slacker son. Did this catalog of slights mean that Big Al loved him most of all?

"What's his nickname for you?" asked Chongo.

"Failure?"

Chongo spread his arms like in a benediction, the smoke from his joint trailing his fingers like incense.

"The Al Mighty giveth and He taketh away."

And now Tommy was making fun of Nine too, piling on, no better than his father and his capos.

"Hey, Nine, I'm—"

"Not you," said Nine, now staring over Tommy's shoulder. "The *clod*."

Tommy turned around and saw Todd entering the CrackBurger, loud and obnoxious, and flanked by two hangers-on. The larger man moved through the world like a clumsy bear snapping saplings and ransacking campsites, either completely unaware of or totally untroubled by the smaller woodland creatures that darted out of his way. A lumbering nuisance.

"Let's get out of here," said Tommy.

"Relax, it's a nice night," said Nine, waving away Tommy's concern. "Look, I know you. You probably have it all worked out in your head. Get to know this girl, cozy up to her in class, become friends. Then, after months or a year or whatever, *then* you'll make your move. And said move will be timid and imperceptible, and too little too late. You'll be so deep in the friend zone by then it'll take a submersible to find you."

"Ah," said Tommy, raising a finger. "You forgot. Perhaps after months of meticulous planning, *she* will make a move on *me*."

"You're not playing hard to get, Tommy." With a flash of his teeth, Nine sheared a french fry in half. "You're playing hard to want."

"Fine. You've effectively shamed me, Romeo. What would you do?"

"First off, the only time I would leave my apartment in my pajamas is if there was a fire in the middle of the night."

"You're zero help."

"A girl like that? Someone else is going to swoop in." Nine looked at his watch for emphasis. "If they haven't already. You want honesty? The world owes you nothing. You know I mean no disrespect to your father, but you've had it pretty easy."

Tommy considered this. "Debatable, but go on. What would you have me do?"

"Man up."

"Strength has nothing to do with gender, and shaming never works."

"I'm talking *direct action*. If you want to ask a girl out, ask her the fuck out. No preamble, no qualifications. Don't spend a year becoming her best friend. It's like your father says: A good plan violently executed now is better than a perfect plan executed next week."

"He stole that from General Patton."

Nine shrugged. "Whatever. Carpe fucking diem. You are the son of Don Alessandro Fugue." His gaze flickered over Tommy's shoulder.

"I'm well aware. He never lets me forget it. And neither do you."

"Don Alessandro Fugue is a great man."

Tommy made prayer hands, closed his eyes, and made a beatific face. "The Al Mighty . . ."

"Be a dick," Nine said with a scoff. "But if your father wanted to ask a girl out, he wouldn't tie himself in knots over it. And if she said no, which she wouldn't, he wouldn't 'woe is me' for months, I can tell you that."

"I'm well aware my father can pull women," said Tommy, putting a little steel in his voice. "It's the being faithful and holding on to them that are tricky for him."

Nine looked at his soda cup a little too long. Tommy's mother, Vittoria, had run off a year ago. "Look," he said finally, "I'm just saying, don't wait for your ship to come in. Swim out and meet it."

"Sounds dangerous. Sharks, rip currents . . ."

"Asshole."

"Jellyfish . . . And when was the last time we ate in this scenario, because cramps . . ."

Nine pushed himself from the table. "I'm out of napkins."

"I have a whole stack right here. Next to my life jacket . . ."

"Sit tight, *Nothing Hill.*"

Something in Nine Ball's devilish smile made Tommy spin in his seat, which is how he realized the gangster was striding right toward Todd the Clod.

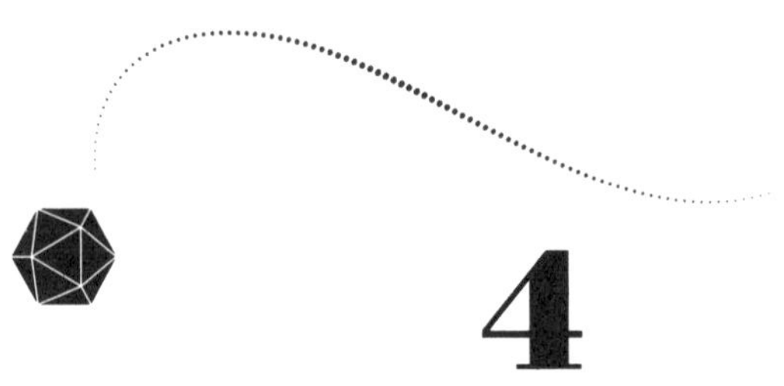

4

Once, when Tommy was eight years old, he was picked up from school by two of his father's associates. Instead of going home, the men brought Tommy to a mall. They took him to a comic-book shop, then an arcade, then bought him a stuffed bunny at the toy store. It was a great afternoon, until he turned around to find the men gone. He had been left all alone, and a nice lady at the toy store had to call the police. When his mother and father arrived with a phalanx of his soldiers, Tommy realized the men had not been associates of his father at all.

The bunny had a card attached. It read, *Nice boy.*

There was no other threat. There didn't need to be.

His father ripped the bunny to shreds right there in the store. As he did with all his emotions, Don Fugue expressed fear as rage. Watching the stuffing fly in the toy store, Tommy was more afraid of his father's reaction than of being left alone.

A week later, a sleepy Tommy was woken in the middle of the night and ushered into his father's study, where several men were gathered. Two men were seated: his father, stationed behind his massive desk, and someone familiar opposite him. This other man was balding, and his pate was dotted with beads of sweat.

"Son," his father said sweetly, as warm and kind as Tommy

had ever heard him. "Have you seen this gentleman before? It's okay, don't be afraid."

The man did not meet Tommy's eye. Tommy did not meet his.

Tommy nodded.

"Did you see him at the mall, son?"

Tommy nodded.

"Good boy," whispered Big Al.

The man tried to stand, but one of his father's men stepped forward and the stranger fell backward into his chair, as if his legs had given out. He groaned.

Big Al nodded, and Tommy was ushered out of the office and back to bed.

The next morning, his father woke him with pancakes.

"Guys Breakfast!" he proclaimed, and Tommy sat at the kitchen counter proudly. Big Al did not explain himself, and, even at eight years old, Tommy knew better than to ask questions. There was a reference to sleepwalking—*it was a dream*—and a promise of Big Al's famous pancakes more often if the prior night stayed a dream.

Tommy nodded vigorously.

"Good boy."

It had ended up being their sole Guys Breakfast.

His father and his associates referred to that period as the Bad Old Days, but it had to Tommy's knowledge been peaceful ever since, Don Fugue's territory unchallenged. But after that day at the mall, Tommy had a succession of babysitters and bodyguards. Large men, sometimes awkward, always fearsome, hulks who hovered over birthday parties and playground visits. Different than all the others, Nine Ball was the latest, assigned when Tommy went off to college, and the closest any of his predecessors had come to being a friend.

Every now and then, the young soldier reminded Tommy he wasn't just a friend.

Nine Ball moved so fast, so sure, that what he did next looked like sleight of hand. As Todd exited the restaurant and walked toward an outdoor table, carrying a tray heaped with burgers and fries and a drink so large it should have come with a lifeguard, Nine walked right up to him, placed a hand under the tray to direct the fire, and let fly with a calorific explosion.

As his food went everywhere, Todd yelled and backed up a step. Because the oaf was so large, he bumped into his two friends behind him and spilled the contents of their trays as well, ensuring he was soaked front and back.

"Watch where you're going," muttered Nine.

"Watch where *I'm* going?" shouted Todd. "I should rip your fucking head off, you skinny little idiot!"

Calmly, Nine looked down at his slick black suit, which didn't entirely avoid the splash. "You got me all wet. . . ." With the thumb and forefinger of each hand, he opened his jacket gingerly and flapped it like a raven shaking water from its wings. He rotated in a slow circle by way of examining the damage done. "I ought to make you pay for the dry cleaning. . . ."

Tommy saw droplets of soda dancing, hitting the patio. He could also see a holstered 9 millimeter at the soldier's back. By the immediate change in posture and attitude of Todd and his two friends, so could they.

Todd's cheeks looked like they had been daubed with Heinz 57. The large man-child had been furious moments before but readily swallowed his reaction now. The appearance was of a monster truck gunning up to speed only to be thrown in reverse. Tommy almost felt sorry for him.

Todd cleared his throat. "Sorry about that," he mumbled.

Nine Ball offered a magnanimous smile. "I thank thee for that. Still, you boys should really be more careful. Someone could get hurt next time."

Then he turned his back to them and headed toward Tommy.

Tommy spun back in his seat. As Nine passed their table and headed for the exit, Tommy saw the soldier biting his lip to keep from laughing. Slipping out of his seat, he followed his bodyguard to the Honda Civic.

A few minutes later, Nine Ball dropped him at his apartment, stepping in to do a quick sweep, per their custom. Tommy offered him a drink, asked if he wanted to play Fortnite or Call of Duty, but he declined. The young man was an early riser, and Tommy had already presumed too much by bringing him to the party. The soiled jacket had to be driving him crazy.

"Say you really did have a moment with that girl. Hypothetically speaking," said Nine with an unyielding expression. "You couldn't bring her back here. She'd get a staph infection."

Tommy looked around at the dishes in the sink, the sticky countertops, the empty chip bags. Whatever was overflowing in the garbage can.

"Opportunity doesn't knock twice," said the soldier. "But if she even knocks once, and you invite her in, you want her to at least feel comfortable enough to take off her clothes."

Before Nine stepped into the night, the two dapped their familiar pattern and Tommy thanked him again for coming out. His partner looked about in another grid search that Tommy recognized and, apparently convinced that nothing on the street was amiss, strolled to his car with calm.

Alone, Tommy considered his options. He was too wired

for video games. It was still early; he could hit Hi-Dive, maybe Herb's Hideout, maybe the DNVR Bar, but he sensed the night had already peaked. He would rather stay at home and parse every nanosecond of his moment with Sanse than drink away the memory of her somewhere public.

Finally, he took a look around his apartment.

"Carpe fucking diem, I guess."

Finding a bottle of Grind, he poured himself two fingers of the coffee-flavored rum. *Only two,* he told himself. Then he found the all-purpose cleaner under the sink and got to work on the countertops. He cranked some Frank Ocean as he scrubbed. He emptied his dishwasher and reloaded it with the dishes from the sink. He poured another two fingers and did a loop of the one-bedroom apartment, filling a trash bag with empty cans and bottles. The more he cleaned, the more energy he had. He felt like a boulder rolling downhill, picking up speed. He poured another two fingers and vacuumed. He continued, wiping and scrubbing and organizing, occasionally catching himself smiling like a loon as he thought about the party. He pressed on, venturing into his bedroom closet to hang the clothes that were piled on the floor.

By now the rum was taking hold and he found himself getting clumsy. He was hanging the last of his clothes when he bumped the gift box on the closet shelf.

Dozens of drawings tumbled out, cascading across the floor. There were sketches of male and female figures, of striking angels and horrid demons, of galloping horses, of mythical creatures. There were drawings of Superman and Spider-Man with Tommy's likeness on them and then, later, from when his taste in comics grew darker and grittier, sketches of him as a Punisher-like character he called Tommy Gun.

His mother could draw anything.

She'd told him when she was younger sometimes people would pay her to draw caricatures in Central Park. As a kid, Tommy had thought that must be the most lucrative job in the world. This she had laughed at.

His mother came from a wealthy Upper West Side family—old New York money—and went to private schools, culminating in New York's School of Visual Arts. But Vittoria Rose Vitali was no hothouse flower. She was a fighter, and whatever she did, she threw herself into wholeheartedly. She was passionate about art, but when handsome Alessandro Fugue met her in a club in New York City, she became passionate about him. And when Tommy came along, she threw herself into being his mother. If Vittoria had a flaw, it was that she could switch these passions too easily, loving something so hard and then leaving it without a backward glance. Art went from a calling to a hobby to a parlor trick used to soothe an irritable child. And by then she had little time for her husband's late nights and extralegal activities, activities that had once titillated her. Vittoria's wild, dangerous husband, who had seemed so alluring compared to her boring Upper West Side life, proved to be just as provincial with his old-world notions of a woman's place. And thanks to the occasional gangland strife, that meant her place was too often locked in their Commerce City, Colorado, mansion for her own protection.

She had traded one gilded cage for another, she would tell him bitterly. Soon, epic fights with her husband became her latest passion, and Tommy felt left behind.

Until she actually left him behind. Last summer, just before freshman year began.

Tommy should have known she was leaving when she gifted

him the box of her drawings with a note telling him to always listen to his inner voice and to follow his passions. She vanished three days later.

Tommy understood her desire to run. Still, he was furious with her. He would have gone with her in a heartbeat, had she asked. Instead, she left him in the care of a monster without so much as a word or a backward glance. When Tommy was being generous, he considered that perhaps she had waited until her son was college-bound to flee, ensuring that he was on a path to freedom before she embarked on her own.

But he wasn't feeling particularly generous at the moment.

He gingerly stacked his mother's drawings, laid them back in the box, and placed the box on a higher shelf. Out of sight.

Momentum broken, he eschewed fingers and poured himself a fist. Then he abandoned cleaning altogether for sleep. Drifting off, he thought of Sanse and her shimmering dress, her electric smile, her warm touch. The room began to spin slowly, and Sanse with it, until he passed out. He dreamed of the party. He dreamed of his mother's drawings come to life. He dreamed of his father standing at the foot of his bed, ordering him to wake up.

Tommy woke up. Blinked.

His father was still there.

"Guys Breakfast," said the Al Mighty.

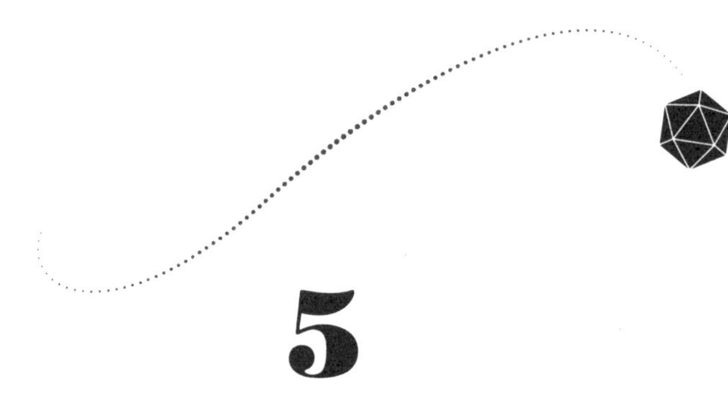

5

Tommy watched his father spread melted butter over a full stack of pancakes at the Red Rooster Cafe, a small diner between I-25 and the Platte. Big Al was always on the hunt for a proper New York diner in the Denver area—and usually critical in his assessment—but the no-frills brick and red-roofed eatery seemed to charm him. Beside the pancakes was a plate of scrambled eggs and sausages and a cup of coffee. Big Al was a man of many appetites, and he was always famished.

The nickname, though, was a misnomer. If anything, his father was on the short side; Tommy had inched past him in his junior year of high school. But Big Al just *seemed* bigger. He possessed rakish good looks with a pugilistic nose, broken from countless boyhood brawls. And he kept in shape, with a lean physique, strong but not showy, the platonic ideal of the tailors who made his expensive suits. Even at this hour, the don wore a bespoke suit. His dark hair, just starting to reveal flecks of gray, was combed back. Like Nine, nothing out of place.

The morning light caught his amber pinkie ring as he doused the full stack with maple syrup. Tommy glanced at his father's other hand and was surprised to see the wedding ring still there. Tommy was also surprised at the surge of anger he felt at the sight of it. Showy, hollow devotion. Too little, too late.

Big Al nodded at Tommy. "You getting anything?"

Tommy swallowed, then shook his head, careful not to be too curt.

"No thanks, Pop. Just coffee." Tommy tried on a smile. "You have enough for both of us."

"Long night." Big Al's return smile was large and wolfish. *"Fun night."*

Tommy didn't want to hear the details. They would likely turn his stomach. He peered over his father's shoulder. At the next table Vincenzo nursed a cup of coffee. The bodyguard looked like a parent sitting at a child's desk on Meet the Teacher night. People's eyes tended to linger on Big Al's movie star looks, but Vincenzo's monstrous frame was what caught those eyes first. The giant was dedicated to two things in life: Don Fugue and dumbbells. His enormous frame and his bulging muscles had earned him the nickname SuperChenz.

"So," said Big Al, finally righting the syrup dispenser after saturating his stack, "how's school?"

"School's good. Finishing up the semester . . ."

The don nodded vigorously before Tommy could finish. It was a sure sign his father wasn't listening and was intent on his pancakes and whatever he wanted to say next, presumably the reason behind his Second-Ever Guys Breakfast.

"So, what did you think?"

Tommy didn't like the question. It sounded final, as if school was entirely in the rearview mirror.

"The first year was . . ." He stopped himself from saying *fun*. It *was* fun, but not because of the girls or the drinking or the partying. It was a *relief*. Living on his own, out from under his father and the tension that always hung over the Fugue household like a shroud. "*Hard*. Hard but rewarding. I'm looking forward to next year."

"Grades?"

"All A's."

Nine Ball always busted his balls about the state of his apartment and his dress and a great many other things, but Tommy knew the priority was to maintain excellent grades. One of his philosophy professors had said that wisdom was understanding the game you were playing and playing it well. *Grades are the game,* thought Tommy. His father would never understand anything in his courses, but he would judge whether it felt like his son was *winning.*

Big Al had never been a fan of college; it was a concession to Vittoria. And with Tommy's mother in the wind, he didn't want to give his father an excuse to renege on the deal.

Big Al shrugged. The question had been perfunctory. "So, you need a summer job, then."

Ah, there it is.

"I do?"

Another bite, another nod. "That was the deal."

"I don't remember that part of it."

"That was the deal."

Tommy suddenly realized how it must feel to borrow money from Big Al and his associates. There's the loan and then there's the vig, excessive and unpayable. Better to never take the loan in the first place. But surely his father wouldn't treat his own son's tuition like a loan?

Then Tommy realized if he had to ask, he already knew the answer.

He slumped in his seat.

Big Al brightened. Mouth full of pancakes, he laughed.

"Relax, kid. It's not like I'm gonna make you wash dishes at the Fuzzy Navel."

Tommy relaxed a little and grabbed his coffee mug. School itself hadn't been threatened. Yet.

"I have a little job I want you to do for me."

Tommy froze, mug halfway to his mouth. In his father's parlance, "a little job" could mean anything, none of it good and certainly worse than washing dishes.

Big Al sawed into his full stack, not even looking at Tommy, but the tone of his father's voice told Tommy that he clocked his son's unease. "Should be a walk in the park for you."

The don forked another wedge of pancakes into his mouth, then spiked a sausage. "With that mighty intellect of yours."

"What kind of job?"

Big Al patted his mouth with a napkin, a delicate gesture at odds with his rapacious feeding. Tommy saw Vittoria in the motion. She had loved her feral husband but had endeavored to civilize him. Or at least teach him some manners.

"We had a game last night with some out-of-towners. *I did well!*" He slugged some coffee and grunted a small laugh. "Very well. And *you* are going to help me invest it."

A joke. Tommy laughed and relaxed further. "Pop, my major is art, not business. I don't know the first thing about investing or finance."

Finally, Big Al turned his full attention to his son. He looked at Tommy as if he was a total idiot. The last kid picked on the playground. The last to get the joke.

"Oh," muttered Tommy. "You don't mean *invest* invest."

Big Al put down his fork. "You ever heard of this Spot-a-Fly?"

"No . . ."

"The music thing."

"Do you mean Spotify?"

His father waved his hand with the pinkie ring. Then he

leaned in and lowered his voice. "You wouldn't believe what I heard last night. Swedish gangs used it to launder money. They bought fake streams or whatever for friendly musical acts. I don't get the ones and zeroes of it all, but Spotify then paid the artists for all the streams, the artist paid back the gangsters, and the money was as clean as an IKEA showroom." He shrugged. "You know, until they got caught."

"So?"

"So Chongo is going to swing by later today with some cabbage. I want some new streams." Big Al took a swig of coffee. "*Revenue* streams. And I'd like you to help me diversify."

Tommy's guts began to roil. He shifted in his seat.

"*Pop*," he pleaded, "I don't know how—"

It must have been a good night indeed for Big Al, because this morning his son's terror was a source of amusement rather than disgust. "That's the point. You're going to learn. Think of it as summer school." He grabbed the maple syrup dispenser and drizzled from high over his plate, like he was a bartender showing off while pouring a shot. "I thought you liked learning. The *bursar* seems to think you like learning. He keeps sending me bills for it. The vig on that shit, talk about a racket . . ."

"Of course I like learning, it's just . . ." Tommy leaned in, his voice an urgent whisper. "I don't want to learn how to break the law."

"I thought college was supposed to expand your mind."

"College is supposed to help me find a career instead of, you know, doing 'little jobs' for you."

"Ah," said Big Al. He raised an eyebrow as he lowered his syrup dispenser again. "You think you're better than me?"

Shit.

"No, Pop, it's not that—"

Big Al Fugue settled back in his seat and scrutinized his son. That full attention was enough to make words dry up in Tommy's mouth. But Big Al Fugue really must have had a good night, because after a moment he offered a genuine smile.

"It's *okay*. I want you to be better than me. Your mother damn sure wanted you to be better than me. It's a nice notion, but it's just that, if you don't put in the reps—a notion. Despite my lack of college, I consider myself a lifelong learner, and one of the most important lessons I've learned is this: Evolve or die. And evolving means pushing yourself outside of your comfort zone. It means you have to work for it."

"I am working for it."

Big Al made a face. "Art school."

"It's a multidisciplinary art program in humanities and social thought for the purpose of teaching future leaders how to inspire and create," Tommy recited. "With a minor in philosophy."

"You need a backup plan."

"Your backup plan is *organized crime*?"

Big Al shrugged. "Consider it a multidisciplinary program. No summer job, no college in the fall."

"That's . . . that's not fair!"

"Fare is what you pay to get on a bus, Tommy." Pleased with the delivery of his favorite line, Big Al gave a little salute with his coffee mug and drank deep. "Come on, don't look so glum. This will be a piece of cake for you. You're young, smart. You're good with computers and phones and shit. You even know what Spotify is. . . ."

"Everybody knows what Spotify is."

Big Al shrugged. "I'm an iTunes guy."

Tommy stared at the Formica tabletop and considered his options. He quickly surmised that he had none. Big Al was still smiling, but Tommy knew his father's temper was mercurial, with few to no intermediate steps between high spirits and low moods. Big Al often went straight from a summer's day to a blizzard, with no gentle autumn to acclimate. Tommy could either risk frostbite—and get pulled out of school or worse—or he could go along and keep his father off his back.

No options at all.

Tommy sighed. "What do I have to do?"

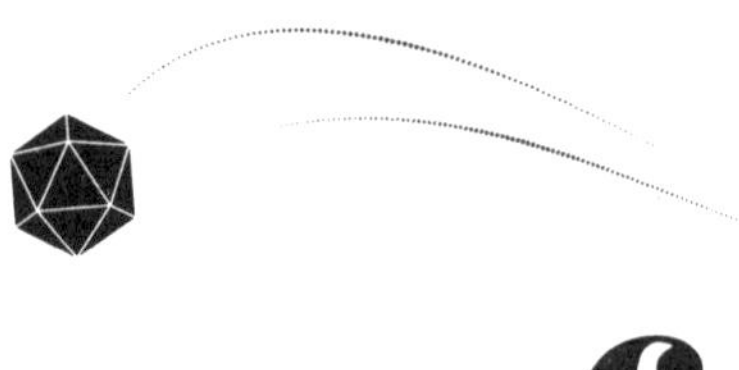

6

The plump brown paper bag sat atop Tommy's scuffed, secondhand kitchen table. It was so plain but dominated the space so thoroughly, Tommy didn't want to touch it. Behind him, Chongo made noise as he rummaged through the refrigerator. Though Chongo was the longtime accountant for the Fugue Family, this was the first time, outside of some algebra tutoring in middle school, that Tommy had ever seen Uncle Bud's "professional" side.

"Christ, kid. You know mold is not a vegetable, right?"

In additional to being a notorious stoner, Chongo was also an unrepentant snacker.

But Tommy wasn't listening. He was still watching the paper bag as if someone might snatch it if he took his eyes off it for a second. Or as if the bag would move toward him of its own accord, like in some horror movie. Tommy needed it to stay in place, to come no closer. He and the bag were locked in a stalemate.

Chongo wandered into his field of vision. He was a solid man in his sixties, bald on top with white hair on the sides. He wore an untucked dress shirt over khakis, where he wiped his hands. "You ever heard of groceries? I'm starving. Next time I'll bring over some brownies."

"I don't know if I could handle your kind of brownies, Uncle Bud. There's a box of mac and cheese in the cupboard. . . ."

Did the bag just lean toward him?

Chongo sighed and put on a pot of boiling water, then pulled up the chair opposite his pupil. It scraped across the floor until finally Uncle Bud sat down. His belly bumped the table, tipping the bag over. Tommy jumped up as if green toxic sludge had rolled toward him.

But it was just stacks of twenty-dollar bills.

Just stacks of bills . . .

"Look," said Uncle Bud, upending the bag and shaking the rest of its contents out. More stacks of twenty-dollar bills tumbled across the table until, laughing, Chongo shook the empty bag for a few long seconds. "They don't bite, Tommy. Come on, sit down."

Chongo reached into the breast pocket of his rumpled dress shirt and produced a joint. "You mind?"

Tommy shook his head, retook his seat.

Chongo lit up, took a deep hit, and let it out. He held the joint out for Tommy. "You need to relax, kid."

Tommy accepted the proffer and took a hit, held it, and let out a long exhale. It was stronger than he expected, but then again, when you were a pro like Uncle Bud, it took a bit more to move the needle.

"Damn," he said, as he shook his head and felt his shoulders drop from his ears.

"Don't tell your father." Chongo winked. "He'd kill me."

"My mother would have killed you too."

Chongo snorted. "That she would have. Boy, your mother . . ." He inspected the cherry at the end of his joint. "You know how people say, 'She lit up a room'?"

"Usually in investigative shows, but yes."

"Well," said the stoner, lost in a moment of reverie, "she didn't just light up a room, kid. She *owned* it. Sucked up all the oxygen and eyeballs. Deadly. Hotter than donut grease and twice as bad for the heart."

Tommy tried to look at the money, but stared at the ceiling instead. "As much as I love super-awkward anecdotes about my mother's hotness, Uncle Bud, can we get back on track?"

"Anyway . . ." Chongo came back down to earth, leaned forward, and gathered the stacks of cash to him like he was scooping chips after a winning hand, which, Tommy had learned, was exactly how the money had come into Big Al's possession the night before.

There were ten stacks in total.

Long night. Fun night.

"What we have here," said Chongo, the joint bobbing up and down from the corner of his mouth, "is ten straps of twenty-dollar bills, consisting of one hundred bills each."

"Twenty grand," muttered Tommy. His voice sounded far away to his own ears.

"Very good, Einstein." Chongo began piling the stacks evenly. He handled the money without a hint of hesitation or self-consciousness. It looked natural; this was a carpenter handling a hammer. Tools felt awkward in Tommy's hands, as did most sporting goods. Big Al was not one to play catch or show Tommy how to change spark plugs. As a result of his lack of coordination and discernible skills, he felt less than his peers, isolated, and as a further result, retreated into comics and games. Subsequently, this only made him more of a disappointment to his father.

He was enthralled as he watched Chongo play with the money with the practiced nonchalance of a magician. For a childlike moment Tommy wondered if Chongo was going to pull a stack of bills from behind his ear.

"All right," said the old man, "you ready for Money Laundering 101?"

Tommy nodded, slightly numb.

"There are so many ways to launder money, it's not even funny, but the principles remain the same."

Chongo pushed the pile of money back to the center of the table.

"The first step is *placement*. We have earned a sum of money that we would prefer to keep low profile, either because its origin is extralegal, or we simply don't want to give Uncle Sam a taste. Regardless, what do we do with it? We need to introduce this sum into a legitimate business. In other words, we need to disguise this dirty money—a term I hate—as legal profit. That is placement."

"Where do you put it?"

"Tons of places. Restaurants, real estate, casinos, nightclubs, cash businesses. It helps to create a shell company, make the cash look like it came from a legit source, but after that, the sky is the limit. Your father never taught you this stuff?"

"Mom wouldn't let him."

Chongo considered this and nodded. Vittoria's reputation was almost as fearsome as Big Al's. The accountant left the table, dumped the macaroni into the boiling water, then returned to his seat to resume his lesson.

"All right, so you've found the venue in which you are going to introduce your ill-gotten gains. The next step is *layering*."

Chongo began to remove stacks from the main pile and place them around the edges of table lengthwise. When he was done, each stack looked like a train car on a toy set.

"The purpose of layering is to create distance from—and confusion over—the original source of the money."

He chose the three stacks in front of him and began throwing them over one another, like a New York City sidewalk hustler performing three-card monte.

"You just keep moving the money, transferring it, again and again. . . ."

Chongo incorporated the remaining stacks farther away on the table into his follow-the-money shuffling. His hands picked up speed, rearranging and manipulating the stacks in a blur. Tommy, high and paranoid, was mesmerized.

"The goal is to keep the money moving, always staying one step ahead. Speed is a force. Transaction after transaction, investment after investment, form after form. Make such a winding trail that's it's impossible to trace where the money came from in the first place. Which brings us to the last part: *integration.*"

Chongo held his hands aloft and rotated them for Tommy. *Nothing in my hands, nothing up my sleeves.*

"I don't follow," asked Tommy.

"That's the point. Take a closer look."

Tommy looked at the bands of money, neatly stacked again. Then it dawned on him. Excited now, he knocked at the center of the table.

"It started here," said Tommy, smacking the now empty center of the table, "and now it's in front of you!"

"Right back where it started, now clean as whistle. All that commotion, all that tumbling . . ."

Chongo took another hit, and as he exhaled, he made a swirling motion with the hand that held the joint. Smoke trailed it in lazy loops. "Round and round she goes, where she stops, nobody knows. . . ."

The avuncular accountant pushed himself up from the table and wandered into the kitchen. Tommy shook his head to clear it and counted the stacks of money. Still ten stacks, two thousand apiece, totaling twenty thousand. He sank back in his chair. When Chongo returned, he clutched a small pot and a large wooden spoon and set them down in front of his pupil. Then he pitched him the small cheese packet. "Mix this up for me, would you?"

As Tommy poured the neon-yellow powder into the pot and began to stir, Chongo re-sparked his joint. When Tommy tried to hand the pot back, Chongo reclined in his chair and said, "Keep going." A minute later, Tommy glanced in the pot and, satisfied it was mixed sufficiently, slid the pot across the table to the accountant.

"See, Tommy? That wasn't so hard, was it?"

"Making you a snack?"

"Laundering this." He waggled the empty cheese packet. "You could have done anything with this cheese, but you *placed* it in the macaroni."

"It comes in the same box, what else was I going to do with it?"

"It's a metaphor, smart-ass." Chongo grabbed the spoon and stirred the cheesy pasta as Tommy had. "Then you layered the shit out of it."

"Until it was fully integrated . . ."

Looking pleased, Chongo shoveled a spoonful into his mouth. "Wax on, wax off, Daniel-san."

Tommy was entertained but still confused. "Thanks for the crash course, but what the hell am I supposed to do with *that* kind of cheese?"

"That?" said Chongo, knocking over the piled stack with a dismissive wave of his hand. "*Please.* I could wash that in my sleep. This is training wheels stuff, kid."

"Then why don't you?"

"*Not* the assignment. Your dad wants *you* to learn."

Tommy realized there was no point in trying to wriggle off the hook any longer. "All right, you taught me the principles. Now, like, what do I do? Practically speaking."

"Do you happen to own a bank?"

Tommy swept an arm wide as if to indicate the rich holdings of his lands. "Sure, it's right next to my casino."

"You could start your own religion. No better racket than a church." Chongo squinted at a stack of cards beyond the boy. "The High—Very High—Holy Order of Pokémon Nerds, since you've done the research."

"Come on, Chongo, help me out here. Where do I start?"

Chongo pondered this. He shoveled neon-yellow mac and cheese into his mouth and mumbled something that sounded like *smurfs*.

"Like the cartoon?"

Chongo pointed the yellow-stained wooden spoon at him. "Smurfing is breaking large chunks of money into smaller chunks, then spreading them around to multiple accounts. Harder to detect."

"Why smurfing? Because they're little?"

"I don't think that's the bit you should be focusing on, Tommy."

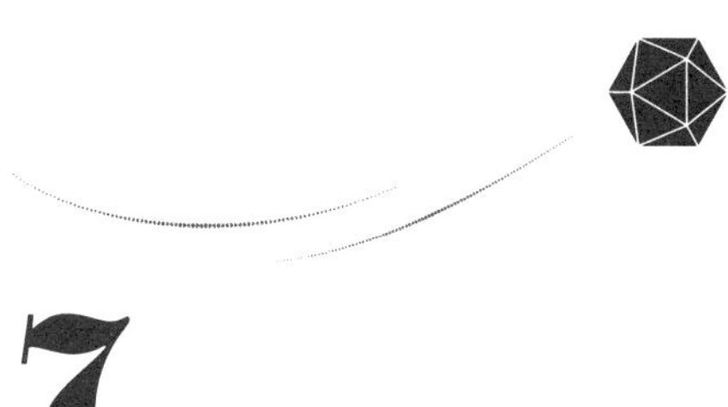

7

Chongo left and the weed wore off, leaving Tommy with a yellow-crusted pot, lingering paranoia, and a lot to think about. He kept coming back to the idea of smurfing, of taking the sum in front of him and breaking it down into smaller chunks. It was the difference between hiding a body and hiding body parts. The more and smaller, the easier to scatter and hide. A lot more work, but safer in some ways.

Jesus, he thought. *My father gives me twenty grand to launder and I'm thinking about feeding bodies into woodchippers.*

He felt like he was teetering on the edge of a very slippery slope.

Dad's just trying to prove a point, thought Tommy. *Once I placate him, he'll get off my back. I'll finish school, then I'll get the hell out of here. Move to the coast.*

He imagined taking Sanse by the hand, taking her with him, like he was a character in the Bruce Springsteen songs his father had played so often when Tommy was younger. The songs had carved channels into his brain: lighting out west on a last chance power drive, astride a motorcycle with her behind him, hands wrapped around his waist, still wearing her flapper dress. It was ridiculous in so many ways—he had no business sitting in a sidecar, let alone piloting a chopper—but even in the solitude of his apartment, Tommy smiled and blushed at the vision.

Then he caught sight of the banded green stacks and sighed.

Tommy wasn't born to run. He was born to do whatever Big Al wanted.

If Tommy ever wanted to get free, he would have to earn it. Which meant earning his father's respect. He hated the option of running like his mother had, and it wasn't like he had squirreled away resources like she must have. So as nerve-racking as this summer job would be, he needed to do it. Just do it and be done with it. He would smurf the shit out of those damned stacked bills, breaking them down to coins if he had to, and scatter them like pennies in a fountain.

After much cajoling for help, Chongo's most actionable suggestion had been gift cards. Loading up gift cards and then giving them to his father to redeem. Chongo seemed to get that a gift card scheme wasn't really laundering money "online," but whether he chose to ignore it or was just tired of thinking for Tommy he offered it up without comment. For his part, Tommy figured that if the pieces of plastic all said Apple or Amazon on them, that would be close enough to "the internet" for his father, who didn't know what he was talking about anyway. Besides, Tommy smirked at the notion of taking the sack of twenty grand, buying two hundred gifts cards of one hundred dollars, and handing them to his father in a duffel bag. Sure, on one level this would be akin to his father ordering him to build an in-ground pool only for Tommy to declare himself finished after digging a giant hole. It was just the first step. And not finishing would *really* be digging a hole for himself.

Still, the gift cards were a first step on the path to what Chongo called *placement*. It would convert the pile of ill-gotten cash to a pile of something else, something that could be more easily absorbed into polite society. He didn't have any sort of plan beyond that, but he figured spending days driving all over the greater Denver metropolitan area buying prepaid gift cards gave him plenty of time to come up with one.

What he really wanted to do was drive around and think about Sanse. Her shimmering dress. Her mischievous sense of humor. Her hand touching his chest as she laughed her bright, warm laugh. Ever since his father took him out for Guys Breakfast, he couldn't afford to spare her a thought, too consumed with getting the man off his back and realizing the only way to do it was to break the law. If he failed at this, he could forget about both college *and* Sanse. Last night was as happy as he could remember being since before his mother disappeared. Now, every moment spent mulling over his "summer job" felt like he was moving further and further away from that crystalline moment with her, and his loneliness grew proportionally.

If he wanted to remain in her orbit, and that of her collective of cool artists like Anibal, and figure out what kind of artist he wanted to be, he had to wash this bag of cash. The only way out was through.

Tommy felt like he was embarking on a dangerous voyage, like he was leaving a warm bright cabin to set out onto the dark plains on horseback, or sailing from a safe harbor to uncharted waters marked on some medieval map by mythical monsters. He tucked his moment with Sanse into his memory for safekeeping, next to the ones of his mother, another golden nugget or piece of eight, and focused on completing the job quickly, avoiding pitfalls, and returning home.

His mind stuck on those medieval maps, and the fearsome

creatures and sea monsters that represented danger or the unknown. Normally, Tommy felt like an NPC in his own life. Like it or not, Tommy now found himself at the center of his very own quest.

He reached for his bottle of Grind, then froze. He reached for a notepad instead.

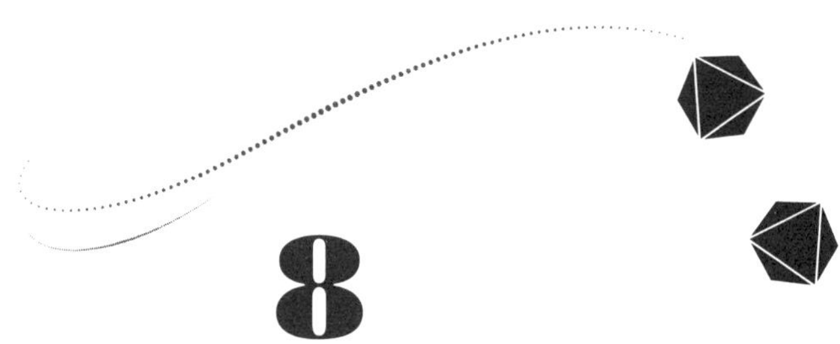

8

"FunFunder?" asked Nine Ball once Tommy got done explaining what the site was. His expression registered somewhere on the spectrum between skeptical and annoyed. "Why can't you just do it the old-fashioned way?"

He and Tommy sat under an umbrella at a taco joint, Nine dressed in another funereal black suit despite the blue sky and the midday sun. He was the living embodiment of the *dress for the job you want* ethos, and apparently Nine wanted to be John Wick. But Tommy was undeterred by the young soldier's dubiousness.

"I was thinking about that guy Anibal last night," said Tommy. "From Sanse's party?"

"Was he the furry?"

"Breadwinner."

"Lame." Nine carefully drizzled hot sauce into the shell. "More your speed than Sanse."

"He made his own comic book and launched it on FunFunder."

Nine was in the middle of a massive bite of his taco, so his eyebrows had to do the heavy lifting. They stood high and with a slight shake of his head issued a dramatic *So?* Tommy had hoped Nine would be more excited, see the possibility. Deeper than that, he wanted his approval. He knew the prospect of Nine thinking he was cool was a long shot, but he would settle for begrudging respect, a first step on the path to genuine friendship. Growing up, being the son of Don Alessandro Fugue made having real friends next to impossible. Who wanted to hang out with the kid surrounded by goons and guard dogs at birthday parties?

"So, you want to make a comic book?" asked Nine.

"We can make anything we want. A freaking calendar where every month is just a different photo of you in another dark-ass suit." Nine's eyebrows did not rest at Tommy's words. "Or, like, a version of Candy Land where Big Al is King Kandy and everybody pays their tributes in Skittles."

"I'm Lord Licorice," said Nine, then pointed a finger at Tommy. "You're Gloppy, bruh."

"Whatever. The point is, FunFunder is just a legit place to introduce the cash. Like a restaurant or a casino. It's the first step."

"Unless you plan on going to FunFunder HQ and handing them a paper bag with twenty large, then it most def is not the very first step."

Nine had a point. Placement, layering, and integration. There would be some legwork that needed to happen first.

"Admittedly, there will need to be some baby steps until the first real step. We're going to need a shitload of gift cards, like the ones that are debit cards that work anywhere. We buy them in cash, then use them for pledges. We create dummy accounts with fake email addresses, and each one makes a small pledge to avoid scrutiny—ten dollars, twenty dollars, fifty dollars, the occasional hundred dollars—and the project is funded. The dirty twenty is now squeaky clean."

Nine went from skeptical to unimpressed, which Tommy took as progress. "Seems complicated."

“It’s simple, but not easy. I called Chongo last night and ran it by him. He says it can work.”

“I don’t know what’s worse, spending the next week fetching gift cards or being a keyboard warrior.”

“It’s tedious, no doubt, but it’s super low-pro. Little exposure, little risk.”

“Except for the internet of it all.”

It was Tommy’s turn to shrug. “That’s like throwing a coin in the ocean. No one will even notice.”

“Thing is, I don’t mind the risk. But I signed up to be a gangster, not a gopher.” Nine looked up and down the street, scanning for a threat that never materialized, then returned to his taco. “It’s the boredom.”

“I mind all of it. Remember, I didn’t sign up for any of this bullshit.”

“No, you were born into it. It’s your birthright.”

“You can have it.”

Nine looked off to the side. His jaw was working, but he wasn’t chewing. Tommy knew he was irritated. The young soldier never missed an opportunity to bust his chops, whether it was his style or his silver spoon privilege, but this was more. Nine may have tolerated Tommy, maybe even had a soft spot for him, but his first loyalty was always to the Al Mighty. He would not tolerate disrespect, not even from the don’s own son. Respect was everything to Don Alessandro Fugue, and therefore respect was everything to Nine Ball.

“Don’t be so dismissive. Some of us would kill for that birthright.”

Tommy held up his hands, a peace offering. “All I’m saying is, this is not my world. This shit fell—”

Nine waved a finger. *“Opportunity.”*

"Fine, this *opportunity* fell into my lap, *hard*. But any risk to me means risk to my father. And no one wants that. I'm majoring in fucking *art*, Nine—this ain't my world. But if I have to do this, and I don't see that I have much choice in the matter, it has to be done perfectly. So, I need your help. Will you help me?"

His companion exhaled. They both knew he really didn't have a choice either.

"I'll help you. I'll help you get the cards. And I'll help you set up some phony handles. Beyond that, it's not like washing money at a club. I can't stick a gun in the internet's face, Tommy."

Tommy nodded a few times. "Trust me. I want to get in and get out. Start next semester pretending this never happened."

"Sounds like One Last Job shit."

"My first job *is* my last job."

"Uh-huh," said Nine, now skeptical and amused at least rather than skeptical and annoyed.

"You'll see. Come on, let me show you what I've started."

Tommy didn't take offense to Nine Ball's naysaying. The soldier played things close to the vest. It simply didn't do in his father's world for gangsters to geek out. But Tommy was determined to bring him around. For Nine to not only find merit in his FunFunder idea, but get excited about it. Tommy would show him.

His discovered the first hurdle to his plan when he arrived back at his apartment.

The lock on his front door was busted.

And the money was gone.

9

"Who knew it was here?"

Tommy answered Nine from near the sink, where he had just thrown up. "Pop." He wiped his mouth with the back of his hand. "And Chongo. Maybe SuperChenz. I don't know."

"Chongo dropped it off?" asked Nine. He paced back and forth in front of the kitchen table, the last place Tommy had seen the paper bag.

Tommy nodded. It went without saying that the accountant would not have stolen money that he himself had dropped off. It was nonsensical. Worse, it would have been a death sentence.

"Shit, Tommy. One night. You had the bag for one fucking night, and it's fucking *gone*? You weren't even like, 'Hey, maybe I should hide this under my mattress,' or something?"

So much for impressing Nine with competence. He would be forever branded as a *mamaluke*. A fool, a fuckup. Someone who couldn't help punching himself in the dick every chance he got.

"Maybe this is part of Pop's initiation?" said Tommy hopefully. "Like another test or something?"

Nine whirled on him, fast. The fierce look in his eye was enough to convey the credence of that theory. It also conveyed something else: fear. It struck Tommy like a knife to the heart.

Despite his wobbly knees and terror-induced nausea, Tommy straightened. "I'll just come clean. Tell Pop someone broke in. I mean, it's true. That's not our fault." He was psyching himself up as he went, standing taller, almost believing himself.

Nine dropped into the chair Chongo had occupied the night before, when the accountant was playing with the stacked bands like they were a deck of cards. He put his head in his hands and spoke low.

"You're his son. There's only so much he'll do to you. Me on the other hand . . ."

Tommy sat down opposite the young soldier. "It's not your fault, though—"

Nine slammed his hands on the table. "*Grow up*, Tommy!"

Tommy fell back in his seat, slack-jawed.

"Do you think Don Fugue gives *a shit* about fault? Or excuses? Or random break-ins? He only cares about one thing: results!"

Tommy wanted to argue, but he knew it was true. His father was always going on and on about overcoming obstacles, personal accountability, radical ownership. Like some twisted Ted Lasso. Tommy took it all with a grain of salt. He never dared contradict his father, but it was tough to listen to the man spouting lofty principles, knowing he bent them to organized crime.

"I'll go to him, face-to-face, tell him it's all on me. You had nothing to do with it. I'll take care of it."

The soldier offered a sad smile that broke Tommy's heart. Whatever Nine Ball really thought of Tommy, Tommy looked up to him like an older brother. Handsome. Half Italian, half Native American, a chip on each shoulder. Ice cold with a molten core, slicing through the world with the grace of a shark. Seeing him so defeated was devastating.

"It was on my watch," he said. "That's all that matters."

The pair stewed in silence for a while—Tommy worried about living it down, and Nine worried about living at all—when it struck Tommy.

"You said *random* break-in," he said.

"Yeah."

"Some jamoke kicks in my door when there just happens to be a bag of cash in here?"

Nine shook his head. "No one would be stupid enough to cross Don Fugue. Not one of the crew. Not even whoever he took the money off of in the game. They might be pissed, but better to lose twenty grand than ten fingers."

"What if the thief didn't know it belonged to the Fearsome Don Fugue?"

Nine laughed a rueful laugh. "You have any enemies I should know about, Tommy Gun?"

Tommy stared at him.

"Oh shit . . ." the young soldier said with a mix of some concern and more amusement.

10

The party was in full swing by the time Tommy and Nine Ball drove past.

"Keep going," said Nine.

Tommy complied, but he stole a glance as they rolled on. It was a garden-style apartment complex, mostly populated by the students from the university; i.e., not people who would mind the noise of an epic rager, which this certainly was. There were two kegs stationed on either side of the wide lawn and a Slip 'N Slide running between them. Buff frat boys in tank tops lobbed beanbags onto cornhole boards. Women in varying forms of undress and with questionable rhythm drank beer or filmed wan TikTok dances.

"Pathetic," said the soldier. "Looks like every cheesy eighties movie where the parents go out of town. No imagination whatsoever."

Tommy parked around the corner and checked to see if anyone could see them. "What's the plan?"

"Get your money back."

"How?"

"Easy. They're going to put it in my hand."

"Why?"

"Trust me." Nine checked his piece a few times in rapid succession. "This is my world."

"Frat parties?"

"Redistribution of wealth." Nine got out and waited for Tommy to join him. "Now lock the car, please. I don't need anything else getting stolen."

The pair approached on foot, Nine striding toward the apartments, shoulders back, sunglasses on, a spring in his step. Even from around the block, they could hear the bass booming like the complex itself was one massive subwoofer. They walked up the sidewalk, drunken revelers on either side. The sun had not yet begun to dip. Despite making up for lost time during his freshmen year, Tommy had never been to a party quite like this one, one that could be described the next day as "legendary" or "epic" or, he thought, glancing at Nine Ball, "killer."

A keg arrived in the back of a pickup truck. A pair of beefy partygoers leapt into the bed to retrieve it.

"What are we going to say?" asked Tommy.

"*We* are not going to say anything."

The pair of keg-bearers shouldered past them. "Coming through," said one of them as they made their way up the walkway to the complex.

"I wouldn't tap that if I were you," said Nine.

The other one looked him up and down. "You just come from court?"

The pair laughed.

Nine shrugged. "Your funeral."

Ignoring the skinny stranger, the keg-bearers replaced the tapped one on the lawn to cheers. Tommy noticed Anibal in the throng of partyers milling around waiting for the fresh keg. The young artist nodded at Tommy and made his way over to them before they entered the apartment building.

"Hey," said Tommy. "How goes your campaign?"

"Let's just say I'm in my Battle of the Bulge era."

"Yikes. That bad?" asked Tommy, but he was distracted, scanning over Anibal's shoulder. Nine was doing the same.

"She's not here, dude."

Tommy stopping scanning and focused on the young artist. "I'm not looking for Sanse."

Anibal smiled a wide, cheesy smile. "I only said *she*. You said *Sanse*. So . . ."

Despite his nerves, Tommy grinned. "Fair enough, but I'm actually looking for Todd right now."

Anibal rolled his eyes. "Caligula, you mean? Dude can't just throw a party; he has to let everyone know it's *his* party." Anibal swept his arm toward the lawn, encompassing the gyrating girls, the football-tossing bros, the beanbags crisscrossing the lawn, and the beach balls sailing through the air, dancing from person to person. "It's the douchebag Olympics."

"Then why are you here?" asked Tommy.

"I'm an inherently curious person." He raised a mock toast. "And by that I mean I'm a hypocrite who likes free beer."

Nine leaned in. He was smiling, but Tommy could detect the impatience. "We'd like to thank Todd for his largesse. Any idea where we might find him?"

Anibal looked at Nine for a moment, appraising him silently. It was one thing to wear a dark suit to a masquerade at a RiNo loft at midnight, but another to wear one at an outdoor party in the afternoon. Still, the kid did not appear fazed, like he saw characters like Nine all the time. "2B. Be careful. He's probably making people literally kiss his ring by now."

Nine strode inside without a backward glance. Tommy rushed after him, calling over his shoulder to Anibal, "Let's catch up later!"

Tommy found Nine on the stairs. His guts roiled. His partner, on the other hand, loped across the landing to 2B, shoving party-goers aside with rote indifference. Tommy caught the irritated glances in Nine's wake and muttered apologies as he passed. By the time he reached the front door, the soldier was smiling. Relaxed.

Nine glanced over, saw Tommy's nerves. "My grandfather broke horses. Same thing, only this is more fun."

Tommy did not share this enthusiasm. From inside the apartment came aggressive, expletive-laden rap, punctuated by the shouting of several men. It sounded like the baying of a pack of wolves. Ever since he was young, Tommy tended to escape into his imagination when things got too rough or scary, particularly during his parents' more spectacular shouting matches. It was just easier to drift off, go somewhere else. That such a dissociation was known as a fugue state inflamed his father. *"A fugue state,"* Big Al would rage, *"is when a Fugue keeps his goddamn head in the game!"*

Tommy caught himself drifting. Eldritch smoke billowing from the bottom of the door, clinging to the cobblestones of some dungeon . . . and Todd a dragon now, hoarding his gold, surrounded by the charred bodies of those who had tried to claim his treasure . . .

Tommy shook his head to clear it.

"We're walking right into the lion's den," he said to his partner.

"Lions, tigers, and bears, oh my," Nine said flatly, then laughed suddenly at this, his mood brighter than Tommy had seen it in a long time.

Nine didn't knock, just shoved the door open and strolled in. After a moment, Tommy followed.

Inside, the smell wasn't of charred bodies but rather the sweet, clashing scent of a dozen different vapes. The music's volume was punishing. Todd sat at one end of a couch, next to an end table, wearing a trucker hat and a button-up short-sleeve shirt over ratty cargo shorts. On the table were Solo cups and handles of rum and vodka and tequila. Arrayed around him were similarly attired bros; Tommy counted a dozen of them. He was scared, but even taking that into account, he didn't like the vibe. Apparently, neither did the women, because there weren't any in sight.

A few heads turned in Nine and Tommy's direction, but Todd was mashing a controller, and everyone was transfixed by the flatscreen, where a first-person shooter game presented exploding gore in 4K splendor.

Nine clocked a large wireless speaker that produced the bone-rattling music on the apartment's small balcony. He walked to it and flipped it over the edge before anyone registered his presence. The aggressive rap ceased upon impact. There was some faint shouting from below, but the party continued.

"That's better," said Nine, stepping back into the apartment.

Every head swung in the interloper's direction at once. It took them a moment to register what had just happened—Tommy barely believed it himself—then Todd got to his feet. Tommy was astounded anew by his size—he just kept unfolding until he stood tall in the small room. His two lackeys from CrackBurger began to get up too. Everyone else looked on. With a swing of his arm, Todd ordered his bros to grab Nine, but as the students rose from their chair, Nine fake-lunged at the group. They all flinched. One fell back into his chair.

Nine strolled around the coffee table and blocked their view of the flatscreen. He smiled.

Todd, still on his feet, spoke up. "Real tough guy with a gun."

"Gun?" said Nine. *"This?"*

He pulled his weapon. Everyone froze, but Nine placed it on the cigarette-and-bong-dominated coffee table and stepped back. It sat equidistant between the two adversaries.

"Go on, big guy. Take it. If you're man enough to take it."

Todd glanced at his friends, gauging their support. Gauging his distance to the gun. Gauging the stranger's reaction time.

Finally, Todd snorted awkwardly and sat down. "Nice try. I'm not putting my prints on that shit. I don't know what you've done with it."

"Yeah, I didn't think so," said Nine, retrieving the gun and tucking it away. "Now. I came for the money."

Todd smiled a Cheshire cat grin. "I don't know what you're talking about."

"Come on, Ty."

"Todd."

Nine nodded a little too vigorously. "You expect me to believe you saved up for this rager, which by the way, looks like the kid from Home Alone's idea of *a really swell time.* A Slip 'N Slide? Return the money now, Ty, and I'll walk away."

"You owe me a speaker, motherfucker."

"*Stunod,*" Nine said quietly, almost to himself.

Tommy's face felt hot, and his stomach dropped. He swore everyone in the room could hear its gurgling. But he remained still, kept his gaze neutral and relaxed, as he had been instructed to on the drive over.

"Do you know who the money that funded this *swell shindig* belongs to?"

"*What* money?" Todd laughed at his own joke, looked around for backup, but there were no laughs or grunts or even smiles of approval.

A palpable sense of nervousness filled the room. Either Todd's crew had been sobered by the appearance of a firearm or they were curious about the strange young man who was outnumbered yet held the vibe in a choke hold. Nine Ball seemed to address the room as much as he did Todd. "Your unintended benefactor tonight has been Alessandro Fugue. Also known as Big Al Fugue, also known as the Al Mighty to true believers. And sometimes referred to in the media as Don Fugue of the Fugue Crime Family. An unfair portrayal . . . but still."

Side-glances. The boys stopped looking at their purported leader and started looking at one another. A new level of anxiety spread throughout the space. The first stirrings of true panic.

"Bullshit," said Todd. He guffawed and looked around.

No one joined in his laughing.

"Mr. Fugue is a legitimate businessman and a major community booster. He is quite magnanimous, but if there's one thing that irritates this upright citizen more than his unkind portrayal in the media"—Nine turned his head and leveled his gaze at Todd—"it's when people take advantage of him."

Nine reached into his jacket. Several of the partygoers flinched, expecting the gun to reemerge, but instead the soldier produced his phone. Looking down as if perhaps dialing or reading something interesting on it, Nine walked around the coffee table and then held its screen up in front of Todd's face.

The clod's face went pale, his jaw slack. "Oh, God . . ."

Tommy didn't know what was on the phone, and did not want to know, but he felt his guts, roiling moments before, calm. His shoulders eased. It was like he had off-loaded his terror onto this big, dumb party kid. He suddenly had to keep himself from smiling.

"Now," Nine said, spinning slowly to face the others in the

room once again. "The Al Mighty is nothing if not fair. If you had nothing to do with this little . . . practical joke, you are free to leave."

Nine clasped his hands in front of him and studied his polished shoes as most of the boys in the room found their feet and scrambled for the door.

"A warning, gentlemen," the gangster said over the din. "This conversation did not take place. By all means, clear the party and recoup whatever you can, but if there's one thing the Al Mighty hates more than being taken advantage of, it is lack of discretion. If I learn that Mr. Fugue's name is mentioned beyond this door, I will be very displeased. And men not as reasonable as me will find you."

"What do we tell them?" asked the boy closest to the door, his hand frozen on the knob.

Nine laughed. "Tell them the cops are on their way."

In a moment, only Todd and the two CrackBurger boys remained. The rest bounded downstairs like a herd of antelope fleeing a lion. Within seconds, the sound of the festivities died down.

As Nine paced in front of the three men and *tsk-tsked* them like a professor to a group of naughty schoolchildren, Tommy felt emboldened enough to walk onto the balcony and peer over at the party. He watched the stampede of frightened frat boys explode from the front doors and fan out, spreading across the lawn. It was like watching *The Walking Dead* or a video game, the message transmitting from person to person like a contagion. He watched the backs of those in line for the keg stiffen. The music, pumping the moment before, fell silent with the finality of a record scratch. Sailing beach balls fell to the ground and rolled to a halt against the trampled landscaping. Todd's posse continued to move through the crowd, scattering the partygoers before them like sharks dispersing schools of fish. Within minutes, the lawn was clear. The posse looked up to the balcony in astonishment, some in confusion, but all with some measure of fear.

Tommy lifted his hand like a British royal.

"Dude," hissed Nine. Shot him a look.

Tommy dropped his hand.

Tommy looked at the boys again.

They stared back.

Tommy did a little test lunge.

They flinched.

Holy shit, thought Tommy, a grin forming.

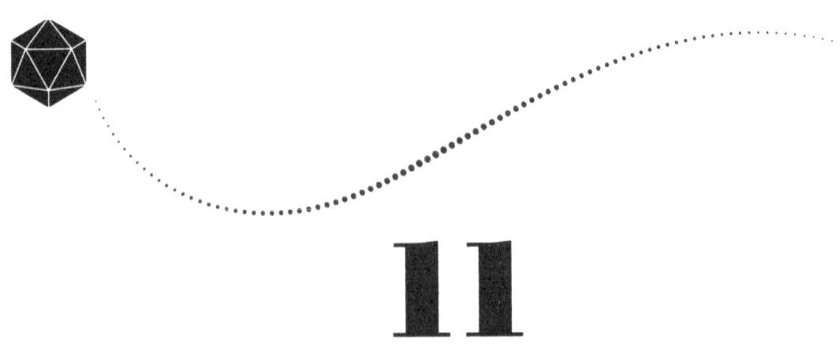

11

Fear is the mind-killer.

Counterpoint, thought Tommy: *It's also a hell of a motivator.*

Nine had been right. In the end, Todd placed the money in the soldier's outstretched hand like it was a little bird landing on Snow White's finger. Nine turned to Tommy and winked, a quick little *I told you so.*

But the bag was light. Seven thousand dollars light.

Nine had been expecting Todd to be short. A DJ, kegs, food, and party props do not just materialize gratis, but being short seven large was more than they had anticipated. And leaving them with a sum of thirteen large seemed like a bad omen.

A little on the nose, thought Tommy. *As if this whole enterprise wasn't already cursed from the jump.*

Despite Todd's pleas that he couldn't come up with seven grand overnight, Nine—all smiles—expressed insincere confidence in the oaf's initiative and creativity and gently reminded him that if he—and by extension Don Fugue—was not made whole, then Todd himself would not *remain* whole.

"I'll pay," the boy had muttered. "I swear."

An aggressive payment plan had been worked out on the spot.

By the time they left the apartment and walked outside, everyone had vanished.

Nine looked at the mess left behind: tipped red Solo cups, paper plates with half-eaten barbecue warming in the sun, flies buzzing. Nine toed a brightly colored water pistol and snorted.

"It's like the Rapture. But for dickheads."

Tommy looked up toward the balcony of 2B. He could hear weeping coming from inside. Another voice, angry, shushed for silence right before the balcony doors slammed shut.

"What am I going to do?" asked Tommy.

"You're going to do your nerd shit. I'll start converting the cash to cards. You said yourself that would take time. It'll take me days to get through the 13K we have. We'll get paid back, good as new, with some interest on top."

"Pop can never know."

"Generally, it's not healthy to keep secrets from the Al Mighty," Nine began, but after a pause added, "but yeah, we're in total agreement."

He held out his hand to Tommy. Nine preferred not to touch people, and when he had to, he preferred the cleanest, least intimate option: the fist bump. Proffering his open hand was scarier to him than walking into a room outnumbered a dozen to one. Which told how Tommy how serious he was, and how scary Don Fugue was.

They shook.

Tommy returned to his apartment, the paper bag lighter, but he was optimistic that the funds would replenish before his father would ever be the wiser. It had been a terrifying interlude, and despite emerging from the party victorious, Tommy was still jumpy and nervous. He imagined a residue of fear clung to his skin like a fine dust. Worse, he was no closer to figuring out what he was going to "sell" on FunFunder. He found a clean glass and poured himself some rum.

"Time to get into the Grindset," he muttered to himself facetiously before he realized he was actually kind of sincere.

He spent hours sketching doodles, snatches of phrases, and half-baked ideas onto a yellow legal pad. There were lots of puns. The rum level in the bottle sank. His blood-alcohol level rose.

He wrote the title of a bogus project at the top of a sheet, adding notes and flourishes, but by the bottom of the page, it became apparent that there was no *there* there. His enthusiasm drained along with the rum. He ripped sheet after sheet from the notepad, crumpled them, and tossed them over his shoulder.

The Photo Journal of Ennui Kitty, a moe-apocalypse story featuring a very cute cat in World War I Paris—

Rip, crumple, toss.

All the Pretty Hearses, a novel of three funerals—

Rip, crumple, toss. Don't even finish the joke.

Zombie versions of Disney princesses.

Rip, crumple, toss.

Princess versions of zombies.

Rip, crumple, throw as hard as possible at something.

He finally flung the legal pad aside like Captain America's shield. He reminded himself that these projects didn't have to be real. They just had to go up on the site and look plausible enough to wash the money and cash out. But despite the events of the past day, his rum-soaked mind, now free of the initial panic of losing the money, kept drifting back to Sanse. He wanted to impress her. And, he found, Anibal too.

This whole summer job might just be a cash grab to his

father, but if stuck doing it, Tommy wanted to do something real. Something he could be proud of. Something that would prove that he could create something on his own.

And stop feeling like a tourist or a poser. Tommy the NPC. Time for some main character energy.

He navigated, stumbling over last semester's textbooks, his way into his bedroom and opened his closet, where he looked for his mother's sketches on the high shelf.

He had photos and videos of her on his phone, but her art? He felt like he was holding shards of her true self—her soul—in his hands. It wasn't just about impressing Sanse. It was also about honoring his mother.

Holding her drawings like religious relics, he made a drunken vow to her that he would, for once in his life, *try*.

He would try, and she would come back for him, and then they could leave together. Tommy remained angry with her, though it felt muted now. She was not the villain here. One breakfast with his father had reminded him of that. If Big Al could casually upend Tommy's life over a stack of pancakes, how much anguish had he put his wife through over the years?

Fuck you, Pop. For running her off.

He carried the drawings gingerly back to the couch, stepping over his scattered books and failed ideas—yellow and crumpled—dotting the floor like land mines. He was in a full wallow now, his anxiety and dread replaced with a deep sadness. He had committed to pouring another drink and staring at her drawings, when he stubbed his toe on a thick philosophy tome: *Serenity Nowish: Philosophy for the Instant Gratification Generation.*

"Fuck," he said, glaring at the academic hazard.

The book was open to a page with a giant compass rose on it.

Tommy blinked.

But instead of marking direction, its cardinal points directed toward virtues: *Wisdom, Courage, Discipline, Love.*

It was a moral compass.

The smaller intercardinal points, nestled between the big four virtues, pointed to four more characteristics.

Curiosity, Zest, Gratitude, Hope.

Tommy was astonished.

In his philosophy class, he had learned what *astonish* really meant. From Latin, it translated to "leaving someone thunderstruck." As he looked from his mother's art to the compass and back again, he felt like a bolt of lightning had cracked the sky and found him in his messy Commerce City apartment. And the electric current fused and animated the disparate drawings, the compass, and the discarded ideas, Frankenstein's monster–style: *It's alive. It's alive!* In his mind's eye he saw a band of fantasy characters, banished to a realm, hopelessly lost, both internally and externally. Instead of the characters being defined by their requisite strengths and skills, these were motivated by what they lacked. Or what they had lost.

Tommy was still dazed and rooted to the spot, but ideas were flooding in and floating past involuntarily. He was in a riptide moving almost faster than he could process.

A bard in search of Courage.

An assassin halfling in search of Discipline.

He fixed his gaze on a pencil sketch, his mother's self-portrait, simple yet exquisite.

An heiress in search of Love.

Tommy did not have time for sadness; the exhilarating wave of ideas battered him. The concept was a little *Wizard of Oz*—each character was defined by their missing piece, sure; but hell, wasn't that all of fiction? Of life? And the characters didn't need to be bound to fantasy archetypes. Time-tossed and agnostic, he could see a twelfth-century samurai with no Zest battling alongside a World War I doughboy who had forgotten what it meant to Hope. And the environment could be designed to be as inhospitable to the campaign as possible. A mage in search of Wisdom battling a mindless horde; a curious knight solving a set of increasingly complex puzzles.

Once all members of the game worked together to collect the broken pieces of themselves—finding the broken shards of their very souls—then . . . *what?*

The eyes of his mother stared up at him from its pencil sketch. She must have done it when she was the same age as Tommy. She was young; her eyes were intent, not yet hardened by her marriage.

Another lightning bolt found him in the lines of her image.

These lost souls didn't just get their shards back and return to their home dimensions or whatever eras they were plucked from. They were brought to the realm by the magic of a lost, imprisoned queen, the rightful monarch of the realm, and they must use all their restored virtues to rescue her. For what was a piece of one's soul regained if not exercised, used, and cherished in a task?

For a moment the flood ebbed, and Tommy sighed. It was all a bit emo. Maybe a little on the nose . . .

But *damn it,* wasn't that what his professors were yammering on and on about—that creativity was about transmuting your life into art? About being authentic to *your* self and *your* vision?

The electric current animating the idea came rushing back. It spread to his fingers and toes, burning off the rum. He dove for his yellow legal pad.

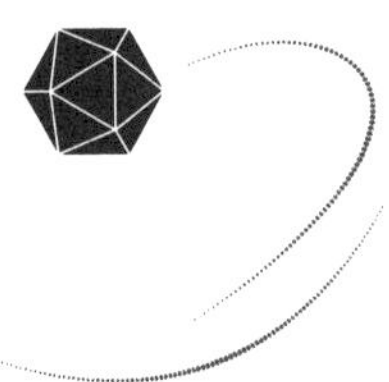

12

"You look like shit, my guy," said Anibal.

The artist sat across from Tommy in the Red Rooster Cafe, the same spot in which the Second Guys Breakfast had occurred, only this time Tommy occupied the space where his father had sat. He had spent that breakfast waiting for the other shoe to drop, so he had not appreciated the place's kitsch before. Stickers of local businesses adorned the tabletops. A vintage Radio Flyer fire and rescue vehicle hung from the ceiling on thin chains. An automated server that looked like a Roomba's taller older brother rolled past, heaped with foot-long burritos.

"You couldn't have gotten too banged up at Todd's. Cops broke it up, I heard."

Tommy shrugged. He was only half listening. Beside Anibal sat Sanse. That was unexpected.

"Oh," said Sanse, leaning in and touching Tommy's forearm. "Do tell, playboy."

Tommy had wanted to infuse his reply with an air of mystery, to provide just the slightest bit of edge, but it didn't suit him. He backpedaled wildly.

"No! No, nothing like that . . ."

"And here I thought you were cool," teased Sanse.

Anibal looked on, amused.

"I'm cool. I'm totally cool. So cool I'm fire, in fact . . ."

Sanse laughed. Tommy wasn't trying to be funny. Words just kept tumbling out of his mouth unchecked, and he silently cursed himself, but Sanse's laughter was warm and sounded like wind chimes on a summer night. "I told you he was hilarious, Ani," she said.

Anibal stared at him, then at Sanse, then back again, his raised eyebrow screaming, *What the hell is going on?*

Great question, thought Tommy.

He had texted Anibal with a plea to meet him for breakfast. He wanted to discuss the finer points of FunFunder. As much as Tommy loved being in Sanse's orbit at her party, it was loaded with pretentious douchebags who wanted to discuss art, or more precisely slag other people's art, instead of actually making it. But Anibal was different. He was making a comic book—seen as lowbrow in snobbier circles—and that he didn't care what they thought showed a confidence belying his small stature and bookish looks. Tommy wanted to bounce his new idea off what he hoped were receptive ears. And deep down, Tommy wanted to be his friend.

But Anibal brought Sanse. Any other day, Tommy would have been absolutely delighted. Hell, he was still delighted, but he was distracted, still lost in the world that was unfolding in his head, still a bit rattled by his father's menacing demands.

"I didn't know you were coming, Sanse," he managed. "I would've worn, um, nicer pajama pants."

More wind chimes of laughter.

"I was texting with Ani the same time you were," she said. "He mentioned you were cooking something up. And I never turn down a free breakfast. So, what genre-mashing, multimedia masterpiece are you planning?"

"It's an RPG."

"A rocket-propelled grenade?"

Tommy nodded. "Absolutely. Did I say art? I meant *arms.* Wait, is this not an arms deal?"

A powerful gust of wind rattled the wind chimes. "Oh, no, you're in the right place," Sanse said. "Ani, did you bring the briefcase with the money?"

Tommy winced at that, took a sip from his coffee cup to conceal that the image was all too familiar. Then he managed, "Despite my attire and aforementioned coolness, I am not, in fact, an international arms dealer. I meant *roleplaying game.*"

Anibal leaned forward, finally interested in the conversation, or perhaps just hoping to banish the awkward flirtation he was being made to witness. "Tabletop?"

"Oh, did I also forget to mention I'm a software designer and created my own massively multiplayer online roleplaying game between Fine Art Fundamentals and Introduction to Moral Philosophy? Fuck yes, tabletop. *Way* cheaper."

It was Anibal's turn to laugh.

Sanse looked from one to the other. "Boys, telling jokes. Ha ha."

"She doesn't grok," said Anibal. "Just another pretty face."

Sanse threw an elbow into Anibal's ribs.

"Okay, okay . . . easy," said Anibal, laughing. "She's not really that pretty." He flinched, anticipating an attack that never came. "So, what are you thinking, Tommy?"

Tommy prepared to launch into an explanation of the game, then stopped. He was suddenly nervous. Vulnerable. If his mother was the game's muse and his father was the game's means, then Sanse was the raison d'être. She was the audience. Part of him had pictured himself as a knight-errant—his armor dented, scorched, and stained with dragon blood—laying his boon, the game, at the foot of her princess throne before her awestruck court.

But that was supposed to be *later*. Like, when he was sure it was actually *cool*.

He hadn't expected her to be wolfing waffles in front of him the morning after he came up with the premise. So many ideas had blossomed in his head last night, with shoots of new ideas bursting forth from them, that he was afraid he would sound as disjointed and nonsensical as a five-year-old telling a joke. Unsure where to begin, he looked at the beautiful girl across the table, smiling in anticipation.

He took a deep breath, looked into her eyes, and asked, "What if I told you, *What was once lost could be found again*? What would you then want?"

Sanse leaned back in the booth, as if someone had knocked the wind out of her.

"Seeing my father again." She looked down. "He's passed."

Nice work, Lancelot, thought Tommy. "I'm so, so sorry. . . ."

She held up her hands, laughing a softer laugh. "No, it's okay. Long time ago. Cancer. I did not have to hit you with that, but we're artists, right? We shouldn't shy away from our pain. We use it all."

Tommy nodded. Even offhand, she answered the deepest questions he posed to himself. In that moment, over a diner booth, he felt like he might burst. It was impossible to love her more.

He quickly turned to Anibal, lest she see it all over his face. "What about you?"

"For my comic to get funded and sell a million copies."

"Why?"

"Why not? It's good."

"Come on, Sanse went deep. You can give me more than that."

"To get the fuck out of here," he said, stretching his arms wide. "To be free. How's that?"

Tommy pulled a folded paper from his pocket and smoothed it out on the tabletop, oriented it to them. It was the page from his philosophy textbook with the compass rose.

He met Sanse's eye.

"For you," he said. "Love."

She raised an eyebrow.

He felt his cheeks redden, but he cleared his throat and pressed on. "If you were to create a character with that history, with that wish, their motivation would be *Love*."

She stared at the compass for a few moments, her full lips pursed in concentration. After a few moments, she nodded.

"I don't see freedom in there," said Anibal.

"To 'get the fuck out of here' is a hell of a motivation, and believe me, no one understands that better than me, but maybe you lack the bravery to leave. In that case, Courage would be the virtue you seek. Or you lack the means or the resources, in which case maybe Wisdom."

"Or you're a scattered, smothered, and covered hot mess," said Sanse, raising her hand.

Tommy snapped his fingers and pointed at her. *"Discipline."*

He felt himself getting on a roll. He explained the rough mechanics of the game, the virtue compass, the patchwork realm, the sets of challenges designed to test or tempt a campaign. His players could be led astray, but with teamwork, they could retrieve the missing pieces of themselves. Become whole.

And save the queen.

"I call it the One Thousand Shards of Tergivers."

Tommy was breathless when he finished and pleased with

himself. He had not been prepared to pitch his creative newborn to the girl he loved, but he'd worked hard to sound coherent and to channel his nervousness into passion. He watched her posture change the more he fleshed out his world, putting her elbows on the table and leaning in as he detailed out the vision. He had nailed it.

"I don't like shards," said Anibal flatly.

Tommy deflated.

"What's wrong with shards?"

"You're not gluing a vase back together. What can you do with a shard?"

Tommy ducked his chin, pretending to mull over the critique, but the rejection stung.

"Plus, no matter what you do, a segment of fanboys will just call it *sharts*—"

"Ani!" yelled Sanse. "Can't you see he's in the middle of a Cat 5 brainstorm? There are no bad ideas in a brainstorm. Don't be a dick!"

"Yo, Tommy," said Anibal, leaning in. "Sanse can do the whole *rah-rah,* drum circle thing, but I assume you wanted me here because you want to take this to the marketplace and—"

"Here we go again with the marketplace," said Sanse, making a jerking-off motion. *"You students don't understand what it's like out there on the mean streets of FunFunder. . . ."*

"There's art," said Anibal, ignoring Sanse, "and then there's commercial art. And when people back or buy your art, they feel entitled to act like a giant, walking dickhole of a comments section."

He stared at Tommy for a long, hard moment. "Change *shards* to *blades*." Then he sat back and smiled.

"That's it?" said Sanse. "That's your big note?"

"Blades are swords, and swords are cool as fuck, bro."

"Blades . . ." Tommy drummed his fingers on the table. "Each sword could be different. Different blades for different virtues. Stylized, personalized . . ."

"The wand chooses the wizard . . ." said Sanse.

Now Anibal leaned forward, excited. "Fuck that. Too passive," he said. "The sword is *inside you*. Like King Arthur's sword in the stone, only the stone is your fucking heart, dude, and you have to pull it out of you all gnarly-like."

He mimed pulling a sword out of his chest, made grunting, gurgling noises.

Tommy laughed.

"Love could be a flaming sword," ventured Sanse.

Her eyes met Tommy's. Both smiled, looked away. The robot server glided past, now stacked with slices of double-layer chocolate cake. Everything felt lighter, sweeter.

"And Discipline could be, like, the hardest magical metal ever. *Disciplinarium* or some shit."

Last night, Tommy had been visited by inspiration. Now, from Anibal, he was getting his first taste of iteration, the next stop on the wheel of creativity. The concept was out of his head and out living, walking around, interacting with others. It was exhilarating.

Tommy pulled out his phone, his thumbs flying across the screen taking notes. "Blades! This is gold. . . ."

"I could draw you some," said Anibal, offhand.

"Seriously?"

Tommy didn't know him well, but he sensed Anibal was struggling to tamp down his excitement. Trying to play it cool.

The artist shrugged. "Proof of concept."

Tommy was delighted but couldn't pay. "It's not like I can . . . I mean . . ."

The kid smiled. "Relax, man. I ain't coming after your IP or whatever. Friends helping friends."

"In that case," said Tommy, a smile spreading across his face, "when can you get it to me?"

"Tomorrow."

"Well, I'd love to stick around and chat with you titans of commercial art, but some of us have summer jobs," said Sanse.

"What's your job?" asked Tommy.

"Don't you fucking make fun of me."

"I wouldn't."

"Caricatures. Kids' birthday parties, bar mitzvahs, weddings. Sometimes in City Park."

Just like his mother. Tommy gave her a wistful smile.

"That's . . . amazing" was all he could manage.

"Fuck you." She laughed. She started digging in her purse, but Tommy quickly threw some bills on the table.

"Breakfast is on me. It's the least I can do."

She pulled out a lip balm and coated her lips while she smiled. "Yeah, I know."

Out on the sidewalk, Sanse gave him a delicious hug. Anibal gave him an approving fist bump. Tommy savored both as he watched them go. He faced west and smiled. Though he couldn't see them behind the buildings, he imagined the Rocky Mountains standing sentry, but he was so buoyant he felt like he could float right over them like a hot-air balloon. Riffing with Anibal, flirting with Sanse . . . was this what freedom felt like?

The feeling didn't last long. Across the street, he saw the skinny, suited figure of Nine Ball leaning against his car.

As Tommy crossed, the soldier doffed an imaginary cap. "Having breakfast with that stunner from the party, I see." Nine pretended to punch his shoulder jovially. "And a third wheel, of course. So tragic."

"Picking their brains. Art stuff."

Nine looked around, eyed a slovenly shopkeeper down the block. "If there's one thing I know about your father, he's private. This isn't one of your group projects, you understand?"

Tommy grunted. "Can *you* draw, Nine?"

"No."

"Know anything about crowdfunding?"

"Nope."

"Game design?"

"Game?" said Nine. "Tommy, the idea is not to *build* a game, it's to *look like* you're building a game."

"I still need enough art and story to make it look good. I'm just putting up some scaffolding, okay?"

Nine considered this. He clearly didn't like it, but whether he conceded because he believed Tommy or because Tommy was the boss's son, he nodded. But with a pointed finger he warned, "Too many people know about this little hustle already. The name of the real game is *discretion*."

"Discretion? You shut down a party."

"Saving your ass. Just keep it low-pro, understand?"

"They're my friends, Nine. It's all good."

"Friends," snorted Nine. "Next time you take the girl out to breakfast, make sure it's *after*, you know what I'm saying."

Tommy didn't need any more dating advice from Nine. Tommy supposed that, to Nine, romantic partners were potential vectors for countless germs, incompatible habits, and headaches. But he was too excited to argue. Being at the diner was kind of like being on a date with Sanse. They were connecting on a creative plane, which had to count for something.

Tommy nodded in the direction of his apartment. "I have to go back and write some copy for the launch. What are you up to?"

"I guess I'm on fucking gift card duty, thank you very much."

Tommy drove home, the whole way feeling that something had fundamentally changed in his life. When he got to his place, he checked that the money was still there, locked away in the closet now. The ideas still popped in his head like fireworks. He opened his laptop, and his fingers flew across the keyboard. Only when he had poured the ideas out of his mind and into a document could he come close to relaxing. When he finished hours later, he was wrung out. He slept.

Overnight, he received files from Anibal: images of all manner of badass, mythical blades. Giant greatswords larger than any wielder and burning with eldritch energy. Daggers with ornately designed hilts. Energy blades that crackled and pulsed off the page. He also threw in some drawings of dashing rogues, four-armed barbarians, terrifying goblins with wide maws and rows and rows of spiky teeth. Anibal had been playing it cool, but he betrayed himself with the images, and their quantity. He was excited too.

The next morning Tommy took a photo of his mother's self-portrait and sent it to the artist with a note: *Can u make her a queen?*

It only took a couple of hours. What had been a sketch from a bored yet beautiful girl came back as an artist's rendering of noble medieval splendor—complete with crown—on a parchment background. It looked like a scroll to be hung above the roaring fireplace of a castle's great hall, or clutched in the hand of a town crier, or held in the hearts of the ancient sailors aboard one thousand ships at sea.

Anibal texted him back: *Let me know when it's live. I'll signal boost.*

That's when it hit Tommy.

Nine Ball's voice practically screamed in his head: *No one is supposed to see this.*

His fantasy was a front, designed to conceal the real game: Discretion: A Money-Laundering Adventure. Chongo had called it the minimum viable product, just enough to make it look good for FunFunder's purposes. At the time he had seriously considered launching ten such half-ass projects, just to spread the pledge sums even thinner, to seem more plausible. But now, thanks to the last twenty-four hours of creative inspiration, and some artistic assists from Anibal, they had created a beautiful, beguiling Potemkin village, one that would have to remain a hollow front for his father's activities.

He jabbed at his screen. A thumbs-up emoji appeared on Anibal's offer to signal boost.

Tommy tossed the phone aside. The thumbs-up was a lie. He would not let Anibal, or anyone, know when Tergivers was live. The more "civilians" who actually knew about it, the more people he would let down when they realized a game would never materialize. He would be a failure at best, a liar at worst.

The thought made him powerfully sad. He had put more heart into the last twenty-four hours than he could remember ever putting into anything. He had applied himself—not something he was accustomed to—and to his surprise, it hadn't felt like work. It felt like flying. He liked it. More importantly, he liked himself.

It was a new feeling.

He told himself he would do it again someday.

In the meantime, as much as he hated it, he would ghost Anibal, come up with some lame excuse. The thought of disappointing Sanse was unbearable, but he convinced himself that she didn't care enough about him to be disappointed. She had tagged along, bored, to humor two nerds for a free breakfast.

As his creative fever broke, reality flooded in. As much as he enjoyed the brainstorming aspect, there would be no game. What did he know about game design and development? Going to college in the first place was Tommy figuring out who he wanted to be, but he was pretty sure he wasn't an entrepreneur.

He opened FunFunder, loaded the copy and the images, and played with the formatting. Seeing it all up there, it looked good. It looked real, which made the whole situation real, and that scared him. He realized how close he had come to actually being on the hook for something. No thank you, sir. He had just finished freshman year and had more studying and self-exploration ahead of him.

When everything was in order, he hit Return.

The One Thousand Blades of Tergivers was as alive as any zombie ever was.

13

Tommy awoke to a sharp knock at the door. He picked up the phone from the bedside table. It read 9:00 a.m. *Maybe it's a neighbor's door*, he thought. *Maybe it's a dream. Or a bird hitting a window.*

He let his head drop to the pillow again. His head, it throbbed. After launching the game, he'd spent the rest of the day drinking. He hadn't bothered leaving the apartment, subsisting on brownies Chongo'd baked for him, pizza, and, later, cold pizza. Now it was time to catch up on sleep.

Bang.

Not a neighbor. Not a dream. And if it was a bird, it hadn't learned its lesson the first time.

BANG.

And the bird was a condor.

Tommy shuffled to the front door in his boxers and a Scott Pilgrim T-shirt. He looked around at the wreckage of his apartment. He hadn't cleaned up the evidence of his initial brainstorming from the other night: empty bottles of rum, wrappers from DoorDashed tacos, and tight yellow wads of paper everywhere—each crumpled-up ball representing a failed idea. It resembled a tennis court after one of his mother's lessons.

Tommy trod quietly as he approached his front door and

looked through the peephole. Some fathers taught their sons how to throw a curveball or change the oil in their car. Big Al taught Tommy to always pay in cash, always sit with his back to the wall in public, and never just answer a door.

Tommy peeped, then exhaled. It was Nine Ball.

He opened the door to the young soldier and the bright morning sunshine.

"Jesus, Nine . . ." said Tommy, shielding his eyes.

"Rise and grind. Your father wants to see you."

"Shouldn't you guys be in your coffins at this hour? Sharpening your fangs or whatever."

Nine didn't laugh. "Get dressed."

"Now?"

"When Don Fugue says your 'presence is requested,' it's not really a request. And since he did not expound with a time, it's safe to assume he meant immediately. If not sooner."

"Why?"

A shrug. "He wants a progress report."

"Okay, okay. Just let me grab a quick shower."

"Tommy . . ."

It was just a single word—his own name—but it was spoken low. Serious. Devoid of affect. Tommy thought of Todd and his posse and their loud, showy brand of masculinity. Puffed-up chests and bellowing and shoving one another around like apes squaring off in a nature special or professional wrestlers cutting a promo.

Let's go, bro!

Do something, bitch!

I'll fuck you up, kid!

It always amused Tommy, because in his world, loud meant festive. When things grew quiet . . . then it was time to worry. The tactical deployment of silence, the heavy quiet that fell when someone overstepped. That one word from his sudden guest, and the vacuum that followed, made the back of his neck itch. The phantom tingle of prey.

It was easy to forget that Nine was only a year older than Tommy, and the same age as most of the meathead frat boys, given that he possessed the same icy chill of his father and associates. *Of course he does,* thought Tommy. *It's in the job description, and someone with Nine's level of OCD would have honed that part of himself to a tee.*

"Right," said Tommy. "No shower. Can I at least put on some pants?"

"No pajamas, Tommy. Find some big boy pants. Don't embarrass your father."

Tommy nodded. He jerked his thumb toward his apartment. "You want to wait inside?"

Nine peered over Tommy's shoulder. Tommy followed his gaze. A shaft of sunlight illuminated the coffee table, revealing splotches of spilled rum and the sticky rings where Tommy had forsaken a coaster, and the dozens of yellow balls that to the soldier probably resembled enlarged bacteria under a microscope.

"Thanks," said Nine Ball, leaning back. "I'll take my chances with the sun."

After a fifteen-minute drive, Nine Ball delivered Tommy to an indistinct building in an industrial park on the outskirts of Commerce City's downtown. Commerce City was no Denver, but this neighborhood pocket made Denver's downtown look like Neo Tokyo. The buildings were low and blocky, like government administration buildings or elementary schools built in the 1970s.

But the area was clean enough, with a minimum of broken glass on the streets and weeds between the sidewalks. It seemed like the DMZ between the moneyed city center and Rocky Mountain Arsenal. Previously a US Army chemical weapons manufacturing center, the arsenal had been cleaned up and now operated as a wildlife refuge. Growing up, it had always been presented as a feel-good story. This morning it felt like laundered history.

Nine held a plastic card up to an electronic card reader. A green light flashed, followed by a click. A sign above them read TESAURO CATERING.

He held the door for Tommy. "What were you expecting, the Fuzzy Navel?"

"My father is a mammary supporter."

"Did you just call Don Fugue a brassiere?"

Tommy laughed.

Nine gave Tommy a look that warned: *No smart mouth beyond this point.*

When Tommy looked sufficiently chastened, Nine continued. "What's sadder than watching a clown put on his makeup?"

"What?"

"Watching him take it off. There's nothing bleaker than a strip club in the morning light. Spilled beer, fake eyelashes, broken dreams. Better to get out before the illusion breaks." He leveled a finger at Tommy's chest, stopping just shy of actually touching him. It was like he was casting a spell, one that would travel through his body until it penetrated his thick skull. Nine spoke with pride. "The Al Mighty Himself taught me that."

"He sure puts the wise in wiseguy."

Nine's face darkened.

"Last one, I promise." Tommy held his laptop up to cover his face and tiptoed past Nine Ball and into the building.

14

Nine led Tommy through a nice entryway to a staged dining room that Tesauro Catering used to demonstrate its ability to host large, fancy parties. Tommy had pictured his father and associates eschewing open spaces in favor of cramped booths in Italian restaurants and smoke-filled back offices of strip clubs, but this was a wide, bright, and cheerful room. Tommy was genuinely surprised. A buffet station running along one wall offered eggs, pancakes, and trays of pastries. Three silver coffee urns gleamed in the morning sun coming through the tall windows on the opposite wall. Taking it all in, Tommy realized that even before he had entered the room, he'd detected the mood: loud, and therefore festive.

He exhaled a breath he didn't realize he was holding.

Tommy could read his father the way mariners and meteorologists read clouds: The tiny contraction of the skin around his father's eyes and their glint when he had received bad news. The slight tilt of his head and licking of his lips when someone dared to correct him. The subtle set of his father's jaw and heavy silence when Tommy's mother wasn't speaking to him—his mother's verbal silence offset by loudness in everything else—which presaged a combustible fight consisting of slammed doors and coffee cups broken on countertops, followed by the staccato stomping of high heels on parquet floors that sounded like the report of automatic weapon fire. Too often, his parents were two supercells on a collision course that could result in a tornado tearing through the house, and Tommy knew before anyone when to barricade in a storm shelter.

But when his father was in a good mood, everyone was in a good mood.

And there was the extreme too, when a good mood tipped into hysteria. When the smiles were a little forced and the laughs came a little too easily. Like everyone had been gassed by the Joker.

If the Tesauro showroom was any indication, his father's mood was in the sweet spot.

Two steps into the room and Tommy was assaulted with bear hugs. The two Johnnies were first in line. Tommy's mother had tried to contain his father's business dealings, but family and Family often bled together. He saw the two Johnnies, for example, as near-uncles like Chongo. In truth, he knew they were Don Fugue's consiglieri. Most bosses had only one senior advisor, but growing up with both men around, it didn't seem strange to Tommy.

Johnny Socks got to him first. Smallish with a warm smile and salt-and-pepper hair, he was called Socks because he grew up on the streets of Philadelphia selling everything that wasn't nailed down, from pretzels to parking spots. But he had started with menswear, hence "Socks."

Socks grabbed one of Tommy's biceps and shook it. "Look at you, kid! What are they feeding you on campus?"

Johnny Reb towered over the both of them. "I can still take 'im," he said in his deep voice. He hailed from Queens but spent the summer of his eighteenth year working at an amusement park on the boardwalk in Ocean City, Maryland. But one summer below the Mason-Dixon Line was all it took. With Maryland considered the Deep South by New York standards, "Reb" had been his name for the last forty years.

From the corner, Tommy received a greeting nod from SuperChenz, the only person larger than Johnny Reb in the room, which he returned with a quick wave. Bicep still sore from Johnny Sock's inspection, he remembered one summer in high school when Tommy wanted to lift weights and Big Al assigned SuperChenz the task of getting his son "swole." It didn't last long. SuperChenz didn't speak much—Tommy only ever remembered him counting off reps and offering cheerful, bro-coded encouragement—and Tommy drifted to other pursuits as he so often did.

Turdo sidled up. Mikey Turdo was his father's second-in-command. Unlike the Johnnies, there was no avuncular love there. Turdo's smiles were always bright but brittle. As much as he pretended otherwise, he had little interest in Tommy. Which suited Tommy fine, because he had little interest in his father's dealings, let alone his underboss.

The formal little man looked Tommy up and down, taking in his collared shirt, his khakis, his dress shoes. He nodded in approval. But Tommy felt like Simba being appraised by Scar in *The Lion King*. "Looking good, Tommy. We're all very excited to hear about your venture."

"Thanks, Uncle Mikey."

Turdo flagged a passing server and relieved him of one of the small plates on his tray. The underboss proffered the plate, loaded with mini quiches, to Tommy. "You need to eat. These chili quiches are fucking divine."

Tommy held up a hand and said softly, "I'm allergic to peppers, Uncle Mikey."

"I'm sorry." Turdo gave his own forehead a light tap. "I keep forgetting about how *sensitive* your stomach is."

It was true. Certain peppers caused him to break out in hives and his airway to close up, so of course, much to the chagrin of his father, his mother had declared them *peppera non grata* in her home. "An Italian who can't stomach peppers . . ." Big Al would mutter and shake his head. Yet another source of embarrassment.

"You know," continued Turdo, "it's a beautiful thing to have a father who wants to bring his son into the family business."

The remark put Tommy on high alert. Perhaps because it was delivered in such a tone that it was clear that him following in Big Al's footsteps was absolutely *not* a beautiful thing to Turdo.

Surely the underboss did not see Tommy as a contender for the throne.

"I, uh, want to pursue art," Tommy offered.

It sounded lame, but it was the first thing he could think of, and he wanted to communicate quickly and clearly that he was in no way competition.

"That's good, Tommy. Real good." Turdo gripped his shoulder, too tight to be familial or reassuring, but light enough to not be a threat. "Where would the world be without art, am I right?"

15

Tommy navigated though the throng of his father's associates crowded around the coffee service, receiving more painful hugs, numerous claps on the back, and even a pinch on the cheek. By the time he found Chongo, his uncle among uncles, he was as panicked as when he first heard Nine Ball banging on his door.

"What the hell is this all about, Chongo?"

"Just a little summit we do from time to time. Old business, new business . . ."

"Yeah, but what am *I* supposed to do?"

Chongo gave him a reassuring look before downing three prosciutto rolls at once. "Just walk him through it, Tommy. You'll be fine."

Another man tapped the accountant on the elbow and the accountant excused himself for a conversation out of Tommy's earshot, leaving him to collect himself. Extricating himself from the crowd of boisterous gangsters, he made his way to the windows on the far wall, passing several long tables topped with gleaming white tablecloths and ornate place settings. The windows were incredibly tall, accenting the pale blue peaks of the Rocky Mountains. Framed as they were in such a room, he had to admit they looked spectacular. No forest fire haze rendering them incorporeal today. Normally, he hated them. The mountain range was always there, a reminder of the outer reaches of Tommy's perimeter, the bitter end of his leash.

A firm hand on his shoulder turned him from the view.

His father was standing next to an attractive, middle-aged woman with jet-black hair in an apron.

"Lori, I'd like to introduce you to the prodigal. This is Tommy. Tommy, this is Ms. Tesauro, the owner of this dazzling establishment."

The raven-haired chef offered her hand. A grip firmed by kneading, pounding, and scooping.

"You can call me Lori." She paused, taking Tommy in, then beamed. "The resemblance is uncanny. Such a pair of handsome fellas. You must be very proud."

There was an awkward pause. Tommy thought she was referring to him, but she was in fact talking to Tommy about his pride in his father.

"Oh," said Tommy. "Yes, *of course*. Very proud. Very *very* proud." He hoped his smile was genuine.

The woman went on without really registering much of what he said. "This business has been in my family for decades. We hit a rough patch, but Big Al helped get us back on our feet. We wouldn't have been able to build this addition without him. What do you think of the view?"

Tommy glanced at the distant peaks again, subtle but undeniable, like a pasture fence or a prison wall. The mountains denied him the West Coast in the same way that the East Coast felt tainted by his father's business.

He also noticed for the first time the two goons outside, walking the perimeter. Big Al's early warning detection system.

"It's really something," he said.

"We call it the Alessandro Fugue Commemorative Showroom," Lori said with a wink.

"Come on now," said Big Al, the picture of false modesty.

Lori Tesauro grabbed Al's upper arm gently. "Can I get you boys anything else? More food? More coffee? Something with a little more kick maybe?"

"Everything is perfect, dear," he said. He kissed her cheek. "I always appreciate your spread."

She smacked his arm and the two of them shared a carnal laugh.

Gross, thought Tommy. He faced the windows and pretended to take in the view while concealing his disgust. *He doesn't even bother to hide it anymore.*

"You boys have fun now," said Lori.

Once the caterer left, Big Al stood by his son at the window, his associates inside milling around drinking coffee and eating Danish, his guards outside keeping watch.

"What's up your ass?" said Big Al as he looked out at the landscape.

"Is she, like, your girlfriend or something?"

Big Al let out a belly laugh and looked at his son. He seemed genuinely tickled.

"Lori? We've known each other a long time."

"That doesn't really answer the question, Pop."

"Listen . . ." Big Al put his arm around Tommy's shoulder and pulled him closer, halfway to a headlock. "People do not remember what you say, they only remember how you make them *feel*."

It was true. Tommy tried to think of the bullshit his father had told him over the years but could only remember how Big Al made him feel: Small. Frightened. Angry.

Big Al spoke quietly in his ear, conspiratorial. "It's like this: That poor woman works her fingers to the bone sixteen hours a day and that's it. She doesn't go out. She doesn't get to put on makeup and let her hair down and dance. She sees the same coworkers every day and her asshole customers. She is a magnificent chef and a hard-working small business owner who takes care of everyone but herself, but beneath all of that? She is a woman. And she wants to be seen. To be appreciated. In every way. It's primeval. So, I tell her she's doing a great job, which she is. And I tell her she's pretty, which she is. And I flirt and she pretends not to love it. But she walks away happy. Everyone's heart is a lock, son. You just need to find the right pick. It can be money, it can be fear, but sometimes, it's just flattery."

Only his father could dress up banging the caterer as some sort of noble deed.

"What was Mom's pick?"

Big Al pursed his lips. He looked as if he had not anticipated the question and didn't like it. Tommy had not anticipated asking it and feared for a moment that his father might explode. Instead, his father took a deep breath and looked out at the spectral mountains, a rueful grin on his face.

"She changed the combination every day, son. If I'd figured her out, maybe she wouldn't have left."

In that moment, as he watched his father scrutinize the mountains—majestic and just out of reach—Tommy actually felt a flutter of pity for him.

Then Big Al brought his hands together in a single, mighty clap. It sounded like a gunshot in the airy room. The chitchat in the room ceased at once. Everyone found a seat. He turned back to his son, a predatory gleam in his eye.

Tommy's father was gone, their fleeting bonding moment over. In his place stood the Al Mighty.

"Showtime. Time for your final exam, college boy."

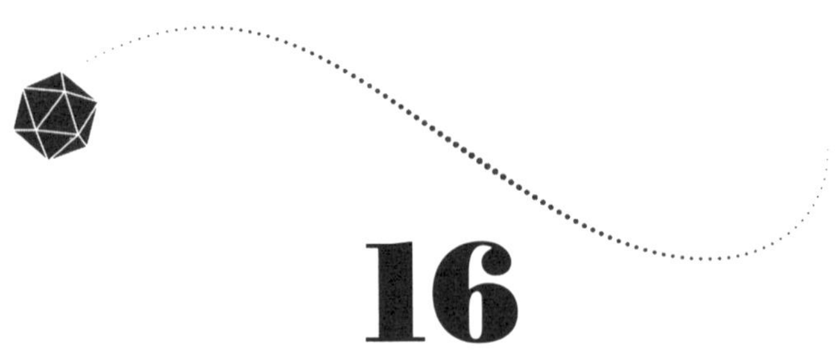

16

"Apple of my eye, fruit of my loins," said Big Al, "Chongo informs me you set out on the digital frontier and have returned with a boon. Please educate these fucking Luddites."

The assembled gangsters snickered.

Tommy had remembered to bring his laptop, fortunately, and, even more fortunately, had something half resembling a pitch deck for Tergivers that he had made to organize his thoughts a little better. He figured he could share it with his dad, but looking at the crowd, he suddenly wondered: *What am I going to do, have a bunch of mafioso huddle around my screen?*

Fortunately, Nine Ball was a details guy. The soldier had anticipated this and brought a small projector in a backpack otherwise stuffed full of random computer cables and dongles. As Nine connected the two devices, Tommy heard a long exhale from the direction of his father. *Impatience.* But Nine worked quickly and precisely and before long Tommy's screen was projected onto a section of the wall where the sunlight didn't reach.

As Turdo's cigar smoke wafted through the projection and distorted it slightly, Tommy panicked anew at how absurd this all was. PowerPoint was as alien to the crew as the finer points of the Racketeer Influenced and Corrupt Organizations Act was to him.

Tommy coughed and began. "I call it—"

Big Al held up a hand and shook his head. The tables were configured in a large horseshoe, with his father seated at the center of the bottom. He gestured toward the wide-open area between the tables.

"I'm sorry?" said Tommy.

"Don't apologize," said Big Al. "Sounds weak."

Nine, sitting next to Tommy, leaned over. "On your feet," he whispered.

Tommy complied. He walked to the top of the horseshoe and entered it. It felt like getting prodded into the Colosseum, the surrounding men less like uncles now and more like bloodthirsty spectators, with the occasional tiger stalking the periphery. Tommy was not fond of public speaking. His father, though mostly an absentee father, was keenly aware of this fact, and was probably playing to it. Big Al cataloged everyone's strengths and weaknesses. It was like he had written up detailed character sheets on all his enemies and associates. Tommy imagined the stats his father had worked up on him.

CLAN: ***The Family Fugue***

CHARACTER NAME: ***Tommy Fugue***

———STATS:———

- STRENGTH: ***Not much***
- WISDOM: ***Dumb as shit***
- CHARISMA: ***Negative***
- PERFORMANCE: ***Please . . .***

The space inside the horseshoe felt too large for him to fill. Enough to trigger spontaneous agoraphobia. Like he was a rabbit on the Eastern Plains, surrounded on all sides by coyotes . . .

He found Nine's eyes. Intense eyes that stared at him, their stillness almost steadying Tommy's flailing mood.

Tommy pointed at the laptop. "Will you run the slides?"

It was the soldier's turn to look uncomfortable. He had not had time to wash his hands after handling the projector. Tommy imagined Nine Ball could see the microscopic germs dancing on the keyboard. Before Nine could touch it, Chongo reached over and slid the laptop toward himself.

"I'll DJ," said the accountant, sparing the young man.

Nine's relief was palpable. Tommy, however, was still on the hook.

"Isn't that better?" asked Big Al. "When you make a pitch, you want to be on your feet. Taking up space. Commanding the room. Your fancy computer can't do *that* for you. What are they teaching you at that candy-ass school of yours?"

Everyone laughed.

To Chongo, Tommy said, "It's the file that says Queen."

The accountant nodded. A moment later, the projector displayed the sketch from his mother that Anibal had improved, rendering her as a crowned medieval queen on parchment. Above her was the title of his nascent game in a suitably dramatic Gothic font. He waited for the gleam of recognition in his father's eye at his mother's likeness.

Big Al stared at the illuminated wall, concentrating like he was indeed trying to pick a lock. "What the fuck is a *Tergiver*?"

"It's just a name."

"Yeah, but what does it mean?"

When Tommy froze, Nine pulled out his phone. "Closest word is *tergiversation,* Don Fugue. Means 'to equivocate.' "

"Would someone please speak English?"

"Using ambiguous language to conceal the truth," Tommy said at last.

"Like saying 'a friend of ours' when you really mean 'mobbed up,' " said Johnny Socks.

"Or someone 'got their badge' when they got made," said Johnny Reb.

Like saying "flirting" when in reality you're banging the caterer, thought Tommy, but he kept his mouth shut.

Big Al looked around the room, his frustration growing.

"Like saying 'I gotta see a man about a horse' when you have to take a shit, Big Al," said SuperChenz.

"A-oh!" Big Al made a face. "We're eating, Chenz. Come on."

"Sorry, Don Fugue."

"Everybody focus. Proceed already, One Thousand Blades of Turducken."

"Yes, sir . . . So the One Thousand Blades of *Tergivers* is a fantasy-based roleplaying game, or RPG. There are all sorts of RPGs," explained Tommy. "There's the original format, the tabletop roleplaying game, or TTRPG—played around a table obviously—and even live-action roleplaying, or LARPing. You may have seen some people LARPing before. . . ."

He paused and looked around the room at the older, heavy-set men with sallow skin and the younger men like Nine Ball, dressed in black, who looked like modern, stylish vampires. Their expressions ranged from dead-eyed to rough.

"Or maybe not. Chongo, next slide, please. . . ." The accountant clicked to another slide, which featured an Anibal original: a fiendish warlock the size of a kindergartener dressed in flowing robes. He noticed for the first time that Anibal had named him Gnorm the Gnome and included a footnote that the *G*'s were not silent.

Tommy chuckled and looked around the room to see if anyone

else had caught it. The gangsters stared at him stone-faced.

"Anyway . . . these RPGs also evolved into complex online versions called massively multiplayer online roleplaying games, or MMORPGs. But for Tergivers—"

Big Al cleared his throat.

The respectful silence in the room found another depth.

"Son, why don't you begin with the FunFunder of it all," offered Chongo. "You know, the *money* . . ."

"Right. So, how many of you are familiar with crowdfunding?"

"Like collection?" asked SuperChenz.

"Good, yes!" said Tommy, pointing at the mobster. "Kind of. Actually no. If you want to start a venture—a film, a comic book, or in our case, an RPG—you can post your venture on a site like FunFunder. You post a description, some art, a slideshow like this one, a video—whatever it takes to get people psyched—and also how much money you need to get it off the ground. If people are into it, they can pledge to fund that venture and get one of the products if you make it. If, after thirty days, you hit your funding goal, you get to keep the pledges. But if not, no money is collected."

"And *that's* when you break some legs!" said SuperChenz loudly, thinking he was being helpful.

Tommy's eyes went wide. "No, Chenz. No. Funders are your investors. You need their money. You don't break their legs."

"So, some jerk-off comes along and does this FunFund," said Big Al, "and I pledge a grand. Walk me through it."

Tommy tried to not take offense, hoping he was not the assumed jerk-off. "Well, you enter your credit card information into the site. Using Tergivers as an example, if I get enough backers and hit my funding goal, which I set at twenty thousand dollars here, if that happens within thirty days, *your* grand is now *my* grand."

"Where's my money in those thirty days?"

Tommy smiled as he watched his father begin to grok it. Big Al always followed the money.

"In your account. Absolutely nothing happens unless I hit the goal. It's just a pledge, Pop."

"And if you hit your goal?" asked Big Al.

"Oh!" exclaimed SuperChenz. "Then we break his legs!"

"No, you fucking dump truck," said Big Al. "That's when he gets paid, nice and legal-like, yeah?"

Big Al looked to his son for confirmation. Tommy had shared many meals with these men over the years, always as a kid, a fly on the wall, but he knew the drill. He was surprised at how quickly he himself fell into the role of rushing to validate the Al Mighty.

"Yes, Pop. Absolutely, Pop."

Satisfied that he had demonstrated a rapid grasp of crowdfunding to his underlings, Big Al sat back in his chair, relaxed. He pointed a finger at Tommy. It was his own peculiar way of pointing, his large pinkie ring preventing him from closing his fist entirely so it resembled the sign of the horns. When pointed down, the horns were meant to ward off bad luck or misfortune when someone gave you the *malocchio*, or the evil eye. But when you threw the horns at someone else, it was an insult. Either way, whenever Big Al pointed, it usually portended misfortune for the pointee.

"You . . ." said Big Al, "you should FunFund a *Star Wars*."

Tommy didn't even know where to begin with that. But as he struggled to find the right words to describe intellectual property, copyrights, and trademarks, Big Al was already off to a galaxy far, far away.

"Now *Star Wars*," said Big Al, "that was a *movie*, am I right?"

Vigorous nods and affirmations around the table.

Yes, Don Fugue . . .

One hundred, boss . . .

Amen, Al Mighty . . .

Tommy was concerned about correcting his father in front of his men, but he needed him to understand the game. The internal conflict contorted his face until it looked like he had indigestion. When a break in the affirmations presented itself, Tommy approached his father, leaned in, and said softly, "Tergivers is more of a *fantasy*, Pop."

"What, *Star Wars* isn't a fantasy? Spaceships and lightsabers and Wookiees? Are you yanking my chain?"

"It's science fiction, Pop."

"It's an adventure," added Johnny Reb. "Inspired by old serials."

"Don't discount the number of Western tropes," said Johnny Socks.

"It's called a space opera," said Nine Ball, whose comment brought silence, whether from shock that he actually weighed in for once, or at the strange terminology, Tommy could not tell.

"Opera?" said Big Al. "This *stunod* over here thinks it's a fucking musical? May I continue?"

The young soldier looked down at the table. "My apologies, Don Fugue," he muttered.

"Did I ever tell you about the first time I saw *Star Wars*?" asked Big Al.

Here we go, thought Tommy.

"I saw it in theaters when it first came out. Your grandfather took me in Times Square . . . but then he ditched. Whispered in my ear that he had some business. Business most likely being a *comare*, let's be honest . . ."

This elicited knowing chuckles from the assemblage.

"And there I am, all by myself in the darkness, having a good time. And then on the screen—with that deep James Earl Jones voice and all decked out in black head to toe—comes Darth Vader. The look. The breathing. The music. He was terrifying. Now, keep in mind, I'm a tot. Your grandfather picks me up and I'm bawling my little eyes out. He brings me home, Ma goes through the roof, *'You stupid piece of shit, how can you take him to something like this, he's gonna have nightmares . . .'* And on and on.

"But there was something about him. I couldn't get this Vader out of my head. Cold as ice and smooth as silk. And stylish as all get-out. I mean, this guy didn't even have to touch you to choke you. *'I find your lack of faith disturbing. . . .'* "

Big Al made the Force choking motion to Chongo. Chongo stuck a finger in his collar to loosen it.

Big Al turned to SuperChenz and Force-choked him. SuperChenz raised his meaty hands to his throat, but his expression remained stonelike.

Big Al turned to Turdo. Turdo gasped obligingly, if tepidly.

Everyone laughed.

"Anyway, that's when it hit me. He's a gangster. A stone-cold space gangster. Literally. He's an enforcer, an underboss to the emperor. And just like that, I understood him in my bones. Even as a little kid. And then I kept crying until my pop took me back the next week. I was *obsessed*. To me, *he* was the show. Not Luke, not Han. Not the cute little droids. From then on, Vader was my guy." Big Al took a bite of Danish. "Until he went soft in that last one. But up until then? Baddest cat in the galaxy."

He pointed at Tommy again. The horns of misfortune.

"You should put in a Jedi like Vader."

"Sith Lord, Pop."

"Irregardless. Continue."

17

When Tommy spoke of the premise of Tergivers, he found his creative juices begin to flow again. He threw himself into the game, its band of broken characters in search of the lost, best pieces of themselves. Their virtues, like hidden jewels, scattered across the landscape and guarded by covetous monsters and unspeakable evils. He kept this part of the pitch tight, wary of his father's attention span and his men's general lack of knowledge about RPGs. But his father was right. He had commanded the room, if only for a minute, and when he wrapped up, he felt great. Breathless, beaming.

"So, it's a *Game of Thrones* pastiche?" asked Johnny Socks.

"I would contend it's more reminiscent of the high fantasy of Dungeons & Dragons," said Johnny Reb.

"D&D is the paragon of the genre," said Socks.

"So dominant as to subsume the genre itself," said Reb, nodding.

"As Kleenex is to the tissue."

"Or Xerox to photocopying."

Big Al glared at the Johnnies. His consiglieri fell silent.

"Fucking A, if I put the money in a bank it would've doubled with interest by now."

There was more scattered laughter, but it was nervous now.

Big Al was losing patience and working himself up, and everyone knew it. Never a good thing. "You know what definitely is fantasy? You assholes thinking I got all day to sit around and listen to this nerd shit. Get to the point already."

"Anyway," said Tommy, spreading his arms to signal his big finish, "I launched Tergivers on FunFunder!"

His reveal was met with indifferent silence.

Tommy looked around for a sympathetic eye or a safe harbor, but the closest he found was Chongo. The accountant made a wheeling motion with his hand.

Keep moving, kid.

"This is where the, um"—Tommy mouthed the words *money laundering*—"comes in."

Big Al rolled his eyes.

Tommy cleared his throat.

"So Tergivers is live and open to pledges right now. I set the funding total at twenty thousand dollars. With Chongo's help, Nine Ball and I have been buying prepaid gift cards and setting up dummy accounts and making small pledges. One pledge per card. Twenty-five dollars, fifty dollars, the occasional one-hundred-dollar pledge. Small potatoes."

Big Al leaned forward and steepled his fingers. His eyes, rolling in irritation moments before, narrowed on Tommy. Laser sharp and focused. "Twenty large, thirty days. Then what?"

"Then we're done. That's twenty grand, free and clear, given to me, which I then turn over to you, Pop."

Big Al trilled his fingertips in their steeple. No doubt weighing everything Tommy had just said. The length of time it would take. The upside, the risk. The juice's worth relative to its squeeze. Tommy searched his father's face, eager for any indication of approval, but Big Al betrayed nothing.

The don next spoke to Chongo, not bothering to respond to his son. "Bud?"

"It's smart placement. FunFunder's funded over three hundred and fifty thousand projects. That's over one hundred thirty million pledges funding over seven *billion* dollars going toward creative work."

Whistles around the U-shaped table, but Big Al remained unexcitable, fixed on his accountant.

"Exposure?"

"In such a big pond, no one's looking for small fish," Chongo continued. "Plus, good layering, it comes back clean. And the fees are way lower than a normal wash. . . . It's pretty tight, Al. The kid did good."

Big Al looked at his son. He did not look inclined to take his accountant's word for it. "Show me."

Chongo's fingers glided across the trackpad. It was so quiet Tommy could hear its faint *click*.

Tommy looked at the glowing image on the wall. His mother's Anibal-enhanced drawing was replaced by the Tergivers listing on FunFunder. There was an Anibal-designed blade on the left-hand side of the page, with the project's current statistics on the right-hand side: dollars pledged so far, number of backers, and days to go. After Tommy uploaded the project the prior night, he'd tested one fifty-dollar pledge to make sure it worked, which meant he and Nine had a month to do the legwork.

But when the FunFunder page refreshed and Tommy saw the updated *dollars pledged* figure, the bottom fell out of his world.

18

$650,000.

The room exploded.

Chongo leapt to his feet, the fastest Tommy had ever seen the stoner move.

"Madone!" exclaimed Johnny Socks.

Johnny Reb let out a long wolf whistle that seemed to pierce Tommy's cranium.

The room spun. The men surrounding him on all sides were hooting and laughing and banging on the tables. The commotion, the clatter of the dancing silverware, *that number . . .*

Tommy felt nauseated instantly, like he was being pitched on the deck of a ship at sea. He placed a hand on the table for balance.

"What the hell?" he mumbled.

He glanced up from his half crouch to gauge one man's reaction: his father's. Big Al wasn't watching his crumbling son. He was still staring at the glowing square on the wall and the massive dollar figure projected in bright green. His expression, which had oscillated between impatience and indifference throughout Tommy's presentation, was changing. A wry smile began to tug at the corner of his mouth. But his eyes still remained steely, like those of a shark closing in on a hooked fish.

"Is that real?" asked Chongo.

Nine Ball overcame whatever microbial misgivings he had and grabbed the laptop, squaring it in front of him. His fingers flew across the keys to the Backers page.

Nine looked up from the screen. "I think it's legit. . . ."

"How?"

"You went viral, dog."

Again Tommy looked to his father, whose wry grin had broken into a full-blown smile. The commendations continued to roll in.

"Chip off the old block . . ."

"Always knew he had it in him . . ."

"I still don't get it, but good on 'im. . . ."

Big Al rose finally. He gestured toward his son. For everyone to look.

"My boy," he said.

Tommy's head and the room were still spinning. He felt like he was going to throw up. "No . . ."

"Six. Hundred. And. Fifty. Large."

"No, you don't get it, Pop. They're just pledges."

"And in thirty days, it'll be six hundred and fifty large. Like you said."

"No—" he said, but his protests were drowned out by the raucous applause and the relentless, bone-rattling table slapping. "We have to take it down. . . ."

No one was listening. No one understood.

Big Al held both hands out in Tommy's direction, as if cupping a tiny baby.

"My boy's first score. I had my doubts, but he just became my top earner overnight—"

The pressure inside Tommy was like nothing he'd ever felt before. *"You don't fucking get it, Pop!"*

The room fell silent. In Tommy's panic, in his desperation to be listened to, to make them understand, he made a critical mistake: He overstepped.

Big Al licked his lips and smiled a gregarious smile, though it didn't reach his eyes.

"Gentlemen, give us the room, please."

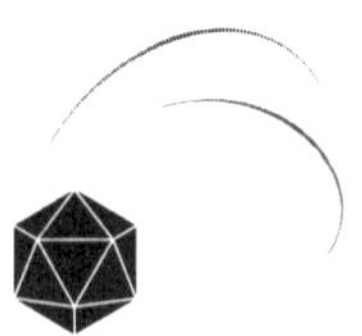

19

Big Al called after the men as they rose silently from the horseshoe. "First timer's nerves, fellas. Let's give him some air. Just give us a minute. . . ."

Tommy put his hands on his knees and tried to catch his breath as the men cleared the room. Hunched over, he saw his father's black wing tips approach.

"Just breathe, son. In and out. Here, stand up. . . ."

Tommy straightened.

Big Al cinched Tommy's throat. Tommy was thrust back rapidly, swept across the expanse of the large room, his feet barely touching the ground. He found his father's face—red and contorted with rage—just before the back of his head smacked the high windows.

Tommy saw stars.

A Feeblemind spell.

His father was blasting his brain, shattering his mind against the glass. Tommy couldn't gather his thoughts enough to put anything into language to make it stop. Real evil space-wizard shit.

When Tommy found his bearings and his vision again, his father's hands were wrapped around Tommy's collar, holding his son against the windows. He felt like he was pressed up against the mountains themselves.

"What don't I understand, smart mouth?" seethed Don Fugue. "What don't I understand?"

He gave Tommy a shove. He bonked the back of Tommy's head against the thick glass again, for emphasis.

"I understand that I spend fuck knows how much on that prissy school so you can insult me, I understand that."

Bonk.

"I understand that my own son disrespects me in front of my men."

Bonk.

"I understand that if one of them dared say such a thing to me they'd be coyote food."

Bonk.

"So, what don't I understand?"

Every time Tommy tried to cohere his thoughts, Big Al knocked him into the glass again and scattered them like Nine Ball's billiards at the break. His vision went haywire. The surprise at seeing the pledge total, the warm glass at his back, the rictus on his father's face . . . last night's pizza and Grind threatening to charge back up his throat. But the idea of throwing up on an already incensed Don Fugue scared his guts back into submission. As his father continued to bounce Tommy's head into the windows—forcefully listing the many things Big Al knew, and repeatedly but insincerely inquiring as to his son's opinion on the gaps in his knowledge—Tommy fought for the right word to make it stop.

"What don't I understand, huh?"

"The heat," Tommy managed.

Tommy's answer only seemed to enrage Don Fugue more. The grip at Tommy's collar tightened. The expression on his father's face darkened. It put Tommy in mind of a black hole, collapsing in on itself, the rage consuming everything in its orbit. He wondered if it was the last thing he would see. In that moment, he wondered, before he could stop himself, if it was the last thing his mother ever saw.

No. Tommy shoved the thought aside.

Don Fugue released his son then. He backed up a step, and paced in front of Tommy, burning off his excess fury, while Tommy caught his breath.

“Talk,” said Big Al, seething. “What heat?”

Tommy rubbed the back of his head. “We can’t stiff them.”

“It’s a bunch of nerds. Who cares?”

“That’s when the leg breaking happens,” gasped Tommy. “Online leg breaking, but still.”

Big Al approached his son again. Tommy backed into the window, bonking his own head. The don’s fiery temper had burned itself out; now his father had gone cold. Subzero. Even with the morning sunlight warming the glass against his back, it gave Tommy a chill.

“Explain it to me like I’m stupid,” said Big Al. He offered a warning by way of a chilly smile. “But not like I’m stupid.”

“If it were just our dummy accounts making the pledges, no one would have been the wiser. Twenty grand in, twenty grand out. Even if there were a few stray legitimate backers, a few unhappy customers are the price of doing business—”

“Wrong,” said Big Al. He pointed those horns at his son, but some of the ice had melted. “Unhappy customers are *not* the price of doing business. No one wants to be in business with someone who cuts corners. Who half-asses it. You think Lori half-asses it when she caters a wedding and serves pasta e fagioli to two hundred people? There’s no fucking traffic on the extra mile, Tommy.”

Tommy thought this was rich, a teachable moment on the ethics of maximum effort while laundering money. But some heat had returned to his voice, which was preferable to his quieter but more terrifying permafrost. Receiving hypocritical fatherly advice was better than receiving concussions.

"Yes, Pop. I didn't anticipate—"

"There's a lot you didn't anticipate. That's the other thing. You have to know all the angles. If everyone else is thinking two steps ahead, you have to think ten steps ahead. *Twenty*. What didn't you anticipate?"

"I had no idea it would go viral. It was just this . . . thing that I thought would be cool."

His father stared at him for a long time. Finally, he said, "Well, clearly some people agree," and stepped back, giving his son some room.

It was as close to a compliment as Tommy had received in some time.

"But now that it's viral," explained Tommy, "with that many backers and that many pledges, if we stiffed them, it would bring a lot of attention. Negative attention."

Big Al nodded, considering this information. Tommy feared a second explosion.

"It was stupid, Pop. I'll take it down."

"You got me all worked up there."

"I'm sorry, Pop." Once again, Tommy couldn't believe he found himself in the position of having to apologize for getting assaulted. He remembered getting the belt once for playing baseball and breaking the window of his father's study. An innocent foul ball. He learned later his father thought it was a potential hit. His mother consoled his agitated father, while he ranted to her about the stresses of his demanding, dangerous job.

Somewhere along the way, everyone had forgotten about the crying little boy.

"650K," said Al with a whistle. "That would have been pretty sweet."

"Again, Pop, I'm real sorry. It was a dumb idea. But if we cancel it now, before the campaign closes, there's no repercussions."

Big Al looked at his son sideways, through squinted eyes. "No repercussions?"

Tommy felt himself on unsure footing. Like walking across a half-frozen lake. Any wrong move, any shift in weight, could send him plunging. "They're just pledges, no one has been charged—"

"No repercussions other than you being a quitter, you mean."

"It's not about quitting, Pop. . . ." Tommy felt his panic rising again, but fought to keep it out of his voice this time. When his father didn't step closer again, he took a breath and went with reason. With math. "If Tergivers gets fully funded, FunFunder takes five percent of everything, right off the top."

"Smart nerds."

"Plus, it's all taxable income."

"Meaning it's clean."

"I'd have to pay artists. There's, like, time and materials. Manufacturing costs. Printing. Postage. Most projects don't break even, Pop, let alone make a profit. It's just a lot of work with no promise of getting a return. To say nothing of being on the hook for actually delivering the game."

"Ah," said his father. A devilish smile, followed by the horns. "Right there."

"What?"

"*The hook*. You've never been on the hook before. You've never had to work before. Not really. Your mother never let me put you to work. You've never had to look a customer in the eye. Sure, you go to class and study, you go to Starbucks and consume, but you've never had to hustle. You've never had to *deliver*."

"What do you want me to do?"

"For starters? Man up." Big Al thumped his chest. "Stop slouching. Plant your feet. Roll your shoulders back. Chin up, chest out."

Tommy complied, doing his best Clark Kent to Superman transformation. It didn't help.

"I gave you twenty grand for a simple rinse. You botched that . . ." said Big Al, scrutinizing his son from head to toe, then starting to circle him like a shark. Tommy remained in place, almost at attention, not wanting to leave his back to his father, but not wanting to turn around to face him either. "But you stumbled upon an investment. I don't get this *Turdgifters* shit, but I cannot deny that it's an opportunity. And Fugues do not waste opportunities."

"I don't think it's going to make a lot of profit, Pop."

Big Al finished his rotation and squared back up to his son. His anger seemed to have dissipated. He was no longer the Al Mighty, but something more resembling a father.

"I'm not talking about the money, son. I'm talking about conquering fear."

Tommy was desperate, eager to wiggle off the hook. "I don't want to throw good money after bad. . . ."

Big Al laughed. "There is no good money or bad money. There is only more money or less money."

"I don't even know where to start, Pop."

"Start where you are." Big Al looked out to the mountains and spread his hands, bathed in morning light. He turned back and added flatly, "Also, Google."

Big Al rested a hand on his son's shoulder, a warm fatherly gesture. Tommy fought off a flinch.

"I will expect my twenty back, right off the top. I will waive the vig."

Tommy deflated again, overwhelmed suddenly.

"Don't worry." Big Al thumped Tommy's chest again. Tommy straightened. "You can use Chongo. Put Nine to work. I'll even give you Porks."

"Porks?" Tommy made a face. What the hell was a Porks? "Can't I have the Johnnies? Just one of them?"

Big Al shook his head. "They have bigger fish to fry. And you don't go to war with the army you want, you go with the army you got."

What began last night as a goof now had an "army" consisting of a perpetually high mob accountant, a wannabe gangster, and a Porks.

Some army.

"Pop, I need artists, more players. . . ."

Big Al considered this. "I might know someone else. Do as much as you can in-house," he continued. "Keep your overhead low to maximize profits. If you need outside help, run it by me first. Understand?"

Tommy nodded.

Big Al poked at a Danish before picking it up and swallowing it whole. "You know I'm not a fan of your college, but your mother insisted. So I gave you a year. You want to return to Jerk-Off U in the fall, show me you want it. Any profits, we split right down the middle. And your half goes toward tuition."

Tommy wanted to protest at the unfairness of it, but he knew better. He swallowed and nodded.

His father gave his son a light slap.

"Good boy." Big Al, the beaming father, fully restored. For a flash, it was an odd version of what Tommy always fantasized their relationship could be like.

The don walked away, and Tommy exhaled. As his father made for the doors to welcome Family Fugue back in, he turned to face his son again. His smile remained, but his eyes were cold.

"Don't forget: You're not just on the hook to the nerds, Tommy. You're on the hook to *me*. So don't screw it up. I'm not Darth Vader. I don't go soft in the final act."

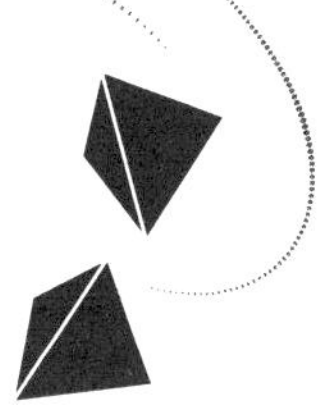

20

Tommy sat in silence during the rest of Don Fugue's meeting, his mind both a million miles away and trapped right there with his father.

"Turdo, gimme a sitrep on the collection routes in Montclair . . ." he heard from somewhere far or near; it didn't matter.

When he couldn't take it anymore, he left the table, pretending to get coffee.

His head was bad enough from the hangover, but now it throbbed from its repeated impact with the window. The last thing he wanted to do was think. Plus, his guts were jelly, and fear set his nervous system aflame. He could feel the psychic hook buried deep inside him. He could squirm and wriggle as much as he wanted, but there was no getting off it. A line his philosophy professor liked to utter as an aside flashed through his mind:

When you argue with reality, you lose, but only one hundred percent of the time.

He remembered laughing at the quote in class, but now, firmly on the hook, its gently mocking tone stung. It was time to quit arguing with reality and get to work.

It was time to gather the team.

He had the first two members already—Chongo and Nine—neither of whom were pleased, but both were smart enough not to whine about it in front of the Al Mighty. During the next break in discussions, they were only too happy to join Tommy at the coffee station to bitch.

"I'm an accountant," said Chongo. "What the fuck do I know about dragons?"

"No dragons," said Tommy. "I mean, I don't know. Maybe there will be dragons? I haven't gotten that far yet."

Nine was even surlier. "Hey, in your game, can I be a captain? Because at this rate, babysitting your ass and playing with dolls, I'll never make capo in real life."

"Enough!" hissed Tommy.

A few of the made men lingering at the U-shaped table turned their heads, then turned back, pretending not to listen. Only Turdo, his father's second-in-command, didn't turn away. His eyes gleamed and a grin formed on his lips as he lingered by the mini-quiche station.

Tommy pulled his new party into the hallway.

He turned to Nine. "Riddle me this, Batman: How much protection money do you collect for my father? Is it more than six hundred and fifty thousand dollars?"

Nine stared at his perfectly polished dress shoes. Tommy could see the soldier's reflection in them, sullen.

"That's what I thought."

He turned to Chongo next. "Tergivers has been up for a day and it's already over half a million dollars. And counting! This is no longer a money-laundering operation; this is a business. I don't know shit about business, but you do. You saw my father in there. He smells blood. Worse, he smells money, which to him goes hand in hand. He's like the shark in *Jaws*, he's not going to stop. And I can't do this without you."

"Fine. I'm in, kid," Chongo said between bites of what was likely his twentieth quiche. "Not like I have a choice."

Tommy looked back to Nine. "None of us do."

"Okay, okay."

"We have to get this game into shape and make sure it actually works. I'm going to get you character sheets to help you create your adventurers. Think of something cool. Be creative. You've all seen movies, even if you haven't played D&D. No soldiers, no accountants. Take it seriously." Before he could stop himself, he said, "Capisce?"

The men nodded. In the swirl of terror, nausea, and pain, Tommy detected a small electric charge running through his body.

He had never given an order before.

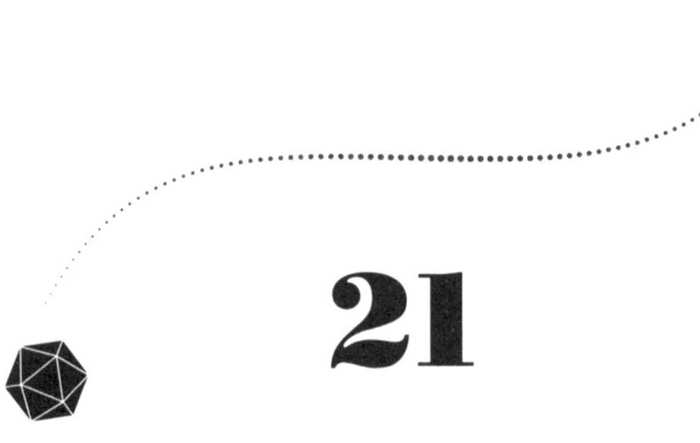

21

Tommy had never been to a strip club before either.

Don Fugue had given his son an address. Tommy didn't think twice when he plugged it into his Maps app. It wasn't until he parked his car and saw the stylized sign with the silhouette of a very buxom, very naked woman that the other shoe dropped.

He cleared his throat and marched to the front door of the Fuzzy Navel.

In the noonday sun, a steroidal bouncer leaned on a stool and scrolled through his phone. Tommy wondered if it was because he was a solitary dude, or because of some perceived deficiency in his size or appearance or demeanor, but the bouncer did not bother looking up as Tommy approached. The meathead simply said, "ID."

Tommy handed it over.

The man scanned it. Apparently nineteen was old enough to enter.

"Know where I can find Porks?" asked Tommy.

At this the bouncer tilted his head up. "Looking for a job?" He laughed. "You're a little skinny to be a dancer."

It had been a day of indignities, and Tommy found that he'd had his fill.

"Take another look at the ID."

"You're good, kid."

"No, not the birth date. The name."

The bouncer snorted but glanced at it. One moment, his sneer was pronounced; the next it was gone. It was like a magic trick. The mass of muscles jumped to his feet—the stool he was leaning on spinning like a top before settling again—and stood at attention.

"Um, Mr. Fugue, I meant no disrespect. It's just, uh, first time here?"

"As a matter of fact, it is."

"Let me take you inside, get you set up."

The bouncer pushed the heavy doors open and led him down a long hallway. This setting was more like what Tommy had expected earlier this morning, going from the always-sunny Denver sky into a dark underworld. At the far end of the hallway, Tommy heard the thumping of bass. Another set of double doors and Tommy was awash in strobe lights: reds, purples, and greens. There were bored, topless women onstage, dancing lazily for a meager lunchtime crowd. Even the customers looked bored. Everyone appeared to be going through the motions, except the mighty bouncer, who was now the most animated thing in the space. He paused to whisper to the announcer, who turned to whisper to someone else. Tommy's eyes followed the whisper trail, not unlike Todd's posse at the party, a one-word flame licking the underbrush until the whole place was ablaze. People cupped their hands over the thumping bass and whispered the *F*-word like a game of telephone.

Fugue.

"Set you up with something while you wait, sir? Drink?"

"Diet Coke?"

"Diet Coke it is, boss. A kicker, perhaps?"

"Got any Grind?"

The bouncer snapped the fingers on both hands, then pointed twin finger guns at him. "My man's in that Grindset. Coming right up."

Tommy smiled, nodded. He could get used to this, he thought.

Then, just as quickly, he thought, *Don't.*

A trio of topless women approached. The first came down from the stage, ignoring the crumpled men who sat around its perimeter. As she fixed on Tommy, he felt his cheeks redden and did not clock the other two women had flanked him until he was surrounded.

". . . was here first."

". . . free country."

". . . look just like your father, handsome."

They swirled and cackled around his head, and he was overcome with the smell of perfume. The competing scents from all three in such close proximity were so thick it made his eyes water.

"I'm Fallon," said the dancer from the stage. She wore cherry-red boots and red bikini bottoms and had platinum-blond hair that gleamed white in the strobing lights. She bent toward him and reached out a red-gloved hand, her pneumatic breasts staying in place despite her contortions, despite gravity. *"Enchantée."*

Tommy shook her hand, averted his eyes. But everywhere he looked there was exposed flesh.

"*'Enchantée?'* Girl, you're from Boulder. . . . Hi, sugar, I'm Fiona," said the dancer on his left. She had jet-black hair and wore blue hot pants. She draped her arms around his shoulders. "You look stressed. How about a lap dance?"

"No thank—"

He couldn't finish his thought. Fingers on his chin pulled his head around 180 degrees to a redhead, all dressed in green, save for a seasonally inappropriate Santa hat. "I'm Merry. How about we go someplace a little more private and we can *both* be merry?"

They continued to talk at Tommy, until he felt like they were swirling around him. The strobing of the lights, the pummeling of their perfumes, their competing whispers in his ear . . . it all bewitched him. He hadn't had a sip of alcohol yet, but it set his head spinning.

"Girls!"

The women jumped. Tommy expected to see a dapper man like his father or a large man like the bouncer, but when the three dancers parted, there stood a diminutive, balding pig of a man. A prominent potbelly shoved itself before him, putting the food stains on his short-sleeve dress shirt on display, framed between threadbare suspenders. His skin was sallow, like he hadn't seen sunshine or touched grass in decades. The man put Tommy in mind of Batman's repulsive villain the Penguin, before the gangster had discovered tuxedos, umbrellas, and monocles.

"Fuck off with thee!" he yelled with a rough, grating voice that was perfectly modulated to slice through the din . . . and through one's brain. It set Tommy's teeth on edge. The man stormed up, one thumb hooked into his suspenders and waving his free hand. The three dancers fluttered off like sparrows flushed from a bird feeder.

"Sorry, kid. Those three get on my last nerve."

"They seem . . . nice."

"Nice," the man snorted. The motion sent fleshy waves rolling across his body. "For the right price, they'll be as nice as you want. Dress 'em up, take 'em to church or the rotary club." He leaned over his shoulder and bellowed in the trio's direction, his voice like rocks in a garbage disposal. *"Maybe they'll keep their traps shut for five minutes!"*

He turned back to Tommy. He cleared the spittle from his cheek with a rough swipe of his hand.

Tommy cleared his throat. "It must be very challenging to, um, be a proprietor."

"Proprietor? That part's easy. Being a pimp, though?" He gave his head a grave shake.

"A pimp?" Tommy squirmed in his seat. He told his father he needed players for a game, and Big Al gave him a pimp. And not just any pimp, but a real-life rock troll. He knew he was sheltered, but never in his wildest dreams did he expect to meet an actual pimp. Especially one who was so brazen about it.

He had no idea what to say.

"I hear pimping, uh, ain't easy."

"Fucking A. 'Do what you love, and you never work a day in your life'? Utter bullshit. More like, *Do what you love for work and work will destroy what you love.* When I was your age, all I could think about was sex. I wasn't much of a prize in the looks department if you can believe it, so it was unobtainable. Now, after years of this . . ." he said, waving his hand to take in the entirety of the Fuzzy Navel, "I'm ruined. I haven't had a solid hard-on since Y2K. I'm officially Post Sex. For Little Porks to even shift, it has to be some truly deviant shit, do you know what I mean?"

"I see . . . *Porks.* All of that is very . . . disturbing, but that's not why I'm here. Have you spoken with my father?"

He shook his head. "Johnny Reb called me, told me to give you whatever you asked. So which one will it be? Or all three of them . . ." He jerked a thumb over his shoulder at the dancers, who were still whispering to each other at the foot of the stage. When they saw Tommy looking their way, they smiled in unison. Tommy imagined a bubbling cauldron before them, each one dropping an eyelash or one of his hairs into it to cast a Binding spell.

"*No!* I mean, no thank you."

It was either Tommy's fear or the notion of corrupting Tommy's soul, but there was a greedy gleam in Porks's eyes that wasn't there before. He hoped it hadn't made Little Porks shift.

He shivered at the thought.

Between sips of his drink for courage, and some looks of confusion on Porks's face, Tommy explained the game as quickly as he could and precisely what he needed from Porks—which was for him to join the campaign. He glanced at Fallon, Fiona, and Merry again, fearing if he didn't escape soon, they might trap him there forever.

After a long pause—or one that felt too long, anyway—the pimp at last asked, "Anyone? I can be anyone I want?"

"Anyone or anything," said Tommy. "Except a pimp."

Tommy promised to send him over some sample character ideas to get him thinking, but Tommy could already see the wheels turning behind the man's beady eyes. It was a lascivious gaze.

"This could be fun. . . ."

"This will be a time commitment," Tommy began, hoping for the possibility that Porks would back out, and complain to his father, or something else that would maybe end close contact with the man. "Your nights are going to belong to me for *quite* a while."

Porks laughed. It sounded like a snort.

"Don't threaten me with a good time."

22

That evening, Tommy sat on his couch, staring at a television he had not bothered to turn on. After a day that included a disastrous morning spent with his father and his goons, and an afternoon with someone named Porks, Tommy could not believe his day could get any worse. Then his phone lit up with a text.

What did u think of the images?

Anibal. Tommy lolled his head against the back cushions. He thought about responding, but he hadn't even told Anibal the "game" was launched yet—which any decent human being would have done if they weren't using it to launder money—let alone that it had gone viral. Worse, if he did respond, Tommy knew it would only be a matter of time before he pumped Anibal for information about Sanse. He wouldn't be able to help himself.

Tommy had been throwing himself a pity party, but now a new emotion had joined the festivities—guilt.

Just then the phone in his hand rang.

Johnny Reb's deep voice filled the line.

"Evening, kid. You free?"

"Of course. What do you need?"

"No phones. Your pop's on a kick about that. Heaven," said Reb, then hung up.

Twenty minutes later, Tommy stood with the Johnnies outside Heaven Creamery on Larimer Street. Socks did the talking while Johnny Reb shoveled raspberry and dark chocolate gelato into his mouth with a tiny plastic spoon. Tommy wondered if their in-person meeting had more to do with Big Al's operational security protocols or the consigliere's notorious sweet tooth, but at least they'd brought him a name.

"Joe?" asked Tommy.

"Galliano," said Johnny Socks, "aka the Stinger."

Tommy's burgeoning party now included a stoner accountant, a wannabe capo, a revolting pimp, and a Stinger, apparently. Johnny Socks gave him the Stinger's location: the UCHealth emergency room in Commerce City.

"What happened?" asked Tommy.

"That's the Stinger." Socks gave a shrug that conveyed, *What are you gonna do?* "I'll let her know she won't need to call Uber."

"Her?"

"Jo as in Jolene," said Johnny Socks.

"And Stinger as in the cocktail," added Johnny Reb, scraping the bottom of his cup of gelato. "Galliano stinger."

"One would hope that the inclusion of Jo in the beta-test party makes Tergivers less male-centered," said Johnny Socks.

"Androcentrism." Johnny Reb looked like he smelled something rotten, shook his head. He tossed the cup into a garbage can. "It's so limiting."

"Roleplaying games provide an excellent opportunity for intersectionality," said Socks.

"What I find interesting is that so many dystopian novels are feminine-coded," said Reb.

"Male dominance has brought society to ruin, and only the love and idealism of an uncompromising young woman can save us from the ravages of late-stage capitalism or environmental collapse."

"Irony, thy name is Katniss Everdeen."

The two consiglieri shared a laugh as Tommy looked on, baffled.

"Are you sure *you guys* can't join?"

"I can only take so much Porks," said Socks.

"And the Stinger scares me," said Reb.

Socks gave his partner a look and then a thoughtful nod of agreement.

Tommy pulled into the parking lot of the UCHealth ER and found a spot. As he approached the automatic doors, he saw a woman with a bandaged hand arguing with an orderly about lighting up a cigarette too close to the hospital.

"Fine, my ride's here anyway, you fascist!"

Oh no, thought Tommy.

"Jolene?"

"It's *Jo,*" she barked. Over her shoulder, to the orderly, she snapped, "And fuck *you* very much."

She tried to give him the middle finger with her bandaged hand, but it seemed to hurt, so she yanked her other fist up and brandished its middle finger like an obscene quick draw.

"Fuck it. Let's go, kid."

Tommy took her to his car and opened the passenger door, whereupon she promptly collapsed into the front seat before reaching out to slam the door shut. Tommy took a deep breath and walked around the car to take his seat behind the wheel.

Inside, he felt like he was sitting next to a hand grenade. He glanced at her. She had high cheekbones and thick eyebrows, and it was clear she was pretty, but any beauty was obscured by greasy hair pulled back in a ponytail, a black eye, and the general demeanor of a bobcat with a splinter in its paw.

"I spent all fucking night in there. Let's go already, Baby Fugue."

"Of—of course," stammered Tommy. "Where do you live?"

She looked at him like he was an idiot. "I'll tell you where to go as we go."

The only words Jo spoke on the ride were terse directions. *Turn here. Make a right. There.* She navigated him to a low concrete building in Commerce City with electric beer signs in the windows. Jo threw open her car door and was marching toward the front door before Tommy had put his car in Park. He hurried after her.

Unlike the Fuzzy Navel, there were no strobing, lurid neon lights providing artificial cheer or the promise of transactional sex in this establishment. The light sources here were anemic, hanging over the bar and pool tables and flickering from the jukebox and pinball machines. Instead of thumping bass, there was loud, blues-inflected rock music, and the men sat in pairs, talking low, or alone, lost in their thoughts.

Jo marched to the bar, held up two fingers. A double shot appeared before her. She downed it before Tommy had found a seat beside her. She ordered another immediately. "And whatever my Uber here is drinking."

The bartender, who looked like he would be more comfortable swinging an axe into a redwood, furrowed his brow. It made his bushy mustache lift on the sides. "He needs ID."

"He's with us."

Not with me, thought Tommy. *With* us. It was more subtle than the employees at the Fuzzy Navel passing the Fugue name from one to the other, but it had the same effect. The man nodded. Moments later, a mug of beer was set before him without another word.

When she had knocked back her second shot, Jolene looked at him head-on for the first time. Her face contorted with what looked like a mixture of pain, wariness, and a note, around the eyes, of deep sadness. Tommy imagined it couldn't have all been from her long night.

"To what do I owe the fucking honor, Little Prince?"

Porks had left Tommy feeling dirty—five minutes in the pimp's presence left him craving a shower—but slightly emboldened. He had his father's blessing to proceed and his party, though imperfect, was growing. If he wanted to succeed, he would need to be bold with this new stranger. He would need to sell. He decided to try out a little marketing.

"What would you say if I told you what was once lost could be found again?"

Her left hand shot out and grabbed him by the collar, jerking him from his barstool toward her. He thought she was going to hit him with her right, and perhaps she was going to, but closing her bandaged hand made her wince. Instead, she bared her teeth, fearsome as a wolf. He smelled the bourbon on her breath.

"What the fuck did you just say to me?"

"It's a tagline," Tommy said, backpedaling. "For my game."

She stared at him hard for a petrifying moment, studying him like she would dirt under her fingernails, then shoved him back onto his stool. Perhaps she had second thoughts about manhandling the boss's son, but Tommy didn't get the sense she gave a shit.

"What game?"

"The Johnnies didn't tell you?"

"In case you haven't noticed, genius, I've been indisposed."

Tommy laughed nervously. "You should see the other guy, huh?"

"Not if you have a weak stomach."

"What happened?"

"I hit a guy who tried out a tagline." She downed another shot that had mysteriously appeared. "Hit him a lot."

Tommy decided to get back on track. As quickly as he could, he described the game and how she fit in. "So, in essence, there's a magical realm, or planet maybe—I haven't gotten that far—where a band of warriors . . . but they don't have to be warriors, per se, they can be whatever you like . . . quest to find these enchanted items—blades—except the blades are really just physical manifestations of the missing parts of their souls. So, you know, fun."

When Tommy was finished, she laughed bitterly.

"Is this the Johnnies' idea? Turdo's?"

"The game was my idea."

"Not the game," she snapped. "*Me.* Was it . . . ?"

She struggled with the words, as if she wasn't sure which title to choose from.

"My father," said Tommy.

She wore a rueful smile. "Ah," she said, but it sounded more like the exhalation someone made when something stung rather than one of understanding. She blinked several times, tilting her face toward the ceiling, and Tommy realized she was doing it to clear tears. He looked away, busied himself with drinking his beer rather than staring at her. It seemed safer. When he looked again, she wore a rueful smile.

"Who else?"

Tommy told her. She nodded at Chongo's name. She didn't know Nine Ball, which would have bruised the young soldier's ego. At Porks's name, she recoiled.

"One wrong word and I'll gut that slime."

Tommy believed her.

23

A young Arapaho called Macarro wakes in a meadow, unsure where exactly he is. He is a rover, a warrior in training, tall and lean and handsome. The last thing he remembers is preparing for initiation rites. He believes that if he becomes a great warrior, like his long-dead father, slain in battle, it will fill the hole in him; the hole feels like a burning pit in his core. He has an aptitude for medicine and senses his true calling lies there, but the hole in him is too large and Macarro will sacrifice that part of himself as an offering if it means he can become a great warrior.

Macarro is brave to the point of recklessness, and loyal beyond reason. He believes the void in him is pride, but it is really acceptance he seeks.

Love.

Macarro is gifted on horseback and skilled in the weapons of the People. When he awakes, he is filled with shame because he thinks he has fallen from his horse in front of the tribe and stunned himself. But there is no horse. There are no weapons scattered around him, save for his war club, and there are no people. He pushes himself to his feet. He is dressed in moccasins and leggings and a shirt, a bear claw necklace and eagle feathers in his hair. His face is painted black and red. He looks fearsome. He does not feel fearsome.

Macarro gathers his bearings. He does not see his beloved Plains. Worse, the sky is purple, like a deep bruise. He does not know if it is day or night. He senses something is very wrong. He feels his first stirrings of fear then, a sensation he detests. A mountain looms before him, its foothills rimmed with a line of jagged boulders arrayed like teeth.

"Now what?" asked Nine.

"Well, what do you want to do?" asked Tommy.

"Go back to my ancestral lands."

"Sure, obviously, but then there would be no game. What about in the short term?"

Nine shrugged.

"Your class are legendary trackers and hunters," said Tommy. "So how about you climb that mountain? See what you can see?"

"Cool."

"You have to climb over the boulders, Nine."

Nine sat straight up in his chair, waved an invisible wand, and proclaimed, *"I climb over the boulders."*

Jo and Porks snickered.

Tommy stared at them all. "I meant this as a session zero, a learning session, obviously. Hence the premade character sheets while we figure things out. But have none of you *ever* played a fantasy game before? *Seriously?"*

"Business school," said Chongo.

"Work," said Nine.

"I was pretty," said Jo.

"Porn," said Porks. Then he chuckled at some internal joke and mumbled, *"Zeroes . . ."*

Tommy sighed. He held a d20 aloft between two fingers like a jeweler. "Okay, this is where *this* comes in. Lady and gentlemen, choose your weapons. . . ."

He pushed a bowl into the center of the table, featuring several types of polyhedral dice. Some translucent, some prisms, some glow-in-the-dark. Porks selected a bright red d20 that looked like its cousin worked a casino's craps table. Jo selected one that was faux mother-of-pearl with the numbers etched in gold. Chongo chose a psychedelic die with swirling colors.

Nine refrained from putting his hand in the bowl and instead reached inside a jacket pocket, pulling out a small leather dice case. When he opened it, six dice set into a foam insert caught everyone's attention. They looked like they were carved from bone, and their glossy black numbers shone even in the indirect light of the room. Nine pulled out the twenty-sided die gently and cradled it in his hand for a moment before realizing everyone was watching him.

"Did you really think I was going to fondle your party bowl of disease? No thank you."

Sensing Jo was about to say something biting and Porks was about to say something disgusting, Tommy spoke first. "*These* are what we use to determine outcomes. Along with your character sheets."

Chongo examined his die. "So what's best, the one or the twenty?"

Tommy smiled. "Fair question. Well, a one is a critical failure—"

"And when you roll a twenty?" Nine asked.

"That's called a natural 20—"

"I like natural twenties," said Porks with a dirty chuckle.

Jo glared at the pimp.

Tommy ignored him. "If you're attacking and you roll a natural 20, your attack is going to hit no matter what, even if your opponent is superpowerful or wearing armor. It's a critical hit. Now a dirty 20—"

"I like dirty twenties even—"

"Don't," said Jo.

Porks fell silent.

"A dirty 20," continued Tommy, "not to be confused with a nat 20, is when you have a roll that *totals* twenty, like rolling an eighteen with a plus two modifier."

"Just when I thought this couldn't get any sadder," said Jo, "you added math."

Chongo fiddled with his joint, muttering, "A dirty 20 is how we got into this mess. . . ."

"Just do an ability check." Tommy nodded at Nine. "Roll."

Nine shook his ghastly d20 for a moment, then dropped it neatly on his character sheet. An eleven.

"What's your ability score for Agility?"

Nine scanned his sheet. "Fifteen."

"Modifier? It's that little number next to it."

"Two."

"Okay. Adding your roll and your modifier you have a thirteen."

"Did I do it?" asked Nine.

"Well, those boulders are relatively easy to navigate, so they have a difficulty class of ten."

Nine smiled. "Thirteen is better than ten, yeah?"

"Way to go, Pythagoras," said Jo.

Nine ignored her. "So, I did it?"

"You did indeed. Onward."

"Let's fucking climb, then."

• • •

Macarro puts the meadow behind him, clutches his war club as if it were salvation, and clambers over the jagged boulders. He springs from boulder to boulder, executing a number of flips. He gains confidence as he ascends, spinning and somersaulting through the air. There is an easier path through the rocks; however, Macarro exults in complicated maneuvers and deft flourishes. Finally landing clear of the jagged boulder field, he begins his hike up the slope to get a better view of his surroundings.

At the top of the slope is a narrow ridge.

And Bellarmina.

Bellarmina is no warrior in training; she is a full-fledged knight, quick to anger, her armor dented and scuffed from countless campaigns. She is dazed and exhausted from the latest in a string of battles for her king. Was she repelling an invasion or quelling an uprising? This place is disorienting, and she finds it hard to remember. She needs some mead to clear her head.

She is brave and dependable, noble even, but the small voice she hears before passing out each night whispers that if she masters herself, she might be able to look at her own reflection in her armor without flinching. She is a living weapon. With Discipline, she might become something more.

She might be a hero.

All she knows right now is that she is bone tired and separated from her fellow knights. She emerges from the wilderness and finds the same bruised sky. A storm must be rolling in. She climbs her side of the slope for a better vantage and encounters, to her mind, a feathered creature with a red-and-black face. Clearly some unholy monster, fueled by dark magic, summoned by her king's many enemies.

Bellarmina draws her sword.

Macarro brandishes his war club.

They circle each other, contemplating their first strikes.

Bellarmina realizes that Macarro is not some ghoul, but is a man painted for war, like the remote highland subjects in her kingdom.

And Macarro deduces that what he had first believed was some mechanized clockwork being is in fact an armored female.

For a moment, they both relax.

Then there is crashing in the wilderness behind them. Strange birds shriek and take flight from the swaying trees. The earth rumbles and shakes. Both warriors note the widened eyes of the other, quickly realizing that the trouble thundering toward them is not affiliated with either of them. An unspoken agreement passes between them. A warrior's code. They turn and face the mighty threat barreling toward them from the woods. Macarro again hefts his club; Bellarmina again readies her sword.

A giant, twice as tall as either of them, bursts from the trees. He is half naked, with long reddish-brown hair and a mighty beard.

He draws in a deep breath and bellows . . .

"My name is Robert Redford and I have two cocks!"

"Wait—*what?*" said Tommy. Looking around the table, he added, "That is definitely *not* on the sheet."

Porks shrugged. "I decided my character has two cocks."

"Why?" asked Nine Ball.

Chongo smirked, a joint dancing in the corner of his mouth as he chuckled, but Jo looked furious.

She pointed a finger at Tommy. "I *told* you," she said, with a look that could burn through steel. Her hands disappeared beneath the table, and remembering her threat to gut Porks, Tommy nearly dove across it.

"Wait!"

Jo froze, though that might have been more because Tommy had knocked over a beer, which careened over the side of the table. Nine popped up to get a towel from the kitchen and Tommy gave him a thank-you nod.

"Porks," said Tommy, trying to keep his tone calm, "your character can't have two cocks."

The pimp looked hurt. "Why not? Show me in your user's manual where it says I can't have two cocks. Oh, that's right, *you haven't written one yet.*"

Technically, Porks had a point. Tommy had spent his time between gathering the team and the first night of their campaign punching up his party's character sheets. He was still working on building the world and sussing out the game's mechanics, scribbling notes as he went. At the moment it was a knockoff of other popular games, his version essentially a loose homebrew building on the work of many others. He was nowhere near developing a unique user's manual, and didn't have the skills to produce one when he was ready for it. But that was a problem for another day. Today's problem was his ornery players. And their redundant privates, apparently.

The only one who put in any real effort was Nine, who actually called Tommy one night while he drove "between drops" and spent a little time talking about his character's backstory. Tommy had been surprised both at the level of detail and that he drew on his Native American heritage, which wasn't something he advertised around the Family. The only leap that Tommy made was giving Macarro a deficiency of Love, which felt less like a leap and more like reading between the lines. Fortunately, Nine approached tonight's gameplay the way he approached everything else is his life: Anything worth doing was worth doing right.

Chongo had thought it would be "kinda cool" to be a druid. Tommy had no objections.

Jo's "I could not care less" had left her sheet mostly up to Tommy.

Although Tommy had come up with Duke Melindo of the Black Lodge, a Home for Gentlemen Diviners—a wizard who claimed to traffic in fine silks, among other items—Porks had just wanted his character to fight and fuck. Out with subtlety; the pimp's character sheet instead read like the journal of a horny middle schooler. The only specifics the diminutive, bald Porks had listed were that he wanted to be a giant barbarian with a flowing mane of hair.

And now, apparently, two impromptu cocks.

"Come on, Porks," said Chongo, "that serves no purpose."

"Says you." He looked over with lewd eyes at Jo. "I can think of plenty of purposes."

Tommy needed to change the subject, fast.

"And Robert Redford?" he asked.

"In his heyday?" said Porks, waving a stubby finger at Tommy. "There was not a more beautiful man, rest his soul."

"But this is a fantasy realm. . . ."

"And in my fantasy realm, my avatar is a dual-cocked Robert Redford."

"You can't name him that."

"Fine. Brad Pitt."

"That's the same principle, you idiot," said Nine.

"Okay, okay," said Tommy. "How about this: We'll name him Bradford. Brad for Brad Pitt, ford for Redford. He'll be the most handsome barbarian that ever walked the planet of Tergivers."

"Bradford the Barbarian . . ." said Porks, nodding. "I dig it."

"I motion to cut off Bradford the Barbarian's extra dick," said Jo.

"Motion?" muttered Nine.

"Jo thinks she's in court," said Chongo with a laugh. "Again."

"Oh, forgive me," she said with false saccharine. "I *roll* to cut off the extra dick."

"You wouldn't dare," hissed the pimp.

In a blur, Jo whipped something gleaming from her jacket pocket. With a few sharp flicks of her wrist a butterfly knife unfurled. She leaned across the gaming table.

Nine braced. Chongo's eyebrows lifted on a two-second cannabis delay.

Porks backed off the table, hands raised. "Easy, Stinger. Just a game we're playing . . ."

Jo offered a deadly smile. "How's this for playing? I cut off one of *Bradford's* little dicks or *your* one and only. Take your pick, Piggie."

Tommy slammed his hands on the table. The d20 before him danced. The grid map raised a few inches and settled back down like a shroud.

"Goddamn it, I'm the game master!"

It sounded petulant and ridiculous to him as soon as it left his mouth, but everyone *did* stop what they were doing and stare at him.

"If I have to remind you why you're here every five minutes, then I'll just call *my father* and he can remind you. I'm sure he won't mind the interruption."

He hated invoking Big Al, but it had the desired effect.

The assembled looked sheepish. Chongo nodded and took a hit. Nine stared into his lap. Porks frowned but took his seat, and

Jo—whose nickname "Stinger" Tommy now grokked—folded and pocketed her butterfly knife.

"I don't need a user's manual," said Tommy to Porks. "I *am* the user's manual as we figure this out, *together*. But one of the rules is that everyone at this table is cool to one another. The only person who harasses players or makes them feel uncomfortable at this table will be me, in my role as GM, steering this campaign. If everyone is going to be free to express themselves and get lost in their characters and this adventure, they can't be creeped out by their own party members. Do I make myself clear?"

Porks made a sour face, but he nodded.

Tommy turned to Jo next. "And I can't believe I have to say this, but do not stab your tablemates. The only thing more important than the psychological safety of my players is their *actual* safety. The only combat will occur *in-game*. Understood?"

Jo folded her arms. "Whatever."

Tommy spread his arms across the table, gesturing to include Chongo and Nine as well. "This table is a *safe* space in every sense of the word, all right? Say it with me."

The rest of the party sulked, wordless.

Tommy held his phone aloft. "I swear to God, I'll call him. . . ."

They all repeated: *"This table is a* safe *space in every sense of the word."*

It sounded like a dirge or a spell without any enthusiasm.

"Thank you," said Tommy. He exhaled. "Now, Jo, roll to cut off Bradford's extra penis."

"What?" screamed the pimp. He jumped to his feet again.

Tommy leveled a finger at him. "You started it. This is how we settle our differences."

Porks looked like he was going to storm off. Tommy raised his eyebrows. The pimp took his seat again.

"Really?" asked Jo.

"Attack roll."

The Stinger looked from player to player; then she smiled and rattled her d20. In that moment, Tommy would have sworn that the sun came out. Until then, he had been too afraid of her to realize how beautiful she was.

She shook her fist, then let fly. Porks clutched his crotch.

The die spun near a twenty before toppling slightly and coming to rest at eight.

"Did I get it?" squealed Jo, standing up and looming over the table. She was beaming, eyes wide, almost childlike. Tommy wished he had better news for her, but maybe he could contrive a win for her anyway.

He snatched Porks's character sheet. "Bradford has a Durability score of eighteen. But Bellarmina has a Precision score of fifteen; with a modifier of two, making ten, that wouldn't be enough. *But* her blade is made of, um, *Sicilium* . . . and it can slice through most objects like a hot knife through butter. . . ."

"What the fuck are you *saying*?" begged Porks.

Next to the pimp, Nine stared at Tommy with a scary intensity.

"I'm saying I'm willing to exercise a little latitude, as game master. You chose a charmed battleaxe as your weapon, yes?"

Porks nodded vigorously.

"I'm willing to make an exchange . . . *if you swear to never mention your character's genitals at this table again.*"

"Anything!"

Bellarmina charges at the giant barbarian, raising her Sicilium blade as she approaches.

Bradford swings back the arm that wields his mighty battleaxe to meet her attack. The axe is forged of metal from the deepest mines of Peccary and can cleave most creatures in twain with a single chop. Only, he discovers his hand is empty. He must've left the damn thing in the woods. Without its comfortable heft that has become like a part of him, he loses his balance and topples backward, exposing his crotch to the sky.

Bellarmina swings. Her enchanted blade connects with the barbarian's fur-lined britches.

Bradford screams helplessly as he tumbles.

There is a deafening clang and a shower of golden sparks as the blade slices clean through his britches but glances off a metal codpiece that he had totally forgotten he was wearing until just this moment. Fortunately for Bradford, it is forged from the same strong Peccarite as his missing axe.

Bradford, as a barbarian, is prone to rages, but in the reverberating silence following the sword strike, there is a clear, unusually wise voice in his normally irrational mind: You can choose to retaliate, in which case, she can strike again, and we'll see how long your super-special cup holds up against a pissed-off knight's enchanted blade, or we can get on with the damn game.

"Verily," says Bellarmina. She looms over the barbarian, flat on his back, her blade poised again for another strike. "No more talk of thy foul nethers."

"A deal's a deal," grunts Bradford the Barbarian. He runs a meaty paw through his hair. "Still totally fucking handsome, though."

Fine. Bradford the Totally Fucking Handsome Barbarian gets to his feet and the lost trio head down the ridge together.

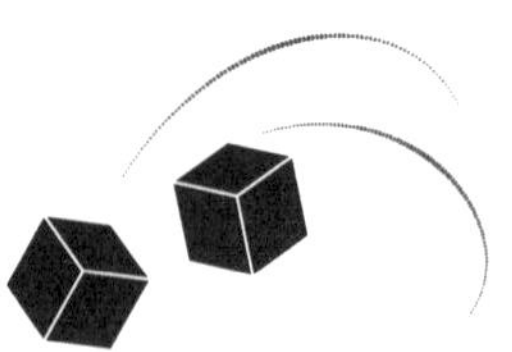

24

It had been a rocky start.

After the session, while Nine discussed his character with Chongo—whose druid had not made an appearance due to the unusual level of cannabis in the accountant's system—Porks pulled Tommy aside.

Tommy prepared to defend his performance as GM.

But Porks beamed. "Kid, that was *wild*."

"I'm glad you had fun."

Porks shook his head, leaned in. "It's not just that. There's something about using my imagination. It's fired me up."

"That's great, Porks."

The pimp tapped his head and offered a greasy smile. "They say the most powerful sexual organ is your mind."

"Oh," said Tommy. "No . . ."

"Oh *yes*. And when that bitch Bellarmina tried to, you know . . . it was a real use-it-or-lose-it moment for me. Remember when I said I was Post Sex? Things are happening for me down there again. I think I'm back, kid!"

I've created a monster, Tommy thought. Then he corrected himself, *Pretty sure he was already a monster, but I've definitely transformed one into a horny barbarian.*

"When are we doing this again?" Porks asked with a little swish of his hips.

Tommy stepped to the side to get everyone's attention and to extricate himself from the carnally reinvigorated pimp.

"Adventurers, considering the sum on FunFunder—"

"Over 700K now," said Chongo.

Everyone but Jo clapped. Tommy grimaced. He had purposely avoided looking at the web page. It just reminded him of the stakes. It put his stomach in his throat like he was on a roller coaster, *tick-tick-ticking* toward the peak, just before the inevitable plunge.

Tommy hated roller coasters.

He forced a smile. "Thanks, Chongo. All the more reason that we meet every night. At least until the online campaign is finished. The more we have done by the time we're funded, the less likely I'll have a panic attack."

Everyone laughed. He laughed along with them, then added, "I'm actually not joking."

He had expected resistance about a nightly appointment, but Jo shrugged, Nine and Chongo nodded, and an eager Porks pumped his fist and said, "Yes!"

With the immediate schedule sorted, Porks left the apartment with his fists raised in victory. Giggling, Chongo and Nine followed him into the night. Jo lingered a beat longer than the rest.

At the door, she turned and faced Tommy. "Mead," she said.

"It's like medieval wine."

"I know what it is. Why?"

"You didn't select a race or type of warrior. You didn't even give me a name. You just scrawled 'bad bitch with a sword' on your character sheet. You didn't really give me a lot to work with."

The hard lines of her face returned. “I can stop anytime I want. Understand?”

“I understand. It’s just a character, Jo. Interesting backstory, you know . . .”

“And Bellarmina. What the fuck kind of name is that?”

It was as much a threat as a question. He thought of her swift motions, one moment her hand empty, the next a butterfly knife appearing. Deadly sleight of hand.

“It’s Italian. It sounded cool.”

“Yeah, but what’s it mean?”

Her chin jutted out, defiant. A dare. Tommy’s heart hammered in his chest.

“It comes from *bellarmine*. It means ‘the one with the beautiful armor.’ ”

The hardened killer stared at him hard for a few moments, tilting her head back, scrutinizing him down the bridge of her nose. Tommy wanted to watch her hands, see if he was about to get stung, but he held her eye.

Finally, she gave a single nod.

“See you tomorrow night, Baby Fugue.”

25

They were parked on a street a few miles west of the Auraria campus. From the passenger seat, Nine squinted at the squat concrete building across the street, then squinted at Tommy.

"I don't like it. It's outside of your father's territory."

Tommy looked at the building again. A tiny tributary of Lakewood Gulch flowed beneath the structure, bifurcating it. Its storefront was filled with colorful posters and the sign overhead blared CARL'S COMICS!

"What do you think is going to happen, a stack of long boxes is going to fall on me? Relax."

"I'd be more relaxed if I did a sweep."

"You'll stand out like a sore thumb in there."

"Because I've showered?"

"Because it's fucking *weird*." Tommy gestured at Nine, his suit. Then he felt a little bad for the kid, so he added, "Besides, they'll think you're John Wick or something and will dive through the windows."

A small smile broke Nine's facade. "Fine, but if you're not out in ten minutes, I'm coming in."

Tommy rolled his eyes and exited Nine's car and crossed the street. There was a pleasing chime when Tommy opened the front door, and he was immediately hit with one of his favorite scents:

old comic book. The chemical decomposition of the paper, the inks and adhesives, and mold all combined to create an aroma he would bottle if he could. *Eau de X-Men.* It reminded him of four-color fights in the skies, heroes triumphing over villains, misunderstood teens bursting with secret promise . . . the perfect escape while his parents raged downstairs.

Batman, deliver me from evil.

A familiar voice from behind the counter snapped him from his reverie.

"Welcome to my secret lair."

Tommy had owed Anibal a call, and when he finally worked up the nerve to reach out, the artist told him they should meet here. Tommy navigated the warren of long boxes to the front counter and proffered his fist for a bump, which Anibal matched. Tommy looked over Anibal's shoulder at a wall pinned with vintage comics, collectors' items, and first issues. There were issues of *The Lone Ranger* from the 1950s, early Stan Lee and Jack Kirby issues of *Fantastic Four*, and a *Daredevil* comic with the Kingpin's face looming over a burning New York City skyline.

"You work here?"

"My father wanted me to get a job. Didn't care where as long as I understand the value," said Anibal, making air quotes, " 'of a hard day's work.' "

Tommy smirked. "Got one of those myself."

Tommy felt terrible for ghosting the artist, but his father had been explicit: Keep it in the Family until absolutely necessary. His father would not want a civilian in Tommy's campaign. His adventurers were not anyone's idea of disciplined; one of them would surely make a stray comment about the origins of the game or some other bit of confidential Family business.

Tommy was nervous. It was difficult to detect where he and Anibal stood.

"Hey man, how's your comic doing?" he asked.

Anibal shrugged as he finished making notes on the condition of an old *Tales of Suspense*, a two-hander featuring both Captain America and Iron Man. Setting the comic aside, he explained, "I don't know if it's going to cross the finish line."

"I pledged. How much do you need?"

"More than you got, but I appreciate it." A pause. "I hear the game is ramping up."

What? thought Tommy. *How would he know?*

"How do you know?"

"I heard you assembled a crew."

Tommy laughed at "crew." If only Anibal knew.

"I have some beta testers."

"I thought I'd get a call. I play, you know. . . ."

There it was. Tommy was pretty sure gossip worked the same in college as in high school, so he was sure his reputation—or more precisely his father's reputation, recently illuminated to Todd—preceded him now. In high school, it dogged him, but going to college he had hoped that being the son of a Mafia don would be like a big fish swimming into a much bigger, murkier pond. Presuming Anibal did know his lineage, it was refreshing that he didn't seem to give a shit about it.

And Tommy *wanted* Anibal to play. But he couldn't possibly add the artist, a civilian, to the campaign. Tommy's crew may have been motley—a stoner, an edgy drunk, a baby gangster, and an elder troll pimp with two dongs—but they were a *connected* motley crew.

Better to keep the world Tommy came from separate.

A balding, middle-aged man emerged from a back room then.

He carried a stack of comics but shuffled like he was carrying the weight of the world on his shoulders. He wore a T-shirt that read I'VE GOT ISSUES and was grumbling about customers not picking up their pull lists; the clearest Tommy heard was "These no-shows are killing us . . ." before Anibal hailed him.

"Carl, this is Tommy, the guy I was telling you about. Tommy, this is Carl. Carl owns the shop."

Meeting a potential new customer did not seem to abate Carl's heavy mood.

"You tell me about a lot of people."

"The game? FunFunder?"

"The One Thousand Blades of Tergivers," added Tommy.

"Oh," said Carl. "That."

"Don't listen to him," said Anibal. "He hasn't smiled since the Bronze Age of comics. His battle cry is 'Meh.' "

"You should check out that half." Carl pointed to the other half of the store, where the shelves were stocked with Magic: The Gathering, HeroClix, Warhammer, Pokémon, and more. "It might help. Sounds like you need it."

Tommy made a face at Anibal. Anibal just shook his head.

"What's that supposed to mean?" asked Tommy.

"I read the comments section," said the storekeeper. "Haven't you? It's *your* game."

"No . . ." said Tommy.

Anibal put a hand in front of him. "Never read the comments section."

"Yikes. Not my problem, though," said Carl, already seeming bored with the conversation. Tommy watched him shuffle off to slip the orphaned pull list pile into poly bags, destined for the back issue bins.

"Never read the comments section," repeated Anibal.

"Well, now I kind of have to," said Tommy. He pulled up the FunFunder app on his phone and handed it over to Anibal. "Here. Go to the comments section, then hand it back."

Anibal raised an eyebrow at the proffered phone.

"I don't want to see the total," explained Tommy.

"Seriously?"

Tommy nodded. "Superstition or whatever." He squeezed his eyes shut.

Anibal took the phone and then let out a long, low whistle.

"The comments are that bad?"

"I haven't moved past that sum yet, player." Tommy opened his eyes and noticed the slightest wince on Anibal's face. "Gotta admit, it's hard not to be a bit jealous. . . ."

"I got lucky is all."

"Shit, I'd bite my arm off for some of that luck. . . ." Anibal scrolled until he found the comments section, then handed back the phone, smirking. "I'd feel bad about letting you read these, but those hundred-dollar bills will help wipe your tears. . . ."

Tommy read what was on the screen, and felt nauseated.

@MinorSpoilers: 1000 Blades of Turd Givers more like.

@MightyKingPython: Playskool's "My First RPG!" Why do they have a World War I doughboy alongside mages? Incoherent AF.

@FearsomeCreature: With the right GM could be interesting maybe @MightyKingPython but def not pledging. Never heard of maker. 0 pedigree. Who the heck pledged it this high? There's not even a section about how you play. It's probably just another diet 5e or chubby 5e who cares.

@MinorSpoilers: You forgot "lazy" @MightyKingPython.

@RedRaven77: I think it's inspired.

@HateNate8: Cuz yur brain dead @RedRaven77 fuck yourself

"Jesus . . ." muttered Tommy.

Anibal waved the comments away. "Every project is like that, especially the successful ones. The more money, the more trolls emerge from under their rocks. Trust me, deafening silence is worse."

Tommy squirmed, then blurted, "Look, I want you to play . . . but everything is really half-baked now. Obviously. I was so caught up in the idea of Tergivers that I probably kicked off the FunFunder a little prematurely. Now I'm reverse engineering, and I'm not much of an engineer, reverse or otherwise."

"First drafts are supposed to suck."

"I know, I know. But I'm not . . . bold. Not like you or Sanse. I've never done anything like this before. I'd rather bang it into some sort of decent shape before I bring you in to look under the hood. I'm really sorry I didn't tell you it was going up."

It sounded good. Because it was mostly true. The apology was real.

But Anibal didn't address it head-on. "That's cool, I guess," he replied. "Besides, I'm in the last week of my own campaign so I can't take my foot off the gas yet with the hustle and promo. And if by some miracle it gets funded, I'm gonna be busy as fuck."

Tommy nodded. It was all he could do. "Yeah, true. Good luck, man." He blew out a breath. "Guess I better look around . . ."

Tommy browsed the game shelves and picked up some game master guides and brought them back to the counter. Carl rang him up. With a heavy sigh and light sincerity, he said in a monotone, "Thank you for your patronage. Keep us in mind for tournaments or whatever. And leave us five stars on Yelp."

Anibal looked on, amused.

Tommy headed for the door, feeling like he had dodged a bullet for now. But something still itched at the back of his mind.

He turned back and asked Anibal, "Hey, how'd you hear about my crew anyway?"

26

"Him?" asked Tommy. *"Him?"*

Back in Fugue territory, Tommy berated Nine Ball in a modest pool hall affiliated with the Family. Relaxed now, the soldier studied all the angles, taking too long to line up his shot. Beside him, watching wordlessly and obediently, was Todd.

"Todd," said Nine, pointing to the bar. "Give us some room, yeah?"

The oaf nodded and lumbered off.

"I ask again: Are you fucking kidding me?"

Nine gave him an even stare. "Never in front of the help, Tommy." He went back to looking at his shot. "He's paying off his debt faster than expected. And instead of being terrified, farm boy over there is intrigued by my line of work. Asked if he could shadow me. Can you believe it?"

"So, you accept interns now?"

"Relax, Tommy." Nine pulled the trigger and they both watched the cue ball strike a purple-striped ball. No balls went into any pockets, so Tommy had no idea if the result was good; he had never understood the game.

"He owes us money," Nine continued. "I'm also letting him buy some gift cards. Do some of the legwork. He loves it. This is how crews get built and I make capo. Two birds."

"I can't even . . ."

"It's okay. He knows if he tells anyone he stole your money, he's fucked. His sense of self-preservation is strong enough that he knows not to cross the Fugues."

"What did you show him on your phone, that day at the party?"

Nine's gun had chilled the room, but whatever was on Nine's phone broke Todd like one of his grandfather's horses. Tommy wasn't stupid; he knew his father and his "uncles" were no angels, but now felt like a good time to know more about the One Thousand Blades of Tergivers' angel investor.

"You sure?"

Was it a photo of a rival with their throat slit?

A dead snitch with a rat jammed into his mouth?

A gangster face down in a ditch with a raw and yawning hole in the back of his head?

His mother?

The thought came unbidden. He shook his head violently.

Nine watched him.

"Just show me," said Tommy.

Nine shrugged, leaned the pool cue against a yellowing wall, and pulled out his phone.

Tommy had expected a garish explosion of Technicolor ultraviolence rendered in 48-megapixel high resolution. His grinning father in a butcher's apron, covered in gore up to his elbows, carving up a rival don like a Thanksgiving turkey. Or worse, Nine Ball doing it for him.

Instead, he saw a black-and-white photograph of a dated newspaper article with the screaming headline *Gangland Massacre in Commerce City*. Tommy zoomed in. The article's text was too small to read, but he could clearly make out the photograph. In it, police officers were milling around what looked like a seedy neighborhood. Before a dilapidated building was a row of be-sheeted bodies on the ground. The police were chatting or performing whatever post-murder rituals they performed while stepping over broken glass and around slicks of blood, rendered in the photo as pure black. He caught one snatch of text bolder than the others: *affiliates of the Delgado crime family.*

From the black and white of the photo and the uniforms, and the makes of the cars, Tommy sensed the image was over a decade old.

The Bad Old Days.

Around the time of the inaugural Guys Breakfast.

While he had no doubt his father was involved in the massacre—pulling a trigger, giving an order, planning an assassination or two—the newspaper article provided just enough distance and the illusion of history for Tommy to breathe a sigh of relief.

"I don't like this," he said, lowering his voice and looking over at Todd. "I don't like *him.*"

"Why? Because you think he likes your girl?"

Tommy's insides burned. Not with nausea for once, but with fury. He was tired of the abuse. Tired of this situation. And tired of Nine, cocky and superior, always being right. But in his bubbling rage, all he could think to say was "She's *not* my girl."

Nine put his hand on Tommy's shoulder and offered a warm smile.

"Tommy, don't you get it? Todd is officially, now and forevermore, your bitch."

Tommy looked over at the bar, where the oaf was nursing a glass of soda and pretending not to look at him. He hadn't thought about it like that.

"Ever heard of keeping your friends close and your enemies closer?"

Tommy nodded.

"Well, it doesn't get much closer than under your thumb. In love and war and everything in between, eliminate the competition. Your pop taught me that. And one way of eliminating the competition is to *own* the competition. Believe me, you don't have to worry about Todd. If you order him to never speak another word to Sanse again, he won't."

Tommy imagined casting a permanent Silence spell on the kid. It was a satisfying notion, but it didn't seem fair.

Then he heard his father's voice. *Fare is what you pay to get on a bus.*

As a kid, Tommy never understood the joke. He'd never ridden a bus. But he was beginning to get the gist.

"He's at your service," said Nine. "And if the game ever needs a fucking orc or a red shirt, *boom,* there's your bitch."

Tommy ran his fingers through his hair, exasperated.

"Does he even know anything about fantasy?"

"Yo, farm boy!" yelled Nine.

At the bar, Todd's head snapped up.

"You know anything about fantasy?"

Todd broke into a large, goofy grin. "I like *Dune.* . . ."

"See, he likes *Dune,*" said Nine. "It's fine."

"*Dune* two chicks at once!"

Tommy stared at Nine.

"It's fine. . . . Trust me, Tommy."

27

They make a strange trio: the young warrior, the medieval knight, and the giant barbarian—yes, who is also uncharacteristically handsome, we get it—approaching the village at the bottom of the ridge. The sky has darkened from its purple to pitch black. The wilderness around them seethes. They hear chittering from one direction. Eerie laughter from another. Eyes burn in the tree line, then disappear as soon as the party whirls to them.

The trio presses on.

Suddenly, Macarro hears the call of his young lover from the Plains. She is cold and lost and misses him. He moves to the dark forest but stops suddenly. More than any other in his small party, he knows what it feels like to hunt. And what it feels like to be hunted. Macarro gives his head a rough shake and stays on the path.

Next, Bellarmina hears the booming voice of her king. He orders her into the forest. She has forsaken her duty, the voice reproaches her from between the trees. She has abandoned the subjects she had sworn a blood oath to protect. Worst of all, she has abandoned him. *The stern words of her liege are like a dagger to her heart. But she knows her king—though severe—is wise. He would not order a trusted, valuable knight into unfamiliar terrain with untested, untrustworthy warriors by her side. She grits her teeth and moves on.*

Bradford pauses and cranes his neck toward the dark woods. He hears the far-off laughter of a woman. When he gets a bead on the direction, he hears a shush, and then another voice begins to titter. The women explain, in overlapping whispers, that they are barbarians like him, large and buxom, and they're so very lonely. They promise him delights unimaginable, paradise on a comfortable bed of moss, if only he'll venture a few feet into the darkness.

"Sounds like porkin' time to me. . . ."

"Porks, no!" yelled Nine.

"This idiot." Chongo leaned over and whispered to Tommy, "Am I ever going to get into this game?"

Tommy held up his hand. *Be patient.* He wanted to see where this would go.

Their second night, and their second official session of Tergivers, was off to a better start than their uneven inaugural session. Nine showed on time. For the young soldier, on time always meant ten minutes early, and tonight he'd arrived twenty minutes early, which Tommy decided to take as an encouraging sign of enthusiasm. Porks practically bounded through the door to Tommy's apartment. Chongo showed up with a CBD quiche, one of Tommy's favorites, and Jolene arrived with a bottle of wine.

"My mead," she'd said to Tommy with a smirk.

Now Jo threw her hands in the air. "How fucking dumb can you be? It's so obvious this is a trap."

"How do you know it's a trap?" asked Porks.

Nine looked like a million sentences had gotten stuck in his throat on their way to exploding out of his mouth. He finally stammered, "Have you ever seen a—a *movie* or a *TV show* or read a *book* or engaged with *any* piece of pop culture, like, *ever*?"

"How have you made it this far, Porks?" asked Chongo. "In real life, I mean."

"Fuck you, stoner. The juice is worth the squeeze. If I'm right, there's two buxom barbarian bitches. . . ."

He cut a quick glance to Jo, but rather than brandish her butterfly knife, she rolled her eyes and topped off her wineglass until it nearly overflowed. All told, an improvement.

"So, what's it gonna be, Tommy?" asked the pimp, picking up a fistful of Skittles from a bowl Tommy had laid out.

"I'm going to let you discover how it unfolds. But as GM, yeah, it's a trap."

"Goddamn it! What do I do now?"

Tommy reached over and plucked Porks's character sheet from the table. "Bradford the Beauteous isn't working with a lot of Wisdom here." He pointed to Porks's hand. "Ability check . . . No, not with the candy, with the d20."

Bradford follows his dicks into the woods. He charges through the trees, branches snapping and whipping back in his face, until he enters a clearing. He realizes his mistake almost immediately. It's dark, and despite himself, Bradford feels something cold climbing his neck: fear.

"Hey, isn't anyone coming with me?" he bellows.

"Not my problem," calls Macarro.

"Fuck thyself," calls Bellarmina.

Seated in the middle of the clearing is a small, sniffling creature.

To a normal humanoid, it would come up to the knee. To Bradford, it's tiny. The barbarian inches closer to investigate the wee thing. When he nears, the creature looks up. It has glowing red eyes and large, pointed ears. It's a goblin, and by the size of it, a child. It stops its soft crying.

The goblin smiles then, its face splitting impossibly wide to reveal twin rows of razor-sharp teeth.

"Guys?"

28

"Shall we join him?" asks Macarro.

Macarro's inner voice—perhaps his ancestors, perhaps his own conscience—tells him that it's something only he can answer.

Bellarmina removes a gauntlet and produces a flask from a compartment in her armor. She takes a swig, examines a fingernail. "I couldn't give less of a shit. . . ."

"I would save you,*" comes Bradford's far-off voice, from deep inside the trees.*

"Bullshit," she says.

"I would! Scout's honor!" pleads the barbarian.

"They wouldn't let you within ten miles of a Boy Scout, you fuckin' perv," says Bellarmina.

"Bell," says Macarro.

The knight dons her gauntlet again and sighs deeply. "Fine . . ."

The pair charge into the woods. Dark, slimy things flee before them. Before long, they emerge into a clearing. They come face-to-face with a large, writhing creature with rippling, convulsing green flesh.

"What the fuck?" says Macarro.

"Kill it," says Bellarmina. She rears back with her sword.

But the pair of warriors realize the beast is not a single creature, but several creatures: a swarm of goblins crawling all over Bradford, burying the barbarian in their reptilian flesh.

"In a hot way?" asks Bradford.

Most definitely not in a hot way. Bradford is overwhelmed.

Dozens of wide maws clamp down on the barbarian at once. Each bite is like a hundred dagger strikes. Sharp claws slash his body as the goblins clamber over one another, trying to find purchase to sink their teeth into his hide.

"I still have my magical codpiece, yeah?"

The two little Bradfords are intact, but he is taking heavy damage elsewhere.

"I'll be fine."

In fact, Bradford is dying.

"Shit. Well, don't just stand there. Somebody do something, you worthless fucks!"

Macarro bounds into battle in his typical fashion, executing beautifully complicated maneuvers, martial arts combinations, and spinning kicks. Nothing is worth doing if he can't look cool while doing it.

And despite her deep loathing for her companion, Bellarmina charges in as well and swings her Sicilium sword. Two goblins fall away. Upon closer inspection, she sees that it was a single goblin, cleaved in two.

"Yes!" says Bradford, his voice muffled from beneath the pile.

His celebration is cut short. The area of Bradford's body the dead goblin had occupied is quickly claimed by another goblin. Like a patch of sand with the tide rushing in, the giant's ruddy flesh disappears again.

"Get the fuck off him," says Macarro, "or I'll kill the kid."

Bellarmina turns to find Macarro, his foot on the throat of the first goblin—the goblin child—his war club raised.

"It's a kid . . .*" says Bellarmina.*

• • •

"There's a *code,*" said Jo.

Given a hundred years, Tommy wasn't sure he could describe the look on her face.

"It's a *goblin,*" said Nine. "There's a code for goblins?"

"A goblin child."

Nine Ball gave her his *Get the fuck outta here* face.

From a gameplay perspective, it was a pretty savvy move. From a human perspective, it cast a chill in the room.

Porks nodded appreciatively to Nine. "Nice bluff, kid."

"Who says I'm bluffing? Rolling to smite the toothy little shit."

During their first session, when Nine truly grokked the game mechanics, Tommy thought he had created a monster. The soldier obsessed over stats, inventoried equipment, memorized weapons ranges, and studied characters' movements and positions. And when he finally chose a move, it was usually overcomplicated. And it had to be stylish. Complex combinations of moves or wushu kung fu or spinning his war club around like a bo staff. Nine's turns took longer than everyone else's, even during heated combat, which elicited a groan from Jo, and caused Chongo to spark a joint and Porks to say, "Time to drain the lizard . . ." But this?

This was surprisingly decisive. And vicious. Maybe Tommy hadn't created a monster. Maybe Nine had been a monster all along.

"You sure?" asked Tommy.

"He's their lookout. He knew what's up. Prone, so advantage."

Nine threw. His bone die rolled across the table and stopped to display a sufficient number. It didn't take much; no need to roll a second time for the advantage. The child's goblin class did not stand a chance against the young warrior's attack.

"Well, what happened?" asked Nine.

Tommy looked at the die. Then into Nine's eyes.

"The goblin's body can't withstand a strike from your club. It practically breaks apart. You weren't expecting that. You are showered with its green blood. One by one, the other goblins detach from Bradford, falling off him and onto their knees in grief. One goblin emerges from the pack and retrieves the lifeless body. A piercing keening rises up from the forest floor as the goblins begin to wail."

Tommy's table fell silent.

"Jesus," muttered Porks.

"Happy?" asked Jo. She turned her shoulder to Nine and took a slug of wine, as if he was a boyfriend who had said something really stupid in public, which in a way, he had.

"What?" said Nine, indignant. "You have to show people who's boss on the streets. You show weakness, you're dead. That little guy was *complicit.*"

To Tommy, it sounded as weak and unconvincing as his own protests that he was the GM the night before.

"This isn't the streets," said Tommy. "We can make it whatever we want."

Nine shrugged, refusing to back down. "Sometimes you have to send a message. The streets, magical forests, fucking Narnia, wherever. Same rules apply."

"You don't know shit about the streets, junior," said Jo.

Nine folded his arms, sulking.

• • •

A dazed Bradford struggles to his feet, blood seeping from his innumerable wounds. He staggers over the goblins, lost in their collective grief, and joins his companions.

"Thanks," says Bradford.

"Had to be done," says Macarro.

"We should get the fuck out of here quick . . ." says the sullen knight.

The trio turns to go back the way they came, but more goblins block their path. They drop from trees, unfurl from the branches, rise up from behind bushes and rocks. In short order, the goblins' grief curdles to rage. They surround the adventurers, empowered by the fury of the small. Countless angry red eyes dot the landscape. The adventurers hear an endless rattling sound, like running alongside a wooden fence with a stick, only many at once. They realize then that it is the clicking of hundreds of goblins' teeth in anticipation.

"Nice work, tough guy," says Bellarmina.

Macarro says nothing.

Even more goblins appear, emerging from the ground, and replenishing in a never-ending supply from nearby caves. The creatures, now legion, inch closer, pressing the trio against a wide tree. Macarro looks up. More eyes appear in the canopy, burning like fireflies. The chitter of their sharp teeth rattles the air like cicadas on a hot summer evening.

Suddenly, a blinding light punches a hole in the night. It's as if a small sun has risen in the heart of the dark woods. It's so powerful, the goblins lurch and stumble, their shadows streaking back as if ripped from their small hunched bodies.

The adventurers cup their hands to their brows and make out a figure at the center of the glare.

It holds a dagger aloft, and the light is emanating from it.

The goblins shriek in terror. Some dive into bolt-holes, scrabble up trees, disappear into canopies. The rest of the legion flee deeper into the woods, chasing their shadows, their high whines trailing them.

And just like that, the swarm is gone. Bellarmina, Macarro, and Bradford are alone with the mysterious figure holding the thin, glowing blade.

"About damn time . . ." says the stranger.

The figure lowers the weapon, its glow lessening in intensity from an inferno to a campfire, until the party can discern its wielder.

The stranger seems to be an extension of the very forest itself, dressed in flowing green robes—

"Tie-dye."

Okay, sure . . . flowing robes that seem to have been made of a process of tying, then dyeing, the cloth with different hues. The stranger seems completely unperturbed by the goblin horde, which, moments ago, was about to devour the trio of shaken adventurers. He goes about his business, using his dagger, now casting as much light as a lantern, to scan the ground.

"Ah," he says, "perfect."

Upon closer inspection, the dagger is actually a spade in miniature, which he uses to dig out a clump of weeds. He sits on a stump, packs a pipe with the weeds, then touches the tip of the spade, now glowing like an ember, to the end of the pipe. A thin wisp of smoke curls upward from the pipe—smelling of the sweet deep green of the forest floor—and permeates the clearing. The stranger draws deeply from the pipe, then coughs.

"That is some righteous shit. . . ."

"Who are you?" asks Macarro.

The stranger's face lights up with a smile as he blows out a long tendril of smoke.

"Garcia, man."

Bellarmina rolls her eyes.

"What are you?" asks Bradford. "Some broken-down old hippie? You don't need no game for that."

The barbarian roars with laughter at his own jest.

Garcia ignores the barbarian and explains to the party that he is a druid, native to this forest. Garcia worships Nature. In return, she bestows many blessings upon him. Like the medicinal weed he is smoking. He lives a peaceful life, tending his garden, communing with the animals, and wandering the woods in search of special herbs. But lately there have been disturbances, even in his remote patch of the wilderness. The skies roil in strange colors. Birds begin their migration cycles too early. Large predators appear outside their normal hunting grounds. The forest floor rumbles and small peaks, like hideous blemishes, erupt from the earth to spew lava.

There is an unearthly magic at play—and if there is one thing a druid is sensitive to, it's magic.

Garcia looks at the bleeding barbarian.

"You know, there are many other gifts Gaia can offer if one only knows how to ask," says Garcia.

Macarro and Bellarmina stare at Bradford.

"What?" says the barbarian.

"'If one only knows how to ask' . . ." says Macarro.

"Jesus Christ," says Bellarmina, "do you need it fucking spelled out for you?"

Bradford is gently reminded that he is covered with scores of goblin bite marks, probably poisonous, and rapidly losing blood.

"Oh," says Bradford. "You got any magic for my wounds?"

"Thought you'd never ask," says Garcia.

He plunges his spade into the nearest elderfig tree. When he pulls it back out, a rivulet of sap oozes out.

"Goblins can be a pest, but are no worse than bees really," he says, giving Macarro a pointed look. "It's not good to go around killing bees."

Macarro looks at his feet.

"All you need is light to deter them," continues Garcia, "and a little of this if you get 'stung.'"

Bradford touches two of his large fingers to the sap stream, sniffs it.

"Natural antiseptic for goblin bites," explains Garcia. "Rarely will the forest present you a problem that it doesn't also furnish a remedy for. Mother Gaia always provides, man. She's like the ultimate dispensary."

Bradford daubs his many wounds with the thick sap. The blood is stanched. The burning sting of the bites dulls. With rest, and no more foolishness, proclaims Garcia, the barbarian will make a full recovery.

"Want to pass any of that magic herb?" asks Bradford.

"Get your own," snaps Garcia.

Garcia does not want to leave his beloved glade, but his Mother Gaia is out of balance and suffering. With one hand she has presented him a problem, and as always, with the other she has offered him a solution: this unlikely band of adventurers.

Garcia accepts the invitation to join their party.

"Finally. Let's get the fuck out of here already," says Bellarmina, and marches back in the direction they came.

"Who died and made her boss?" says Macarro, but he falls in behind her nevertheless.

"Fucking hippie," snorts Bradford.

"Saved your dumb ass," says Garcia.

29

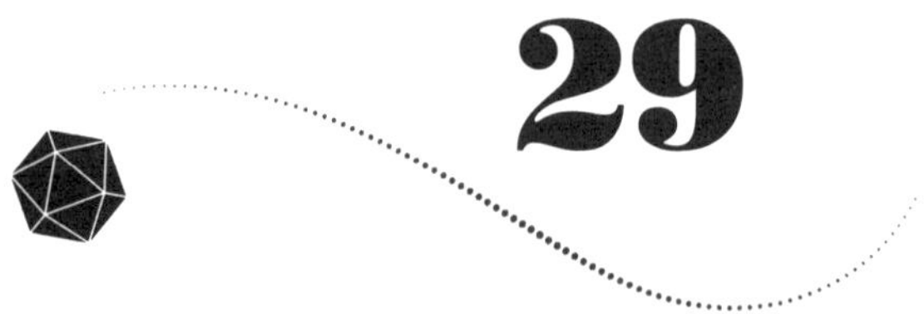

The One Thousand Blades of Tergivers was coming together.

Over the next few sessions, Tommy navigated his band of adventurers, in fits and starts, out of the forest to a village in the shadow of the mountain. They found a sketchy tavern where a variety of races consorted over wagon wheel tables. Nimbuses of candlelight illuminated the features of many different faces. Like a watering hole in the savanna, it teemed with life—dwarves, elves, fey, half-orcs—and also danger. It seemed like any one of the patrons could lunge across a table with a terrible snap of their jaws. Everyone was on edge. Even those who weren't as sensitive to nature as Garcia felt something was amiss. It made the populace pulsate with a nervous End Times energy.

Naturally, Bradford wandered off in search of wenches. Macarro tried to rig a card game with a band of fey. Bellarmina got into a scuffle with an arrogant NPC—"*You think you're better than me?*"—in a way that made Tommy think fast and come up with a whole backstory behind the insignificant stable hand. Garcia traded some magical weed with a bard for a floating compass that displayed virtues as its cardinal points rather than directions.

The compass pointed toward Wisdom, and the players followed it back out into the woods.

The game had direction now. Literally.

Better yet, Nine, Jo, Porks, and Chongo stopped fighting the scenarios so much and began to gel. They still bickered and broke out into the occasional skirmish, and side quests abounded—usually Porks wanting to investigate the world of Tergivers' seedy underground—but they were beginning to grok their characters' stats, the mechanics of the game, and the larger narrative. They were having fun. Even Jo went from sloshed by the end of a session to pleasantly buzzed.

Nine had moved so fast into testing the mechanics—mechanics that were still being written for each situation—that Tommy found himself making things up on the fly, trying to recall helpful approaches from when he'd played old game systems in middle school and some ad hoc systems people had tried online. He thought he could use a little time to let some concepts coalesce in his brain, and since the game was coming together so well, he decided to give his players a rare night off.

Which was when he got a text from Sanse asking to hang out.

He stared at his phone, as if he were holding his own magical compass.

He agonized over the composition of the return text.

Would love to, he thought about writing.

No! Can't say love*, you idiot. Not in any capacity, not yet.*

Or simply: *Sure.*

Way too casual, cool guy.

Tommy needed to show he was game but not eager, mysterious but not aloof, cool but not cold. Hell, this was harder than planning the next session. He realized he was taking too long. He settled on a response: What did you have in mind?

• • •

The meetup was not what he had in mind. He had not allowed himself to dream that it would be just the two of them—having his hopes dashed would kill him—so he'd tricked himself into thinking Anibal would join them. But when he met her at the comedy club down on South Broadway, a strip lined with dive bars, arthouse bookstores, and punk rock donut and cupcake shops, he was aware he was in *her* space. Seated at a tiny lounge table for two, he realized—first with delight, then with budding terror—that this might be a date. Like a *date* date.

He had never been on a date before.

Tommy cursed himself. He had spent even more time on his wardrobe than on his text, tying himself into knots. He would not make the mistake of dressing like a homeless samurai again, but if he listened to Nine's advice, he'd be in a suit, which would be overkill for sure. He figured he would split the difference and settled on noncommittal jeans, designer sneakers, and a polo. But after one look at her—spellbinding in the tea-light set on the table, wearing another unique dress, care taken with her hair and makeup—he realized that noncommittal was a cop-out.

A tiny, angelic Nine Ball appeared on his shoulder in a puff of cloud and shook his head, admonishing him.

Always commit, Tommy. There's no kill like overkill.

On his other shoulder, a devilish Nine Ball appeared in a flash of fire and brimstone.

What do you want from me? The angel's right, numbnuts.

Sanse ordered an iced tea. Tommy did the same. Tommy stole a glance over the top of a menu, caught her doing the same. They both smiled, blushed.

Definitely a date.

Hidden behind his menu, Tommy banished the imaginary Nine Balls on either shoulder to psych himself up. He told himself to forget about the clothes, and every other misstep in his life. None of it mattered. He didn't have much experience, but he recognized a pure, incandescent moment when he saw one and he was not about to fuck it up.

"So," he said, "thank you for texting."

"Thank you for coming!" Sanse beamed. "Everyone else thinks things like this are cringe, but I love performers—music, theater, poetry. All of it. You never know what you're going to get at these things. Besides," she said with a flash of a smile, "Anibal gets to hang out with you all the time. It was my turn."

Tommy laughed. "I don't see him that much. But I'm more than happy for you to take the lead."

She smiled at this. "How are you guys doing? With the game, I mean. I heard that it was doing, like, insanely well."

He held up his hands, almost panicked. "Please don't tell me!"

"Tell you what?"

"The number."

"Okay . . ."

"I'm sorry, I just . . ."

Calm down, Tommy. Don't be a fucking weirdo.

He took a deep breath, caught the faint lilac of her perfume. He decided to level with her. A little. He knew enough to know that if he couldn't open up, at least a bit, nothing with her would be real.

"The pledge money really stresses me out." Porks had slipped during one of the last sessions: $880,000. God knows what it was now. "Everything about it stresses me out, but the money in particular. It's like a trigger. Bad dreams . . ."

Most nights, he dreamed of his mother's eyes or of Sanse's smile. Sometimes, he dreamed that he was inhabiting the patchwork world of Tergivers, but more than once, he dreamt that he was sitting at a desk on a beach, taking a timed test. Suddenly, the lazy waves lapping his feet were sucked out to sea. Stranded fish flopped. He saw a wall of water in the distance. It grew closer. Tommy looked down at his paper, rushed to fill in the dots of his multiple-choice test, looking over at the mighty wave every few answers. When he heard its roar and the shadow fell over his shoulder, he woke up in a cold sweat.

Knocking on the door to a million.

He didn't need to be Freud to realize the game was stressing him out. After that first dream, he'd ordered his players not to tell him the pledge total. He was serious. The ballooning sum freaked him out, stultified him. He would allow himself some brief celebration when it was funded, but until then, he would ignore the tsunami as best as he could. It was head down, nose to the grindstone time.

After talking to Anibal, he'd read some more comments, which led to him clicking through to some articles about the game's meteoric funding rise, and so he'd stopped going to the FunFunder page altogether. He dictated the necessary updates to Chongo or Nine; when Big Al had checked in and asked if there was any way to juice the intake, they also added some stretch goals. Tommy stopped checking email too—agents were already beginning to circle his inbox like slick sharks, detecting distant promises of money in FunFunder's vast ocean. He just wanted to focus on the end product, getting as much done and making the game as airtight as possible in that liminal time between launching and receiving the money.

"There's the creation aspect of the game," he continued, "which I have to admit is really fun. Like, exhilarating. But then there's the commerce side and . . . the more I think about that, it just . . ."

"Locks you up?"

"Yeah," said Tommy. "Exactly. I just need it to be good. I need it to be great. And it's not even close to being ready."

"Well, tonight is about recharging your battery. It won't be great if you run out of creative juice."

If tonight was about recharging his battery, just sitting beside her at the little dark nightclub table threatened to overheat it and melt it to slag.

"And if you want it to be perfect," she continued, "then it's never going to be ready. At a certain point, you're going to have to ship—"

"We're not even close to shipping. The postage alone will be crazy. . . ."

The waitress came by, saw that the duo were clearly no further along in ordering the food, and flitted off to another table.

"I don't mean *literal* shipping," Sanse said after a pause and a laugh. "I mean it as a concept. Every artist, sooner or later, has to figure out when a project is done, and turn it over to the universe or the public or the marketplace or whatever, and then you move on to the next project. If I wanted every sketch to be perfect, I'd never get out of the park. Don't let the perfect become the enemy of the good."

Wow, thought Tommy.

"Wow," said Tommy.

"You're teasing me," she said.

"No! I'm not. You're just verbalizing all the crazy that's swirling around my brain."

"You have friends, you know. We can help. I'd love to help. . . ."

"You would?"

"Of course I would. You're actually doing the damn thing, Tommy. You're not posturing like so many of the other art-holes in school or blathering like the professors telling us to pay our dues. You're not asking permission. It's exciting. Who wouldn't want to be a part of that?"

She placed her hand over his.

He felt the lead plates in his battery begin to short-circuit.

"And maybe I can give you something else to dream about?"

Fireworks erupted behind his eyes. Stray thoughts arced in his mind, then exploded all at once in a Technicolor display he hoped wasn't visible on his cheeks.

Her hand. On my hand. She likes me.

It's about money, she just wants in on Tergivers.

Who cares?

Maybe she just wants to be friends.

Fuck you, her hand is on your hand, dipshit. She's smiling, waiting. Is she leaning in? Holy shit, she's leaning in.

"Ladles and jelly spoons!" a loud voice shouted through the club speakers.

By instinct, Tommy and Sanse looked toward the stage, where a cheesy, over-caffeinated MC in a Hawaiian shirt and electrified hair hyped the crowd, reminding everyone to drink heavily and tip their waitresses, and then introduced the first volunteer of open mic night.

Tommy shifted his fantasies momentarily from Sanse to choking the MC to death, but then found Sanse again. He turned to her, ready to resume inching his face closer to hers, but she remained facing the stage, eager for the show. The moment had passed.

Tommy took one last longing look at her profile: doe eyes wide and full lips parted in an anticipatory smile. She looked utterly without pretense or judgment, ready to receive the first performer with a generosity of spirit that was completely alien to him and made his heart swell. The kiss could wait. In truth, if he left with only this image of her, he would be grateful. He took a mental snapshot, pocketed to treasure later, and faced the stage too.

Where he saw a drunken Jolene Galliano approaching the microphone.

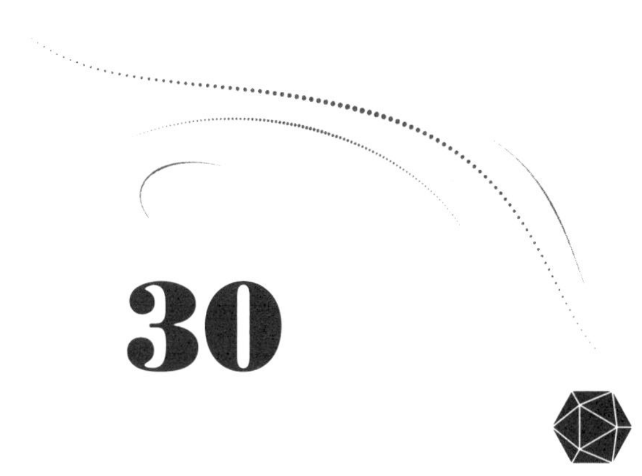

30

Tommy jolted in his seat.

"Are you okay?" asked Sanse.

"Sorry." He rubbed his thigh. "Old war injury."

She smirked. "*You* should go up there."

By the look of Jo, he might have to. Thanks to his highly combustible parents, Tommy had grown so keenly sensitive to the rhythms and tells of other people he knew there was a problem instantly. Though Jo was dressed in her usual attire—boots, jeans, leather jacket—he could pinpoint where she was on the shit-faced spectrum before she even reached the microphone stand. There was Caustic Jo, who stormed into his apartment before a session, eager to have a drink. There was the Ball-Busting but Affable Jo, who loosened up after a few glasses of wine and even took a leadership role. And there was Sloshed Jo, who yelled she was *perfectly fine* when Tommy the Tight-Ass ordered an Uber for her at the end of the night.

"What the fuck is up, Denver?" she yelled into the mic.

Hoots rose from the surrounding tables.

"My name is Jo, I'm Italian, I'm drunk, and I am all out of fucks to give."

Turns out Tommy did not need his finely calibrated drunk barometer after all.

"As you can tell by my name, my father wanted a boy. Which is only fair, because I didn't want a lowlife piece of shit for a father. Actually, Jo is short for Jolene, which meant my father also wanted a redneck."

Some mild laughter from the crowd.

Tommy leaned forward in a defensive crouch. He cupped his chin in his hand, hiding a wince. He had played soccer for a couple of seasons as a little kid. Once a season, everyone had to take a turn as goalie. You either loved it or you hated it. If you loved it, you were a born goalie. But if you were like 90 percent of the kids, you stood there, praying the game stayed at the other end of the field because you knew that at any moment everything could go wrong and the other team would get the ball and make a break for it. Seeing Jo up there, he felt like a kid again, stuck in goal and watching with dread as the other team stormed his way.

"I'm kidding. My dad was great. He taught me all sorts of useful shit. How to change a battery, how to win at cards, the best ways to dispose of a body . . ."

More laughter, uncertain this time.

"Trips to Home Depot were a real education, let me tell you. 'Daddy, why do you need so much lye?' And he's all, 'I like to make my own soap.' Can you believe it? I should've known better—he lived in a studio apartment with no pots, two towels, and one bar of soap with pubes on it—but until I was thirteen I thought the motherfucker invented Irish Spring."

That received a genuine, warm laugh.

"Look, I'm not saying he was a hit man, but he had a punch card at the funeral home."

Tommy couldn't believe what he was seeing. Was she nuts? Did his father know about this? Tommy readily admitted he was risk averse, but this was crazy. He could see absolutely zero upside to a gangster getting up onstage and airing her dirty laundry, even for laughs.

"Now, scientists, they'll say that the apple doesn't fall far from the tree, and to be clear, I am not saying I'm a hit man. . . ."

Nervous laughter. Tommy leaned forward.

"Because that's gendered. I prefer hit person. I will also accept hit *lady*," she said with a curtsy.

"She's not bad," whispered Sanse.

From the stage, Jo continued. "I'm kidding, I'm kidding. I'm not saying I'm a hit woman, but if I was it would really suck. I'd have to give up one of my passions: killing people for free."

There were a few scattered laughs, but now a few groans thrown in.

Jo pressed on. "Do what you love, and you'll never work a day in your life. That's what Dad said, anyway, before sentencing. . . ."

The laughter-to-groaning ratio had flipped, and a heckler or two popped up. One loud woman jeered, *"Thank you, next!"*

Even from the back of the room, Tommy noticed Jo's jaw clench. One of her tells.

"I'm not saying I'm a hit woman, but if I was"—she pointed into the corner of the room—"I would do *that* fucking bitch pro bono."

Uh-oh.

The resulting groans far outnumbered the laughs, with a few shouts thrown in.

"I'll be right back," said Tommy. "Bathroom."

"Sure," said Sanse, transfixed by the slow-moving car crash onstage.

Tommy took a circuitous route around the room, heading toward the bathrooms, trying to get into Jo's eyeline.

The loud woman's date did not find Jo's banter amusing. "Get off the stage, you drunk bitch!"

Sober, Jo was an unflappable member of her father's crew, but Tommy knew that, with a few drinks, she could be easily baited. And her temper was something to behold.

"Look," Jo said, and the microphone screeched with painful feedback. "I don't go to your work down at the glory hole and tell you how to do your job, pal."

Tommy moved toward the stage. He made frantic knife-slashing motions across his throat, but she was focused on the jeering couple.

"Keep it up, you little shit. *This* Jolene doesn't just take men, she takes them the *fuck out*—"

"Fuck you!" yelled the man. Several others in his table's vicinity agreed and joined in.

"Fuck me? Fuck you!"

And with that, Jo dove into the crowd.

Tommy sprinted between the small cocktail tables and intercepted Jo before she reached the hecklers' table. He grabbed her arm. She wrenched it free and reared back with a savage elbow strike toward his face. Fortunately, Jo's normal lightning-fast reaction time was slowed by drink. Tommy, sober, dodged. Still, the elbow missed by an inch.

"Hey! Jo! It's Tommy!"

She stopped in her tracks. She turned to face him, and blinked.

"Oh. Hey, Tommy." She smiled a dreamy smile, like his sudden appearance was a pleasant surprise in the midst of a calm forest. "What're you doing here?"

"What am *I* doing here?"

But the table of hecklers, all on their feet now, were still spoiling for the fight that Tommy had interrupted.

"Thank you all so much for participating in tonight's immersive performance art experience!" Tommy announced and started clapping at both Jo and the table of angry patrons. "Wasn't that fun, everyone?"

"I don't get it," said the heckling woman.

"You wouldn't, bitch," Jo spat, suddenly angry again.

"Still in character, ladies and gentlemen!" Tommy clapped and nudged Jo along with his hip. To her, he whispered, "Let's fucking go. Now."

Sanse caught up to them as Tommy pulled Jo out of the fray and toward the venue's sad excuse for a greenroom.

"Tommy, that was so brave."

"Tommy, that was so brave," repeated Jo in a high voice, cracking herself up. She was slurring her words now. "She's a cutie, Tommy."

"I'm sorry about all this, Sanse. She's one of my father's, um, coworkers."

Jo wagged a finger in Sanse's face. "I'm not saying I'm a hit woman, but if I was . . ."

"Isn't she hilarious?" said Tommy, and spun Jo away into a chair as other comedians looked on.

Sanse looked Jo up and down, clearly charmed. "She's really committed to the bit."

"Sure is. Look, I'm really sorry, Sanse, but I can't leave her like this. I need to take her home."

"Let me help you." She took both of Tommy's hands in hers.

He stared at them.

Holy shit, both *of her hands . . . She really likes me.*

This absolutely sucks.

He squeezed her hands, and against every instinct he had, let them go.

"No, no. That's really sweet," he said, then lowered his voice. "She's very combustible."

"I can handle myself," Sanse said quietly.

"I know," Tommy said. "She just doesn't like new people. It's cool, I got it."

Tommy smiled, but the sadness must have been palpable on his face, because Sanse touched his cheek and said, "Don't worry, you get a do-over."

He brightened.

Sanse hugged him goodbye, leaving Tommy alone with the drunk enforcer.

"Do-over," snorted Jo.

"Shut up, you."

Tommy drove Jo to her apartment on the edge of Commerce City in silence, until finally, she said, "I think the set started off okay."

"That bit where you threatened to whack a heckler needs polish."

"It's crowd work."

"If your crowd work includes leaping into one to fight it, then your crowd work needs work. Next time, maybe lead with 'Hey, where are you from?' or 'What do you do for a living, ma'am?' or 'How long have you two been going out?' Or better yet how about not having a next time? Are you fucking nuts, getting onstage like that?"

"Maybe."

From the corner of his eye, Tommy saw her open and close the hand that was bandaged when Tommy had first met her.

"Is that why you were in urgent care that day?"

"More or less."

Tommy laughed ruefully and shook his head. "Unbelievable. Does my father know about your hobby? The Johnnies?"

She shook her head.

"Don't be so sure. I don't know much about the criminal underworld, but I'm pretty certain comedy clubs and strip joints are cousins. Word travels, Jo." He shook his head. "Jesus, I thought *Porks* was dense."

He expected another elbow strike aimed at his head, but he didn't care. He was incensed and on a roll now. She'd sabotaged his date with Sanse and jeopardized herself. He looked over at her, but the alcohol had made her docile, remorseful.

He sighed.

"I know enough about my father to know that he would probably not appreciate you getting onstage and talking about that stuff. Even in jest. It invites scrutiny. And, no offense, but that's at least two occasions where your set ended in a fistfight. Do you have a death wish or something?"

He stole another look. Passing headlights revealed she had tears in her eyes.

"It's like a high-wire act. I could kill or I could bomb." She shrugged, like either option was fine to her. "I'm telling the truth up there. Kind of. I feel creative, alive. Free."

Tommy understood more than anyone the desire to be free of his current circumstance. Free of his father. But he wasn't reckless enough to stage a one-man show about it.

Jo looked over at him. Her voice was thick with tears and whatever she had been drinking. She was very drunk but forced the words out.

"I haven't done a set since the day you picked me up. I didn't need to. . . ." Her eyebrows knotted, as if the words were either too hard to find or too hard to say. "The game is good, Tommy."

Damn it, he thought. Jo was an alcoholic hit woman and an adrenaline junkie, and Tommy had accidentally created Tabletop Roleplaying Therapy. *Alcoholics and Adrenaline-Junkie Mafia Hit Women Anonymous.*

Then he had given her the night off to fend for herself. And *anonymous* went right out the window.

"Sorry about your date," muttered Jo. "She's real cute."

Tommy sighed. "Yeah."

They got out and he guided her to the threshold of her apartment, where she dropped her keys. Tommy picked them up for her, but she dropped them again. As Tommy tried the different keys in the lock, Jo leaned against the wall and laughed at him.

Finally, hitting upon the right key, Tommy tried to help her off the wall, but she shoved past him. "M'fine," she growled, any momentary vulnerability bottled back up and locked away.

Tommy followed her inside. The apartment was sparsely furnished, and its chief decorations were empty wine bottles stacked like bowling pins on her kitchen counter. As she walked through the ascetic space she dropped her leather jacket on the floor. Tommy heard a clank, saw her butterfly knife spill from it. He collected the blade, slipped it back inside the jacket, and gently hung it over the back of her threadbare couch.

He peered inside her bedroom. She had already flopped onto her bed.

"Fuck off with thee, Boy Scout."

"Okay," he said. "Good night, Jo."

He turned to leave.

"Wait!"

He turned back.

"Boots!" She kicked a leg out at him.

Tommy returned to the foot of her bed. He unzipped a boot, set it down.

"Firstborn of the Al Mighty," she said, laughing. It was not a kind laugh. "Look at you now, Baby Fugue."

Tommy took hold of her other foot, eager to get the hell out of there.

Look in the mirror, you surly—

On the bedside table, he saw a picture of a much younger, happier Jo, laughing and holding an ice-cream cone. Beside her, arm slung around Jo's shoulder, holding her own ice-cream cone, and her wide mouth caught mid–explosive laugh, was his mother.

He dropped Jo's leg, her boot still on, and snatched the frame from the bedside table, held it up to the light. Jo was beyond caring. Her eyes were closed. Her insult chamber was empty. She was off to Neverland.

Tommy studied the picture for a long time.

"You look like her," mumbled Jo. "Pisses me off sometimes."

Tommy was surprised she was still awake. She was still very drunk, her voice thick, and she was fading, but coherent. For the moment.

"You were friends?"

"I looked after her a long time ago. Like your boyfriend Nine does you. For all the good it did. And what's lost can't be found again. Not in real life, Little Prince."

"I wish my father hadn't chased her away."

Jo's breathing slowed and deepened. He waited a moment

longer, then pulled out his camera and took a photo of the picture in its frame. He left the bedroom for the kitchen, filled up a large glass with water, and set it beside the picture. Carefully, he removed her remaining boot.

Jo stirred. Her voice was far off, half caught in a dream.

"... wasn't chased away ..."

Tommy forgot all about Sanse then, his anticipatory nerves, the electric current of her hand on his, their warm embrace at the end of the night. The sly promise of a do-over. Gone even was Tommy's recollection of jumping into the melee to grab Jo, her deadly sharp elbow sailing just past his nose.

Instead, it felt like she had punched him in the gut.

Jo was his mother's bodyguard. And it was highly unlikely something would happen to his mother without Jo's knowledge. Or her complicity.

Tommy stood there, staring at the sleeping woman, waiting for more. But nothing more came. She began to snore, and after a long moment Tommy left, locking the door behind him.

31

Macarro, Bellarmina, Bradford, and Garcia follow the floating compass from adventure to adventure. The catch? Its direction only reveals itself to one of them at a time, and that adventurer must convince the others in the party to follow it. Arguments abound. Bellarmina is brash and does not like to take orders from anyone save her homeland's king. Macarro overthinks everything and tries to remain ten steps ahead—he is not one for leaps of faith. Bradford, lacking Wisdom, has the opposite problem. He is firmly rooted in the moment, reluctant to pursue any course of action not obviously in his immediate self-interest. And Garcia the druid, lacking Courage, prefers to avoid scrapes, smoke his magic weed, and proselytize about nature.

"Pododу's nerfect," he says, and blows a smoke ring.

The compass lights up for Bellarmina, its cardinal point of Discipline flaring and pointing to a mountain peak on the horizon. But the peak is larger than the rest, a massive black triangle silhouetted by a golden thread. Scanning harder, they see the thread is the light of fires outlining the mountain.

In the distance it thunders. The earth quivers. Lightning strikes illuminate the peak for a moment at a time, hinting at its true, terrifying scale.

It's a massive, fearsome volcano.

"Nope," says Garcia.

But the compass flares, insistent. That way lies Discipline.

"We're going," says Bellarmina.

"Like Mount Doom," says Macarro. "In Lord of the Rings."

It's not Mount Doom. It's a very distinct, nonderivative thing the characters are seeing.

"Mount Dread?" offers Garcia.

Fine. Whatever. Mount Dread.

The adventurers leave the forested area and head toward it. The transition is sudden. In a matter of steps, they leave their pastoral patchwork of dark forests, green meadows, and gently blowing grasslands for a scorched and jagged realm.

The party moves closer and closer, picking their way over the bleak, lifeless terrain. They spend days walking over jagged rocks and around massive pumice stones, the size of cottages, hurled from the volcano during its constant, spectacular eruptions. Finally, they arrive and begin their ascent.

"This juice better be worth the squeeze," says Bradford.

The compass only grows brighter.

They forge onward, up the slope. They must stop periodically as the mountain shudders, as if trying to shake them free. Its rumbling is deafening, as if Tergivers itself is clearing its throat.

Bellarmina, in the lead, hears a mighty crack *and looks back to see the mountainside has split apart. Bubbling rivers of lava separate the party: Macarro and Garcia stand on one rock island, Bradford another.*

"No problem," says Garcia. "I'll just summon up some serious wind to blow us back together."

But as Garcia begins to swing his spade around, Macarro notices the growing waves of lava crashing against their craggy island. Instead of flowing back, the waves remain, solidify, and darken.

"What the hell?" says Macarro.

Magmins.

Sizzling black magma creatures intent on burning everything they see . . . The magmins call the volcano home and do not appreciate trespassers. Garcia uses his spade now to blow them off the rock, and Macarro uses his war club like a bat to knock them back, but as soon as one magmin is repelled, two more burble up and wash onto the rock to take its place.

Alone on his rock, Bradford contemplates how he can join the fray, but beside him a large pumice stone starts to move of its own accord. It grumbles and unfolds, and a stone giant towers over the barbarian. In a deep, gravelly voice, the giant bellows that it does not like to be awakened from its slumber. Bradford and the stone giant trade mighty blows.

"What about me?" asks Bellarmina.

The only answer comes from the compass. Pointing upward. Toward Discipline.

Toward the crater. She does not want to leave her party behind, but she realizes there is no choice. With great effort, she climbs and scrabbles to the rim of the volcano. The heat is so intense, she can feel herself cooking inside her armor. It buckles and warps. Her fine hair singes.

"What am I supposed to do?" mocks Bellarmina. "I'm not throwing myself in."

To the side, a portal opens. She approaches. Through it, she sees her old kingdom. All she has to do is step through and she can go home.

"I don't get it."

• • •

“I don’t get it,” said Jo.

“What’s to get?” said Tommy. He looked around his living room, pretending to be bored. He had turned the walls surrounding the gaming table into vision boards, hanging posters of exotic landscapes and mythical creatures to help inspire his players. Tonight, before they arrived, he’d hung Anibal’s drawing of his mother as queen and placed it directly in Jo’s line of sight.

The enforcer hadn’t revealed anything else about her connection to Tommy’s mother, and he knew she wouldn’t. Not without leverage. And the only leverage Tommy had was the game. If he was going to learn anything, it would be here, in the seat of his power. It wasn’t much, but it was all he had.

He sat back in his chair and stared at her.

“I think we’ve taken your character as far as we can.”

“What the fuck does that mean?”

Tommy laughed. “Come on, don’t take it personally. Fallen knight in search of redemption? A little one-note, no?”

“Bellarmina’s not one-note. . . .”

“Look, all I’m saying is that to complete this game, I’m going to have to cycle through a lot of different archetypes. . . .”

Jo’s most common facial feature was a smirk, but for once, she looked wounded.

But something inside her recovered quickly. “What about these assholes?” she snorted. “They wouldn’t last ten seconds without Bellarmina.”

“Consider it parole. Time off for good behavior. This takes up a lot of time and we both know you’ve got other things you can be doing.” He gestured toward the door. “All you have to do is walk through the portal and you can be reunited with your king.”

"I know what you're doing," said Jo.

"I'm glad you do," said Nine. "Because I have no idea."

"What's going on?" asked Chongo.

"Sounds like a little malice in the palace," said Porks. "Wait, you two aren't . . . you know . . ."

Any other night, Porks's comment would have resulted in Jo's butterfly knife making a sudden appearance, but that night she ignored the pimp. She stared at Tommy instead.

"Don't," she said.

Tommy dropped his nonchalant good cheer. "Individual characters don't mean shit. It's about the game, and while we've veered away from the topic a bit and focused on the blades, ultimately the game is about *finding the queen*. And if you're not willing to play the game, then you are no use to me. Do you understand?"

Jo picked up her wineglass.

"Put the fucking glass down."

She glowered at him, her face contorting with rage. The rest of the table sat in tense silence, looking from Tommy to Jo and back again. Tommy half expected her to lunge across the table. He didn't care.

"Are you in or out?" he asked.

"I'm fucking here, aren't I?" Jo tried for her customary bravado, but it sounded more like a sullen teen.

"Did you have anything to do with the queen's disappearance?"

"No!"

Nine consulted his notes and his character sheet. "Did I miss something?"

"Yeah," said Chongo. "The vibes got real heavy all of a sudden."

Porks looked between Tommy and Jo, rapt.

Tommy ignored them all. "Do you know where the queen is?"

"I don't," she said. "I swear."

He considered this as the rest of the party waited in silence.

"Then tell me something else of value," said Tommy. "Something about your king."

Bellarmina gazes into the portal of her homeland—sees the cobblestone streets, the high stone walls of the castle, her king's banners ruffling in the wind . . .

Then she turns her back on it.

She approaches the crater's rim. The lava belches in great, sizzling bubbles below.

Tell me a story, *says the volcano.*

The heat is punishing, relentless, so much so it brings tears to her eyes. She raises her forearm against the bright glow of the magma. Then she begins her story.

"My king was not always a king, you know. And he was not from some royal bloodline. He was just a commoner. An ambitious hothead. Legend has it, long before he ever met his queen, the young man lived in a village with a powerful cleric. The cleric was loyal to the order of the day and paid many tributes to the old *king. Then one day, the young hothead, still in his teens, heard the cleric had . . . an unnatural fondness for the youngsters of the village. He asked around, discovered that it was an open secret. Such was the money the cleric brought into the kingdom. He was told the cleric was untouchable. Besides, no one wanted the karma of harming a holy man, even one as corrupt—in every sense—as this piece of shit.*

"But the young hothead had no such misgivings.

"One night, he stole into the cleric's temple, bound his mouth and hands, and marched him deep into the darkest woods, sanctions

be damned. When they reached their destination, the hothead removed the covering from the cleric's mouth. The holy man was outraged. All 'Don't you know who I am?' and shit like that. When the cleric realized all his bluster and threats of eternal damnation didn't mean a thing to the young man, he resorted to begging. Finally, the cleric began to cry. He told the young hothead that he was sorry. Finally, he sobbed that he was afraid.

"Only then was the young man satisfied. He smiled. And shot the cleric in the back of the head."

A hush falls over the mountain. The magmins stop their assault. Macarro and Garcia look up toward the rim. Bradford and the stone giant pause their fistfight.

"Happy now?" asks Bellarmina.

Throw your sword in, *commands the volcano.* It belongs to me now.

Bellarmina looks at her Sicilium sword, tosses it in. It doesn't even make a splash on the surface of the lava. It falls through the air one minute, is lost in the steam the next.

Exhausted, Bellarmina turns from the rim and begins the trek back down.

There is a deeper rumbling then and the most violent shaking yet, presaging the mightiest of eruptions. The volcano is going to blow. The adventurer begins to run, scrabbling down the mountainside. Suddenly, there's a lightning crack from inside the crater. The sound sharpens and tapers into a high whine, the whistling sound of a missile streaking toward Bellarmina. She braces for impact, expecting to get run through with jagged lava rock.

Instead, a smoldering sword pierces the ground before her.

"What the fuck is this?" asks Bellarmina.

Forged deep inside the planet and thrust up from the roiling currents of underground magma, her weapon has cooled itself into a shatterproof obsidian sword.

Of the One Thousand Blades of Tergivers, this is the Blade of Discipline.

If you're going to wield it, *the volcano booms,* you must promise to be worthy of it.

Bellarmina considers the cost, then nods.

Swear it.

"I swear."

She grabs the hilt and pulls the obsidian blade from the mountainside. It feels good in her hand.

Spent, she moves toward her comrades. The magmins see the blade and bow before her. The stone giant nods and lies across the lava as a land bridge, allowing Bradford to rejoin Macarro and Garcia, and then stretches again to reunite them all.

The adventurers, shocked into silence, follow Bellarmina with her new blade, back down the mountainside without a word.

32

Against his better judgment, Tommy pulled up the FunFunder app, navigated to the comments section, and checked in with the Geek Chorus again. The debate raged on, but it remained mostly one-sided.

@MightyKingPython: Would take structure and set class systems over this drivel any day.

@MinorSpoilers: Rules lawyer

@MightyKingPython: Don't see you pledging @MinorSpoilers

@FearsomeCreature: Focusing on virtue is interesting. Will wait and see.

@MightyKingPython: Interesting enough for you to pledge @FearsomeCreature?

@FearsomeCreature: Ha! Negative.

@RedRaven77: Savages, all of you.

@HateNate8: I'll savage u

Tommy sighed. He couldn't put it off any longer. He needed help.

He needed someone to design the *Tergivers Game Master's Manual* and the *Tergivers Player's Guide*, complete with illustrations for the monsters they were coming up with daily. Checking the listing, he saw Anibal's FunFunder comic hadn't been funded, and while he felt bad for the artist, he was excited at maybe this meaning he'd have time to do work on the RPG.

But it still required permission from Big Al, of course.

He called his father.

"Hey, Pop. I need to run something by you."

"Better make it quick, Tommy Gun. I'm in New York."

"Again?"

"Everyone has a boss, son. Even a Boss. What's up?"

Tommy explained the urgent need for an illustrator and a designer.

"How fucking hard is it to design a game board? I can draw you Monopoly in, like, ten minutes. . . ."

Tommy assured him it was far more complicated than that. A game people were paying fifty to one hundred dollars a pop for required graphically designed booklets, loaded with fabulous depictions of fantastical characters and detailed maps. They were basically the product—the essential physical artifacts of Tergivers—and without them, people would feel ripped off. Plus there were the stretch goals his father had asked for—once they were explained to him—meaning a bunch of extra merch and whatnot to design.

"Do you really need *two* people? Can't one of your little art buddies do you a solid?"

Tommy smiled, the trap sprung.

"Now that you mention it, Pop, I do have a friend who is both an illustrator *and* a designer. Two for the price of one, I suppose. . . ."

There was a pause on the line. He could picture his father's intense glare as he mulled it over. That glare could cause grown men to wilt as they waited for an answer. Tommy was glad his father was across the country.

"You trust this kid?"

Before Tommy could answer, he heard a woman's laugh. Faint, in the background. His father not quite fully cupping his hand over the phone and issuing a savage *Shhhhh*.

"Look, son, I'm in a meeting."

"He's great . . . but we have to pay him something. It's a big job."

More muffled conversation in the background; then a distracted Big Al came back on the line.

"Fine, fine. Set it up with Chongo. Don't get ripped off. I gotta go."

The line went dead. Tommy felt both elated and like he had to take a shower. He had wanted to broach the topic of bringing Sanse on board too, but that would have to wait. Still, the call was enough of a victory for one day.

He called Anibal before he had even worked out what to say. He thought their exchange at the comic book shop went as well as could be expected, but he wasn't sure he was completely on solid ground with the artist. It was hard to tell; the kid played things close to the vest. And Tommy certainly had not given Anibal reason to trust him.

When Anibal answered, Tommy blurted, "Will you please join Tergivers?"

"Thought you'd never ask," said the artist.

• • •

Thirty minutes later, Anibal arrived at Tommy's apartment with what looked like a wooden briefcase. Anibal unfolded it, making Transformers noises, revealing a portable easel. It carried dozens of colored pencils and art supplies.

"Let's fucking *go*," said Anibal.

Running the sessions had given Tommy a charge, but this was even better: mainlining pure creativity and having a partner. Their days settled into a routine. At long last, they began organizing the manuals. Anibal would come over in the mornings and he and Tommy would flesh out everything about the world of Tergivers—the game's mechanics, its internal logic, landscapes, the races and classes—codifying what Tommy was developing with the players in the evening sessions.

Is this what it felt like for Lennon and McCartney? he wondered. *Is this what it feels like to have a real friend?*

After the first week of this new routine, Tommy felt so energized that he asked Sanse out to an early dinner. This time, he eschewed jeans and sneakers and went full-out: dress pants and shirt. They met at the first downtown Korean barbecue place that popped up in his hasty Google search. Sanse looked gorgeous as usual. The lighting was low, and the food, grilled tableside, made it feel intimate. He hoped to slip back into the romantic vibe that had been so rudely shattered at the comedy club.

"Is your friend okay?" asked Sanse.

Berserker Jo strikes again, thought Tommy.

"She's fine," he said, trying to brush the topic off with a dismissive wave. "She had too much to drink, and I think some friends put her up to it."

"How do you know her again?"

"Business friend of my family's."

"And what's your family's business again?" she asked with a smirk.

Tommy's parents had sat him down at a very early age to have The Talk. Not about the birds and the bees, but about how to answer questions about his father's line of work. Big Al had explained that he worked for a very large business headquartered in New York City and that he operated its franchises in the greater Denver area.

Tommy was eight.

"Franchise?" young Tommy had asked. "Like McDonald's?"

"That's right, baby," said his mother. "Very good."

Big Al said, "Yeah, only it's like a McDonald's for the little guy. Like, not everyone can afford the same burger as everyone else, so we make deals. Or maybe it's not good for some people to be seen eating hamburgers, so we give them their hamburgers around back."

Tommy felt confused. "Who doesn't want to be seen eating hamburgers?"

"Vegetarians, baby," said Vittoria.

Tommy nodded.

"And maybe we put different toys in the Happy Meals, because some people don't like that cheap plastic shit."

"Language, darling," said Vittoria.

"McDonald's for the little guy," said Tommy. "Like Robin Hood?"

Big Al snapped his fingers. "*Exactly*. And just like Robin Hood, we don't trust the Sheriff of Nottingham, who is always trying to pick the little guy's fucking pocket—"

"Darling."

"You know what I'm saying. . . ."

From that moment on, the rules were set when discussing his father's livelihood in public. Be vague, deflect, evade.

The first rule of Fugue Club: You do not talk about Fugue Club.

"Waste management." Tommy made a face and gestured to their food. "It's not very appetizing."

Sanse raised her eyebrows, then affected a New York accent and pulled a tough face, mugging for Tommy. *"'If I was a hit woman . . .'"*

"Okay, okay," Tommy said, laughing. "So, we're Italian. It's an unflattering stereotype."

"*Tommy*. I'm not dumb. I have Google."

She was smart and stunning, and stared at him with her big, beautiful eyes that shone with amusement, until he squirmed.

"If I'm going to date someone," she said, "I need him to be honest with me. . . ."

Tommy felt a jolt go up his spine. She said *date*. She was saying the quiet part out loud. He stopped himself from whooping and making a fist pump.

"I understand," he said, meeting her eyes fully. "If there's one thing I *can* tell you, I am nothing like my father."

Sanse smiled and put her hand on his.

Tommy tried to play it cool. It was still early in the evening. Anibal should be gone, and it would be another couple of hours before the crew came for that night's session.

"Do you want to come back to my place?" he asked. Not wanting to seem too impertinent, he quickly added, "To see the game."

"I would love to. To see your game." She gave him a knowing smile.

• • •

After what felt like forever, between the suddenly too-slow pace of meat grilling and the drive back to his place, they arrived at his apartment complex. Without preamble, she took his hand on their way to the door. Tommy beamed.

Until he opened the door.

Anibal was still there.

Worse, he was there with three half-naked women.

Fallon and Fiona were caught mid-embrace on the floor. Fallon's red bikini bottoms were accented with knee-high Uggs, a cheap fur coat, and a headband with fuzzy animal ears.

Fiona wore a revealing metallic minidress, her eyes painted in heavy blue-and-silver eyeshadow. She looked like a clubgoer from the distant future.

Standing on Tommy's couch, looming over them, was Merry. She was dressed in a chain-mail bikini and a shell belt and swung a Nerf sword over her head. She looked like a sexy version of Red Sonja, which, even in the moment, Tommy realized was a redundancy.

He blinked.

They weren't cavorting. They were wrestling.

Tommy blinked again and looked to Anibal, seated at his easel in the corner, sketching madly, his face pure bliss.

The girls weren't just wrestling, Tommy realized, they were posing.

Merry was the first to see him frozen in the doorway, keys dangling from his finger, a stunned Sanse by his side.

"More prisoners!" yelled the stripper. "Take them to the breeding pens!"

"What the fuck?" blurted Tommy.

"Silence!" yelled Merry. "Seize them!"

Fallon and Fiona leapt toward Tommy and seized him. Sanse

came to her senses then. She dropped his hand like it was covered in bugs and stormed out.

"Sanse, wait! I can explain!"

But the girls tackled and wrestled him to the ground. The liquor on their breath was as biting as the shock of the scene.

"She's a cutie, Tommy. . . ."

"Not as cute as me . . ."

"Off with her head . . ."

"Let me up!" yelled Tommy. "Let go!"

He bolted for the door. He arrived just in time to see Sanse's taillights speeding away.

Numb, he closed the door and walked back inside. He fell into his chair at the game table. The girls watched him, quiet suddenly.

Anibal tried to explain. "It wasn't my idea. . . ."

Just then, Tommy heard the toilet flush. The bathroom door banged open, and Porks emerged, buttoning up his pants. "Oh, hey, kid. Just thought I'd help you guys make those manuals really pop. By the way, I think you're outta TP. . . ."

33

Anibal had insisted Tommy come to his home for dinner. Or more precisely, Anibal's parents had insisted Tommy come for dinner. It had been a full day since his date ended in disaster and Sanse had still left him unread.

Tommy checked his phone before he got out of the car in the circular driveway of a palatial home in Cherry Hills Village, south of Denver. He'd begun checking the GPS when he first hit the nice homes with wide lawns and privacy hedges, and he took one last look to make sure he had the right address, but this was it.

He followed the long walkway to the front door, admiring the gardens on either side—the kind that no matter how much money his father made he would never bother with. It had been a point of contention between his father and his mom. She was bold and artistic and had grand plans for their home, but he never veered too far from the ethos of the Neighborhood: nice but nothing too flashy.

Tommy stepped up to the house. Suddenly the artist came out and brought Tommy to one edge of the porch, where a small statue of a lion stared out over the lawn.

"Damn," said Tommy. "This place is sick."

Anibal waved away the compliment and plowed ahead with his apology.

"Tommy, again, sorry about Sanse, man. I swear I had nothing to do with it. I was just packing up my stuff when Porks showed up with them."

Tommy held up his hand. "Don't worry. Between you and Porks, I'll take your word for it. Have you talked to her?"

Anibal shook his head. "She won't return my calls either."

"Sounds like you were caught in the blast radius too."

"Also," said Anibal, looking over his shoulder toward the front door, "could we not talk about this in front of my family?"

"Wait, I'm confused: You *don't* want me to bring up strippers at dinner?"

"Ha! Best fucking night of my life— *Hi, Mom!*"

Anibal's mother had appeared at the door. She wore cream slacks, a silk dress shirt, and pearls. Her hair was pulled back in a perfect ponytail and her smile was dazzling. She looked as if she'd stepped off the cover of a magazine, the same one Tommy's mother could have modeled for: *Stunning Middle-Aged Women in Casual Clothes That in No Way Actually Seem Casual and Who Also Look Like They Own a Yacht.*

"Mama, this is Tommy Fugue," said Anibal, his posture suddenly improved. He also had developed manners, something Tommy had never seen in him before. "Tommy, this is my mother, Maria."

Tommy could also deploy manners when the situation demanded. From a very young age, he became accustomed to dressing up and standing in ballrooms and catering halls, being seen and not heard. An accoutrement to his glamorous mother and her husband who, though a savage, could wear the hell out of a suit. It was a childhood of endless dinner parties and torturous nights spent in too-tight dress shoes and itchy pants. It was one of the reasons Tommy dressed in what Nine called *homeless chic*, though he was willing to admit that perhaps he had overcorrected.

Tommy took her hand lightly and shook it.

"Pleased to meet you, ma'am. Your home is breathtaking."

"This one has manners, Ani. I like him."

She led them across an expansive marble foyer. Tommy, under his breath, said, *"Ani."*

"Remember, only pretty girls are allowed to call me Ani."

"Oh, do your models call you Ani?" whispered Tommy.

"Shut it."

They entered a massive kitchen that resembled Maria's outfit—light, gorgeous, and spotless. The dozen well-appointed cabinets along the walls made Tommy imagine a wide range of kitchen implements and secret ingredients at the family's disposal. For all her other abilities, Tommy's mother had never been a cook, and it wasn't like Big Al was going to stand around stirring sauce.

A handsome man with a lion's mane of salt-and-pepper hair and a matching goatee rummaged through one pantry.

"When are we eating, my love? I'm farting fresh air!"

Maria rolled her eyes and gave him the light, perfunctory slap that said that this was the thousandth time he had made such a joke, and that he should turn around and meet his guest.

"Tommy Fugue, this beast," she said with an eye roll, "is Emiliano, Anibal's father and the man who tricked me into marrying him."

Emiliano clutched his heart as if stabbed. Another eye roll from his wife. Then the man bounded over and grasped Tommy's hand.

"It is an honor to meet you, young man. Anibal has told us all about your project—"

"*Campaign,* Papa."

A small chuckle. "I'm sorry, son. I did not realize you were waging a war."

"Well, we are, sir," said Tommy. "We're currently engaged in a pitched battle with an undead kraken. And Anibal is depicting it all beautifully."

Maria squeezed her son so hard that she grunted with the effort. Anibal pretended to hate it.

After a few more minutes of niceties—Tommy feeling obligated to compliment practically every corner and element of their house—a serving person he hadn't noticed before proclaimed that dinner was ready. They all moved to an ornate dining room dominated by a crucifix so large it rivaled the one in his own family's dining room. Maria and Emiliano peppered Tommy with questions about the game and the world of Tergivers. The normally tight-lipped artist described their process with abandon. They listened intently, proud smiles on their faces. Tommy realized Anibal must have received enormous support from his parents over the years.

Must be nice, he thought.

"You know," said Emiliano, "when I was a boy, Dungeons & Dragons was not as universally beloved as it is today. In the eighties, there was this *satanic panic.*"

"Papa . . ."

Maria narrowed her eyes. "That's terrible." She placed her fork on her plate, made the sign of the cross, and turned to her son. "Anibal, tell me there are no devils in your game."

Emiliano laughed behind his napkin.

Tommy bailed out his friend. "Mrs. DeLandro, I promise this game is one hundred percent Satan-free."

Well, all but twenty thousand dollars of it, he thought.

• • •

Tommy offered to help clear the dishes—and assist Anibal with his defense of the game—but Maria would not hear of it. Mother and son left the dining room, Maria whispering urgently to her son, and Anibal balancing dishes behind her while trying to explain the difference between Lucifer and a lowly Tergivers demon.

"I love winding her up," said Emiliano, "but don't let her fool you. She's the boss. Do you like books, Tommy?"

Tommy nodded, and Emiliano led him to his study, lined with beautiful inset bookshelves that reached the ceiling. It looked more like a library than one man's study. It even had one of those rolling ladders to reach high shelves.

"This is amazing. . . ."

Tommy, seeing everything these days through the lens of Tergivers, noted details he could incorporate the next time the party had to visit a wizard's castle or glean secret knowledge in a monastery that preserved texts against the at-large forces of ignorance.

"Take a seat, young man," said Emiliano, settling behind a polished walnut desk the size of a small aircraft carrier, and gestured for Tommy to take the leather club chair opposite. He glanced toward the door to the study, and confident they were alone, leaned forward and steepled his fingers.

"I wanted to thank you personally for reaching out to my son and allowing him to help you on this project. My apologies—*campaign*."

"He's doing me a favor, sir. I'm no artist and he's incredible."

"I wish the *pendejos* on FunFunder felt the same way. He was devastated when his comic was not funded. I must admit, I never understood it myself, but Anibal was heartbroken."

That surprised him. When Tommy had offered his condolences to Anibal about the comic, it had elicited no more than a shrug from the quiet artist. Then again, Tommy realized he should know better than anyone that appearances were not always what they seemed.

"Maria begged me to fund the whole damn thing myself. In the final days, watching him mope around, I will admit I was tempted." Emiliano offered a wistful smile then. "But Anibal never asked. He wanted to do it on his own. I respect that. Heartbreak can be good for a man. Make him stronger, more resilient. But two heartbreaks in a row?"

Emiliano looked at Tommy then, and in the low light of the study, his eyes looked black and dangerous.

"Oh no, sir," said Tommy. "That's not a problem. The game is already fully funded. More than fully funded."

Emiliano nodded. "I heard," he said, though the news did not seem to cheer him.

"A young artist has to protect his reputation. No one wants to attach their names to a . . . half-assed endeavor."

"I assure you, sir. I am not half-assing Tergivers. This game is everything to me. I am bringing my whole ass to it."

"That is very good to hear. Ani is bringing his whole ass to it as well."

"Absolutely he is, sir."

"And you would agree that for the entirety of one's ass one should be compensated accordingly, yes?"

"I . . . yes?"

"I am glad to hear that, young man." Emiliano smiled at Tommy, then cocked his head as if to study him from a new angle. "You know, I forgot to mention at dinner that your father and I know each other."

The hair on Tommy's arms stood on end.

"You're . . . friends with my father?" asked Tommy hopefully.

Emiliano plucked a crystal-handled letter opener from a matching crystal base and began to play with it. Twirl it, flick its sharp point, wave it for emphasis. It mesmerized Tommy.

"Friends?" said Emiliano, laughing. It was a good-natured laugh, the kind one might give when a child asks an outlandish question. *Oh, Tommy, kids say the darnedest things.* "Maybe you would say we are more like . . . in the same industry. One might say business rivals. Your father's 'sales territory' is the east side, while Delgado territory is the west side."

"I'm sorry," said Tommy, swallowing. *"Delgado?"*

"Of course."

"But . . . but Anibal's last name is DeLandro."

Emiliano laughed and waved the hand that held the letter opener, piercing the rest of Tommy's notions like a balloon.

"A necessary contrivance. The Delgado name can draw unnecessary attention in this region, and I want my son to concentrate on his studies and enjoy himself—within reason—during his time at college. Sometimes the name of the game is discretion."

Tommy grew queasy, wiped his palms on his pants.

Anibal DeLandro was Anibal Delgado. Of the Delgado Crime Family. Of the Bad Old Days Delgados.

Oh my God, thought Tommy.

"Oh my God," said Tommy.

Emiliano noted Tommy's expression and laughed once more.

"Oh, it's not as bad as all that. Not anymore anyway. The Delgados and the Fugues have had our disputes in the past, but it's been peaceful for a good long while now. Everything has been clearly delineated, you see. It is good for everyone to know where they stand."

The darkly appointed study began to feel more like a dungeon than a kindly wizard's home, and the grand house surrounding it more like a labyrinthine castle in a hostile kingdom.

"That is why I wanted to have this conversation with you. So that," said Emiliano, waving the tip of the letter opener between them, "we know where each other stands. Do you know much of your father's business, Tommy?"

Tommy shook his head.

"Ah," said Emiliano, and nodded. "Anibal has never shown any interest in my business either. He prefers his drawings and comic books and games. I will admit, there is a primitive part of me that takes offense to his lack of curiosity, that wishes he would be more of a man . . . but that is just pride talking. It helps when a man has an evolved wife to keep him in check. I am far from perfect. Between us, this comic was his last chance. I would of course let him finish school—I am not a monster, after all—but I was going to make him become more familiar with the daily operations of the Delgado Family business. I will not allow him to graduate into nothing and with no prospects. I do still have some pride, and it would not allow for that."

He pointed the tip of the letter opener at Tommy.

"And then you came along. He doesn't know it, but you bought him a small reprieve. You have shown me that perhaps there can be a livelihood for him in this . . . *fantasyland* after all."

Tommy heard himself say, "I'm glad to hear that, sir." His voice sounded hoarse and far-off.

"As long as his contributions are rewarded." Emiliano smiled warmly, then his magnanimous warmth faded. "I would hate for my son to be taken advantage of in general, but by a member of the Fugue Family . . ."

Emiliano stared at the blade of the letter opener. He stopped short of drawing the blade against his own throat. He didn't need to.

Tommy swallowed, sat up straighter in his chair. He tried to sound professional, reassuring. "My accountant is drawing up paperwork to pay Anibal as an independent contractor."

Emiliano made a face as if Tommy had just passed gas.

"Independent contractor sounds so . . . unseemly. The way Ani has been talking about it, it sounds much more like a creative, fruitful *partnership*. Wouldn't you agree?"

Damn it, thought Tommy. That *was* how he saw it, if he were being honest. It would not, however, be how his father would see it. At all. Don Fugue would see it as a very polite, very charming shakedown. And the streets would run red.

Tommy cleared his throat.

"I'll see what I can do."

Emiliano nodded. "I'll be reviewing any documents personally."

"Of course."

Emiliano dropped the letter opener into its crystal base, then slapped his hands on the desktop. "Ah! It feels good knowing where everyone stands, yes?"

Tommy nodded, though he did not feel good at all.

34

Bradford is the last fighter standing. Floating before him and his fallen comrades are a trio of banshees. They are luminous, floating above the stone floors, long hair obscuring their faces, their once-flowing dresses now spectral rags hanging from thin, ghostly frames.

"You'll be mine forever," the first coos.

"No, mine," hisses the second.

"You will fall in love with me, traveler, or else," wails the third.

"I'm listening," says Bradford.

Voices from somewhere remind Bradford of the last time he went off half-cocked and tried to hook up in the forest. He nearly became goblin food.

"So, this is not hot?"

No, definitely not hot. They are basically floating ghost zombies, and they want to turn Bradford into one of them. Their power is their wail. It's incredibly painful and will drive the barbarian mad.

"Never mind, then. I already have three women who nag me to death," the adventurer says, seemingly to nobody.

The party was already in bad shape before the banshees. Bloodied and severely weakened by a pack of werewolves, they found an old fort in the nick of time. It was large and defensible, perfect to recover from their wounds and hold off the werewolves until morning. But mere steps inside, the old, rotted floors gave way, plunging the party into a subterranean labyrinth . . . and the banshees' home.

Once the daughters of the fort's paranoid commander, they were locked away in the lower levels, hidden away from the soldiers by their overprotective father. The daughters lived their entire lives as captives, never experiencing love or light or joy.

Garcia is unconscious from the fall. Macarro is heavily lacerated from his tangle with the werewolves. And Bellarmina has been knocked out by the banshee's wail, so jealous were they at the sight of another woman.

Bradford tries his usual attacks, but his blows sail through their incorporeal forms. He is alone, lost in the dark. He can feel his life essence fading. It is as close as the party has ever come to perishing.

"This could really be it?" asks Bradford.

This could really be it, *Bradford realizes.*

"Wait . . . What if I make a sacrifice? Can I transfer my health to the team?"

Perhaps.

Bradford plucks Bellarmina's Blade of Discipline from her fist. In his large hands, it is but the size of a dagger. He closes his eyes and takes a deep, sorrowful breath. The banshees float around him in a circle, eager.

"What's happening?" mumbles Macarro.

"You all say I run off half-cocked. Maybe that's the answer."

Garcia opens one eye.

Bellarmina props herself on one elbow. "Oh, I've got to see this."

"For my comrades in arms! For Tergivers!"

With a mighty roar and a quick flash of the blade, Bradford the Barbarian unmans himself by half.

• • •

"No fucking way," said Jo.

Chongo chuckled, shooting mini plumes of smoke with each laugh.

"I did not see that coming," said Nine.

"Me neither," admitted Tommy.

"Odin plucked out an eye for wisdom. What I just did should make me the wisest motherfucker ever. That should definitely earn me the blade."

"It's just . . ." began Tommy.

"Come on!" yelled Porks. "What more do you want?"

"Porks, I was only going to make you solve a puzzle."

The pimp looked crestfallen.

"Oh."

The banshees, who are susceptible to offerings, float in circles around the discarded member and screech at one another.

"It's mine!"

"No, mine!"

"He gave it to meeee. . . ."

They pause their attack on the adventurers, such is their preoccupation with the strange object.

Bradford fits his codpiece and loincloth back in place and says, "Let's have it, then."

A deal's a deal.

Suddenly, there is a flash of light, illuminating the warren of corridors around them. Even the banshees shield their spectral eyes. When the light recedes, a large, beautiful sword is revealed, its tip buried in the gaps of the stone floor. Bradford reaches for it and pulls it from the stones with ease.

"Fuck yeah."

The blade is highly reflective, almost like a mirror, and it looks strangely alive. Bradford examines it closer and sees there's script on its edge, but it flows and changes like a living book.

Congratulations, *reads the blade.* For your selflessness, your devotion to your comrades, and your . . . unexpected solution to your quandary, Tergivers bestows upon you its Blade of Wisdom. To use it, you must remain just, wise, and in service to the queen.

"Whoa," says Bradford.

Also, congrats on avoiding a TPK, *the blade-writing adds.*

Bradford wonders over this last message, but not for long. The covetous banshees quit their arguing over their new plaything and fly at him, reaching for the sword. Bradford brandishes it before him. He is about to rear back for a mighty swing with his new weapon when the banshees catch their reflection in its polished blade. If there's one thing a banshee can't stand, it's her reflection. The trio shrieks in pain. One covers her eyes. Another plunges her hands into her matted hair as if to keep her head from exploding. The last rends her tattered gown. Unable to bear the pain, they flee down the corridor, their cries and eerie spectral glow trailing behind them, until they are no longer in sight.

Slowly, Macarro, Bellarmina, and Garcia get to their feet. The revived warriors stare at Bradford and his new blade in stunned silence.

The barbarian beams. "I'm wise now."

35

Bradford's "sacrifice" left Tommy thinking. What would he do for those he cared about? How far would he go to protect them? In light of the example of a porn fiend who gave up half of his complement of fictional genitals, what would *Tommy* accept and what would he let go of?

On his way home after their dinner, Tommy had confronted Anibal on the front porch, grilling him about his revealing chat with Emiliano. Anibal had sworn he had no idea about their fathers' feud.

"Do you expect me to believe that?"

"Tommy, I want nothing to do with any of my father's gangster shit. My comic was supposed to be my ticket out. And then when that failed, I was stuck. Until you came along."

Tommy stared him down. "That's pretty goddamn convenient, man. You could've at least told me your real name. Especially when you learned about *mine*."

"I know, I'm sorry. It's just . . ." Anibal stared at his shoes. "You're the first real friend I've had."

"Bullshit."

"It's true. Do you think kids were lining up to hang out with the weirdo guarded by sicarios and Spanish mastiffs?"

Fuck. Talk about feeling seen, thought Tommy.

And just like that, as with Tommy's phone call inviting Anibal to join the game, the tension dissipated between the two of them. Perhaps, Tommy wondered, *that* was actually the power of friendship.

"I'm pissed . . . but I understand," said Tommy. "From now on, no more secrets."

"I'll swear on a stack of Bibles."

Tommy shook his head. The only thing that was sacred to the both of them was the game. "On Tergivers."

Anibal put his hand on his heart. "On Tergivers, then."

Bradford's "sacrifice" also left Tommy wondering: How much shit would he eat to get Sanse to talk to him again?

A lot of shit, he decided. As much as it would take.

He hoped she was as forgiving of him as he was of Anibal.

He thought about sending flowers, then had a second thought: better to deliver them firsthand. Then a third thought. Was showing up uninvited with flowers pushy? Creepy? Had the third-act grand gestures and desperate gambits of rom-coms warped his sense of what was acceptable when trying to win a girl back? But surely there was something else he could do besides the flurry of *Can we talk* and *I'm so sorry* texts he had sent already. He'd considered asking for Nine's opinion, but he already knew what he would get: a wholly unsatisfactory answer, heavy on bravado and light on empathy, with an insult thrown in for good measure.

My advice? Ignore her completely. There are plenty of fish in the sea and you're a great white. Well, your father's a great white, you're more like one of those nurse sharks, all docile and shit. But still a shark of some sort. Forget her, dude.

Not an option, Nine.

But he did have some dignity. He sent one final text:

You're angry, I get it. But I swear, I was just as surprised as you were. I had nothing to do with it. Neither did Anibal, really. And do you honestly think I would invite you over if three strippers were going to be there? This will be my last text, but I wanted it on the record that THAT is NOT my thing.

He paused. "Fuck it," he said.

YOU are my thing.

He put the phone down but scooped it back up when he saw the three dancing dots. His first sign of life in days.

"Come on," he said, willing a positive message to materialize.

Come over. Let's talk.

He nearly broke a land-speed record getting to Sanse's loft, stopping only at a grocery store to pick up two dozen roses. He gripped the large bouquet in his hand, careful around the thorns, as he waited for her to come to the door. They felt like a flimsy weapon to go into battle with. He closed his eyes, imagined him winning her over, the roses transforming in his hand into the Tergivers Blade of Love.

Suddenly, there she was. He had hoped she would open the door with her nose red from crying, her hair messed up from sleeping too much from depression, cheeks hollow because she was too bereft to eat.

Who are you kidding? he thought.

She looked incredible. No tear-streaked makeup, not a strand of hair out of place. She didn't just look beautiful; she looked pristine. Her lips, shiny with gloss, were pressed in a firm, impatient line.

He felt like he'd just rolled a natural one. His confidence score plummeted.

Of course she hadn't shed any tears for him. She had always been out of his league, and it had been a miracle that she had ever been interested in him in the first place. He needed to fix this fast before she completely came to her senses.

He thrust out the flowers too quickly. She flinched.

"Sorry," he said, clearing his throat. "These are for you."

"Thank you," she said with zero enthusiasm.

She took them, then walked deeper into the loft to the kitchen island. She found a vase, filled it with water, and started snipping the stems off at an angle. She didn't invite him in, but she hadn't kicked him out either.

Ability check.

He took three steps into the loft. "Again, I just wanted to express how sorry I am. I was furious too and kicked them out the second you left—"

"Tommy, I just don't think this is going to work out."

"Sanse, I told you I had nothing to do—"

She held up her hand, scissors suspended by two fingers.

"Let me finish. I believe you. I do. I don't think you're some psychopath sex fiend who invited me over when you had three strippers at home."

Tommy nodded dumbly in agreement, repeatedly. "I am definitely not a psychopath sex fiend. Ask anyone."

"But why were they even there to begin with? And it's not like I'm judging them—I'm sex positive—I'm judging *you.*"

"But I didn't *do* anything."

"You're not being honest with me. I told you, if this is to go anywhere, I need you to be honest with me. I go on a date with you and one of your father's friends goes into a *Sopranos* routine and tries to start a brawl. I go to your apartment, and three naked women are posing for Anibal. *I told you.* What the hell kind of game are you making? What the hell kind of game are you *playing*?"

Tommy sighed. He had to come clean—as much as he could—or this would be it.

He would not let his father take Sanse from him too.

"Fine! My family is not like other families, is that what you want me to say? My fifth birthday party was at a racetrack. My father pressed money into my teachers' hands at parent-teacher conferences. He thinks *Goodfellas* is a Christmas movie. Do you understand what I'm getting at?"

Sanse nodded slowly.

"Because of his *line of work,* he's very overprotective, okay? Then when my mother left last year, his overprotectiveness went into overdrive. He's like a helicopter parent, if the helicopter is an Apache gunship. So, when I created this game, he would only let me test it with people who he knew and trusted. Friends of the family, so to speak. It's a miracle I got him to sign off on Anibal."

A miracle at the time, he corrected himself silently. *Now,* after breaking bread with the don of the Delgado Crime Family, it seemed like just another in a long string of curses.

"That's why I've been cagey. I wanted you to be involved from the jump, but it's complicated." Tommy exhaled. It was as much of the truth as he could share. If that didn't work, there was nothing left to do.

"Your mother left?"

Tommy nodded.

"Where is she?"

"No idea. She just . . ." said Tommy, rocketing his hand up like an airplane climbing, "took off. No call, no note, no looking back. Haven't heard from her since."

"I—I didn't know that. . . ." Sanse looked nauseated suddenly. She put down the scissors. "I'm really sorry. And that doesn't, like, worry you?"

In his darkest moments, in his deepest fears, it did worry him. But he was not going there with Sanse. Or anyone.

His mother was out there somewhere. She had to be.

Tommy shook his head. "They were crazy about each other, with an emphasis on *crazy*. She left before, just never this long. Wherever she is, she is sick of my father's crap."

He looked at Sanse. His voice radiated with a growing anger.

"Does it sting? Absolutely. Did I wish she took me with her? Of course. Do I blame her? Not at all. Because I'd have done the same damn thing. And as soon as I can, I will. I want to go to California and maybe Tergivers can get me there. But in the meantime, I have to make it perfect. I have to play ball. I have to do what my father says. If that means I have to beta test with his drunk muscle and the manager of a strip club, then that's what I'll do. But mark my words, the first chance I get, I'm out of here. And then, when I'm free, Mom will find me. Maybe she's just waiting for me to get free too."

He stared at her, his eyes burning.

"Is that enough honesty for you?"

Sanse said nothing. Her arms were crossed at her chest, but less in fury and more to hold herself against a chill.

"Never mind," said Tommy. He turned for the door. "This was a bad idea. You don't have to understand my life, but you don't get to judge it."

She ran toward him then, threw her arms around his neck. It caught him by surprise. His hands floated up, hesitating for a moment; then he hugged her back. It felt good. He couldn't remember the last time he had been held like this. He never wanted it to end.

"I'm sorry," she said, pulling back.

There was her face then, inches from his. Her lips were parted, luscious and shiny with gloss. *Carpe fucking diem.* He went in for a kiss. She met him tentatively at first, then kissed him back hard.

Oh my God, it's happening! he thought. *It's really happening!*

It was the flip side of the coin of getting his head smacked against those high, majestic windows. His thoughts swam. His heart pounded in his chest. The world was bright, its sounds and colors too rich to process. The delicious pressure at his lips, its pleasant burning, how the kiss left him breathless.

Then it all became too much for him. Like that day at the caterers, his senses dialed up past their breaking point.

His throat began to close.

His legs gave way.

"Call Nine," he said, as he fell away from her. He passed out before he could add, *one one.*

36

"Where is he?"

Even groggy, Tommy registered the change. He didn't have to see outside of his small, curtained alcove in the UCHealth emergency room to feel it. It was like a bow wave pushing ahead of a massive ship, shoving everything aside. Or more appropriately, like a large jungle predator charging through the forest, the smaller prey fleeing before him.

"Where is my son?"

Tommy heard the sharp sound of curtains down the corridor being yanked back, of a hunter getting closer. And a stampede of dress shoes in its wake.

"What the hell is that?" asked the nurse, looking over her shoulder.

The doctor looked irritated at the commotion, but she ignored it, focusing instead on her patient. She flicked the IV bag that was slowly feeding him antihistamines. In her other hand, she held a syringe. Tattoos of ravens flew up her arms, and for a moment Tommy wondered if she was real, or another citizen of Tergivers.

"I know you got some epinephrine in the ambulance, but I think we need some steroids too, okay?"

She spoke loudly but sweetly. Like he was a child. In the moment, he found he did not mind.

"I'm sorry," said Tommy weakly, struggling to keep his eyes open.

The doctor offered a kind smile. "For what?"

Just then, the curtains flew back in Tommy's alcove. The nurse jumped. The doctor, syringe still in hand, froze.

"For that."

Don Alessandro Fugue's face was a mixture of fury and relief. Tommy had seen that precise blend only once before, when his father had picked him up at the mall years ago. Turdo, Johnny Reb, and Johnny Socks filed in behind him. SuperChenz was too large to fit inside with them. More soldiers orbited around outside, like satellites to a planet.

"Whoa, whoa, whoa," said Don Fugue. "What is that? Where's the doctor?"

"Sir, *I* am *Doctor* Rachel Liang," she said. "And this is a corticosteroid to reduce inflammation for an anaphylactic allergic reaction, and if you calm way down, I will administer it."

"Statistically speaking, there are more female ER doctors than male," said Johnny Reb.

"I find it refreshing," said Johnny Socks.

The don pointed at the men with his finger horns. "Shut the fuck up, you two." He turned back to the doctor. "I want to know what's going on. *Now*."

The doctor turned to the nurse. "Amy, go find the on-duty police. Let them sort this out."

SuperChenz blocked Amy's path. "Not so fast."

Before Dr. Liang could protest, Nine Ball squeezed past SuperChenz and into the alcove with a shaken Sanse. Tommy saw her and his heart flared, cutting through his drugged haze. Suddenly, he didn't need the adrenaline anymore. But she looked upset, her earlier put-together visage now blown apart. Her eyes were puffy, and her nose was red, as he had hoped for earlier. But actually seeing her like this made him feel rotten for ever wishing it.

And worse, she looked afraid.

"Pop," said Tommy. It was still difficult to breathe. Harder to stay awake. "It's okay. . . ."

Don Fugue held up his hand to his son and strode over to the young woman.

"Who are you?" asked Don Fugue.

"She's a friend of Tommy's," said Nine. "She brought him in."

It grew quiet. Quiet enough for Tommy to hear the whir and beeping of the machines around him. He heard his father say low to her, "It's fortuitous you're here. Because if you had something to do with this, you won't have very far to go anyway."

Sanse's lips quivered.

"Doc," muttered Tommy, "hit me."

Dr. Liang looked around the room, shook her head, and bent to inject the steroid.

"Now," said Don Fugue, seething, "what happened?"

Sanse began to babble. "I—I don't know. He came over and we were talking. And then we—we kissed. And it was great at first, and then he just sort—sort of passed out. And he started having trouble breathing."

Don Fugue cut a quick glance to Nine, his anger threatening to boil over again.

The soldier quickly turned to Sanse. "Did he eat anything? Drink anything?"

"No," said Sanse. "Nothing to eat or drink, I swear!"

"You're not supposed to leave him," growled Big Al at the young man.

"I'm sorry, Don Fugue. . . ."

His father's anger was volcanic. Once enough pressure built up, there was no turning back. It needed to be expressed. Huge chunks of rock would be hurled skyward. Rivers of molten lava would rage, scorching everything in its path. A towering plume of dark smoke would blot the sun. Bystanders be damned.

Tommy could tell an eruption was imminent. Unless . . .

"Lip gloss," he said. No one heard him, but he felt the steroids kicking in. He felt suddenly as if he'd drunk a pot of coffee. His body started to shake. He thought he might vibrate off the bed. An eruption of his own bubbled.

"Nine, lip gloss!"

Nine grabbed Sanse's bag and started rifling through it. He produced a tiny pink tube and held it up.

"Plumper," said Nine.

Johnny Reb snatched it from him.

" 'Warning: Intense Heat. Lasting plump,' " read Reb. He passed it to Socks.

" 'Plump It Up extreme lip-plumping gloss with chili pepper delivers a powerful heated sensation and plumping effect. Available in eight heated shades.' "

"Pepper . . ." said Don Fugue.

"I believe this is the culprit," said Johnny Socks, brandishing the tube. "Chili pepper–based Pink Zing."

"I would venture to say," said Johnny Reb, "that the real culprit is society's unreasonable, unrealistic beauty standards for young women."

Socks nodded gravely. "Insidious and systemic."

"You're a lovely young lady," said Reb. "You don't need to put this shit on your face."

Tommy's body began to shiver as if he had the chills. "Pop," he said, "I'm okay, really—"

Don Fugue held up a single hand. It silenced the room. Even Dr. Liang and the nurse went still.

He gestured at the Johnnies, and they passed him the tube. He glanced at it, then turned to Sanse.

"You mean to tell me that this lipstick contains pepper and you kissed my son, who is deathly allergic, with your plumped-up, pepper-laced lips?"

Sanse's face quivered, her eyes brimming with fresh tears, but she nodded. "I'm sorry, Mr. Fugue. I had no idea he was allergic. . . ."

Big Al exploded into laughter.

For a moment, Nine, Turdo, and the Johnnies looked stunned, but quickly they burst into laughter as well. The soldiers outside the alcove laughed along, not knowing why, and this caused a fresh round of maniacal laughter inside the alcove.

Sanse looked confused.

Big Al leaned over to the bed and gave his son a few hard pats on the shoulder. "My boy! Doc, is he gonna be all right?"

Dr. Liang appeared to be digesting what was transpiring.

"He had a bad reaction. We gave him two shots of epinephrine, intravenous antihistamines, and a steroid to move the process along. He's going to be very tired later, but yes, he will be just fine."

Turdo pointed to Tommy's crotch. "Big Al, it could've been a lot worse!"

A fresh round of laughter rolled through the gangsters.

Tommy's father pulled a roll of cash from his pocket and

peeled off some bills. He pressed some into the doctor's hand. "Sorry about that, Doc. Really appreciate you . . ."

"Sir, I'm a doctor. We don't take tips."

"I'll take a tip," said Amy the nurse, stepping forward.

Big Al grasped her hand, put some bills in it, and shook it. "Get yourself a new defibrillator or something. Nine!"

Nine Ball sprang to his don's side. Big Al peeled off some more bills. "Here, go get some drinks. We're celebrating."

"Absolutely not!" said Dr. Liang. "This is an emergency room."

"Come on," said Big Al. "What about food? Long night, you ladies gotta eat, right? Pizza? Steaks? Donuts?"

Dr. Liang stared down the mob boss.

"I could eat."

He peeled off more bills and gave them to Nine. "Feed the whole floor—even the people we put here."

Amid the fresh laughter, Tommy watched his father approach Sanse again.

"Young lady, please accept my sincerest apologies for frightening you."

Sanse tried to smile. "That's okay, Mr. Fugue."

"You see, my son is my world, and the thought of him hurt . . . Well, I lost my cool and I'm sorry. I'm sorry for the misunderstanding, and I owe you."

Tommy summoned what little dignity the situation allowed him and called Sanse over.

"I'm so sorry about this." He leaned in, fighting off tremors, and whispered, "Do you see what I'm dealing with now?"

Sanse laughed, the relief in her face palpable. "I don't know. They seem kind of fun."

"Get out while you can."

He expected her to flee without a second glance, but she grabbed his hand instead. "I can stay. At least until the keg stands start."

Tommy's alcove became a party. Dr. Liang popped in occasionally to check on him, weaving her way through capos and soldiers and consiglieri wolfing pizza and celebrating Don Fugue's son's budding romance. Despite her orders, covert flasks were passed around. It was both humiliating and exhilarating.

Tommy declined a flask when Turdo offered and at some point, he fell asleep.

When he awoke, it was dark in his alcove and he was alone save for his father, who had pulled a chair beside his bed. Gone were the Johnnies and soldiers and even Nine.

"You're awake," said Big Al.

Tommy nodded, groggy.

"We'll get you out of here soon. The doc's coming back with the discharge paperwork and instructions." He paused. "She's a real nice lady. Tough, but nice."

"Sorry about all of this," said Tommy.

"Why are you apologizing?"

Tommy considered this. He wanted to say *Force of habit*, but he did not want to set off his father, who seemed so subdued in this moment.

"Never apologize," said Big Al. He poked Tommy's leg under the blanket with his finger, but playful, not rough.

"Never?" said Tommy. "Come on, Pop."

"Well, *you* shouldn't. I could've apologized to your mother more, if I'm being honest. Besides, you're not the one who barged in here like a *chooch* and scared that nice girlfriend of yours and turned this place into a three-ring circus. So, for that, Tommy . . . I am sorry."

Tommy nodded. There were times when his father had flown off the handle before and realized it later, but that usually resulted in a gift or his father being twice as nice the day after or pretending it never happened in the first place. But he had never apologized before.

Big Al stood suddenly, did a quick circuit around the small alcove, a tiger in a cage. "I'm sorry for a lot of things. Seeing you like this scared the living shit out of me. I know I can be an overbearing prick, but all I've ever wanted is to keep you and your mother safe. This world is tough, and I worry sometimes I haven't done the best job of preparing you. Or maybe I overprepared you, I don't know. Either way, the harder I try, the bigger mess I seem to make. . . ."

Big Al collapsed into his chair again, exhausted from the effort of explaining himself. Tommy saw him rubbing his forehead, but he realized that he was trying to conceal his eyes, which were shining.

Then Don Fugue summoned whatever bluster remained and jabbed his son in the leg again, this time more insistent.

"You've got a good heart. You don't apologize for nothing to nobody. You're a good boy and I love you, okay?"

"I know, Pop."

For a few moments, they listened to the beeping of the machines around them, the quiet bustle of the staff outside, the low murmuring of the mobsters standing sentry.

"That girl," said his father. "She's nice."

"Where is she?"

"I had Nine drive her home. She didn't want to go. She didn't cut and run." He gestured to the curtain and, presumably, the leadership structure of the Denver Mafia behind it. "Even after all this. I respect that."

"She's great."

"Yeah?" said Big Al, a smirk spreading on his lips.

"Yeah," said Tommy. He blushed. Even in the low light, his father picked up on it.

"First kiss?"

"Pop."

"Well, we gotta make it up to her. After all this? Does she like flowers? We'll turn her place into a fucking greenhouse."

"No love bombing, Pop."

"What the fuck is that?"

"Wildly grand gestures. Crazy flattery. It's . . ." He was going to call it manipulative and emotional abuse, but he remembered all the times he would come home from school to discover a roomful of roses for his mother or a car with a bow on it after some huge blowout. "It's too much, Pop. I don't want to scare her away."

"Love bombing," said Big Al, considering it. "I think someone put one of those under my car once."

Tommy raised his eyebrows, then Big Al started to laugh. Tommy did too. He couldn't help it.

37

As the doctor had promised, Tommy slept deeply. He dreamt of both his mother and the game, conflating the two just as he did during his waking hours. She was calling him from the Plains, like the goblins had to his adventurers, beckoning him into the dark. There was no moon. He kept walking and walking, stumbling on the uneven ground, tall grass whipping his face, out where the predators roamed.

"Where are you?" he called.

I'm down here.

Tommy froze, then began to push and pull the grass aside to get to the ground. It was like trying to machete through a jungle. The grass sawed his hands. When he cleared enough aside to see the ground, his mother wasn't there.

Oh honey, I'm deeper than that. . . .

He woke with a start. He was drenched in sweat. His head felt thick, his throat clammy. He looked at the time—it was mid-afternoon, well past the time for Anibal to have been there. He walked out to the living room. Sometimes the artist let himself in and got to work on his own, but not today. Anibal had not shown up. *Just as well,* thought Tommy. He could use the day.

He put his phone on Do Not Disturb and spent the rest of the day preparing for that night's session.

• • •

Nine was the first to arrive that night. He was alone.

"Hey, man," said Tommy at the door. "Weird night, huh?"

Nine gave Tommy his serious smile. It was devoid of mirth or warmth. A stranger might think it was polite. Tommy knew better.

"No session tonight, my man," said the soldier.

"Why not?"

"Don Fugue wants another update."

"He just saw me last night."

"Last night wasn't about business. Tonight is."

Tommy wanted to make another joke, like the morning of his presentation, but something was off. Maybe it was last night's allergic reaction; maybe it was the dark dreams. The whole day had felt laced with dread.

"I'll change."

"I'll wait."

Tommy dressed smarter than last time: pants, dress shirt, dress shoes. He was trying to step up his sartorial game in front of Sanse, and somewhere along the way he realized he liked how it made him feel. He had even begun dressing up for his nightly sessions.

He looked in the mirror, blew out a shaky breath, then followed Nine to the car.

Nine drove in silence to Commerce City. Tommy didn't bother to ask questions. Nine wouldn't have answered anyway.

"He just wants an update on the game," declared Tommy, trying to reassure them both.

"Sure," said Nine.

He cut a sideways glance to the young solider. Stoic, betraying nothing. Did he know more than he was letting on? Sometimes his friend was maddening, inscrutable. He found new sensations bubbling up from the lake of fear in his belly. Irritation. Indignation. Pride.

"How's Todd?"

"He's coming along."

"I meant his debt to us."

"He's square," said Nine. Then the soldier turned his head to Tommy. "Todd's one thing you don't have to worry about."

That chilled Tommy. They drove the rest of the way in silence.

Nine pulled into the parking lot of the Fuzzy Navel. Save for a few cars, the lot was empty. The neon sign of the silhouette of a naked woman lounging in a martini glass, high heels kicked high, was dim. Tommy would have preferred the caterer's place. Nine, though trying to conceal it with his typical cool bravado, looked equally ill at ease.

The soldier killed the engine. They sat in silence for a moment.

"Here?" asked Tommy.

Nine shrugged. *"Tommy."*

"Right. *This* Al Mighty doesn't explain things in stone tablets. Got it." Tommy clapped his hands to psych himself up. "The debt's paid off," he said. "The sessions are going well. The art is coming along. You're lining up vendors. It's good. It's all good. . . ."

Never mind Anibal's direct connection to the Delgado Crime Family.

"Sure," said Nine. He stared out of the windshield. "All good."

They got out of the car. Nine marched to the main entrance, where a large bouncer normally stood guard, but this night the doors were unattended. Nine tried them, found them open, and held one open for Tommy. The young soldier looked at his shoes as Tommy passed, his face locked down tight.

They entered the long, dark hallway into the main space. Tonight, there were no lurid lights or sounds of the bass bumping from deep inside the club. It was as quiet as a tomb. They stumbled forward in the half darkness, Tommy's nerves ratcheting tighter with every step. They approached the hostess's podium, and found it unmanned as well. Around the corner was the club proper.

"I think the back rooms are through there," said Nine.

Tommy took a deep breath and rounded the corner, where he was assaulted by an explosion of light and sound.

"Surprise!"

Tommy stumbled back to riotous laughter. His wild eyes took in the room, the lights pulsing again, the music booming anew. Everyone was there: The remainder of his RPG party, Chongo, Jo, and Porks. Anibal too. Turdo, his father's second-in-command. The Johnnies. All of the soldiers who had been at the ER the night before and several more, some Tommy had seen over the years, many he hadn't. Fallon, Fiona, and Merry were there too, along with dozens of other women in bikinis and hot pants.

In the center of this circus was the ringmaster: Big Al. His father stood on the stage where the women usually danced, microphone in hand. Behind him, on a giant screen, was a digital clock.

"There he is: The man of the hour! My boy!"

Everyone cheered, then followed Don Fugue in a rendition of "For He's a Jolly Good Fellow."

Tommy turned to Nine. "What the—"

Nine burst out laughing. "Dude, you should've seen your face. I thought you were going to shit yourself."

"I think I did. What the fuck is going on?"

"You don't get it, do you? It's been thirty days! When the clock strikes midnight, Tergivers is officially fully funded!"

Tommy faced the stage and noticed the giant digital clock was counting down to midnight, New Year's Eve–style. All the dread drained from his body. Relief flooded in. A giant, dopey grin lit up his face.

Nine shook Tommy's shoulder. "You did it, numbnuts!"

When the raucous crowd had sloshed through its final "which nobody can deny," Big Al addressed the crowd again.

"Boys, get up here."

Tommy and Nine made their way to the stage. Tommy thought his back would bruise from all the drunken claps he received as he weaved through the crowd.

"Nine, I need you to DJ," said Big Al, then pointed to the laptop that ran the clock. "Tommy, here. Come here."

Tommy stood beside his father, who put his arm around him.

"Be honest, were you nervous?" Big Al held the microphone to his son's mouth.

Tommy leaned forward. "Little bit, Pop."

The drunken crowd erupted into laughter.

"Listen to him. He still gets nervous walking into a strip club!"

The crowd laughed even harder.

"I feel like a friggin' game-show host over here."

One of the Johnnies called out, *"Family Fugue!"*

"Ha!" Big Al pointed into the crowd. "*Family Fugue,* I like that." Then he swept his arm in a wide gesture toward the screen. "All right, Nine Ball: *Tell him what he's won!*"

Nine's fingers flew across the keys and the large screen displaying the digital clock changed to the Tergivers page on FunFunder, with its new total, which Tommy had scrupulously avoided since the first week of the campaign.

The crowd gasped. Then the roof came off.

"1.6 million dollars!" yelled Big Al.

It was a good thing his father's arm was around him, because Tommy's knees nearly buckled. He shook his head, as if trying to clear his vision, but the sum remained.

It was real.

1.6 million dollars

"This kid!" said Big Al, beaming. "This fucking kid!"

His father hugged him roughly, kissed him on both cheeks. Then he faced the crowd again.

"In all seriousness, I am so fucking proud of him. I don't want to get into it, but it's no secret we've had a rough year. But he put that big brain of his to work and persevered. All he needed was a little *push. . . .*"

At this, the soldiers, most of whom had been at the caterer's breakfast meeting, howled with laughter. Big Al, on surer emotional footing now, continued.

"A little push, and half a chance. And you turned nothing into something. 1.6 mil worth of something." He pointed at the screen. "You made that shit happen. That's what Fugues do. Never forget that you're a Fugue through and through."

Big Al held a glass aloft. "To Tommy, my beloved son *and* my top earner . . . *cent'anni.*"

The crowd responded in kind, all hoisting their glasses and wishing Tommy health for one hundred years. His father finally let him offstage, to rapturous applause. Nine appeared with two shots in his hand. He handed one to Tommy and they clinked glasses.

"A little Grind," said the soldier. "For that Grindset."

"To the Mighty Macarro," said Tommy, and they tossed back their drinks.

Then it was an odd procession line of his father's crew and the half-dressed workforce of the Fuzzy Navel congratulating him. A new drink was thrust into his hand, and nobody would let it get down to half before it was swapped out for a fresh one. Pretty quickly, he realized he would need to pace himself, but a pleasant warmth began to spread across his face. He felt good, loose. There was a break in the crowd and the three strippers forced their way to him, screaming with excitement.

He screamed back.

Fiona hugged him tight. Tommy let her; it felt nice.

"I'm so proud of you, Tommy. *Ah-mazing.*"

"Thanks, Fiona. Anibal did a great job with your sexy flesh-golem pic."

Not to be outdone, Fallon elbowed her aside, wrapped her arms around his neck, and squeezed hard. With her augmented breasts, the weaponized hug felt more like the grip of a boa constrictor.

"Don't forget me at midnight, cutie."

"Okay," wheezed Tommy.

Tommy braced for a third hug, but instead Merry grabbed his shoulders and shook him.

"Thank you so much, Tommy."

"For what?"

"Thanks to you and Anibal, I got into cosplay. Superheroes, anime, horror. I'm making a shitload of money on OnlyFans. My topless Poison Ivy went viral." She leaned in and whispered in his ear. "Don't tell the girls, but I'll be able to leave this shithole soon."

Tommy wasn't sure how to feel about that, but happiness for her was mixed in there somewhere. "Good for you, Merry."

"Also, let me know if you ever need an extra player. I'm working on a succubus with daddy issues." She squared up to his face and took a step closer. He could feel her breath on his cheeks. "We can have a private session first if you want. I can come in character."

"Uh . . ."

Tommy felt a firm hand on his shoulder. He turned and saw his father.

"Ladies, allow me to steal my son a moment, would you?"

Don Fugue to the rescue—something Tommy never imagined he would think. His father steered him through the crowd to a quiet corner of the club where the bass was less bone-rattling.

Nine appeared with two more shot glasses, handed them over, then melted back into the crowd like a wraith.

"Good kid, that Nine," said his father. "He doing right by you?"

A thought came unbidden to him. Tommy realized that with a word he could blow up Nine's spot. Like bodyguards and handlers of the past. When Tommy had complained, they were transferred out—back to whatever illegal shit his father had them doing before—and someone rotated in. The thought terrified him.

"He's the best, Pop. You have no idea."

"Good, good. Listen, I gotta get out of here. New York is breathing down my neck, so I'm wheels up first thing in the morning. But this party is yours. Till the break of dawn, you know what I mean?"

"Can I ask you a question?" ventured Tommy. "About work?"

Big Al narrowed his eyes, suddenly wary. "Shoot."

"Does New York know about the game?"

"That?" Big Al laughed. "Look, I always pay my dues and kick back upstairs. But it's a gig economy. Everybody's got a side hustle. Let's just say this is a Fugue Family secret. What New York doesn't know won't kill them."

Tommy nodded.

"Anyway, I'm gonna go, but I just wanted to say again how fucking proud I am of you. If your mother could see you now . . ."

Where is she? thought Tommy.

"Where is she?" he blurted. The copious amounts of rum had emboldened him. Or made him careless. Or Tommy had gambled that his father was in more of a wistful mood than a vengeful one.

His father pinched the bridge of his nose. He did that sometimes in the seconds before he exploded, but his father seemed exasperated, not enraged.

"I don't know."

Tommy's limbs felt like they were on a two-second delay thanks to the alcohol, but he watched his own hand reach out to his father's shoulder, and hover there, before finally clasping it and giving it a warm shake. Big Al looked at him, almost startled, then pulled his son in for a bear hug. After a few moments, he let him go.

"I can tell you this. If your mother could see you now," he said, gesturing around the club, "she would fucking murder me. But she'd be so proud of you."

"Maybe someday she'll come back and tell me herself."

"Wouldn't that be nice?"

"Pop, can I ask you a favor?"

"Anything, kid."

"Can Sanse join the party?"

Big Al looked around, saw the trio of strippers on the edge of the crowd eyeing the pair of them.

"A little like bringing sand to the beach, no?"

"No, I mean the Tergivers party—the game. I really like this girl, Pop."

"I'm just busting balls, son. If she can roll with all of this, then she's very special indeed. Just do me a favor and use protection, okay?"

"Pop!"

"I mean Benadryl, Romeo. Like just put it all over you. But yeah, that too." His father pointed at him then, his large pinkie ring jutting his little finger to the side. The inadvertent throwing of the horns. "And be careful. More than one gangster walked into an ambush following his prick around."

"I'm not a gangster, Pop."

Big Al laughed and spread his arms wide, taking in the entirety of the celebration, all for Tommy's big score.

"Keep telling yourself that, kid."

38

Tommy woke late the next afternoon with a vicious hangover. He stumbled into the kitchen to pour himself some water, then doubled back to the bedroom to retrieve his phone from the nightstand. Last night, after he had watched SuperChenz down two bottles of wine at the same time and found himself cheering the hulk on, he'd texted Anibal to delay their creative session until the afternoon. Anibal, also hungover, suggested they wave off the afternoon as well. They agreed: Maybe even cancel that night's game too.

As soon as he picked his phone up, it rang. Tommy winced at the sound, but a smile formed on his lips when he saw the caller.

Sanse.

His smile evaporated when he answered. She was crying.

Tommy panicked.

"What is it? What's wrong?"

"It's Todd," she cried. "He's missing!"

Oh, thought Tommy. *Is that all?*

"How can he be missing?" asked Tommy. "He's a grown-ass man. Hell, he's like seven feet tall."

Physically, thought Tommy. Mentally, he probably still hovered around the eighth grade, but Tommy refrained from sharing his assessment.

Through tears, Sanse explained that the last time his roommates saw Todd was when he was leaving to run errands the previous afternoon. He was supposed to return to their apartment to change before a party, but he never showed. He never came home that night, and no one had seen or heard from him all morning. No calls, no texts, no Snaps. Location turned off.

"That is so not like Todd," she said.

He didn't like the sound of this. *Even idiots love their phones*, thought Tommy.

"It's been over twenty-four hours," she said. "They've filed a missing persons report."

Tommy liked the sound of that even less, though he didn't have time to dwell on it. There was pounding at his door.

"Sanse, let me call you right back."

"But Tommy, I—"

The pounding was insistent.

Maybe it was the oaf himself—he certainly knew where Tommy lived—but he doubted it. Sanse's call set him on edge, made him nervous. Tommy was pretty sure it was the Tergivers party that Todd had been going to, but he didn't tell her that.

Tommy squared up to the door. His father had always wanted him to keep a piece in his apartment, just in case, but Tommy had refused. He almost wished he'd listened.

He moved to the peephole, peered through.

It was Nine Ball.

"I see you in the peephole, numbnuts," yelled the soldier. "Open up, damn it!"

Tommy exhaled. He threw off the chain and his minder bounded in. Nine slammed the door behind him, latched the chain again. He was out of breath.

Nine was moving too quickly for Tommy's hungover brain to

process. It was like jump cuts in film. One moment the kid was at the door. The next he was at the sink, downing a glass of water. The next he was back across the room, pacing.

"Someone took a shot at me! I had to get off the street and yours was the closest spot."

Tommy couldn't help himself. He looked toward the door.

It dawned on the soldier then what he had done. "Fuck," said Nine. "I'm sorry. I have to get out of here."

"You're not going anywhere," said Tommy. "We'll wait until dark, then we'll take you to my father's house. You'll be safe. Let me call him. He should be in New York by now, but—"

"If he knows I came here instead of the Navel or the pool hall or any of the other Fugue spots, he'll kill me himself." His voice dropped to a mumble. "This was just the first place I thought of. . . ."

"Do you think you were followed?"

"No, man. I swear."

"All right, just . . . just let me think for a second."

But his phone rang again. This time it was his father.

"You okay?" asked Big Al.

"I'm fine, Pop. I heard from Nine, though. Someone took a shot at him."

"Where?"

Tommy mouthed, *Where?*

Nine pointed down.

"South Side," said Tommy.

"Shit," his father seethed. "Is he okay?"

"He's fine. What the hell is going on, Pop?"

"I don't know, but I'm heading back to find out. I'm getting reports of disturbances in the Force all over the place. Someone shot up the entrance to the pool hall. They painted a giant *thirty* on the side of the Navel. Some animal even threw a brick through Tesauro Catering Alessandro Fugue Commemorative Showroom. I love those fucking windows."

"What's 'thirty'?"

Nine Ball, who was pacing in the apartment, stopped cold.

Thirty? he mouthed.

Tommy put his father on speaker and made the *shush* sign to Nine.

"I don't have time to explain. I'm coming home. Until then, everyone is on high alert."

"What do you need me to do?" Tommy surprised himself by asking. It just came out. Years of conditioning.

"Stay put. Tell Nine to make sure he isn't followed, then get over to your place. Order pizza."

Relieved, Nine put his hands on his knees and blew out a long, silent breath. He took off his jacket, folded it, then collapsed onto Tommy's couch.

"I need Porks at the helm of the Navel and Jo on the streets cracking heads. Plus, I don't need Fugue associates coming in and out of your door every day. Tergivers is on temporary hiatus."

On one hand, Tommy felt a small spark of pride. He had never actually heard his father say the name of the game correctly before. On the other, he had work to do; the game had just got funded. Tommy was really on the hook now.

He fought to keep the whine out of his voice. "For how long?"

"Until I say so. *This,*" said Big Al, before ending the call, "is no game."

Tommy turned to Nine Ball. "Now that that's sorted, he said shit's popping off all over. Someone painted a *thirty* on the Navel?"

Nine loosened his tie. "It's a tag of the Rolling 30s. Occasional muscle for hire. But that doesn't make any sense. . . ."

"What's their beef?"

Spotting the *Dungeon Master's Guide* in a stack of books next to the couch, Nine said, "Let me put it this way. The 30s are mostly Lawful Evil. Like most sets, they have a code. It's a fucked-up, cruel-ass code to be sure, but they operate within a set of rules. But if they're somehow disrespected, or someone higher up lets them off the chain, they are only too happy to go full Chaotic Evil. But even so, they're not stupid. They wouldn't make a run at Don Fugue without backing—"

They heard a *whoosh* sound. Nine picked up his phone, studied the screen, and sat up straight.

"Oh shit," he said. *"Shit."*

A package had been delivered to the Fuzzy Navel. Porks sent Nine a photo of its contents: a T-shirt with a crest of crossed swords. Above the crest was printed ROLLING 20S.

The shirt was bloody.

"Rolling 20s?" said Tommy, confused. He looked at Nine. The fear in the soldier's eyes returned. "What did you do?"

"Fuck," said Nine. *"Fuck fuck fuck."* He sprang from the couch, started pacing again. When he passed something that wasn't set cleanly at ninety degrees, he turned it to order.

"Nine, sit down, talk to me."

The soldier stopped but did not sit. "I ordered Todd to have T-shirts made for the party. I thought it would be fun. I didn't specify what to put on them, just something to do with the game. Of course, that giant dipshit would choose a play on words that would invoke the wrath of a fucking motorcycle gang."

"How would they even know?"

"The streets have ears, Tommy. And Todd has a big mouth. I'm going to *kill* that hayseed."

"Someone may have beaten you to it. Sanse just called me. He's been missing since yesterday."

Nine didn't react at first. It was like he had absorbed too much bad information at once and a circuit breaker tripped in his head. Tommy glanced down, saw the soldier's fingers move. On both hands, he was tapping his thumb to each fingertip—index, middle, ring, pinkie—then back again in quick succession.

He was stimming. Other than some habitual straightening and his constant cracks at the uncleanliness of Tommy's apartment, Nine usually kept his compulsive behaviors in check. Then again, Tommy had never seen his friend this stressed before.

"I just started a gang war over a fucking T-shirt," said Nine. He went and got another drink of water, then sat at the game table in his familiar spot.

If he wanted Nine to focus, Tommy would need to redirect him. He took his chair at the table too. "Let's assume Todd is still alive."

"That's a generous assumption. The 30s don't play."

"It's just a bloody shirt, some broken windows, and graffiti so far."

"And a shot at me."

"But they missed. It sounds like if they really wanted to kill you, you'd be dead. So, they want something. What's their motivation?"

"Their motivation? Tommy, this isn't a game."

"Oh, but it is." He slapped a character sheet down on the table in front of Nine. "Give me everything you know about the Rolling 30s. Stats, races, classes, strengths, weaknesses, affiliations. All of it."

Tommy didn't know what he was doing, but it worked. Given

something to concentrate on, Nine lost himself building a profile on the gang. As with Macarro, Nine went deep. When he handed back the sheet, it was dense with detail. Tommy read it and his stomach dropped when he reached the neatly printed section titled Affiliations.

"Shit," muttered Tommy.

"What is it?" asked Nine.

"Come on, I'll explain on the way."

"Don Fugue ordered us to lay low. Where are we going?"

Tommy grabbed his keys. "Side quest."

39

"Are you fucking kidding me?" yelled Nine.

As he drove down University, Tommy looked out the window to try and avoid Nine's gaze. It helped somewhat, but when they passed a small shopping area where every store seemed to have the words *Bonnie Brae* in its name, he was disoriented all over again.

On the plus side, Nine was back to his old self. With a course of action, he had snapped out of his stimming. On the negative side, he was furious.

"Anibal is Anibal *Delgado?* Son of *Emiliano* Delgado."

"Surprise." Tommy lifted his hands in mock frivolity.

"The Emiliano Delgado who is Don Fugue's chief rival in Denver?"

"I'm sorry I didn't tell you."

A few minutes and some nearly pastoral house plots later, they spotted Anibal waiting in the roundabout in front of his family's mansion. Tommy parked the car and the artist rushed over to him.

"Tommy, I had nothing to do with any of this. You have to believe me."

"I do," said Tommy.

"Jesus Christ," said Nine Ball. "Peas in a pod, you two. Do you have any idea how fucking naive you both sound? How do you know this wasn't a Delgado plan from the start, Tommy?" The gangster leaned closer to Tommy by way of leering at the suspect in question.

Tommy was afraid to touch Nine, but he raised a finger for emphasis. "Because *he's* not the one who decided on party favors that could get people killed. Look, it doesn't matter how we got here, only that we do everything we can to end it. So, stop arguing with reality and get with the program, okay?"

Nine made a face but said nothing further.

Tommy turned to Anibal. "Will he talk to me?"

"Of course."

The three of them moved to the front door, but Anibal held up his hand to Nine. "You should wait here."

"No fucking way, pal," said Nine. "I don't leave his side."

"Nine, it's okay. It's just a friendly chat. It's not like he's going to chop me up and bring me out in pieces." Tommy looked at his friend. "Right?"

The artist nodded.

"I was hoping for a more full-throated affirmation, Anibal."

Once inside, Tommy followed the artist to Emiliano's study. Outside the door, Anibal turned to him. "Again, I swear I don't know what's going on. I don't think my father does either."

"But you can't say for sure."

After a moment, Anibal replied, "No, I can't. I love my father. He's a great father, but sometimes I'm afraid he's not a good man. His business, his dealings . . . they're like a black hole. Everything gets sucked into it. Do you think I want my friends pulled into this shit? To jeopardize the game?" The artist shook his head. "No way."

"On Tergivers?" asked Tommy.

"On Tergivers," said Anibal.

Tommy nodded. It was the only oath he could count on.

Anibal knocked on the study door. A rich voice ordered them in.

Behind the massive desk sat Emiliano Delgado, looking like the cat who swallowed the canary.

"Young Master Fugue, to what do I owe the pleasure?"

"I'm afraid there's been a terrible misunderstanding, and I'm hoping a cooler, wiser head can intercede, Mr. Delgado."

"What is the nature of this misunderstanding?"

Tommy suspected that Emiliano Delgado knew all about the Rolling 30s assaults on Fugue establishments. And that few moves on the streets were made without the crime boss's knowledge.

Tommy cleared his throat and explained anyway. The end of the Tergivers' thirty-day campaign, the subsequent surprise party, and the incendiary T-shirts.

"I would laugh," said Emiliano, "if it weren't so careless. Did you know any of this, son?"

"No, Papa. I swear."

"It's worse," said Tommy. "We think they have our friend."

"Friend?" asked Emiliano. He looked skeptical.

"One of our classmates," said Anibal.

"He's a civilian," said Tommy. "Wrong time, wrong place."

"Wrong T-shirt, apparently," said Emiliano. He steepled his fingers and let the moment, and Tommy's anxiety, draw out. Finally, he said, "Let me make an inquiry."

The crime boss crossed the study to a quiet corner and spoke a few clipped sentences in Spanish into his phone. He did not wait for a response. He hung up and returned to his desk.

"I suppose congratulations are in order," said Emiliano. "For your funding. Though I'm starting to reconsider if this game is more trouble than it's worth."

"This has nothing to do with the game, sir."

"That would seem . . . untrue. And what of our discussion?"

"What discussion?" asked Anibal.

Emiliano held his hand up, silencing his son without even looking at him.

"My accountant is drawing up the agreement," Tommy said.

"Your father's accountant, you mean."

"My father knows nothing about it."

"Don't underestimate fathers or the extent of their knowledge."

Emiliano's phone rang. He listened. After a few moments, he said, "Gracias," then hung up.

"I have good news. Your classmate lives."

"Thank God," exhaled Tommy.

"For now."

"What does that mean?" asked Anibal.

"Certain conditions will have to be met. However inadvertently, you have disrespected the 30s and they have their honor."

"How do I fix it?" asked Tommy.

"With a token of respect."

"How much will this token cost?"

Emiliano smiled. "Twenty thousand dollars."

Great, thought Tommy. *Another dirty 20.*

"I will be happy to broker this for you, of course."

Tommy didn't like the sound of that. He waited for the other shoe to drop.

As if reading his mind, Emiliano held up his hand once more. "I am not going to exploit you in your moment of need, Mr. Fugue. I only ask that you honor my son with a contract. As a partner."

"Papa!" said Anibal. "Our friend is in trouble."

"What's the saying? It's not called 'show friends,' it's called 'show business.' By midnight."

"I'll try."

"Do or do not. There is no try."

What is it with gangsters and Star Wars? thought Tommy.

He nodded. He had no leverage. No other choice.

"Of course, Mr. Delgado."

"Once I receive the contract, I will text you a location. You will have to retrieve him yourself, as a sign of sincerity."

"How do I know it's not a trap?"

"Because unlike the Fugue Family, I am neither rash nor careless. I have no desire to return to the Bad Old Days."

Tommy fought off a shudder. He remembered that carefree afternoon in the mall, eating too much candy, and the darkness that followed.

"Peace is good for business," he heard himself say.

"Very wise," said Emiliano. He nodded toward the door. "I recommend haste. I only have so much sway over the 30s. They grow bored easily, and they have a plaything."

Tommy headed for the door, pulling his phone from his pocket. He swiped past the worried string of texts from Sanse on his lock screen.

Emiliano called after him. Tommy stopped in the doorway.

"Truth be told, I don't even remember how the Bad Old Days started. A territorial dispute? A cross word in a bar? Was it over a woman? Whatever it was, the response was not proportional to the offense, and all that blood has washed the memory away. Move quickly, but with care."

"Understood, sir."

"No, I do not believe you do. The shirts were made at a screen print shop well inside 30s territory, and by extension, Delgado territory. A very foolish place for a Fugue associate, or friend, to find himself. That is some truly bad luck, my young friend."

"Yes, sir."

"I don't believe in luck. Some may see the return of the Bad Old Days as an opportunity. Watch your back, Mr. Fugue."

40

Macarro walks ahead, descending the stone stairs of the dungeon. Torches burn in sconces, creating a dotted trail of light leading a new adventurer deeper into the darkness.

Ahead of Macarro and his comrade marches a lone kobold, leading the way. The pair were granted safe passage to the dungeon, but every so often, the lizard-like kobold looks back at them and flashes a carnivorous smile.

A chill runs up the new adventurer's spine.

"Let me do the talking," whispers Macarro.

The comrade nods, unsure.

The kobold reaches the bottom of the staircase and gestures through the door with a clawed hand.

"After you," he says with a snort.

Macarro passes through unmolested. The new adventurer squeezes by the creature, his skin erupting in gooseflesh as he passes closely. Afraid his claws will grab him, afraid of a bite. Afraid of everything.

They enter a large chamber, stacked high with wooden crates filled with goods. A dozen or so more kobolds laze against them or sit at a table drinking mead and playing cards or loom over their captive.

The oafish peasant is seated in a battered wooden chair,

dressed in torn rags and draped with heavy chains. His mouth is stuffed with cloth and crisscrossed with chains. There are cuts and dried blood on his face. One eye is swollen shut.

Yet he lives.

One of the lizardmen sits at the head of the table. Even seated, it is obvious he is larger than his brethren. His shoulders are bunches of rippling muscles. The twin horns on his head are taller than the others' horns. His teeth are longer and sharper. He has wings that, unfolded, would eclipse him.

King Kobold.

He does not rise at the visitors. Rather, he leans back. His chest shakes and he emits a dry huffing sound. The new adventurer realizes King Kobold is laughing.

"Well, well, well," says the king. "Who has graced us with their presence?"

From the table, someone hisses, "Fresh meat."

The kobolds snicker.

Macarro speaks up. If the young warrior hopeful is afraid, he does not show it. His voice rings loud and clear.

"I am Macarro. With me is Prince Thomas, scion of the Fugue Clan, firstborn of the Al Mighty himself. We have come to parlay."

"Macarro," repeats King Kobold. "You're the one with the quick reflexes."

King Kobold made a sign of a gun with his claw.

"Had I wanted to end you, know that I could have. I do not miss. I just wanted to watch you dance." More dry huffing. "And dance you did."

Macarro does not take the bait. "Thank you for agreeing to meet with us."

"Don't thank me," growls King Kobold. "Thank Highest Lord

Delgado for granting your safe passage. He is the only reason we've not stripped the little flesh you have from your thin bones. Yet."

Macarro pitches a satchel between them. It tones like a bell on the stone floors of the dungeon.

They were able to rouse a slumbering Garcia to quickly produce the scroll Highest Lord Delgado required. Garcia also reluctantly parted with twenty thousand in treasury gold. He had many questions, but the prince had no time to answer them, saying simply, "Please trust me."

Reluctantly, the druid agreed.

"We gratefully accept your terms—twenty thousand for the peasant—with our most sincere apologies," said Macarro.

One of the smaller kobolds snatches the satchel and brings it to the table. The other kobolds dive in, grabbing fistfuls of coins and sniggering.

King Kobold slams his clawed fist on the table. His minions recoil.

"Did you really think it would be that simple?" he growls. "You come into our realm? Impugn our honor?"

"I assure you, that was not our intent," says Macarro. He points to the chained, beaten oaf. "And that one is a civilian."

"He did not sound like a civilian," responds King Kobold. The more irritated he grows, the more his wings unfurl. "Running his mouth, bossing everyone around, making demands of the staff." King Kobold points a long, sharp finger at Prince Thomas. "Throwing this one's name around. And for this!*"*

There is a torn box on the long table and the king swipes a red rag from it. His face contorts just holding it, and he bares his fearsome teeth, as if it pains him just to touch it. He pitches it at Thomas's chest.

Thomas catches it, unfurls it. He sees the crossed swords and the crest of a clan called the Rolling 20s.

"That crest! On those colors! What is this if not a deliberate provocation?"

"It's . . . it's just a game . . ." stammers Thomas.

"Prince Thomas," warns Macarro. "Silence, please."

"What does the little scion say?"

King Kobold strides over to Thomas and looms over him, a full two feet taller. His yellow eyes burn down at the prince. Thomas focuses on them so as not to concentrate on the rows of pointy teeth. He hears them clicking in the kobold's head, eager.

"You reek of fear, little scion. Fear and Fugue are two of my favorite flavors. You will be a delicacy. I will roast you over a spit and savor you. . . ."

The gang leader rained threats down on Tommy.

He was massive, as wide as he was tall and rippling with muscles. He wore a leather cut with the 30s crest on the back and a patch on the front that read KING. His head was shaved and mirrored sunglasses hid his eyes even though it was dim in the garage. He smelled of diesel and smoke.

Dragon's breath.

He came closer. *"Oh, is this a fucking game to you?"*

The smell and the proximity had short-circuited Tommy's Tergivers dissociation, revealing the dungeon as a grimy garage, the kobolds as gangbangers, and Tommy as a pampered rich boy. He tried to retreat back into it, but the leader was shouting into his face.

"Tell me what kind of fucking game it is, bitch!"

Tommy swallowed.

"A TTRPG."

The 30s soldiers all looked at each other questioningly.

"What the fuck did you just say?" asked their leader.

"It's a tabletop roleplaying—"

"I *know* what a TTRPG is, *bitch*. But what's it like? Fantasy? Steampunk? Dystopian?"

"Uh," said Tommy. He looked at Nine. Nine gave a tiny shake of his head that communicated, *I have no idea what's happening.*

"Players are pulled from different realms and timelines on a patchwork planet to seek out their missing virtues, fulfill their potential, and rescue a captive queen, and it's . . . like really fun. . . ."

The gang king reared back and stared at him down his nose. Tommy forced himself not to wince as he waited for a blow.

"Anything like Mansions of Madness?"

"What?"

"Running around a haunted house, investigating spooky shit? Yo, that shit's my *favorite*. Your game do shit like that?"

"Well, it's more . . ."

"Tommy," said Nine.

"Yes. In fact, we just had a session with a haunted fort."

"Haunted by what?"

Tommy cleared his throat. "Banshees."

The gang leader gave him the gas face. "Banshees are wack. I rock with that cosmic horror shit. Existential dread. Stuff that breaks your mind. We run sessions in here sometimes. . . ." He looked around the shadowy rafters and shivered. "Spooky! Yo, Lovecraft was racist for real, and that's a big problem with his legacy, but sometimes you gots to separate the art from the artist, feel me?"

"He feels you," interjected Nine. "All of which brings me back to the matter at hand. My friend there was celebrating our game getting funded on FunFunder—"

"Whoa, you got that shit *funded*?" The leader stepped forward and thumped Tommy's chest. "That's dope, Little Fugue!"

There were murmurs of assent around the table.

"Thank you," said Tommy. "That's very kind."

"Anyway," said Nine. "As a surprise, Todd over there was making T-shirts as party favors and—"

"The Rolling 20s is for the d20," said Tommy, "and . . . *surprise*."

"Are you for real right now?"

"Nonfiction," said Nine.

"I'm for real, sir," said Tommy.

King bent at the waist as if someone had sucker punched him. When he straightened again, he gasped for air. Then he shrieked with laughter.

"This fool?" He ran over to Todd, helpless and bound. "This fool right here?"

Todd's unswollen eye bobbed around, following the leader, eager like a puppy's.

"The twenty he's rolling is a fucking d20!"

"A d20, yes sir."

"And college boy here put that shit on a *shirt?* On the South Side?"

"Unfortunately, sir."

"Oh my goodness." King guffawed. He wiped his eyes. "Oh my *goodness*! That is the most hilarious shit I've ever heard."

Nine interjected. "Hilarious, right? I'm hoping that based on our mutual affection for roleplaying games and farcical misunderstandings, you will see fit to let bygones be bygones and set our clueless friend here free."

"Oh, for sure I'm keeping that money, though."

"Of course," said Nine. "For your trouble. And you'll cease all hostilities against Fugue places of business? Seeing as how this was the action of a dumb *chooch* with no common sense?"

"Twenty large for the best laugh I had in a good time ain't bad for a day's work. Cut him loose."

One of the gang members slid from the table and, with a couple of flicks of a blade, severed the lines tying Todd to his chair. Todd ripped the duct tape covering his mouth and spat out his gag. He grimaced but made no sound. He looked around, unsure if this was a trick, then limped over to Tommy and Nine.

King scooped a T-shirt from the box and tossed it to Todd. It hit his chest and fell to the ground. With effort, Todd bent over and picked it up.

"We're gonna burn the rest, but you can keep that one. You earned it." He turned to his crew. "Big Boy got jumped into his own gang. He's a Rolling 20 for real now!"

The crew exploded into laughter.

Todd tried to smile, but his split lip began to bleed again.

Nine gave a final thanks and then guided the other two to follow him. The cackles followed the trio out as they turned toward the corridor and the exit.

"Yo," called King, "not so fast."

They froze. Tommy turned around.

"Bring your game by when it's out. I'd love to give it a try."

"You'll get one of the first printings, Mr. King, sir."

"Tight. You're a'ight, Little Fugue."

As soon as they were in the corridor, Todd began to stammer thanks and excuses, everything coming out in hyperventilated sobs.

"Shut the fuck up until we're outside," said Nine through clenched teeth.

They passed through the labyrinth until they found the exit and bounded through it. Tommy gulped the fresh night air, relieved to be out of the diesel-smelling garage, and felt the satisfying tactile crunch of the parking lot gravel beneath his feet. They passed an assortment of vehicles in various states of repair. He saw two tow trucks. Tommy couldn't tell if the operation was an auto-body shop, a tow company, or a junkyard, and then thought, *Probably all of the above: chop shop.* They passed through a gate in the chain-link fence surrounding the lot and Nine slid behind the wheel and Tommy climbed into the passenger side. Todd had barely folded himself into the back seat when Nine floored it, spraying gravel jets and a plume of dust behind them. They remained silent until they were out of the neighborhood and back on the highway.

Tommy pulled his phone from his pocket. The texts from Sanse continued to pile up, her worry increasing with every message. He texted back: Been out looking. Don't worry, I'm sure he'll turn up any time now.

"Thank you," said Todd quietly. "You were really awesome, Tommy."

"I'm really sorry that happened to you, Todd."

"Fuck that," said Nine. "What the fuck were you doing running your mouth?"

Todd began to answer, but Nine cut him off. "You know what, I don't want to hear it. Your nickname ain't 20s, it's Twelves."

"Twelves?" asked Todd.

"Dozen know shit, dozen say shit, dozen do shit. This never fucking happened, like a d12 roll. You understand?"

Todd nodded.

They drove the rest of the way to Todd's apartment complex in silence. The oaf got out of the car and shuffled across the wide lawn.

"Yo," called Nine. "Put some ice on your eye. You'll be fine."

"Okay," said Todd. "I'm real sorry, guys."

"Get some rest," said Tommy.

"Thanks again. You're a good guy, Tommy."

But sitting there, passenger in his own car, Tommy wasn't so sure anymore. He hadn't liked Todd, and he had relished Nine completely owning him that night with the burgers and again during his party, but seeing the guy standing alone under a streetlight now, stooped and beaten and broken, was too much.

Tommy felt rotten.

A little over a month ago, he was just an art student. And now, whether he wanted to admit it or not, he was working for his father and cutting side deals in secret with the Delgados and the Rolling 30s. He had heard in a philosophy class that you were the average of the five people you spent the most time with. If that were the case, he was the average of a wannabe capo with OCD, a slimy pimp, a stoner accountant, an alcoholic enforcer, and the son of a rival cartel boss.

Tommy looked at Nine. The soldier looked grave. Tommy wondered if the night had taken as much of a toll on him.

"You want a burrito?" asked Nine. "I'm fucking starving."

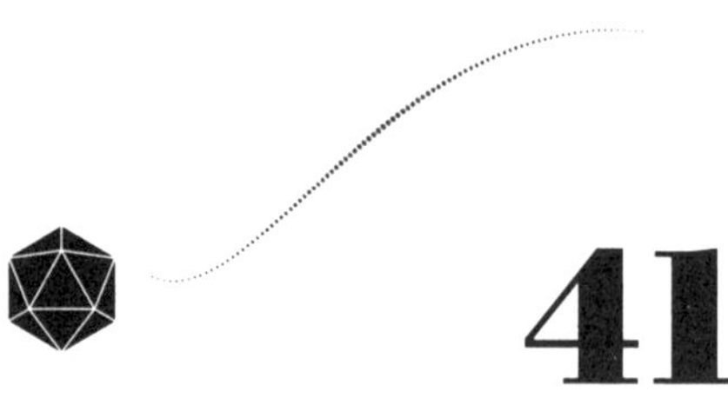

41

Peace on the streets meant gameplay could resume. Tommy tidied his apartment, hung more Anibal art, and realized he had not touched his gaming console in weeks. His living room, while now decorated entirely in fantasy trappings, was utilitarian: If it did not involve Tergivers, it was stuffed into a closet, jammed into a drawer, or kicked into a corner. The gaming table was the center of the space and his world.

He called the crew and told them to report to his apartment at the normal time. Jo was leery, but Tommy assured her it would be fine. Then Sanse called.

"Did you hear?" she asked. "Todd got mugged."

"Mugged," said Tommy, putting the necessary amount of surprise into his voice. "That's terrible."

"His roommates said he woke up this morning, packed a bag, and left to drive home to Kansas. It doesn't sound like he's coming back."

"Wow. That must have been some mugging."

"I'm just glad he's okay. Anyway, are you free for dinner?"

"I have a session tonight. Everyone's coming over."

"Oh. I thought I could cook. At my place."

At my place. "I can always push them back an hour or two."

"Sounds like a plan. I should warn you, I'm a terrible cook.

But I'm an incredibly warm and inviting hostess." She let that linger for a moment before adding, "See you later."

Holy shit, he thought when she hung up.

"Holy shit!" he said to his empty apartment.

It was happening. Today was the day. He was going to lose his V-card. He realized he had no idea what to do.

Anibal arrived for their daily brainstorming session. He thanked Tommy for the contract and apologized for his father pressing him the night before, but Tommy waved it all away.

"That doesn't matter right now! I'm going to Sanse's for dinner . . . and I think it might happen."

"What might happen?" the artist asked as he began pulling notebooks from his backpack.

"It."

"Oh." Anibal made a face. "You think?"

"She says she can't cook, but that she's an incredibly warm and inviting hostess."

"Tommy, she's talking about her vagina."

"Right? It's code, right?"

"That's totally code for vagina. You cracked the code, Tommy."

"I cracked the code," said Tommy in wonder. "Now what?"

"How should I know?"

"I mean, she's . . . Sanse. Gorgeous and glamorous and I'm, well, *me.*"

"I will admit, I do not have a ton of experience in this area, but just do the best you can for as long as you can."

"Easier said than done."

"Wait a minute, you said you're 'you.' What if you weren't?"

"Huh?"

Anibal gestured to the walls, adorned with his own renderings of different swords, intrepid heroes battling demons and dragons, and posters of dramatic landscapes. Looking around, Tommy realized his apartment resembled the side of a 1970s airbrushed van.

"Use your imagination," said Anibal.

"Dude, having sex with Sanse is already beyond my wildest imagination. It's so outlandish it makes Tergivers feel like a documentary."

"That's what I'm saying. It's beyond *your* imagination." He plucked a blank character sheet from the gaming table and flapped it in front of Tommy's face. "But maybe not someone else's."

A smile spread across Tommy's face. "I might know a guy. . . ."

Prince Thomas arrives at the fair maiden's door in his finest garments, bearing a bottle of wine in one hand and fresh cut flowers in the other. The past few days have been a succession of battles with dragons, but at long last, it seems he will be awarded a boon. Even so, the noble prince wants the maiden to know it's not just about the boon; he is in love.

But to declare it before or after? That is the question. So much of their courtship surprises and confuses him.

He is still debating when she opens the door. He stands a little straighter.

She is radiant. Her hair is up, decorated with small flowers. She looks like the maiden of honor in a spring fair. She sees the flowers in his hand and the faintest shadow passes her eyes. She looks wistful, almost sad, and pulls him in for a hug. After a few moments, he tries to pull away to kiss her, but she holds him tighter. His manhood subsides. They stand like that for several minutes.

There is so much feeling there.

It feels right.

"I love you," he says into her hair.

She squeezes him tighter still.

"I've always loved you," he says.

She releases him and she touches his face. There are tears in her eyes.

He wants her to say it back. She gives him a deep, longing kiss instead. Then she takes his hand and leads him to the bedroom without another word.

She walks ahead into the darkness. He follows.

A light illuminates the space suddenly, revealing two bandits lying in wait.

42

His first thought was *ambush.*

His next was the garage the night before.

But I fixed it, he thought.

Then he dropped the flowers, stepped in front of Sanse, and raised the wine bottle by the neck, ready to swing.

One of the men stepped forward. He was middle-aged, shorter than Tommy but hefty, and with a bushy mustache. The other man leaned against the bedroom wall, appraising him with cool eyes. He was tall and rail thin. He looked like he subsisted entirely on caffeine and nicotine. He reminded Tommy of Ichabod Crane's sinister older brother.

"It's okay!" said Sanse. She jumped between the men and Tommy, putting a hand on his chest. "He's okay. Right, Tommy?"

Tommy lowered the bottle. He had spent his entire life around gangsters and associates of gangsters. These men were neither. One good look at their puffy eyes and cheap suits and he knew.

Cops.

The mustachioed man backed off then, a smile playing on his lips. The man was solid and looked aggressive, putting Tommy in mind of a honey badger. Small but spoiling for a fight.

Tommy turned to Sanse. "What is this?"

"These men are detectives and—"

"No shit, Sanse. Why are they here?"

"We just want to talk," the taller man said. He nodded to a chair in the corner. "Have a seat, Mr. Fugue."

Tommy's father never really played catch with him or took him on camping or fishing trips. They had never poked under the hood of a car together. But Big Al Fugue did impart some lessons to his son, and the most important one flew up from the depths of his childhood unbidden.

Don't talk to the cops.

"No."

He turned on his heel and walked out.

Sanse caught him before he reached the front door.

"Tommy, just hear them out—"

"Don't touch me," he hissed. "You've been playing me this whole time? You're a cop? Are you even an art student?"

"I'm not a cop, Tommy."

"She's a sketch artist, kid." Honey Badger surfaced in the doorway to the bedroom. "And she's going to make one hell of a cadet."

Sanse shrugged.

The taller detective slid past his partner into the loft's main room, but only by a few feet, staying well back from the windows.

Tommy speared Sanse with spiteful eyes. "You can have her."

He turned for the door once more and flew it open.

"Before you walk," called the short detective, "don't you want to know what happened to your mother?"

Tommy whirled on him. Before he knew it, he had already taken three steps back into the loft. No doubt doing exactly what they wanted him to do, but he didn't care. He drew closer to the short detective—still careful not to get close enough to give the cop an excuse to defend himself—and drew to his full height. In that moment, he truly felt like Prince Thomas, regal and burning with righteous fury at someone daring to invoke the queen's name.

"What do you know about my mother?"

Behind him, Sanse quietly closed the door.

"There's what we think and what we can prove, and sadly, kid, there is a vast gulf between them," said Honey Badger. "For example, we *know* that little Dungeons & Dragons racket you're running is from ill-gotten gains, but we couldn't give a shit about that. Because we're actually on the same side. We want to help you locate your mother."

"Very generous of you. Vaguely threatening me with bullshit before offering me assistance I didn't ask for."

"Smart kid," said the tall detective.

"Smart mouth, more like," said the short one.

"Look, we apologize for getting off on the wrong foot. I'm Detective Ancelotti," said the tall one. "This is Detective Howard. Tell us, when was the last time you heard from her?"

"She fell off everyone's radar last summer," Detective Howard answered for him, as if Tommy didn't already know. "Isn't that right, Tommy?"

Tommy stared at Detective Howard, hatred in his eyes. It had been nearly a year. It made no sense at all, and he knew it, and he knew they knew it. Then he looked back at Detective Ancelotti.

Finally, Tommy smiled.

"Nice try, detectives. Have a nice night."

He strode for the door.

"I'm going to say the quiet part out loud, Tommy," said Ancelotti. "We think your father had something to do with your mother's disappearance."

Tommy's shoulders bunched around his ears, as if his back was sunburned and they'd just slapped it, but he didn't turn around.

"And deep down, you believe it too," added Howard.

He flung the door open and as soon as he was in the hallway, he broke into a jog. He heard the door open behind him, feet chasing him down. He thought the detectives were going to haul him back, but it was Sanse tugging at his arm.

"Tommy, please come back."

"I can't believe I told you I loved you." He jerked his arm away. "I'm such a fool. But you? You're worse."

He continued marching down the hallway.

"I can explain," she called after him.

"Yeah, you're a fucking liar," he said over his shoulder.

"The Fugues killed my father, Tommy."

Tommy halted.

"Don Fugue didn't pull the trigger," said Sanse, "but he may as well have."

Despite himself, Tommy asked, "How?"

It was telling, he thought, that his first response wasn't *Impossible*, or *You have the wrong guy*.

"My father was a low-level earner for the Delgados. He wasn't much of a father, but he was all my mom and I had, and I loved him. I was nine. I deserved to grow up with him. And he deserved to be more than cannon fodder in a gang war."

She pulled her phone from her pocket, poked around, then held it up to his face.

"Look!" she cried.

It was a picture of a young Sanse, sitting in her father's lap, his face turned down to look at his laughing angel. Tommy registered his proud smile, his sharp features, his bald pate, and recognized him immediately.

Son, have you seen this gentleman before? It's okay, don't be afraid.

Did you see him at the mall, son?

Tommy felt like he'd been hit in the chest with a sledgehammer. He couldn't breathe.

"Tommy, please, I never meant to hurt you," she said. "I've been sketching for the police for a couple of years. Trying to get justice for people, or at least bring them peace. *They* approached *me* on this—"

"I—I can't do this right now. . . ."

She rushed forward and held his face in her hands. He hated himself for it, but he still relished her touch.

"I swear I have feelings for you. But your father took a parent from each of us, Tommy."

He wrenched away, fell back.

Can't breathe. It felt like someone had cast Suffocation on him. He needed to get out of there.

He bolted.

"Where's your mother, Tommy?" Sanse yelled, and the sound felt like a Force bolt striking him in the back.

He barely made it outside before everything in his stomach came up in a fetid rush. When he finished retching, he climbed into his car and sped away. After a few blocks, he pulled over and allowed himself to come apart. Hot tears ran down his cheeks. He sat like that for a while, feeling both guilty and like an utter fool, wondering what to do next.

After what felt like forever, he drove home.

Tommy paused outside his apartment. The last thing he wanted to do was to run a game tonight. He already felt the dark tendrils of depression enveloping him, like they had when his mother first left.

Or went missing, he corrected himself.

He just wanted to crawl into bed. He would tell them all he was sick, ask them to leave. He opened the door and noticed the light was different. He thought a bulb had burned out. His eye was drawn to the corner with the standing lamp. SuperChenz stood there, immovable, in his normal pose—hands crossed in front of his groin in the posture Tommy called the fig leaf—and his massive presence created an interior eclipse, blocking the majority of the lamp's shine. Tommy then looked to the game table. Half of the team was already seated; Anibal and Chongo had not yet arrived. Among them, making himself comfortable in Tommy's chair, the game master's chair, was his smiling father.

He'd become quickly accustomed to Big Al's warm smiles after his stint in the emergency room and the FunFunder party.

This was not one of those smiles.

"There's the little mastermind himself," said Don Fugue. "We've been waiting for you."

43

The dark lord sits in Prince Thomas's seat at the head of the scarred wooden table, assuming the throne as his own. Horns rise from his dark mane, and black velvet wings drape over the high-backed chair. His father doesn't look real, but he is somehow the realest thing in the room, as if all the shadows there have swirled together to become flesh. The dark lord offers a half smile, and Prince Thomas sees the glint of a fang.

"You have nothing to say to your father?"

"I wasn't expecting you, my lord. You did not use your sending device to warn me of your coming."

"No devices this night." The dark lord taps his pointed ear. "One never knows who listens."

The dark lord's goliath circles the table then, collecting the band's sending devices, one by one, stopping at Thomas. The prince looks from the goliath to the dark lord, then places it in the goliath's massive palm.

SuperChenz stomped off to the bedroom with the phones. Tommy looked back to his father, sitting at the head of the table, immaculate in his dark suit, the only pops of color a lavender tie and matching pocket square, tucked and folded so crisply it looked like it could draw blood. Tommy shook his head, then gave his father a comic, exaggerated stare.

"Sorry, Pop. Like seeing a teacher at a restaurant. Took a second to compute."

Porks helped him with an awkward smile. Jo looked warily from father to son and back again, reading their micro expressions for signs of impending violence. Nine stared straight down at the tabletop, like he was waiting for the executioner's axe. SuperChenz returned from the bedroom—without the phones, noticed Tommy—and took up a position in the corner, blocking a lamp and darkening the room once more.

"Take a seat," said Don Fugue.

"You're in my chair," joked Tommy.

"Oh, *forgive me*," said Don Fugue, standing with mock contrition. "Force of habit. You see, I never sit with my back to a door. I always want to keep an eye out for threats. But I guess that doesn't apply here, right?"

Tommy didn't like this at all. His father's drop-ins were rare, but not unheard of. It was the cold smiles, the ambiguous speech, the subtle mockery.

His father was playing with him. Teasing him. Like a cat with a mouse.

Or testing the fences like a velociraptor in Jurassic Park.

Moments ago, Tommy had felt like a shroud had settled around his soul. Now he felt like he had touched a live wire. The depression lifted instantly, replaced with the electric current of fear coursing through his body. Fight-or-flight.

He took his usual seat, tried not to show his fear.

"I wanted to see my investment in person," said Don Fugue. "A million and a half for this?"

He looked around at the littered game table: soda cans,

half-eaten bags of chips, stats sheets, dice, slips of scribbled-on paper, and beta versions of 3D-printed miniatures of the characters. “Not much to it.”

Another slight. At the party, Tommy had never seen his father so proud of him. In the wild fear that galloped through his chest like a band of horses, a tiny fire started. He was angry. He was tired of ambushes. And after all the work he had put in, and the danger and heartbreak and loss, he didn’t appreciate anyone running down Tergivers.

Not even his father.

“Maybe you just don’t get it.”

Tommy half expected his father to launch across the table.

“So, deal me in.”

Tommy cleared his throat. “It doesn’t work like that.”

“No cards?”

“Not how you’re thinking.”

Don Fugue thought on this, nodded. He pointed at one of the mini-figs.

“Are the LEGOs required?”

Tommy took a breath. “They’re called mini-figs. But nothing is required. All you really need is a good imagination and a set of dice.” He touched his temples and then held his hands aloft. *“Theater of the mind.”*

“I’m not a theater kind of guy.”

“The figures help you orient yourself. Where you are in relation to the rest of your party . . . It helps to calculate distances for spells. Combat can be difficult to picture.”

“For some.” Big Al picked up a mini-fig, held it up to the diminished light, and examined it. “Can you sell them?”

“One can.”

“Can *you*?”

Porks chuckled like a good little boy.

"It could be a potential revenue stream. We haven't gotten there yet."

"I thought this game was about imagination. . . ."

Jo offered a wan smile, like she'd swallowed something that didn't agree with her, then looked over at SuperChenz, who stood in the corner, as immovable and immutable as the Rockies.

"Anyway," continued Big Al, reaching into his dark jacket, "I didn't bring a figure. Will this do?"

Big Al placed a 9 millimeter pistol on the table.

Porks stopped grinning. Tommy fought not to glance at Nine to gauge his reaction. It would be a tell, a sign of guilt. His father was trying to intimidate them. The only course of action Tommy saw was to pretend it wasn't working.

"That's not permitted."

"That's the funny thing about guns: They don't ask permission." His father laughed amiably. He looked at the other players, saw they were not laughing along. "Wait, is he for real?"

"They're not in charge," said Tommy. "I am."

"Is that so?"

"I'm the lead storyteller. I'm the GM. I run the game."

"You may run the game, but I own the table."

"My game, my rules."

Big Al pursed his lips. He nodded slowly, appearing to consider this.

"Storyteller," he said finally, "I have a story. A gangster and a priest walk into the woods at night. The priest turns to the gangster and says, 'I don't like this. I don't like the woods. I'm afraid of the dark.' And the gangster turns to him and says, 'How do you think I feel? I have to walk out of here alone.' "

When no one at the table laughed, Don Fugue slammed his palm on the table. The mini-figs danced. The empty soda cans toppled. The players jumped.

"Lighten up," he bellowed. "It's a joke! It's funny, right?"

Still, no one laughed. The new player fixed his gaze on Tommy, but the smile had left his face.

"Guess you had to be there."

Tommy glanced at Jo. She met his gaze, which was as much as an acknowledgment as she could offer.

Alongside the stampede of fear, the small wildfire of anger grew.

Tommy fought to keep his voice steady and calm. Firm yet respectful. Cheerful even.

"This a fantasy game, Pop. Whoever you are does not matter. Whatever you've done does not matter. Because at this table—in my game—you can be whoever you want, do whatever you want. You can even be a hero."

Tommy's father smirked.

"But it's hard to imagine you're a cleric battling a horde of monsters when there's a real piece on the table," Tommy went on. "It kind of shatters the illusion, locks everyone up. No disrespect."

"Don't get constipated on my account." Big Al gestured toward the weapon. "Go ahead."

Tommy, holding eye contact with his father, reached for the gun. Big Al smiled as Tommy removed it and set it on the floor beside him.

"What now?" Big Al asked derisively. He had mastered saying a lot with very little. Those two simple words were both a question and a taunt.

Tommy reached back across the table and placed twin

twenty-sided dice, the same gunmetal black as the pistol, in front of his father.

"Roll for initiative."

Big Al picked the dice up, examined them. He shook them, tested their weight. Then he placed them back on the table.

"Nah. You know what? I have a better idea. Let's go for a drive."

A fresh tide of fear washed in, extinguishing Tommy's burgeoning anger.

"But, Pop . . . everyone's here . . ."

"Give them the night off. You've done that before, right?"

Tommy looked around. No one was going to come to his aid this time.

"Porks, Jo . . . you're dismissed," his father said. Everyone at the table stood, gathered their belongings, and headed for the door. "Not so fast, Nine. You hang back."

Nine returned to the table. To anyone else, Nine would have looked as calm and cool as ever, but Tommy noticed the slight slump in his posture. It was resignation. A dead man's walk.

Big Al got up and walked around, put his hands on Tommy's shoulders, gave them a firm squeeze. Then he bent over and retrieved his pistol from the floor.

"I have a surprise for you two," said Big Al.

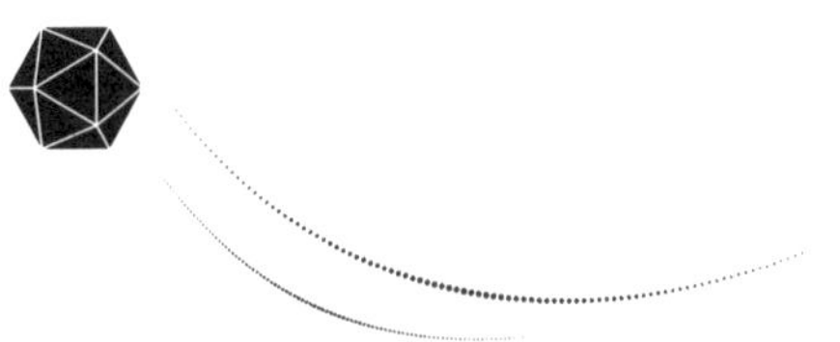

44

They got on Sixth Avenue toward I-70, SuperChenz hunched over the steering wheel of the big black SUV, Big Al in the passenger seat beside him. Tommy and Nine rode in the back. No one spoke. Gone was his father's false cheer, his menacing quips, his probing provocations. They would have been preferable to the heavy, oppressive silence that felt like an extra passenger.

Going westward, the view before the SUV was blacker than black, the foothills blotting out most of the sky ahead. As they hit 70 and climbed those foothills, Tommy could see a little more of the Rockies themselves, the ever-present sentinels that boxed him in. Then it was fully dark, and the black mountains claimed a bigger quadrant of sky; the SUV sped inexorably onward, leaving the civilization and comforting lights of Denver behind. He watched the pine trees tick by. The air grew colder, but his father made no move to correct the cabin temperature, and Tommy wasn't about to ask. He wanted to reach for his phone, call for help, but he remembered it was back in his apartment. Even if he did have it, he had no one to call and nothing concrete to tell them, only a black pit opening in his stomach.

Perhaps he should have heard the detectives out. Perhaps he was too hard on Sanse. Now, speeding west into the darkness, he would have given anything to speak with her again.

Somewhere west of Genesee, SuperChenz exited the highway. From there, he followed signs to a trailhead, and each new road constricted further until they were on a thin dirt lane, bouncing through the woods.

Tommy looked at Nine.

The soldier stared straight ahead.

Finally, the SUV ground to a stop and SuperChenz cut the engine. A deep silence rushed in, the only sound the ticking of the cooling engine and the only light the twin beams of the headlights illuminating a trail before them.

"Here we are," said Big Al, but he made no move to exit. "I know you're curious about things, Tommy. About my business."

Tommy cleared his throat. "Not really . . ."

"Today is Take Your Son to Work Day." Don Fugue turned around in his seat then. "Don't ask questions if you can't stomach the answers."

With that, he opened his door and exited the vehicle and walked away.

Tommy and Nine looked at each other.

"It'll be okay," said Tommy, low.

"No," said Nine. "It won't."

"I won't let him hurt you."

Nine took a deep breath and opened his door. Tommy got out too. Don Fugue and SuperChenz were gone, receded into the night in their dark suits. There was a spear of light then, SuperChenz activating a flashlight up ahead. In the glow, Tommy saw the two of them standing by an unmarked trailhead.

"Colorado is getting too crowded," called his father. "It's good to get away from everybody now and again."

SuperChenz set off down the trail, his bulk blocking the

beam, but Tommy could see the ambient glow bouncing off the trees on either side of the bodyguard.

As Tommy and Nine approached, Don Fugue activated his own flashlight.

"Vwoom," he said, imitating the hum of a lightsaber.

He slashed it across Tommy's body, then Nine's, making the electrical crackling sound, then chuckled to himself. For a fleeting moment, Tommy hoped his father's good cheer had returned.

"Saddle up, nerds," he said.

Tommy paused, unsure what to do. But when Nine said softly, "You heard him," they both entered the trail.

They followed the bouncing lights that were like will-o'-the-wisps beckoning them into a dark forest. It reminded Tommy of one of the earliest Tergivers sessions. He didn't think goblins would be lying in wait to tear him limb from limb.

It might be worse. And unlike that session, there would be no wizard to come to their rescue. And he doubted there was another surprise party for him at the end of the trail.

"We ain't got all fucking night, Tommy," his father called.

He rushed to catch up. Nine was close behind his father. The don walked with ease down the trail, even though he wore expensive dress shoes. Tommy got the sense that the trail was well worn. His father had been here many times before.

SuperChenz swept his flashlight back and forth like a metal detector. The trail was wide enough to allow the big man to pass, but it still felt claustrophobic. The moving lights gave the illusion that the trees were swaying, their limbs reaching out and swiping at them.

Tommy tripped and fell. Neither SuperChenz nor his father stopped or even slowed. Tommy scrabbled to his feet. When he caught up, the men had exited the trail and were standing on the edge of a meadow with tall grass. The darkness was not as oppressive here, leavened by starlight and a waxing crescent moon. Tommy let go a breath he hadn't realized he'd been holding.

Then he saw the figures in the center of the meadow.

He registered the narrow silhouette of Turdo. He saw the familiar shapes of the Johnnies, one slight, one large, standing side by side. He saw a smattering of men, some figures he recognized and some he did not. Young soldiers in tracksuits and short sleeves, unprepared for the chilly Colorado night. The sun could add twenty-five degrees to the coldest of days, but the reverse was true too. With the sun's exit, the world could get back to its true temperature. Tommy surmised the men had been up here when the sun was high. Waiting for him.

Tommy also noticed a deep, dark pool of perfect black. He saw the shovels beside it. A few stuck into the ground, poking up like empty flagpoles, the vanguard of the dark kingdom colonizing the meadow.

There was a large dirt mound, a foothill in miniature. Beside it was a large sack. When he drew closer, the sack moved, its upper half pivoting toward him. Tommy blinked. His eyes adjusted and he saw it wasn't a sack but a man on his knees. Tommy moved closer still and recognized the cargo pants and perpetually rumpled dress shirt, more rumpled than usual.

"Chongo . . ."

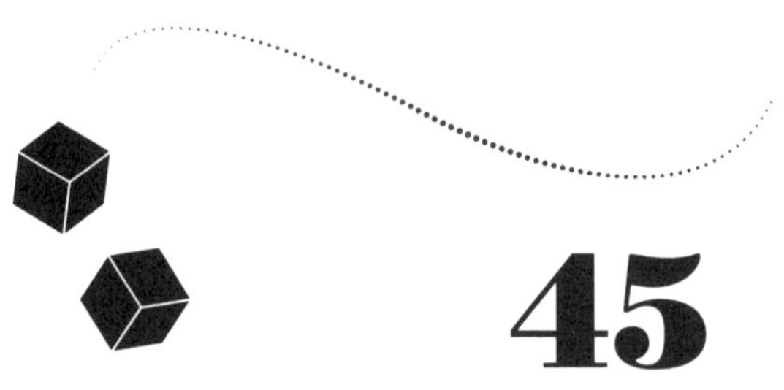

45

"Hiya, kid," said the accountant. He looked sheepish, embarrassed to be seen in such a state. His clothes were dirty and his hair was askew. And his hands were bound behind his back. The old man's voice was hoarse, too. From effort, Tommy realized with dread.

He had dug the hole.

"What's going on?" Tommy heard himself say.

At the approach of Don Fugue, the men who had been lounging or leaning against trees snapped to attention. They gathered around. There was Chongo and the hole, then there was his father pacing around both, and then a ring of men. Concentric rings. SuperChenz put a hand on Tommy's and Nine's shoulders and moved them into the innermost ring.

"What is going on, indeed?" repeated Don Fugue. "That is the question."

Solemn nods in the rings of men.

Don Fugue continued to pace.

"Boys, it is with great regret that I must inform you that Bud here has been caught skimming."

Tommy heard someone say *tsk-tsk* but couldn't tell who in the darkness.

Don Fugue halted. A stillness fell over the meadow. Even the animals quieted and the wind died in the trees.

Deep within Tommy, words formed. *It's only money*. He was working on pushing them out when his father burst into laughter.

"But who trusts an accountant who doesn't skim a little? I'd think something was wrong with him if he didn't!"

He thumped Tommy in the chest as he passed, a little too hard to feel paternal.

"That's table stakes in this thing of ours. What are you gonna do? No, we're gathered here tonight because Chongo has been talking to the cops. What do we call someone who talks to the cops?"

"Rattus norvegicus," said Johnny Reb.

"The common rat," said Johnny Socks.

"That's facts," said Don Fugue, continuing his circuit. "And not only did he talk to the cops, but he turned them on to my beloved son. My pride and joy."

Don Fugue squared up in front of Tommy.

"How long did you know she was a cop, son?"

"She's not a cop."

"Don't mince words, boy," warned Don Fugue.

"Tonight," said Tommy. "I went right home, and you were there."

"You expect me to believe that?"

"On my mother."

His father stared at him. "You should have come to me straightaway."

Then he resumed his circuit, lecturing everyone again like a malevolent professor.

"This *game*," he boomed. "It's got everyone all fucked up! So listen up! If there is an issue, if there is a concern, if there is a problem, you come to *me* right away. Do not pass Go. Do not collect two hundred dollars. Go right to *the Al Fucking Mighty*!"

The outburst echoed in the trees and stirred the night birds.

Don Fugue stared at his accountant bitterly. Chongo stared into the black hole, holding his breath.

"I'm tired of games. It's time to get back to *business*. It's time to return to first principles. Do I make myself clear?"

There were more head nods and murmurs of assent.

Don Fugue paused again in front of his son. At some point in his circuit, the pistol appeared in his hand.

"Did I ever tell you about the first time I saw *Star Wars*?"

"Yeah, Pop," said Tommy, his mouth dry. He fought back tears.

"You know, my favorite scene isn't even in that first one. It's in the *second* one."

"Empire," said Johnny Reb.

"The rare sequel that rivals the original," said Johnny Socks.

"The very one," said Big Al. "Darth Vader has Luke Skywalker out on that ledge or whatever. . . ."

He looked over at a clutch of the younger soldiers, shivering in their shirtsleeves and tracksuits. "Spoilers: Vader tells Luke that he's his father. He even offers Luke a seat at the table. Join forces, power immeasurable. They can run the whole galaxy."

He turned back to his son. "Do you remember that?"

Tommy nodded, not trusting his own voice.

"But he had to teach him a lesson first."

Tommy's eyes grew wild.

"Give me your hand, son."

Tommy shook his head.

"I promise. It won't hurt much. It'll be fine."

"No."

Don Fugue glanced over Tommy's shoulder. That's all it took. SuperChenz seized Tommy from behind. Tommy yelled and struggled, but it was like fighting the side of a building. Tommy looked down, saw his feet were off the ground. The mighty goon held him with no apparent effort.

"Nine," said Don Fugue. He jutted his chin at his flailing son. "Hit him."

"Sir?"

Don Fugue stood there, unmoving, the pistol pressed to his thigh. "I won't say it twice."

Nine squared up in front of Tommy. Tommy stopped his fighting and stared at his friend. No sooner did Tommy stop wriggling than Nine popped him in the face. It clipped Tommy's jaw. Tommy had so much adrenaline pumping he barely felt it.

"Again," said his father.

Nine threw another hook. This one caught him in the temple and his world dimmed. He fought for air, but SuperChenz's vise-like grip was relentless.

Tommy's head lolled and he blacked out for a moment.

When he comes to, Prince Thomas is still held aloft by the orc, the massive creature's limbs as unyielding as a stone wall. His head throbs. It takes him a moment to realize the orc's mighty paw is clasped around Thomas's hand, squeezing. And that something has been pressed into it, and the orc is holding it in place.

The crossbow.

An impersonal, mechanical implement, the weapon lacks the

beauty and grace of a blade. Thomas would never touch such a thing of his own free will and he wonders, in his stupor, why it is in his hand.

Garcia, the humbled druid, kneels. His tie-dye robes are spread out around him. His eyes are closed, as if in prayer. Finally, he opens them and looks up at Thomas.

"I'm really sorry, kid."

"Is it true?"

"I never meant for any of this to happen," says the druid. "You were always a nice boy."

The orc raises his hand, and with it, Thomas's hand with its crossbow.

"I don't care what you did. We have to do something!"

"Nothing to be done. Live by the sword, die by the sword."

"Please!" pleads Thomas. "Figure something out! Cast a spell!"

But Garcia is not one for conflict. He never was. He guided his fellow adventurers through the fractured realms of Tergivers, led them to food and shelter, patched their wounds after battles, entertained them with ribald tales. He doesn't deserve this.

From somewhere the druid produces a sprig of elderweed, and takes a deep inhale.

"Been waiting for the other shoe to drop for so long," he says, before blowing out a large cloud, "it's practically a relief. Maybe I'll get to see the queen again. In the next realm. I'd like to think so."

Facing death, the being of nature and friendship looks as serene as Thomas has ever seen him.

Thomas fights madly, but the orc levels his arm for him. The creature's finger, as strong as an iron prison bar, worms its way into the crossbow's trigger guard.

"No!" screams the prince.

"It's okay, kid. No hard feelings."

Just then, a flash of lightning strikes the ground.

Tommy looks toward its target. What had been a shovel, sticking out of the earth, is now a sword. It is massive and its blade glows a deep bloodred.

The Blade of Courage.

"Well," said Garcia. A wry smile lifts one corner of his mouth. "Would you look at that. . . ."

There is a deafening roar then, far more than should be produced by a crossbow. Thomas squeezes his eyes against it. A bitter tang fills the meadow. When the prince opens his eyes, Garcia is gone. Only the hole remains.

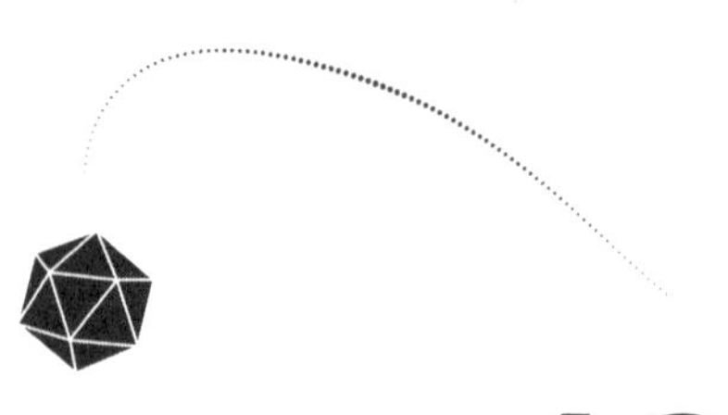

46

SuperChenz released Tommy. One moment, Tommy was held aloft, the next he was a lifeless heap on the ground. He was on his side, head in the dirt, just feet away from the hole. Tommy tried to scream, but he succumbed to shock and could not make his mouth work.

There was the snapping of fingers and then the next sound was shovel heads—manned by the young, shivering soldiers—impaling the dirt mound, followed by the deep, hollow puffs of earth landing at the bottom of the grave. And on Chongo.

From the ground, Tommy saw polished dress shoes and pant legs with razor-sharp creases approach. Don Fugue squatted in front of him, blocking his view of the morbid work.

"Darth Vader took his son's right hand for the Empire. I just took yours."

His father pulled the perfectly folded lavender pocket square from his suit jacket like a dark magician. With it, he gently plucked the pistol from his son's hand.

Tommy hadn't realized he was still clutching it.

"Not that you ever would, my son," he said, "but just in case you had a notion about talking to that pretty little bitch ever again or to her cop friends . . ." Don Fugue held the pistol gingerly in both hands on its silk-handkerchief bed in front of Tommy's face. "Well, glass houses and all that."

The corners of the handkerchief folded around the pistol, concealing it. Making it disappear.

Don Fugue nodded to SuperChenz and the man-mountain bent over, picked Tommy up, and righted him like he was nothing more than a toppled mini-fig. Tommy's legs were still shaky, but Nine moved in beside him, in case he might fall.

Don Fugue looked at the two of them for a moment.

"Come on," he said, and started back toward the hole in the trees that marked the trail.

SuperChenz followed.

Tommy started to walk, but he had only made it a few steps before he bent at the waist and threw up in the tall grass. After throwing up leaving Sanse's loft, there was only bile left.

Nine moved to help him, but Tommy swatted his hand away. As soon as he was able, he stood straight, wiped his mouth, and took a deep breath of mountain air. They marched on in silence.

When they reached the SUV, it was already idling, SuperChenz behind the wheel, and Don Fugue in the passenger seat. No sooner had Tommy and Nine climbed in than the bodyguard rocketed forward, spraying twin jets of dirt behind them into the red glow of their taillights.

They rode in silence. Tommy didn't look at Nine, but as they graduated from dirt road to paved backroad to highway, to Denver and civilization and safety, Tommy noted in his peripheral vision that the young soldier's shoulders had relaxed slightly.

Finally, they arrived in front of Tommy's apartment.

The SUV idled. His father did not turn around.

"Rebellion cannot be tolerated."

But after the line, Don Fugue's voice softened again, like it had in the emergency room and the surprise party. Just another loving father imparting wisdom and solace after grounding his son. Another teachable moment: "I don't expect you to understand, but one day soon, I promise you will."

This hurts me more than it hurts you.

Finally, to Nine, he said, "Clean him up."

And then Tommy and the soldier were on the sidewalk and the SUV was gone.

47

"Did you know that was going to happen?" asked Tommy.

"Get inside," said Nine.

"Did you fucking know?" he raged.

Tommy knew the soldier didn't want to have this conversation on the street. He didn't care.

"No," said Nine finally. "I knew something bad was going to happen. To be honest, I thought it was going to be me in that hole."

Tommy stared him down, but he knew it was true. Nine was unresponsive in the SUV on the way into the foothills, practically catatonic, speeding to what he thought was his doom.

The soldier pointed to Tommy's face. "Sorry about that."

They were both on thin ice with Don Fugue. But Nine wasn't the man's son, so his ice was thinner. He did what he had to do in that meadow to stay alive. Tommy didn't like it, but he understood.

"Your hands are dirty, Tommy," said Nine.

"Fuck you. That was against my will, and you know it."

"No, they're literally dirty."

Tommy looked down but didn't see anything on his hands.

"Gunpowder. Traces. Don Fugue said we have to clean you up. Don't touch anything."

Nine let himself into Tommy's apartment and led him past the game table. The soldier continued to the rear of the apartment and the bathroom. He turned the faucet on and waited for steam to rise from the sink.

"Wash your hands," said Nine. He shoved past Tommy and paced outside the bathroom door while he waited.

But Tommy wasn't done raging.

"Chongo wasn't some imaginary goblin, Nine. He was our *friend*."

Nine shuddered then, but he said, "Friends don't rat out friends." Almost as if Tommy wasn't there and he was arguing with himself. Like he was still in the back of the SUV. Or standing in the meadow, staring at the hole.

"So, he deserved to die?"

"This isn't a game, Tommy. And I'm not your fucking playmate. I'm not Macarro, okay? In the real world, I work for your father. My first loyalty is to him, understand? I'm whatever *he* needs me to be."

Tommy didn't care.

"You're nothing but a tool to him, Nine. He'll use you, until you get dull or break or he finds a sharper, shinier tool, and then he'll throw you away without a second thought. It's what he does. Like Chongo. *Like my mother*."

Tommy couldn't believe he'd finally said it out loud, but there it was. Tommy was still reeling with his own revelation when Nine exploded.

"Will you please just wash your fucking hands already?"

Tommy complied. The fight was already leaving him. His head felt thick, battered by betrayals and numb from the fatigue. He lathered up and scrubbed vigorously. Beside him again, Nine rummaged through Tommy's bathroom cabinet. When Tommy had dried his hands, Nine handed over nail clippers.

"Over the toilet," ordered the soldier.

Tommy squatted in front of the toilet and trimmed his nails. As he did so, Nine turned on the shower. More steam filled the bathroom. When Tommy was finished with his nails, Nine said, "In," and walked out.

Tommy stripped and got into the scalding shower.

Through the door, he heard, "Scrub your hands again. The nail beds, the fingertips, between your fingers."

Tommy didn't move. He just let the hot water wash over his head, his shoulders. Whatever had been powering him through the night finally gave way. He imagined his energy washing right off and swirling down the drain. It had only been hours since Sanse revealed she was working with the police. That Tommy himself had marked her father for death. It felt like weeks. And now Chongo, his uncle, was dead by Tommy's own hand.

The cops had gotten to his uncle too. All to target his damn father.

They could have the bastard for all Tommy cared.

"I tried . . ." On the other side of the shower curtain, Tommy heard Nine clear his throat. "I tried to knock you out. So you wouldn't have to . . . you know. So you *wouldn't be able* to . . . I really tried."

The tears came then. Tommy opened his mouth and racking sobs came out. He didn't care if Nine could hear him or not, but at last he picked up the bar of soap as he had been told and scrubbed his fingertips where the trimmed nails revealed thin crescents of exposed skin.

When he climbed out of the shower, Nine was by the toilet,

scrubbing the floor and looking for stray nail clippings. The reek of bleach filled the bathroom.

"Leave the towels," said Nine. "I'll take them."

"Go easy on the bleach," said Tommy.

"He said to clean you up."

Tommy stared at the young soldier. He had always looked at him as an older brother, though he never would have admitted it to him. Tommy had never once wanted to be like his father, but he admired Nine Ball. Cool and detached, and where Tommy floated through the world, Nine sliced through it like a shark. More than admiring the soldier, Tommy aspired to be like him.

Now, as he watched Nine on his hands and knees, scrubbing feverishly and pressing his face to the floor to spy for nail clippings, he saw that the young acolyte was just another bent soul twisted to his father's will and losing the battle with his own demons. He wasn't cool. He was broken.

"Nine," he said softly. "No one is coming."

But Nine wasn't listening. He continued scrubbing, the trash bag beside him filling up with wet paper towels.

"Clean you up," muttered Nine. "He said to clean you up."

Tommy walked past him and into the bedroom, where he knew sleep would not find him.

48

Sleep did find him, and the next morning Tommy awoke to heavy pounding on his door.

It was like he had simply blinked out of existence. There were no dreams. No reliving his losing struggle against SuperChenz, no replaying his dead uncle pitched into a hole in the earth, no morbid extrapolations such as a zombified Chongo clawing his way out of his grave seeking retribution. There had been no nightmares at all—*the first night's free,* thought Tommy—but the knowledge waited for him as soon as he opened his eyes, like a hound at the foot of his bed, eager to be fed.

The pounding.

Nine, thought Tommy.

But as Tommy passed into the living room, he found Nine stirring on the couch. Nine looked rumpled and not well rested. The idea of the fastidious soldier spending the night on the couch in Tommy's oft-derided apartment was more fantastical than any of Macarro's feats in Tergivers, but there he was. It spoke to Nine's general state of exhaustion. But when he glanced around, Tommy noticed the apartment was spotless. It hadn't even looked this clean the day he'd moved in.

More heavy pounding.

Nine swung his feet to the floor and reached for the pistol

that sat within reach on the coffee table. His hand was bright red from the bleach.

With his other scorched hand, Nine held his finger to his lips. *Be quiet.*

Nine padded to the peephole in his socks, elbow bent, pistol pointed at the ceiling at the high ready. He peered through and let the gun fall.

“It’s the gorilla,” he said, and tucked the pistol behind him.

“What the fuck is he doing here?” asked Tommy. He backed away from the door.

“Relax,” said Nine. “If he was going to do anything, it would’ve happened last night.”

Nine opened the door.

SuperChenz stood there, blocking the sunlight, with a pair of normal-size soldiers flanking him. The monstrous bodyguard stared at Nine for a moment, then ducked his head beneath the doorframe to enter. When he saw Tommy, his eyes lit up.

“Hey, little man,” said SuperChenz cheerfully, as if last night had never occurred. “Your pop wants you home for a while. What with all the crazy on the streets, you know? Safer that way, bruh.”

Tommy thought he could not feel worse after Sanse and Chongo, but now his father was taking away the last scrap of freedom Tommy still possessed.

“I . . . I can’t,” he said.

“That’s okay. These two can help you pack what you need. It’ll just be for a little while.”

“No, I mean I have commitments. I have Tergivers sessions to run.”

It sounded stupid even to him, but he wasn’t thinking clearly or quickly, and it was the first thing that popped into his head.

SuperChenz brightened, so very happy to be helpful. "Don't worry about that, Tommy Gun! Your father's already thought of everything."

Then he turned to his two companions, clad in tracksuits, and pointed to the game table. "Box it up."

One soldier began to sweep the dice and miniatures into a duffel bag while the other grabbed the character sheets and notes, crumpling them.

"Whoa!" yelled Tommy, rushing forward. "*Take it easy!*"

SuperChenz reached out and smacked the soldier with the papers on the back of the head.

"Be careful! Tommy here is a certified genius for real."

He turned back to Tommy. "Don't worry, little bro. I got you. Oh, I almost forgot. Your pop wanted me to give this back."

SuperChenz handed over a phone to Tommy.

Tommy stared at the new device and tried to give it back. "This isn't mine."

"It is now. Don't worry, same number, same everything. Just a little more airtight."

"What about me?" asked Nine.

SuperChenz looked at Nine like he had forgotten he was there.

"What about you?"

That evening, Tommy looked around the dining room table in his father's home. Though he had grown up there, the dining room was as foreign a room in the house as could be. As a family, on those instances when he and his mother and father ate together, they took their meals at the kitchen table. The dining room was reserved for his father's meetings or giant holiday parties, where Tommy was meant to be the ornamental child of a mob king and his queen.

He could not think of a more stultifying room.

The game grid, which had dominated the game table in his apartment, looked like a small island on the polished wood. It made Tergivers—a land of infinite imagination and possibility—feel small. It made Tommy feel foolish.

From the head of the table, he took note of his fellow adventurers. They looked equally miserable.

To his right, Porks squirmed like a child, swiveling in his oversize chair and craning his neck every few minutes to survey the large ornate room. It was obvious he had not spent much time here, if any. Vittoria had put up with all manner of gangsters coming in and out of her home at all hours—that was part of the package of being a Mafia don's wife—but she had clearly drawn the line at strip club proprietors and pimps. Beside Porks sat Jo, ramrod straight in the high-backed chair, her glass of wine carefully centered on a coaster. With her perfect posture and bearing, it was like Bellarmina the knight had switched places with her.

To Tommy's left, Nine was slumped in his chair, exhausted and sullen. Even Macarro was paralyzed; the character could barely take two steps without Nine rolling for agility checks and peppering Tommy with questions about the landscape and their marching order. It put Tommy in mind of the mountains, of stumbling along in the dark, horrified at what he had seen. Of what he'd done. He stifled a shudder.

There were several empty chairs at the long table, but the one next to Nine sat like a vacuum or a low-pressure system. Their eyes all stole glances at it; clearly their thoughts swirled around it. Bands of repudiation lashed at them all in waves.

Every few minutes, a young, tracksuited soldier wandered past the doorway. Tommy wondered if he was meant to protect or intimidate the party. He wondered if Nine was angered by his presence, or jealous.

There was no point arguing with reality, so he decided he might as well begin.

He gestured toward the empty chair and cleared his throat. "Chongo won't be joining us anymore—"

"Tommy," said Jo softly.

"We know, kid," said Porks, matter-of-fact.

"We need . . ." began Tommy, and tears welled in his eyes before he knew what was happening. He rubbed his forehead to cover his face, but his voice cracked. "We need to talk about Garcia."

With that, he broke down. He felt a hand squeeze his arm and was surprised to find it was Jo.

Another guard walked by, peered inside.

Nine got to his feet. "What the fuck are you looking at? Keep moving, bitch!"

The young guard snorted. He had been one of the ones manning a shovel the night before. His lip curled over his teeth in a sneer. He leaned against the doorframe, planting himself.

"Get out of my eyeline, junior," said Jo, "or I'll gut you where you stand."

The guard suddenly stopped smiling. He disappeared as quickly as if she had cast Banishment.

"The next wave," grunted Nine. "No fucking respect."

The small exchange allowed Tommy to recover. He wiped his eyes, then cleared his throat.

"We have a few options. We can make him an NPC that stays with the party. He can retire from adventuring and go back to his forest to commune with nature. Or he can die in battle or off-screen. We can even hold an in-game funeral for him. But I don't want to just *decide*. I want it to be all of us. Together."

Jo took a gulp from her wineglass. "I don't fucking know. Whatever you think is best."

Nine shrugged. "I don't care."

Porks remained silent.

"Come on, guys. I know it's trivial with everything going on. . . ." He looked back toward the empty doorway. "It began with the five of us, and I don't know how else to honor him."

"Honor him?" said Porks. *"Honor him?"*

The diminutive pimp wiggled out of the large chair, bumping the table and knocking over the mini-figs. When he finally extricated himself, he yelled, "Are you *fucking serious,* kid? I don't even want to acknowledge the son of a bitch. I vote we pretend he was never even here. But if we don't, then I say Garcia the high holy wizard goes out just like the motherfucking rat who played him."

The man's sudden vehemence took everyone aback.

"Jesus, Porks, the kid's just trying to be nice," said Jo.

"Yeah, well, fuck that. I'd be more than happy for Bradford to behead the duplicitous druid with the Blade of Wisdom."

"Spoken like someone who never got their hands dirty in real life," said Jo.

Porks waved away the barb.

"There's a *code*. You know that better than anyone, Stinger."

Jo stared into her wineglass. She had no retort for that.

Porks turned to Tommy. "He didn't just betray the Family, he betrayed Tergivers," he said, sweeping his hands over the grid spread out on the table. "He betrayed Bradford and Macarro and Bellarmina. Let me tell you about the man you're all boo-hooing over. Who do you think tipped off the cops about our first night off?"

"What do you mean?" asked Tommy.

"Do you think your little girlfriend just *happened* to text that night? And she just happened to suggest a comedy club, where this one over here pretends she's Sarah Fucking Silverman?"

Jo glared at Porks.

"Oh yeah, I know all about your little hobby. The problem is so did Chongo, who spilled it to the cops, who then had their girl call Tommy. Who the hell knows what you were blurting onstage? Thank God it was probably just the drunken garbage you usually spout. And by the way, if these sessions are any indication, you're about as funny as cancer of the prick."

Jo rose slowly from her chair. Tommy and Nine tensed. It was a dangerous thing to push Jo Galliano, and Porks had crossed a line. But the squat little man pressed on.

"Come *on*, you two!" he shouted. "Didn't that seem a little too convenient? A little too much of a coincidence?"

Jo still looked at him with murder in her eyes, but she remained rooted to the spot.

"And I overheard Chongo tell that idiot hayseed about the T-shirts. Chongo told him exactly what to put on them—the logo, the colors, everything. Even where to get them . . . deep into Delgado territory. I didn't think nothing of it at the time, but putting two and two together, all that was fucking catnip for the Rolling 30s."

Tommy and Nine shared a glance. Both of them looked back toward the doorway. A new soldier passed, peered in, but kept moving. Jo took her seat again, practically collapsing into it with the revelation of the full depth of Chongo's betrayal.

"Everyone runs their mouths around good old Porks. People just love to underestimate me. Think I'm a clown. Or the worst, pretend I'm not even there, beneath their notice. *Oh, don't worry, that's just Porks.* But everyone makes the same mistake: They think I traffic in women, but what I really traffic in is information."

He turned to Tommy with a rueful smile.

"Everyone except for your father. Don Fugue is a very smart man, and game recognizes game. He had his suspicions that he had a leaky boat, and asked if I might join this merry little band, keep my eyes and ears open. And sure enough, I struck gold."

He jerked a stubby thumb at his chest.

"*I* found the rat. . . . *Me.*"

Tommy stared at Porks in horror. Yet another informant in their midst. Was anyone in his life who they appeared to be?

"Why would Chongo do it? Why set up Todd? Why set me up?"

Porks shrugged. "Who knows why rats do what they do? Tell me," taunted the pimp, "have you seen your farm boyfriend lately?"

Tommy cleared his throat and tried to play it nonchalant. "The other night. He's heading home for the summer."

Porks nodded with mock gravity as he pretended to absorb the new information. "That's funny. Word out on the street is the 30s rolled him up."

"I don't know what to tell you."

He leered at Nine. "I also heard some smooth talkers got him back."

Tommy and Nine stared at Porks, who looked only delighted with himself. A Cheshire cat grin with a pair of sparrows caught in his teeth. In Tommy's peripheral vision, he noticed Jo looking from man to man, her brow knitted, wondering what the hell was going on.

"The thing with information is," said Porks, "having it makes you smart. But knowing when to share it, and more importantly, when not to share it? That's *real* wisdom, Tommy."

Tommy couldn't know just how much Porks knew. Did he know Anibal's real identity? It wouldn't take much, so it was possible. More than possible. But he couldn't have known about Tommy's negotiations with Emiliano, could he?

Regardless, it sure as hell sounded like a veiled threat.

Before he could respond, Jo leaned forward and put her elbows on the table. She cracked her knuckles.

"If you're so wise, troll, you'd know it was time to shut your fucking mouth already."

He held up his hands. "Sure thing, Stinger. That's enough fun for one session. I gotta get back to the club anyway. Tommy, I'd check on your farm boy. If I was in Chongo's spot, and I'm sure glad I'm not, I wouldn't have wanted any loose ends."

He headed for the doorway, then thought better of it. "How's this? How about Garcia just disappears. One day, he's here. The next . . . just gone. Just like in real life, yeah? These things happen, and everyone moves on. It's for the best. What do you say, Tommy?"

Porks stared at him, smirking.

Tommy stared back, seething but helpless.

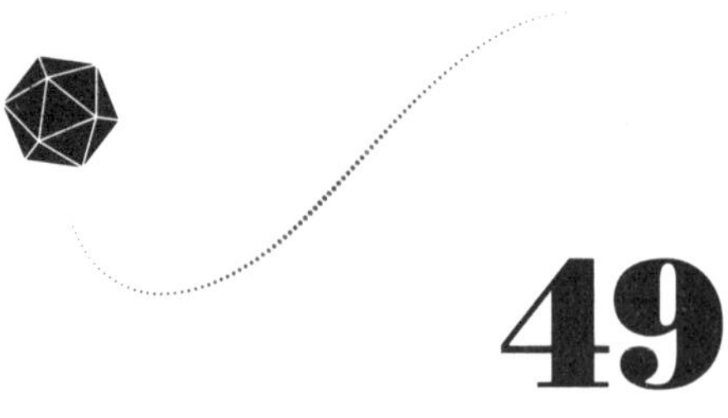

49

Posters of superheroes and manga and sci-fi movies on the walls, Lego builds and busts of favorite characters on shelves—most of the same accessories still adorned Tommy's bedroom as when he left. When his father had finally relented and let him go to college and get his own apartment, Tommy didn't waste a lot of time packing. When you have a chance at escape, you don't stop to collect your personal belongings. You pull the rip cord, ride that big yellow evacuation slide to safety, and run like hell from the burning wreckage.

But now he was back, stuck in the same old cell of his childhood prison, like the past year had never happened at all.

If he was being honest, he wished it hadn't.

His father had finally, irrevocably, revealed himself to be the devil he truly was. He had taken out his friend, using his own son as the murder weapon, before taking the literal murder weapon for "safekeeping." It was no longer difficult to imagine how his mother disappeared. What Tommy had kept deeply under wraps, buried in a dark corner in his mind, was now pushed to the fore. The subtext was text. His father killed her. Tommy didn't just want to hurt Big Al; he wanted to destroy him.

But he couldn't hurt his father, not really. He knew that. When it came to his father, despite all his rage, he was still just a nerd in a cage. He couldn't take Don Fugue head-on. Not yet.

But Porks? He could fuck with Porks.

He could hurt the pimp.

Everyone did what his father told them to do, but Porks reveled in it. Tonight, he lorded his information over Tommy with glee. And he was going to blackmail Tommy with it.

Deep inside Tommy's chest, his tiny spark reignited. He was so tired of feeling weak, of feeling scared, of waiting for a hundred different shoes to drop, that he welcomed the spark. He cupped his hand around it and gave it gentle puffs of encouragement. He lay on his bed, staring at the ceiling until it grew into a brushfire. Tommy imagined it becoming a conflagration, turning everything in its path to ash.

He sprang from the bed then and threw open the doors to his closet. He found a black suit on a hanger. Seeing it only added fuel to the fire. He had learned in philosophy class that it was easier to feel anger than heartbreak.

Because anger felt good.

No matter how many tracksuited young goons patrolled the hallways, and despite his feelings about the place, this house was Tommy's boyhood home. He knew it better than just about anyone. He opened his door and peered down the long dark hallway, half expecting to see a guard posted by his door. But Tommy wasn't a prisoner, not literally. Or at least not yet, anyway. He crept down the wide staircase. From the kitchen, he heard the banter of the new crop of soldiers. Boisterous laughter that signaled Don Fugue was not currently home. That made things a little easier.

Tommy could have crossed the wide foyer to the front door and outside, where his car was parked, but there would be two armed guards there for sure, and another two in the gatehouse.

Perhaps they would let him pass. More likely, they would politely insist he return to the house.

Sorry, sir. Don Fugue's orders.

Tommy eschewed the front door and his car beyond it and retreated deeper into the first floor, slipping from room to room, toward the rear of the house. He opened the sliding glass door that emptied onto the patio and poked his head through, looking for figures or movement. There was no one on the patio. At the edge of it was a massive in-ground pool. The water glowed a deep red, from fiber-optic lights rimming the pool beneath the surface. Tommy watched the red slowly turn to orange. Then the orange turned to yellow, and the yellow became green, then blue, then indigo, and violet. The violet then softened to red again, and Tommy set off across the sweeping backyard as the entire spectrum repeated itself languidly.

There were trees that stood at intervals at the fence, which Tommy had used on those occasions when he snuck out as a child. He had a favorite and headed for it. He was almost there when a pair of sentries crossed the lawn with their flashlights.

Tommy ducked behind the trunk of the tree. The flashlights weren't shining directly toward him but started at the far corner of the sprawling grounds. Tommy blew out a silent breath. They weren't looking for him. It was just a perimeter check. He climbed the tree quickly, remembering the handholds and footholds from his youth, made slightly more difficult in dress shoes, but he found himself at the top of the wide, high wall in seconds. He spotted the first quarter moon, fuller and brighter than the night before, then dropped over into another rich neighbor's yard. He waited for the men to pass on the other side of the thick wall, their voices fading and the glow of their flashlights bobbing along, then sprinted across the neighbor's back lawn.

Only when Tommy was a few blocks away did he order an Uber. It arrived within minutes and dropped him at his apartment. He fit the key into the lock and nearly cried with relief when he entered. It had only been less than a day, but it felt like seeing a long-lost friend. This was his home. He gazed at his game table, which should have been littered with Tergivers paraphernalia, swept clean.

Angry again, he gathered some supplies into his backpack and ordered another ride.

After a few more stops, the last Uber dropped him several blocks from his final destination.

The Fuzzy Navel.

He walked the rest of the way, a shadow slicing through the night. One block out, he donned the samurai mask from Sanse's party. He'd felt like an idiot the last time he wore it. Slides and pajama bottoms and an old hoodie. Now as he fit it over his face—horned and fanged and bloodred—it no longer felt like a costume. It felt like an extension of him. No longer was he an NPC or a gullible fool or even Prince Thomas, the hapless and helpless scion of a dark king.

He was a smartly dressed demon on a mission of vengeance.

He waited in the dark of an alley across the street, taking station in a small, fenced-in square with a dumpster for company. He peered through the fence as the hours ticked by. His fury kept him warm and focused . . . for the first hour. Sometime during the second, his purpose ebbed. Deep into that second hour, he started to feel foolish. Nagging thoughts strafed like low-flying airplanes overhead, dumping water on his burning forest fire.

You're fooling yourself.

You're just a boy in a suit, playing dress-up.

You even brought a mask.

His phone buzzed. An incoming text.

Tommy, I'm sorry how it all went down. I never meant to hurt you. I have feelings for you too. I need to talk to you.

The text from Sanse reminded him of the stakes, made him doubt himself more. *What am I doing out here?* he thought.

Then the next text came in like another wide-bodied plane, dipping just above the flames, and opened its belly. But instead of water, it emptied gasoline onto the blaze.

Please, Tommy. Todd never made it to Kansas.

The sudden influx of rage made Tommy grab the fence to steady himself. He took deep breaths through his nose, blew them out roughly through his mouth to get ahold of himself. When he got his vision cleared, he saw Fiona, Fallon, and Merry exit through the front doors of the Fuzzy Navel with a bouncer. The bouncer bent back toward the front door, fit a key into the lock, and escorted the Strippers Three to the nearly empty parking lot. The bouncer watched each woman get into her car and exit the lot. When the last dancer drove away, he folded himself into his SUV and left as well.

With that, the lot was vacant. No sign of Porks or his car.

Tommy threw open the gate and strode across the street. He followed the facade of the building until the adjoining alley, then walked along the club's wall until he found a small window just overhead. He leapt up, boosted himself on the sill, and peered in. It looked like an office.

Porks's lair.

There were lots of papers on his desk. Sloppy bookkeeping. Even better.

Tommy hopped back down and retrieved the crowbar from

his backpack. He swung it over his head, squeezing his eyes shut as he did so. He heard a pleasing tinkling sound, felt the patter of shattered glass against his resin mask. After all this time creating, it felt good to break something.

He waited for an alarm. None sounded. That didn't mean a silent alarm had not triggered. He needed to move quickly.

Still, he had to be careful with his next step. The mason jar, the gasoline, and the wick. He lit it with great care. He was no revolutionary. He barely had experience with lighting a grill, let alone a Molotov cocktail. The last thing he needed was to catch his sleeve on fire and burn to death in the alley beside his father's strip club. That was not the revenge he was hoping for.

He pitched it carefully through the broken window.

He heard it smash on the inside, and waited.

Finally, he heard a *fwump*. Like the sound of a gas burner lighting after several seconds of ticking. A moment later, a warm glow emanated from the Fuzzy Navel's office.

Tommy smiled and jogged back up the alley.

As he crossed the street, he heard the peals of smoke alarms.

On the far sidewalk, passing the dumpster, he turned and allowed himself one final look at the club. The warm glow had reached the second floor's windows. Tendrils of smoke curled upward from the alley. It was a beautiful sight. On a winter's night, it might even look welcoming.

Tommy didn't kid himself that the loss of a single establishment would be a critical hit to his father's criminal empire, but he still had a modifier or two up his sleeve. He might be able to pull off a dirty 20 yet.

It was time to send some emails. It was time to get New York involved.

The building burned, the demon mask frozen in a garish smile.

50

Despite his lack of sleep, Tommy got out of bed feeling energized. He showered, dressed in slacks and a crisp dress shirt, and headed to the kitchen for coffee. The number of soldiers milling around the house had doubled overnight, but there was no more boisterous laughter. It was as if the grand parquet floors were covered in eggshells.

"Morning, everyone," he said. He smiled as brightly as morning on the prairie.

The three goons in the kitchen flinched at the sudden noise of it.

"Why the long faces, gang?"

"Your father . . ." ventured the most senior soldier, "isn't having a great day."

"Been there," said Tommy. "Where is he?"

"Study."

"Perfect." Tommy set off in the direction of the study.

"Now might not be the best time, Mr. Fugue. . . ."

"Who knows?" said Tommy over his shoulder. "Maybe I can cheer him up."

Tommy strolled down the hallway to his father's lair. He noticed over a dozen surrendered cell phones on the console table along the wall, a product of his father's increasing paranoia.

The door to the study was closed, but he heard his father's voice inside. It was raised, barking orders, and punctuated by curses. As a boy, and even as recently as a week ago, if he'd heard such a commotion inside his father's study he'd know to get away, as fast and as far away as possible.

Today, he rolled his shoulders back, fixed a smile, and strolled inside.

Unlike Emiliano Delgado's warm study—rich and inviting like a wizard's library—his father's was cold. Sleek and austere, its color palette consisted of gray with black accents, metallics and leather. The only decorations were the framed movie posters on the wall: a sinister-looking Jimmy Cagney clutching a revolver from *Angels With Dirty Faces*; the Holy Trinity of Ray Liotta, Robert De Niro, and Joe Pesci from *Goodfellas*; and a new one Tommy had never seen before: a close-up of Darth Vader, pointing at the viewer, with the slogan YOUR EMPIRE NEEDS YOU.

This morning, the study was standing room only with gangsters. His father sat behind his black desk, ready to spring from his seat. Turdo was there, the two Johnnies too. Half a dozen other captains and lieutenants stood around them in a ring. Beside the door, looming like a plinth, was SuperChenz.

"Hiya, Tommy," the giant whispered, still cheerful.

"Hiya, Chenz."

With everyone else, Tommy's entrance produced the same effect as a record scratch. Most of the men froze. All talk ceased immediately.

Tommy realized he hadn't actually seen his father since that night in the meadow. The chief luxury of living in a mansion was that there was plenty of space to avoid the people you shared it with.

Don Fugue looked at him briefly, then said, "Now's not a good time."

With that, he turned his attention back to his coterie, already preparing his next verbal salvo.

Tommy didn't move. "I'm here to learn," he stated. He said it as clearly and powerfully as he could without risking disrespect.

He sensed the tension of the men in the study ratcheting tighter as Don Fugue scrutinized his son from behind the desk, his eyes narrowed, his lips parted. Everyone expected a squall. But Tommy understood one thing they didn't: Every father is cursed with ego, and none more so than Don Alessandro Fugue. What father doesn't want his son to follow in his footsteps?

Don Fugue raised his chin as he continued to examine his son. Finally, he said, "No phones."

"I left it in my room, Pop."

"Even so. Chenz."

SuperChenz patted Tommy down quickly, and surprisingly gently, with hands the size of dinner plates.

The plinth returned to his original position. He gave his boss a quick nod, then resumed the fig leaf stance.

Don Fugue turned to the Johnnies. "Sitrep."

Johnnie Reb began the situation report. "Sometime last night, after closing, some prick firebombed the Navel. Porks is still there, talking to the fire department."

Tommy fixed the appropriate amount of alarm to his face as his father watched him.

Johnny Socks chimed in. "Don't know yet if it can be salvaged, or if it needs to be torn down. Regardless, it's out of commission for a year. At least."

"That's unacceptable," said Big Al. "The Navel brought in

a lot of revenue, both legit and otherwise. He may not look like much, but Porks earned. I want contractors on-site before the smoke clears."

"Yes, Don Fugue," said the Johnnies in unison.

"Was anyone hurt?" asked Tommy.

Another record scratch. Everyone's heads swiveled toward him again, their expressions running the gamut.

Appreciation from the Johnnies. *Kind of you to ask.*

Apprehension from the capos. *It's best not to speak out of turn.*

Irritation from Turdo. *Who fucking cares?*

And concentration from his father. Trying to override his default setting of *Kids should be seen and not heard* with the young man before him who, despite some missteps, voluntarily walked into his study and spoke with his whole-ass chest.

"No casualties," said Johnny Reb.

"This time," added Johnny Socks.

"This isn't petty vandalism anymore," said Don Fugue. "This is a serious escalation. Those Rolling 30s fucks would not pull something like this without the express permission of Delgado. That bastard gave the go-ahead, I can feel it."

Tommy made sure not to react. He knew the blame would most likely fall to Emiliano Delgado. He didn't like it, but he just needed to buy himself time.

"Why does anyone ever step out of line?" asked Turdo. "They sense *weakness.*"

Big Al gave his second-in-command a murderous look.

Turdo held his hands up. "No one here is saying that, Don Fugue. But for some reason, the Delgados are interpreting it as such. Before, the 30s were merely probing. When we didn't immediately react, they felt emboldened. Now," said Turdo, looking over his shoulder and scanning the room until his gaze found

Tommy, "maybe they feel our eyes are off the ball. And we find war at our doorstep. We must retaliate."

"'The greatest victory is that which requires no battle,'" said Tommy.

Turdo's lips curled back in a sneer, which he quickly covered with a chuckle. "I didn't know they taught Advanced Gang Warfare at UC these days. All due respect, Tommy, that's a lovely sentiment and all, but we're dealing with real problems here."

"Sentiment?" Tommy laughed. It was a loud, good-natured laugh that filled the room. "That's not me, Uncle Mikey, that's Sun Tzu!"

Tommy walked deeper into room, head up and chest out, moving with the confidence of someone with nothing left to lose.

"I'll admit that UC does not teach Advanced Gang Warfare, but they do teach philosophy." Tommy looked at the Johnnies. "Surely you guys know Sun Tzu."

The consiglieri shared a look.

"Chinese military general and strategist," muttered Johnny Reb.

"Wrote *The Art of War*, dating back to the fifth century BC," added Johnny Socks.

"How many defeats did Sun Tzu suffer?" asked Tommy.

"Zero," said Reb. "He was a real one."

"*The* OG," said Socks.

"*The Art of War* has been dropping bangers for two thousand five hundred years," said Tommy. "Like 'He will win who knows when to fight and when not to fight.'"

Tommy began to stalk the room, his energy building. He paced in front of the capos like a drill instructor at inspection. "And 'Who wishes to fight must first count the cost. . . .'"

Don Fugue looked on silently, eyes narrowed.

"And 'There is no instance of a nation benefitting from prolonged warfare.'"

"So, you propose we do nothing?" asked Turdo, incredulous. "Is that your solution?"

This elicited the quickest of sideways glances from Don Fugue, but Turdo was too busy challenging Tommy to notice.

"I'm just asking you to apply some lateral thinking."

"The fuck is that?"

"Let him finish," said Don Fugue.

"Apologies, Don Fugue," said Turdo quietly.

"Lateral thinking is solving problems indirectly. Creatively, instead of step-by-step logic. Right now, you have a few data points." Tommy moved his fingers like he was holding an invisible ball, bouncing from one instance to the next in a straight line. "The Rolling 30s tagged a building with some graffiti . . . they busted a window . . . they took a shot at Nine. . . . Step-by-step logic would dictate these are all connected and you should respond accordingly, which would further escalate the situation. But what if the firebomb was unconnected?

"What if it was a disgruntled customer? Though I'm sure the Navel's clientele are solid, upstanding citizens and not at all creeps," he said, rolling his eyes for effect, "there might be a few rotten apples. Maybe one of the girls shot down an incel who holds a grudge? I know the club would never *officially* deal in narcotics, but perhaps someone felt shortchanged? Hell, listen to me and my unconscious bias. Maybe it had nothing to do with the Navel's clientele at all. It could've been some religious freak on a crusade. I'm just saying you don't have to attend every war you're invited to."

Tommy wound up beside Turdo.

"But what do I know? I'm just a college boy whose lateral thinking earned 1.6 million dollars."

Don Fugue leaned forward in his chair and steepled his fingers.

"Interesting theories. Generous even. But what if it *is* exactly what it looks like? What if it is an attack? What does Sun Tzu have to say about that?"

Tommy approached his father's desk.

"'Let your plans be dark and impenetrable as night, and when you move, fall like a thunderbolt.'"

Don Fugue reclined in his chair.

Finally, he smiled. "Take five, everyone. Tommy, you stay."

The capos and soldiers at the back of the room filed out wordlessly, SuperChenz urging them forward, reminding Tommy of a snowplow, clearing everything from its path. The Johnnies nodded at Tommy and headed for the door as well. Turdo, the last to leave, glared one last time over his shoulder before sealing the door behind him.

Father and son were alone.

"Late bloomer," said Don Fugue.

Tommy narrowed his eyes and cocked his head at this.

"The chip." Don pointed at Tommy's shoulder. "Was starting to wonder when it would show. But you're a Fugue, so it was inevitable, I guess."

"Believe it or not, Pop, I don't love getting talked down to. Especially in front of an audience."

"A healthy dose of *fuck you* is powerful rocket fuel for a man. They really teach you that Sun Tzu stuff in school?"

"Wait until I tell you about the Stoics. They'll blow your hair back."

Don Fugue pushed himself up from his chair and walked around the front of his desk, drawing closer to his son.

Fresh fear, like ice water, flowed through Tommy. But he held his ground.

"Look, son. About the . . . *unpleasantness* the other night . . ."

Oh, you mean when you put a gun in my hand and made me murder my uncle? That unpleasantness?

The twin points of Tommy's jaw flared. He didn't try to hide it. He wasn't auditioning for the role of sycophant. He was trying to earn his father's trust again, because earning trust meant getting closer, getting access. And getting access meant finding answers. Answers about what really happened to his mother. Answers about how to destroy his father's business, and with it, his father.

"I don't expect you to understand, kid. But one day—one day soon—I'll explain everything, I promise."

"What's to understand? He was a rat. He jeopardized the Family. And my game. And the money from that game."

Don Fugue took this in, nodded slowly. "All true. Doesn't make it any easier, though, does it?"

Tommy looked at his shoes. After a moment, he shook his head.

"When you've been at this as long as I have," said Don Fugue, "you learn to compartmentalize. It's a muscle. One you build over time."

Don Fugue rested a fatherly hand on his son's shoulder. It took all Tommy's willpower not to recoil.

"It gets easier, son, I promise."

"I was thinking about taking some business classes next year. In addition to art and philosophy. Round out my education." He gestured around the study. "Make me more useful around here."

Don Fugue raised his eyebrows. "You still want to go back to college?"

"That was our deal."

"I just figured with the game and the money, why bother? You're already on your way. What do you need college for?"

Tommy allowed a little steel into his voice. "You have to stop demonizing school, Pop. How many fucking idiots are walking around America these days? No offense, but most of your crew thinks Sun Tzu is an entrée at Chopstickers."

His father chuckled at this. Tommy pushed his luck.

"Tergivers bought me sophomore year. After the other night, I think I'm entitled to graduate."

"Entitled? Let's not forget you got played by the first girl to shake her ass at you."

Tommy took a deep breath, as if he was gearing up for an argument.

But instead he said, "You're right."

Big Al looked surprised. "I am?"

Tommy nodded. "I learned, the hard way, the difference between book smarts and street smarts. I never want to be in that position again. When I said I needed to round out my education I wasn't just talking about college. When's the next time you're going to New York?"

"Next week."

"Take me with."

Don Fugue turned his head and looked at him sideways, as if trying to get a better view of him with his peripheral vision.

"What about the game?"

"Gameplay is in good shape. Nine's lined up suppliers. Art is coming along. I can take a few days."

Don Fugue scratched his chin.

"Now might not be the best time to go. Between the 30s, our former accountant, and now the Navel, there's bound to be some pointed questions. New faces might not be welcome."

"I don't need to be in the meetings, Pop. But the dinners, the nights out? Everyone knows deals aren't made in the boardroom. They're made on the golf course. That's the real education anyway."

Don Fugue pretended to mull it over. But Tommy remembered his father's advice.

Everyone's heart is a lock, son. You just need to find the right pick.

He knew all too well the pick that pried open Don Alessandro Fugue's heart was pride. Finally, his father smiled.

"Son, when I said evolve or die, I wasn't kidding around. This thing of ours, it's at an inflection point. The old ways are dying, Tommy. It's all diminishing returns. As hard as it is to admit, I need help dragging this Family out of the fucking pool halls and strip joints and into the future. I need *you*. Even when I could trust Chongo, his ideas were getting stale. I didn't just give you that money as a cute summer project. It was a proof of concept. Maybe I should have said that from the beginning, but you weren't ready to hear it. But you're listening now, aren't you?"

Tommy nodded. "Yeah, Pop. I'm listening."

"Everything is going to make sense, I promise." Big Al squared up to Tommy, grabbed his shoulders, and gave his son a little shake with every word. "I just need you to trust me. Yeah?"

"I trust you, Pop."

Big Al held Tommy at arm's length and scrutinized him. Finally, he released him.

"Okay. Bring Nine too. You don't roll anywhere without protection. Not now."

Tommy made a show of rolling his eyes, but he'd got what he wanted.

"We good?" asked Don Fugue.

"We're good, Pop. Can I go now?"

The don nodded. Tommy headed for the door.

"That bitch . . ." his father called after him.

Again, Tommy seethed, but it played in his favor. Sanse had betrayed Tommy, broken his heart. But his father had her father killed. He didn't get to call her a bitch. He would put that on the don's tab, but for now, he had to play it carefully.

"She reach out to you?"

Tommy thought about lying, then thought better of it.

He nodded. "Last night. She texted. Apologizing, begging to talk. She has feelings for me. All bullshit. I blocked her."

"I'm sorry. I know better than anyone the sting of betrayal."

Tommy paused at the door, his hand still on the handle.

"Even so," said Tommy, "I don't want her harmed."

"She may be a snake, but she's a civilian snake. There's a code, Tommy."

Tommy nodded and moved to leave.

"Find yourself a girl you can trust and build a life with. That's what I did with your mother. Despite everything, I still cherish every moment I had with her."

Tommy's back was to his father, so he couldn't see the man's crocodile tears. Nor could Don Fugue see the disgust that contorted Tommy's face.

"Thanks, Pop," he said, and walked out.

51

Nine was uncomfortable.

Tommy had seen him irritated before, angry, stimming, even fearful enough for his life that he shut down, but he had never seen the soldier *jumpy*. As they stood in the security line, Tommy watched his companion shift his weight from foot to foot and crane his neck looking around.

He thought about trying to distract Nine by joking about all the conspiracy theories surrounding Denver International Airport, and how the ubiquitous construction notices made jokes about them. But instead of Illuminati and Blucifer talk, he asked simply and, he hoped, compassionately, "Nine, are you afraid of flying?"

Nine shook his head. "TSA."

"Well, the best way to get their attention is to look as nervous as you." Tommy's voice dropped to a whisper. "Please tell me you don't have a, well, *you know* on you."

"I'm not a fucking idiot. And I'm not afraid. I just don't like disrobing in public for the amusement of the federal government." He undid his belt and dropped it in a plastic tub. Next, he removed his black dress shoes. He grabbed another tub gingerly, with his fingertips, and carefully folded and placed his jacket inside.

"This is vile," he muttered.

Tommy was prepared to rib Nine but thought better of it. He imagined Denver International Airport was the tenth circle of hell for someone with OCD: chaos, with a heaping helping of germs.

It had been frosty with Nine since the night with Chongo, but he tried to remember that Nine was just another victim of Tommy's father. The soldier just didn't know it yet. Tommy peered ahead, where the don and SuperChenz had already sailed through the magnetometers and were collecting their belongings. Turdo and the Johnnies had taken an earlier flight.

"Ever flown before?" asked Tommy.

Nine shot him an accusatory look. When he realized Tommy wasn't asking to make fun of him, he shook his head.

"Just follow my lead," said Tommy. "It's a piece of cake."

Ahead, Don Fugue had already passed through security and stood with his roller bag beside him. He caught Tommy's eye, pulled a sour face, and tapped the face of his Rolex.

Let's go already.

When they all reunited, his father seemed as jumpy as Nine, only with anticipation rather than dread. He was impatient, but in good spirits.

"Let's ditch this cow town, boys. The Big Apple awaits."

Don Fugue and SuperChenz boarded first: first class.

When Tommy and Nine finally boarded, a pretty flight attendant was already serving his father a mimosa. He hoisted it toward them as if to offer a toast.

"What can I say, boys? Rank has its privileges."

Tommy pointed to SuperChenz. "What about him?"

"He's my registered service animal, and in case of emergency, my personal flotation device. And he literally cannot fit in coach."

Tommy rolled his eyes and shuffled past. They found their seats in the main cabin and Tommy began pulling his in-flight entertainment out of his backpack: his iPad, noise-canceling headphones, and *The Art of War*. He stuffed them in the webbed seat pocket and looked at Nine.

The soldier had nothing.

"Didn't you bring anything?"

"I'm on the clock."

"Jesus Christ, Nine. You think I'm going to get jumped by the Rolling 30s at thirty thousand feet?"

"Pretty sure your pop wouldn't appreciate me watching the in-flight movie."

"You're seriously going to raw-dog this whole flight?"

Nine made a face. "I don't raw-dog anything."

"There's a better chance of you seeing a goblin on the wing than my father setting foot in coach. Nine. Relax."

Nine shrugged. Whether he agreed or not, he had already made up his mind.

"Fine," said Tommy. "Up."

"What?"

"At least take the window seat so you have something to look at. It's a four-hour flight, you student."

"Really?" A jubilant smile broke out on the soldier's face, one he quickly suppressed. "It's not my assigned seat, though."

"No one checks, Nine."

"Well, if you don't mind . . ."

They stood and do-si-doed in the tight aisle.

It was one of the few moments Nine's boyish joy broke

through, reminding Tommy that despite their differences, Nine Ball was only a year older than him. And for a moment, it felt light and easy between them, like it had been before Chongo's murder.

"You two idiots done playing musical chairs or can I sit down now?"

They looked up and saw Jo walking down the aisle. She slung her carry-on, which looked like a cross between a giant purse and a navy seabag, into the overhead. Tommy could tell by her movement and her speech that she was inebriated, or well on her way.

"What are you doing here?"

"I assume it's to babysit you two jagoffs."

"*I'm* here to babysit," said Nine.

"From the window seat, rookie? I could slit Tommy's throat before you even put your tray table in its upright position."

Tommy touched his throat. Jo flopped into the seat across the aisle.

Nine leaned over Tommy and hissed, "Yeah, well, I would never lower my tray table. They have more than eight times the number of bacteria per square inch than the lavatory flush buttons. Shows what you know."

"Oh yeah?" Jo unlatched her tray table, and it dropped open. She rubbed her palms on the surface, then rubbed them on her breasts. *"Ooh, bacteria . . ."*

"Guys!" hissed Tommy. "Knock it off. It's a long flight."

A flight attendant appeared, his smile perfunctory and fleeting as he moved through the cabin. "Ma'am, please raise your tray table until we're in the air."

"Sorry about that," said Jo. "Hey, could I get a red wine?"

"Ma'am, we're getting ready to take off. And it's ten o'clock in the morning."

"Good point. Screwdriver, then." She offered a smile that was meant to be friendly. "When you get a chance."

The flight attendant shook his head and drifted on.

Jo eyed Tommy's iPad. "You got *Angry Birds* on that?"

Tommy sighed and handed it over.

52

Tommy, his father, and the rest of the group arrived at a high-rise hotel off Central Park. The lobby was pure Gilded Age glamour, all marble and gold and chandeliers. Tommy had never seen anything like it, and by the awed look on Nine's face, neither had the soldier. Jo grumbled about a nap and left for her room, and Big Al and SuperChenz left to procure new phones.

"Again?" asked Tommy.

"Have you had your phone in your possession the entire time?" asked Big Al.

"Yeah?"

"What about the airport metal detector?"

"Yeah, but that doesn't count."

"Oh, you trust the federal government now? If it was out of your hands and out of your sight, it counts."

"Come on, Pop, isn't that a little paranoid?"

"He who controls information reigns supreme, Tommy. There's only one person who is more powerful."

"Who's that?"

"He who controls himself." He pointed from Tommy to Nine, his pinkie ring glittering. "No calls or texts until tonight, capisce?"

Tommy and Nine nodded and watched Big Al exit the lobby,

SuperChenz lumbering behind him, leaving the pair with a couple of hours to kill before dinner. Minutes later, the young soldier stared out of their shared room's windows, overlooking the park. "I mean, we're right here. . . ."

From one of the beds Tommy stared at the ceiling, his fingers interlaced behind his head. He glanced at Nine. "A little on the nose, don't you think?"

Nine looked at Tommy. "What do you mean?"

"Like *obvious*. Touristy. Why don't we just go to the M&M's store in Times Square while we're at it?"

The soldier deflated a little, then recovered quickly, turning back toward the windows. "Yeah, totally. Cornball."

Tommy waited a beat. "I still kind of want to check it out, though. . . ."

Nine turned around. "Yeah?"

"They have a zoo and everything."

Nine tapped at his phone. "Yo, they got red pandas! Those fuckers *kill me,* bro."

"Actually, I want to hit that M&M's store too. You could make some with little nines on them."

Nine tried to play it cool, but the smile was a dead giveaway. "I mean, if you want . . ."

Five minutes later, they dashed across West Fifty-Ninth Street, past a line of horse carriages and the musky smell of the animals, feed, and manure, and into Central Park. Within the space of a few seconds, they plunged into Manhattan's verdant oasis. They marched north, sharing a path with joggers, bikers, and dog walkers, until they passed beneath a narrow stone-and-brick arch.

Inside its short tunnel, Tommy said, "I think I saw this in a movie once," his voice bouncing off the stone and brick.

"Probably somebody got whacked," said Nine. *Whacked* echoed until they emerged.

Back in the sunshine, Tommy observed Nine, who observed everything else, his head swiveling around, for once not scanning for threats, but out of sheer boyish wonder at the sight of people picnicking on the rolling green. His mouth was wide, smiling, and despite his reason for traveling to the city, Tommy found himself grinning too. The soldier pointed to a large outcrop ahead. "What's that?"

"Looks like a big ol' rock," said Tommy.

Tommy had witnessed the murder of Chongo, had burned down the Fuzzy Navel, and was in New York under false pretenses. Nine had watched the accountant's death too, and though he hadn't participated in the strip club's firebombing, Tommy was certain he had engaged in his own share of illegal, violent activity. Yet, presented with a giant rock, both were reduced to gleeful boys, unable to resist climbing it. Tommy scampered to its peak first; Nine's smart suit and polished leather oxford shoes were not designed for rapid urban mountaineering.

Momentarily alone, Tommy took in a 360-degree view of Central Park and the high-rises that formed its perimeter, penning him in. It reminded him of the Rockies, the ever-present physical reminder of the limits of his freedom. He tried to shake the feeling and instead focused on the wide playground before him, teeming with carefree children darting between the swings and seesaws. There were climbers and water features and happy families all around, and in the distance, he spotted caricature artists stationed at their easels, selling their wares.

That's when he saw her. Standing beneath a tree, watching the artists. Even in shadow, her auburn hair burned like a flare.

Before he knew what he was doing, Tommy scrabbled down the grooved face of Umpire Rock, just as a breathless Nine arrived at the top. The exasperated soldier called after him. "Come on! These are Hugo Boss, not Hokas, dickhead!"

But Tommy wasn't listening.

He scrabbles down the face of the jagged mountain. Already, lava has begun to ooze between the outcrop's striations.

He leaps from ledges and over crevices, dodging the startled subjects of this new kingdom. When he finally lands on the grass, Macarro's call now faint and far behind him, he runs flat out across the field to the tree. Flowers bloom as he passes. The field telescopes, the copse of trees seemingly receding the closer he draws to it. When he arrives, she has vanished. He looks around, spotting her again in the crowd. He sprints for the queen, reaches her, grasps her arm to spin her around . . .

There was a flash of her arm and Tommy felt the impact in his stomach, his air escaping from his mouth in a loud rush. He staggered backward.

"Get the fuck off me, creep!"

The redheaded woman carried a large purse, which she reared back to swing into Tommy's face like a mace.

Nine arrived and jumped between the two. "Hey! *Hey!*"

"Get away from me!" she shrieked.

"Sorry," said Tommy, coughing, trying to catch his breath. "Mistake."

The redheaded woman, who appeared to be in her twenties, did not look convinced by Tommy's sputtered apology. She wound up to swing again. Nine put his hands up to block.

"Wait! Stop! He thought you were someone else!"

"I don't give a shit. Don't be grabbing women in Central Park, asshole."

The woman stormed off. Nine clocked a group of onlookers staring at the two of them. "Come on," he said, trying to help Tommy straighten up, "we better dip. . . ."

Tommy shrugged him off. "I'm fine!"

Tommy turned his back to Nine. He felt like an utter fool. He took deep breaths to fight back tears as he looked up at the buildings lining the park, as inexorable as prison bars. He started back the way they had come. Nine fell into step behind him. Tommy marched past the rock, the arch, the horses and their carriages.

Finally, he abandoned the park and the last kernel of hope that his mother still lived, more ready than ever for what came next.

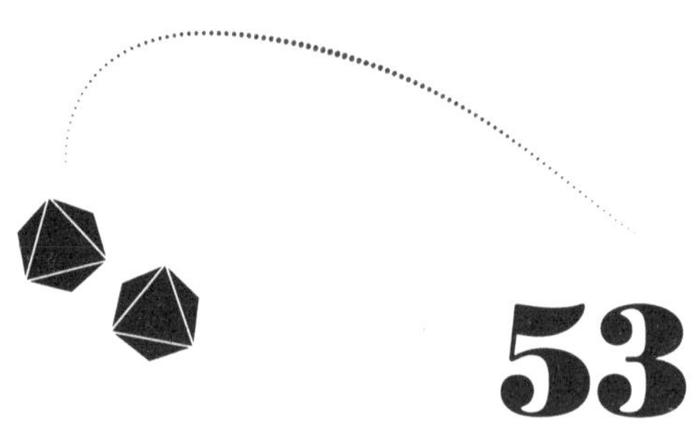

53

The motley crew of Tommy, Don Fugue, Nine, Jo, and SuperChenz, all with shiny new phones, set out on foot for dinner in Hell's Kitchen. The only impression of Hell's Kitchen Tommy had was from *Daredevil* comics: moody, gritty, and infested with gangsters and ninjas and superpowered assassins. And somewhere high above, perched on a rooftop wooden water tank, was the blind vigilante, dressed in bloodred and using his other senses—heightened to a supernatural degree—to detect threats. He could read a regular newspaper with his fingertips as if it were braille. He could hear a scream in an alley six blocks away. And he could identify scents as finely as a shark detecting a drop of blood.

If Daredevil were up there now, wondered Tommy, *how would his radar sense handle all the weed below?*

A haze of cannabis hung over the wide boulevard. Men arm in arm promenaded, boisterous and laughing. The storefronts were crowded with international restaurants, dispensaries, and festive nightclubs.

The Hell's Kitchen of his childhood imagination had been the epitome of noir.

The Hell's Kitchen of reality was decidedly neon.

Not at all his father's scene. He thought perhaps Big Al had taken a wrong turn. He half expected him to explode right there on the corner.

Instead, the don turned around and spread his arms wide. "Isn't this fucking great?"

Tommy didn't know what to say. Instead, he just looked around, his mouth slightly agape. Big Al laughed at him and slugged his arm.

"Keep up, greenhorn," he said, and dove into the teeming crowd.

They arrived at a storefront with a brightly lit sign that read CHEESEBOAT.

"What's a cheeseboat?" asked Tommy.

"Trust me, it's gonna knock your dick in the dirt."

"I prefer to keep it clean, thanks. I guess I was expecting something a little more . . ."

"Italian?"

"Well . . . yeah."

"Believe me, we'll be spending plenty of time on Mulberry Street, but tonight is about fun."

They stepped inside, off busy Ninth Avenue, into the bistro, and were greeted by a heavily tattooed man with an ebullient smile.

"Shota!" cried Big Al.

"Alessandro!" yelled the man.

They embraced and exchanged kisses on each other's cheeks.

Tommy and Nine shared a look. Neither could quite believe they were witnessing this side of Don Fugue. The don seemed radiant, alive. Joyful. Perhaps it was the lights, the noise of the street, or the contact high, but Tommy felt like he had fallen through the looking glass.

"Boys, welcome to the best Georgian restaurant this side of Williamsburg."

Both men laughed uproariously. Tommy and Nine looked confused.

"Williamsburg is our other location," said Shota. He extended a hand. Tommy shook it, noticed several tattoos of cats on his forearms.

"Best fucking khachapuri in the world," proclaimed Big Al.

"The owner's mother's recipe."

"What's khachapuri?" asked Tommy.

"He's never had khachapuri?" asked Shota.

"What, I'm gonna pop his cherry in fucking Denver?"

Shota led them through the long, narrow bistro. They passed an alcove with a cityscape mural populated by cats and CHEESEBOAT written in the stars. Tommy eyed his father suspiciously. He wondered if the don had been somehow dosed, or perhaps replaced with a doppelgänger.

They emerged into a courtyard festooned with string lights overhead and ensconced by walls painted in festive colors. Turdo and the Johnnies, already waiting in their dark suits, looked out of place and relieved to see the rest of the party arrive. The men stood and kissed each other's cheeks, safely reunited in New York City.

If Don Fugue was concerned with the troubles back home, he didn't show it.

"Let's blow some young minds, Shota. Bring these boys two traditionals to get started, a prosciutto, a meatball, and that honeycomb brie. And a couple of bottles of Barakoni."

"Coming right up."

"Oh, and, Shota? Bring me a glass of Putin's Tears."

Shota's smile was infectious. "You got it."

Once Shota returned with the bottles of red and Big Al's jalapeño-infused tequila cocktail, Tommy felt safe enough to pry.

"What is this place?"

"Your mother always brought me to Hell's Kitchen. She got really bored with solemn Italian restaurants filled with dusty old gangsters."

Tommy gritted his teeth. He couldn't stand his father invoking his mother. He changed the subject before anyone noticed.

"So, what's tomorrow all about?"

"A meet with the Family."

"Yeah, but . . . I don't really know what that means."

The Johnnies looked at their boss with furrowed brows, confused.

"When it came to Tommy and the business, Vittoria maintained a strict separation of church and state." He sank back in his chair and raised his Putin's Tears at the Johnnies. "Go on. Explain it to him."

Tommy leaned forward, elbows on the table, eager to learn. The Johnnies looked at each other, wondering where to begin. As if they had sorted it out telepathically, Johnny Socks launched into a brief history of the Five Families.

"The five outfits operating out of New York City are Bonanno, Colombo, Gambino, Genovese, and Lucchese."

"Which are we?"

Johnny Reb's eyes grew wide, and he looked at Don Fugue. "Seriously?"

Instead of taking umbrage, Don Fugue, with cocktail in hand and lounging in the colorful courtyard, simply shrugged. "I told you he was sheltered."

Johnny Reb shook his head.

"We," said Socks, "are Gambino."

Nods around the table and raised glasses.

"So, tomorrow is like, what, a Gambino sit-down?"

"Whoa," said Reb. "Nothing so life or death. Think of it like a quarterly performance review."

"Though there are some concerns," added Socks. "The Old Man does not like to hear of trouble on the frontier. We are here to assuage his concerns."

Don Fugue waved it off. "And we will."

"Don Coniglio loves your father," said Reb. "Thinks he's a cowboy or something."

"Don Coniglio thinks I took a covered wagon to Colorado."

Everyone laughed.

Reb continued, "Your father is being humble. He's in line for a promotion."

Tommy looked over at his father, who wore a wry smirk. Big Al shrugged.

"What I don't get is, with Five Families, why is there not constant fighting?"

Socks took over. "Each family has a demarcated territory. And specialties. We all work very hard not to step on each other's toes."

"Or at least not get caught stepping on each other's toes," said Reb.

"But that's what the commission is for," said Socks.

"Commission?" asked Tommy.

"The heads of the Five Families," said Reb.

"They're like a board of directors, if you will," explained Socks.

"Or Knights of the Round Table, if you prefer," said Reb.

"Who gather every five years, or as needed, to discuss family business, mediate conflicts, whatever."

"Over time, the Five Families have expanded to include outfits from Chicago or Buffalo, and they usually contract again."

"Occasionally," said Socks, "other families will rise to a level commensurate with the Five, and they are unofficially designated the Sixth Family."

The Johnnies paused then and looked at their boss. Don Fugue stared into his drink, a smile teasing his lips. Tommy looked from consigliere to consigliere, then back at his father again.

"Wait," said Tommy. He looked over his shoulder to scan the otherwise empty courtyard, then leaned in and dropped his voice to a whisper. "Are we the Sixth Family?"

The Johnnies shifted in their seats, suddenly uneasy.

Don Fugue cut them off with a raised hand before they could answer.

"No," he said.

"Officially," said Reb.

"For the record," said Socks.

"Unofficially and off the record?" asked Tommy.

"We are loyal members of the Gambino Family," said Reb.

"Your father was sent to Colorado to expand the franchise and he has exceeded beyond Don Coniglio's wildest dreams," said Socks.

"Under his leadership," said Reb, "the Commerce City footprint has grown bigger than all other Gambino territories outside of New York, and in a fraction of the time."

"The Old Man said, 'Go west, young man.' And so I did," said Don Fugue. He tilted his half-drunk cocktail toward his son. "Remember, Fugues don't half-ass it, son."

"We bring our whole ass," said Tommy.

Don Fugue winked.

"By the numbers alone," continued Socks, "the Family Fugue could be considered the Sixth Family."

"Should be," said Reb. "To not acknowledge it is to argue with reality. Even Don Coniglio recognizes it. Your father is the Old Man's favorite and so he allowed the growth. Encouraged it."

Socks chimed in. "A Sixth Family, independent but with deep ties to Don Coniglio, would only strengthen the Gambino position, essentially going from a fifth of the seats on the commission to a third."

"Things were on track," said Reb, "but then . . ."

Johnny Socks cleared his throat.

"It's fine," Don Fugue said abruptly before draining his drink. "Things stalled . . ." He reached for the wine, filled his glass, then with a raise of his eyebrows offered to top off Jo's glass. She nodded. "When your mother took off."

"Sensing an opportunity, the Delgados and their proxies have been nipping at our heels ever since," said Reb, irritated.

"Fucking hyenas," said Socks.

"People talk," said Don Fugue. "They think I am weakened. They think the streets—my streets—are slipping. This talk delights my enemies, gratifies the other families, and concerns Don Coniglio. But it's just talk. We're here to reassure him."

"How?" asked Tommy.

"Family, for one. I've been doing some thinking and I've had a change of heart. Tomorrow morning I will introduce Don Coniglio to my pride and joy, the blood of my blood."

"Me?" asked Tommy. He swallowed. This was not part of the plan.

"Yeah, you," said his father with a laugh. "Who else, rookie?"

Shota arrived with the khachapuri: Trays of Georgian bread formed into the shapes of boats, knots twisted on either end. Inside each bread boat was boiling cheese and butter, to which Shota added an egg yolk that he whisked with a flourish, the egg cooked immediately by the piping-hot cheese. It looked decadent.

Don Fugue raised his glass. Everyone followed suit.

Tommy smiled uneasily.

"To my intelligent, handsome, and strong son. Loyal, just like his father. I will show Don Coniglio that the Fugues are a united front."

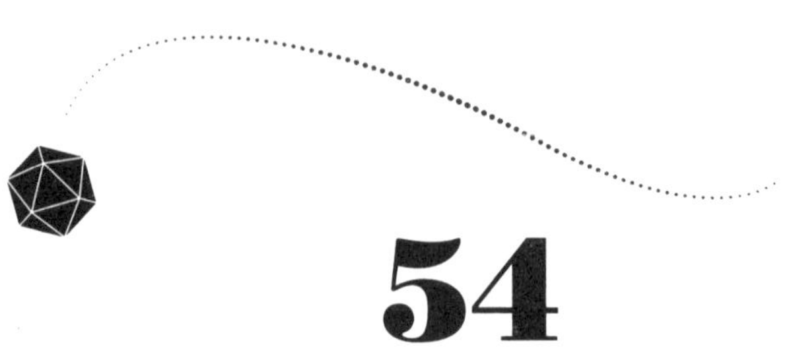

54

Tommy awoke before dawn, terrified and exhilarated in equal measure. Fortunately, the surprise Georgian feast of bread and cheese had inadvertently helped Tommy with his plan. In the next bed, Nine slept soundly.

Thanks, Shota.

A few hours from now, a black car would be taking them to their meet with Don Coniglio and the various high-ranking members of the Gambino Crime Family, where Tommy would be introduced as the firstborn son of Don Alessandro Fugue. To Tommy, it sounded like the gangster version of a bar mitzvah or a debutante ball. Little Tommy's all grown up. He's a Big Boy Criminal now! As he quickly and quietly gathered his belongings in the hotel room, he smiled to himself, wondering what kind of gifts one received at a gangster coming-out party. Brass knuckles? Holsters? Those machines in the movies that count cash really fast?

His father and associates kept vampire hours. With a little luck, he would be back before anyone was awake, the seeds of his freedom planted.

Tommy had never unpacked his roller bag. It stood at attention by the entryway, ready to escort him out into the wild unknown. He padded to the door with his shoes in hand. He moved the swing bar, then placed his shoes on the floor. He put a hoodie against the lock to muffle the sound, then quietly and carefully unlocked the door. The dead bolt still sounded as loud and threatening as a bolt action rifle, but the bread and the cheese had plunged Nine into too deep a sleep.

Tommy grabbed his shoes and roller bag, propping the door open with his hip, and slipped out. He held his breath as he closed the door from the outside. Once the door settled, Tommy stepped back. He still held his breath. His heart pounded. He waited for Nine to burst from the room.

But the door remained closed. No sound came from inside.

Tommy let out a breath.

Then he ran to the end of the hallway in his socks, clutching his shoes in one hand and his bag in the other. He jabbed the elevator button three times in quick succession and hopped from foot to foot as he fumbled with his shoes. When the doors slid open, he took one last look down the hall, still waiting for Nine to fly out, then plunged inside the elevator. Three more jabs to the *L* button and the doors closed with an excruciating lack of urgency.

When Tommy reached the lobby, he looked around the grand foyer for signs of his father's coterie. He expected to see SuperChenz standing like a medieval guard before the revolving doors to the street, a double-headed axe in one hand and a spear in the other, proclaiming Tommy must best him in hand-to-hand combat to escape the glass tower.

"Checking out, sir?"

Tommy jumped—"Fuck!"—but it was just the concierge, who looked very concerned suddenly.

"No, no . . . I'll be back," he said reassuringly, but he put his head down and strode faster toward the front door. It took all his willpower not to sprint. Once he hit the sidewalk, he broke into a run. He headed south, away from the park, and jogged the remaining blocks—his roller bag rattling along behind him on the uneven sidewalk, making too much noise. Every time he glanced backward, he expected to find his father and an army of goons in hot pursuit.

A faint rose-colored glow was visible down the cross streets to the east. He arrived at the Sheraton Times Square, sweating and out of breath.

He checked into a business suite already booked under his name. He'd supposed it was what one used in these situations. He was here to conduct business, after all. He bought a coffee in the hotel's café, still looking over his shoulder out of habit, then rode the elevator to an upper floor. It was a spacious suite, far more than he needed, but his father had always told him to project strength and affluence. Despite all his father's bullshit, that nugget still sounded enough like gold.

There was an expansive sitting area, a large conference table surrounded by ten plush chairs, tasteful corporate art on the walls, and strange vases on the coffee and side tables. There was a separate bedroom with a king-size bed he was too wired to use. He took a sip of his coffee and waited. It was now daylight.

Time to get ready.

This was never the plan. He would have preferred to fly to New York on his own, without his father ever knowing, but ever since Chongo's demise, Big Al wouldn't let Tommy out of his sight. So before the Don Coniglio sit-down, Tommy had to skim a little time for a sit-down of his own.

Tommy retrieved a carefully folded suit and dress shoes from his bag. He buttoned his crisp dress shirt in the reflection of the windows as he scanned the city. He tried to locate Hell's Kitchen, the site of his last family meal. Beyond that, he saw glimpses of the gray vein of the Hudson River, the skyline beyond it. He stared west as the day continued to brighten, and realized he could not remember the last time he'd looked west and didn't have his view blocked by mountains on the horizon. He took a deep breath and let it out, still nervous, but feeling a little freer already.

He cinched and straightened his tie. The first call came.

"Dude, where are you?" asked Nine Ball.

"Out for coffee."

"What the fuck? You've been gone since I got up. We're leaving soon."

He'd assumed Nine would rise early, but he could hold him at bay. "Just sightseeing on my own. Don't make a thing about it."

"The sit-down with Don Coniglio got bumped up. We're leaving in an hour."

Tommy's heart slammed in his chest. He forgot to breathe. If he hurried, he could make it back to the other hotel before his father knew he had gone. He took a breath, then another. Looking down on Seventh Avenue from the sanctuary of the suite, it seemed fitting. Inevitable.

The only way out was through.

"I'm sorry, Nine. I'm not going."

Tommy could picture Nine on the other end of the phone, already pressed and dressed, hair tied back. Immaculate and sharp as a cutting edge. He could picture him trying to remain calm, closing his eyes, and fighting hard to keep his tone even.

"I need you to listen to me," said Nine. "This is a big day."

"I know it is. It's a big day for me too."

"You know what I mean. There's family and there's Family. We don't air one's dirty laundry in front of the other."

"Pop will make an excuse."

"No, Tommy. He won't. It'll be bad. Real bad. For both of us. These are the kinds of people who do not like surprises."

"You're there, I'm not. This isn't on you. Even he'll see that."

"Does Don Fugue strike you as particularly reasonable?"

It was as close as Tommy had ever heard Nine get to besmirching his don.

"Please, Tommy," he said. "I can cover for you for a little bit longer. Say you got turned around."

"I'm sorry, Nine."

"Tommy . . ." said Nine, his voice dropping to a whisper, "I'm going to have to tell him."

"Do what you have to do, Nine. No hard feelings. Seriously, good luck."

Tommy ended the call.

The next call came a few minutes later, as he knew it would.

55

"*Son.*"

It was just a single word, spoken over the phone, but Tommy could tell everything. Just as he could detect Nine's suppressed anxiety, he could detect his father's stifled fury. That the don wasn't screaming down the phone told Tommy he wasn't alone. He could picture the Johnnies exchanging nervous glances in their hotel lobby, watching their boss tense as he gripped his cell phone. Maybe Nine was there too, staring at his shoes, shamed. Jo would be there as well, maybe hungover or itching for a drink, but coiled and ready to lash out. Like a maestro detecting an off note, Tommy heard the barest hint of embarrassment, maybe even fear, in his father's contained rage.

Despite everything, it made Tommy want to sprint back to his father's hotel, spin some tale, and beg forgiveness. It wasn't too late.

Only, yes, it was. He remembered every wound delivered by his father then. His summer job laundering money. His rictus as he bashed Tommy's head against the windows. Sanse, his first love, forever tainted. Chongo, deep in the foothills somewhere west of Denver, his life just another sick lesson from his father.

And his mother, gone almost a year now. How many lessons had his father taught her?

Had he taken her up into the foothills?

Tommy realized his eyes were squeezed shut. He opened them. The sky was a crisp blue as far as the eye could see, the summer haze not yet risen. Inside, Tommy felt as cold and still as ice.

"Good morning, Pop."

"Nine says you're out for a stroll and may have gotten turned around. These things happen. But you need to come back. Now."

"I'm afraid I can't make your big mobster meeting this morning. I have my own."

"Heh." He could visualize his father's mirthless chuckle. Quietly, so only Tommy could hear: "What the fuck does that mean?"

"It means I have a previous engagement."

"Get your ass back here right now." The demand was through gritted teeth.

"No."

A deep breath. Then, quietly, again just for Tommy: "Then I'll have to take it out on Nine Ball."

"He had no idea."

"Then he's not much of a babysitter, is he? He'll need to be repurposed."

Tommy spun around the expansive room, suddenly feeling helpless. He ended up staring back out the windows. Instead of feeding his panic, the vague threat to Nine fueled his anger.

"For absolutely no reason I can discern, Nine is completely loyal to you, and that's how you'd treat him? Don't you ever give a shit about anybody but yourself? If that's how you treat your most devoted soldiers, I'd hate to see how you treat your enemies. Oh wait, I already have."

"Who are you meeting?"

"That's my business."

"FBI? ATF? NYPD?" Big Al's voice grew louder and more hostile with each organization. "I knew you were weak, but I never thought you'd rat out your own father."

Tommy snorted. "You honestly don't get it, do you? I don't want anything to do with your gangster bullshit. I never have."

Tommy heard heavy breathing through nostrils over the line. His father, a bull, ready to charge but with no matador in sight. Ready to knock down skyscrapers until he found him. But when Big Al spoke again, his voice was calm. Gentle. Almost conciliatory.

"I don't want to hurt the boy, but I will, Tommy. Nothing and no one will keep me from my family. So, here's how it's going to be. For every minute you don't tell me where you are, I will break one of his fingers. Chenz?"

Tommy pictured his father's hill giant. Cheerful one moment—*Tommy, you're looking swole, little dude*—blank and compliant the next. Dully and lifelessly dispensing violence as if in a trance.

As you command, Don Fugue.

SuperChenz would have zero qualms with crippling Nine Ball. He'd probably even compliment him on his physical therapy afterward. *Get in those reps, Nine. A setback is just setting the stage for your comeback, bro.*

"Wait." Tommy gritted his teeth. "Sheraton Times Square."

"Room."

"2110."

"We're already in the lobby. See you in a sec."

"What?" Tommy spun toward the door, as if they were already banging on it.

"I was testing you. Predictably, you failed. Next time you decide to defect, turn off Find My Phone first, *stunod*."

The line went dead.

"Shit," said Tommy. He looked at his phone as if it had betrayed him.

His heart beat wildly, his panic flaring. He looked around the room searching for weapons. But there were none. Only lamps, vases, and a couple of circular stone structures on the glass tables that looked like magic rocks one might find in Tergivers. Tommy could use some enchantment, but the only power they contained would be to hold papers in place. And the only items in his pockets were his wallet and the d20s that he had kept on him for campaigns but had taken to carrying as good luck charms.

So much for that.

No, he thought. His own father would not kill him in a luxury suite on the twenty-first floor of a fancy hotel. He was a fucking mob boss, not a psycho serial killer. And if SuperChenz tried to drag him out, he'd scream bloody murder.

I will stand my ground, he vowed. *For Mom.*

He took several deep breaths, blew them out slowly. He walked to the door, opened it, and flipped the swing bar to prop it open. He returned to the high windows, leaned against them, and folded his arms across his chest.

Bring it on, Pop.

One moment, the room was empty. The next, his father pushed in, followed by his entourage: SuperChenz towering behind his don. A sheepish Nine. A wary Jo.

They spread out, flanking him. SuperChenz, dressed in an ill-fitting suit and tie for the meeting, took his position blocking the door. Nine and Jo fanned out to either corner of the suite. Don Fugue, dapper as ever in black business attire, circled the expanse of the room, appraising it. He looked impressed.

"Nice digs, kid."

"Don't worry," said Tommy. "I'm paying for it."

"Oh, you're paying for it all right."

"What do you want, Pop?"

"What do I want? If you're going to stab me in the back, at least have the decency to look me in the eye. Chenz, check him for a wire."

"A wire? You came to me, you idiots. . . ."

But SuperChenz had already crossed the room. He was surprisingly swift and graceful for his size. He tried to pat Tommy down, but Tommy swatted at his hands. "Get the fuck off."

"Chenz, quit playing."

The bodyguard grabbed Tommy's shirt front with both hands and spread his arms. He barely had to put in any effort. The buttons of Tommy's dress shirt popped and shot across the room. Tommy grappled with the bodyguard's wrists, but it was like trying to budge an elephant's leg. Chenz lifted Tommy's undershirt, revealing no wires. SuperChenz let go and Tommy pushed himself away from the bodyguard.

"No wires, boss."

"I can see that, Chenz. Thank you."

Tommy tucked his ruined shirt back into his pants and straightened his tie, trying to restore some of his dignity. He burned with rage.

"I'm not here to rat you out, you fucking monster. If I never have to speak your name again, it will be too soon. I'm trying to start a new life. As far away from you and Commerce City and the Fugue Crime Family as humanly possible. I'm nineteen years old and I'm leaving."

"Oh, so you're a big man now? Is that it?"

"I'm more of a man than you'll ever be."

"Yeah, yeah." Don Fugue headed for the door. "We're leaving, come."

"I'm not going anywhere."

Don Fugue lost his temper and whirled around to face his son. *"I do not have time for this shit, Tommy,"* he bellowed. "There is a lot more going on than you think, and I absolutely do not need your insubordination right now, so you can throw your little temper tantrum later. *We're going.*"

The mob boss looked at his bodyguard and jutted his chin toward his son.

SuperChenz stepped forward.

Tommy backed a step. "Don't you fucking touch me."

"Chenz," his father called. "Grab him already."

"It was me!" blurted Tommy. "*I* torched the Navel."

Don Fugue cocked his head. Narrowed his eyes.

"You?" He pointed at his son. The sign of the horns again. "*You* burned down my club?"

"Thunderbolt, motherfucker."

Don Fugue lunged for his son.

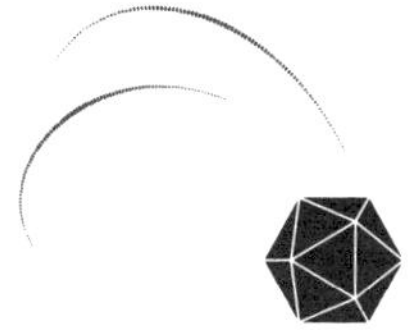

56

This time, Prince Thomas was readied. Seizing the initiative, he caught his charging father. Shifting his feet and twisting at the waist, he grabbed his father's wing in one hand and palmed Lord Fugue's head with the other, then smashed him into the tall window. A low reverberation filled the room as his father's head bounced off the glass.

How does it feel, my lord?

Thomas didn't have time to celebrate. The dark lord rebounded off the window, grunted, and seized his tunic. Together they toppled over a glass table. Thomas landed on his back; his father landed on top of him. The tabletop shattered, showering them with broken glass. Lord Fugue raised his fist high, his pale face now puce with rage. Thomas saw one of the strange rocks on the floor. He got his hand around it.

Alas, it wasn't stone, but resin. Disappointing, though it made the thing easier to heave.

He swung it into the side of his father's head. A loud sound filled the room. Either the piece cracked or it was his father's head. Either way, the result was the same: Lord Fugue fell off Thomas and landed on the floor, dazed. The prince sprang to his feet. His father shook his head, stunned, and placed his palm on the toppled table's frame for balance. He touched two clawed fingers to the side of his head, testing for blood. He looked confused. Then the confusion melted in the heat of his rage.

Thomas scooped up the resin paperweight.

"Chenz," said Lord Fugue. "Take him."

At this, the goliath—stunned by the prince's revelation and the sudden explosion of violence—came to his senses. He lunged for Thomas. Thomas turned to face his father's manservant, his cracked-resin and non-magical paperweight cocked. He knew it would be like hitting a tarrasque with a twig, and he braced for impact.

It never failed to amaze Thomas how light on his feet the goliath was. How quick.

But Bellarmina was in another league.

Tommy had never seen someone move so fast. She sprang from her corner and crossed the room before the giant made it two steps. In one fluid motion, she shot her boot forward like a piston into the goliath's leg and pulled it back again in a flash. He crumpled. It looked like a bridge collapse.

"My knee! My fuckin'—"

But she was already behind him with her butterfly knife at his windpipe, ready to do critical damage, cutting him off mid-howl.

"One flinch and you'll taste Bellarmina's blade."

"You bitch—"

Bellarmina's arm tensed slightly. A thin red line bloomed on the manservant's throat. A single crimson tear trickled to the giant's collar.

"Hush. This is a family matter."

"'Kay," he panted. "Okay . . ."

Father and son both watched the scene, stupefied, too quick for them to process. Lord Fugue got his wits about him first.

"Goddamn it, Nine. Help me!"

The young warrior was rooted to the spot. He stared at his lord, whose face was mottled with fury.

"Don't just fucking stand there, you stunod. *Stop him!"*

Macarro looked at Thomas, the torment evident in his eyes.

The warrior closed his mouth, took a deep breath, and his face once again became the blank mask of a loyal soldier.

But instead of stepping forward, he took a single step back.

Nine Ball looked his don in the eye and shook his head.

The smallest of gestures, but seismic. Thomas blinked and saw his friend.

In that instant, an exquisite sword appeared: Tergivers' final artifact. Its silver hilt was bejeweled with turquoise and bone, and its blade shone so brightly in the sun's rays it looked to be composed of pure light.

The Blade of Love.

Macarro nodded at his friend and his friend nodded back.

Tommy faced his father again. Just the two of them now.

Don Fugue found his feet then, his chest heaving. "Fine," he spat. He dabbed two fingers to the side of his head, in the hair above his ear. They came away red. He pulled the pocket square from his jacket, shook it out, and wiped his fingers. "I certainly don't need anybody to teach college boy here a lesson."

He stripped off his jacket and began to roll up the sleeves of his dress shirt.

"Class is in session, Tommy Gun."

Big Al put up his fists, rounded his shoulders forward, and advanced in a perfect boxer's stance.

Tommy imitated him. They circled each other.

A second into it, Tommy remembered that he was not a

fighter, but his father was, and a savage one at that. The man grew up poor on the streets of New York City, and he never let his son forget it. He had to scrap for every dime, every advantage, and every bit of respect he ever got.

Don Fugue came in fast with a jab.

But it was a feint. He swung fast and wide with an open right hand. The smack was hard. It rattled Tommy's teeth and sounded like a thunderclap in the suite. The impact startled him more than it hurt him. But the sting followed immediately after, like a deep cut that takes a moment to bleed.

"You like that?"

Tommy touched his cheek. Don Fugue danced away.

"You may get A's in art, boy, but you're sure as hell failing self-defense."

He wanted to hurt his father, but he didn't know how. He lacked the skill, the coordination. Tommy quickly put up his fists again, fear and fury battling it out in his guts. As he hesitated, his father came in again, swinging his right hand wide. Tommy went to block, but this time, the left found him. Another stinging slap that shunted him to the side.

He stumbled, barely keeping his feet.

Tommy knew he was too in his head. He couldn't script this like a campaign. Now was not the time for plotting and design. It was time for combat.

He yelled and charged his father, swinging wildly.

Don Fugue laughed as he ducked the blows sailing past him.

"Better . . . I'll give you a D for effort. . . ."

Tommy kept swinging, a torrent of blows. None landed. Don Fugue danced maddeningly out of reach. Laughing.

"*Whoa.* That one almost got me. Tell you what. D-plus . . ."

The taunts only made Tommy angrier. He swung harder and faster. He charged in deeper, then wound up for a haymaker.

Leaving his middle unprotected.

The rabbit punch to his side collapsed him. What little air he had after his futile assault jetted from his mouth.

He fell to one knee.

He looked up just in time to see his father's hand, eclipsing his vision.

The next moment, he was on his back, the side of his face on fire. He tried to get up, but his father knocked his hands away and sat on his chest, pinning Tommy's arms with his knees. Tommy tried to wrench free; then he felt his father's hands around his throat.

His father was choking him.

"I told you," screamed the don, "I don't have time for this!"

Tommy struggled, the pressure of his father's fingers digging into this windpipe. His father had been toying with him before—humiliating him more than hurting him—but now Tommy couldn't breathe. Spittle rained down on Tommy's face as his father lost himself in a berserker rage.

"Your disrespect!"

Don Fugue bumped Tommy's head against the floor for emphasis. His vision swam. *His father was a dark lord again, fangs bared, eyes burning with malice.*

"Your disloyalty!"

Another bump. Back to Big Al, spittle flying, veins flaring in his neck and forearms.

"Your lack of faith!"

Tommy's arms were pinned to his sides helplessly. He had no weapons, and no means to grasp them. All he could feel was the pair of d20 in his pocket. His father's tirade was now lost to the sound of blood rushing in his head. Darkness began to creep around the edges of his vision. *His father, Dark Lord Fugue again, shadows gathering around him, the last thing he would ever see.*

"Do you realize how much I've sacrificed for you?"

Tommy saw Macarro approach, grab the dark lord's shoulder. "He can't breathe. . . ."

The lord's fist shot out blindingly fast. The backhand sent the young warrior sprawling.

But it was all the opening Tommy needed. In hitting Nine, Don Fugue had surrendered a fraction of leverage, enough for Tommy to make one last desperate lunge for freedom. He jerked his arm free and jammed a d20 into the mouth of his still-roaring father.

The effect was immediate.

The dark lord found his feet instantly, his son forgotten, his hands clutching his throat. Wheezing and gagging. His pale face turned redder.

Tommy rolled over, gasping for air and reflexively protecting his throat. He thought he might throw up or faint or both, but he pulled himself to his feet. His vision cleared. When he turned back to his father, Don Fugue reared back as if for a massive sneeze. Then the mob boss hunched forward, hands on knees, and retched the die onto the floor.

It rolled until fifteen was face up.

"Got your modifier right here," said Tommy. He clenched his five fingers into a fist and smashed it into his father's face.

There's your dirty 20, Pop.

Tommy's blow caught the don on his cheek as he was still stooped and coughing. His father went down.

Tommy scanned the floor and spotted the resin paperweight.

He wrapped his hand around it, tested its weight. Again, not stone, not magic, but another bash to the head would keep him down. A second might kill him.

Better make it three, Tommy thought as he staggered toward his father.

He heard a chorus of warnings.

"Kid, no," said Jo.

She even allowed her captive, knife still at his throat, to issue a caution before tightening up on the knife again. "Little guy, don't—"

Nine got in his path. "I can't let you kill him."

Tommy shoved him out of the way. He shuffled toward his dazed father, still on his hands and knees across the room.

Behind him, the sound of the hotel door opening.

Everyone but Tommy turned toward it. Silence fell over the room.

A housekeeper or hotel manager witnessing him bludgeon his father to death was not ideal, but it was better to go to jail than live a second longer with his father's boot on his neck.

He hoisted his makeshift weapon over his head, ready to deal some bludgeoning damage.

Then Tommy heard a voice that stopped him in his tracks.

"My darlings, must you play so rough?"

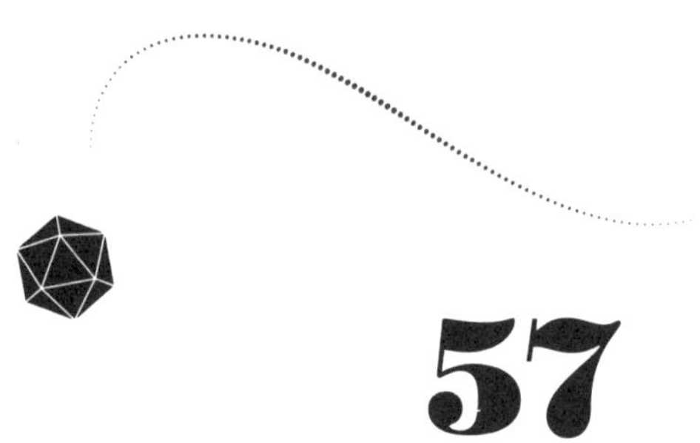

57

The queen stood in the threshold, an emerald cloak over her shoulder and a crown atop her head of flowing auburn hair.

Tommy shook his head.

Vittoria Rose Fugue was still there.

His mother was still there. She wore a sharp emerald suit and a crisp white shirt, her red hair down and flowing over her shoulders.

"My baby boy," she said.

The magic rock fell at his feet, his father and their battle forgotten. He ran to his mother and threw his arms around her neck.

"I thought you were dead," he sobbed.

"My beautiful baby boy."

He pulled away, held her at arm's length.

"You're real. I thought he . . ."

She touched his face. It instantly cooled the stinging of his cheeks from his father's blows. Mom, making everything better.

"Are you hurt?"

"I'm okay, but . . ."

He turned back to his father, who was rising again.

There was blood in his hair. His tie was askew. Yet he looked sleeker and more dangerous than ever. His fists were balled, his muscles tensed. But his eyes were focused on Vittoria instead of Tommy. He panted through his nose like a beast, a jaguar locked on its prey. He didn't approach directly, but loped toward her from the side, circling.

Tommy retrieved his weapon from the floor.

"Stay behind me, Mom."

When he looked over his shoulder, she was gone.

The queen had slipped from behind him, and moved in tandem with the dark lord, revolving in the same circle, maintaining distance from her evil husband. Her chin was up, her upper lip pulled back, revealing her white teeth. Regal yet fearsome. Her hair glowed when she stepped into a patch of sunshine through the windows. Thomas saw her hands. Bloodred nails—painted the same color as her lips—extended like claws. She was the picture of defiance. A righteous phoenix.

Before Thomas could stop her, the queen rushed her husband. The dark lord charged too and the two warriors collided in the center of the room.

They attacked each other savagely. Her nails to his face. Biting him. His arms flailing around her . . .

It took Tommy a moment to realize the warriors were kissing.

His father made low exhalations, panting, like he was still that jungle cat. He heard his mother's soft moans. They embraced each other, their hands fevered and pawing each other.

Nine walked up beside Tommy.

"What," said Tommy, "is happening?"

"It looks like . . . foreplay?" said Nine.

At this, the pair separated. Barely. Vittoria took Big Al's head in her hands and inspected his wound.

"Let me see," she said.

"I'm fine," he growled.

"Hush."

When she determined that her husband wasn't going to expire from their son's attack, she made a sour face at him.

"Must you be such a brute?"

"I get a little carried away sometimes, babe. But you'll see, he's tough now. Tough enough for the truth anyway."

She parted from her husband then and drifted across the room to Jolene, whose jaw was still hanging open.

"Hello, old friend."

Jo finally lowered the knife from SuperChenz's throat. He scampered away as quickly as possible, his busted leg trailing behind him. The man attempted to stand next to Don Fugue, who shooed him away without a second look.

Jo fought to compose herself, but it was a losing battle. Her voice trembled; her face contorted.

"You're alive," she said.

Vittoria embraced the enforcer. Jo flinched, with her hands frozen in midair. Then, slowly, Jo thawed again and wrapped her arms around Tommy's mother. She squeezed with such ferocity, it could count as a chiropractic adjustment. When Jo released Vittoria, tears streaked the Stinger's cheeks.

Vittoria approached Nine next.

"Who is this, then?"

She stared at him intently, but not unkindly. The soldier straightened, standing a little taller, as if at attention.

"That's Nine. Nine Ball," said Tommy.

"What's a Nine Ball?" asked Vittoria dryly.

"He's Tommy's Stinger," said Jo.

At that, Vittoria's face softened from formidable to warm. She clasped Nine's hands in her own. "Thank you for taking such good care of my baby."

Nine pulled his gaze away to look at his shoes. Tommy realized it was because he was blushing. Don Fugue had never thanked him. To his shame, Tommy couldn't remember if he had either.

"It's my honor, ma'am," said the soldier.

With that, Vittoria turned and faced the room, all eyes on her, everyone still dumbfounded. SuperChenz tried to balance on one leg, gritting his teeth.

"Alessandro," snapped Vittoria, "tell your dog to sit or put him out of his misery already."

Don Fugue looked at his bodyguard as if seeing him for the first time. He shook his head in disgust and pointed to the couch. SuperChenz nodded gratefully, hopped across the room, and collapsed into it. The furniture let out a groan of protest.

"I know we owe you an explanation," said Vittoria.

"We?" asked Tommy.

"Your father and I."

He cut his eyes to his father. "You *knew*?"

His father stared back hard, his jaw clenched. The rage had dissipated from his eyes. Mostly. He exhaled through his nose, nodded.

Tommy glanced at the makeshift weapon on the floor, gauged the distance, and thought about resuming his plan. His father watched him, reading his mind.

"Boys," said Vittoria. "Eyes on me, please."

Both men complied.

"Where to begin?" asked Vittoria rhetorically. She looked at her husband. "Does he know about the rat?"

"Just the one."

"Ah," she said. "Chongo." She pursed her lips and shook her head. Her sad look wasn't of heartbreak, but of disappointment.

Such a shame.

"You know about Chongo?" asked Tommy.

"When it comes to the Family," said his father, "there is nothing your mother doesn't know, son."

Tommy's gaze settled on her again, commanding the center of the room in her emerald suit, her hair coiffed and aflame, her nails polished and perfect, her makeup still flawless. The picture of power and composure.

It was then he noticed that, even after nearly a full year of separation from her son, she had not yet shed a single tear.

"It's one thing to skim," said Vittoria. "But *betrayal*?"

When Tommy looked confused, his father said flatly, "He was in love with your mother."

"Always was," said Vittoria. "Since before you were born."

"Not that I could blame him for that, eh?" said his father. He looked at Vittoria with a wolfish smile. She returned it.

"So, he had to *die*?" asked Tommy. "Because he had a crush on Mom?"

"Honey, I know you're upset, but please try to listen to your father."

Big Al looked at Tommy, raising his eyebrows. *Well?*

Subtly, with Tommy barely noticing, Jo and Nine had taken up positions on either side of him. Whatever happened next, they had his back.

Tommy relented with a nod. *Fine, truce. For now.*

"Bud had some interesting things to tell the Johnnies before he went one toke over the line, son," explained the don. "It's true. He carried a torch for your mother. It's only natural. I can forgive the coveting. But acting on it? Plotting?"

"He made a pass at me once," said his mother. "When you were little. He was very drunk at a party. Enough to confess his feelings. I left before someone overheard and he wound up getting himself killed. He paid me a visit the next day to apologize profusely—very gentlemanly—but to also stress that his feelings were real. I let him down as easily as I could but told him he could never speak of it again."

Tommy glanced at his father. He looked fit to dig Chongo up and shoot him again.

"In retrospect," said Vittoria, "I was too gentle."

"So, when the real rat came along," said Big Al, "Bud was his first recruit."

"Real rat?"

Vittoria and Big Al looked at each other, having an entire conversation with their eyes. Vittoria nodded finally, giving permission.

"Your Uncle Mikey," said Big Al.

"Turdo?" said Tommy.

Ever since Tommy was a kid, he never liked "Uncle Mikey"—a moniker his parents had forced Tommy to bestow on his father's second-in-command. Tommy couldn't stand the man because it was so obvious the man couldn't stand him. Always with the backhanded compliments, the sneering smiles, the vague or veiled threats. Offering him peppers.

Nine shook his head in disbelief.

"Infame," muttered Jo. Tommy didn't know much Italian,

but he had heard the word used before to describe someone wicked or disgraceful. A traitor.

"They formed a pact years ago," explained his father. "They started skirmishes with the Delgados. Secretly, of course. Using outside, unaffiliated muscle. Then they did the same to us, making it look like Delgado retaliation."

"But why?"

"Their plan was to destabilize the streets enough," explained Vittoria, "that your father would be taken out. Either by a Delgado bullet or a New York demotion. With Alessandro out of the picture, Turdo would be next in line."

"And Chongo would have a clear path to my queen," added his father.

"That's crazy," said Tommy.

"That's love," said Vittoria. "And ambition."

"Everyone's heart is a lock, son."

"Regardless, it produced the desired effect," said Vittoria. "Both families were whipped into a frenzy. Gang warfare."

"The Bad Old Days," said Tommy.

"Precisely," said Vittoria.

"But then they took it too far," said Don Fugue. "They took my son."

His father met his eye. Tommy saw rage, but also fear. Even love.

Tommy remembered that look years ago when his father and his men stormed into the mall to find Tommy. And again, when he stormed into the ER after his peppered kiss.

That look said, *No one will* ever *harm a hair on your head.*

No one but me.

"We'll never know if the guys who took you were paid by

Turdo and Chongo or by Delgado goons. But by that point, it hardly mattered. By those days, it was shoot first and forget about the questions altogether."

But Tommy knew. One of those men was a low-level Delgado goon: Sanse's father.

Porks, of all people, sprang to mind: *The thing with information is having it makes you smart. But knowing when to share it, and more importantly, when not to share it? That's* real *wisdom, Tommy.*

He kept his mouth shut and listened.

"Your father rained righteous hellfire on the streets. His rampage was so swift, so legendary, that everyone retreated. And peace prevailed," said Vittoria. She said it in a hushed voice filled with wonder. Admiration. And possibly lust. That did his head in more than Big Al's blows. His sainted mother, who cuddled Tommy following his father's storms. The creative spirit who drew and painted and told him fairy tales, who pretended they were royalty. Her, a queen trapped in a tower, and him, her exiled prince and righteous heir to the throne.

Now he wondered if perhaps he was seeing her truly for the first time.

"My family was under threat," said Big Al. "I did what had to be done."

"And you did it *marvelously*, darling."

At Tommy's shoulder, Nine whispered, "Are they going to start making out again?"

"The Delgados backed way off," said Don Fugue. "And the rats fled down their bolt-holes."

"Turdo played the loyal, obsequious Number Two, eagerly helping your father settle scores, and poor besotted Chongo disappeared into a cloud of smoke for years. We never would have been the wiser," said Vittoria.

"Until someone took a shot at us last year," said his father. "Both of us."

"What?" asked Tommy. "How did I not hear about this?"

"We were protecting you," said Vittoria.

"A father does not burden his child with his struggles," said Big Al.

"But you'll put a gun in his hand and pull the trigger?" asked Tommy, incredulous.

Vittoria turned to her husband, raised an eyebrow.

Don Fugue shrugged. "Parenthood is a process."

"Turdo wouldn't wait forever," continued Vittoria after a brief pause. "After years of biding his time, he grew impatient. And greedy. He wasn't content to be Number Two anymore, not with us on the cusp of becoming the Sixth Family. He wanted it all, and finally he had the keys to the kingdom: full access to all our operations and supply lines. Gambling, loan sharking, protection . . . an empire worth millions for the taking. Tens of millions. With us gone, he would be next in line. It's not like *you* were ready. Not yet anyway.

"Turdo may have been next in line on the org chart, but he was never the true heir. The rightful heir. A Fugue. And though Chongo had long ago given up hope he would ever win my heart, he had no choice but to go along. Turdo owned him."

"The timing, the location, the nature of the attempt on our lives . . . it was all privileged information," Big Al said. "We knew we had a rat. Or several. We didn't know who, just that they were well placed. So, your mother devised a plan. Since forces were trying to destabilize the Family, we decided to steer into the skid."

"So, I left," said Vittoria.

"Just like that?" asked Tommy, his question more an accusation.

"I'm so sorry, my baby. It had to be ambiguous, and more than that it had to be convincing. It broke my heart, but I didn't dare reach out. We couldn't trust devices. We didn't know how deep the rats burrowed. We couldn't trust electronics. I took a risk just commenting on your FunFunder page, but I had to . . ."

Tommy remembered then. One of the rare bright spots in the Tergivers comments section.

"RedRaven77," he whispered.

Vittoria smiled, while Don Fugue plowed ahead.

"I told everyone she was tired of my indiscretions. All bullshit, by the way. Before I took an oath to the Family, I took an oath to this woman. I mean, come on, look at this fucking goddess over here. She's hotter than spaghetti all'Assassina."

He crossed the room to his wife's side and kissed her passionately. She groped him in kind.

"But Ms. Tesauro . . ." said Tommy, confused. He saw it with his own eyes: their hugs, their carnal smiles, their knowing looks.

"A facade," said Don Fugue, "which we have perpetrated for years."

"Mafia infidelity is baked into the culture. To be *without* a *comare* would arouse suspicion. Bosses, soldiers . . . they would not fully trust your father otherwise."

"It's an outmoded form of masculinity that I find distasteful, but it was all part of your mother's plan. Besides, she'd cut off my pepper if I ever tried that shit for real."

"This is true."

They clasped hands and beamed at each other.

"Now," said Vittoria, "a mother leaving in the dead of night, not telling her only child . . . it's not natural."

"You're fucking right it's not natural!"

"Language," said Don Fugue.

"But that was the entire point, Tommy," said Vittoria, moving toward her son. "We needed people to think something was very wrong."

"Deep into a night of drinking, I would hint that maybe *I* was the one who'd tired of *her*—as if such a thing was possible, my heart—and let people draw their own conclusions. . . . And start spreading rumors. Which is just how we wanted it."

"Your father had to look rash, dangerous. Unstable. Because we knew about the rat, we knew it wasn't the Delgados this time, but we couldn't afford any more challenges while we rooted out the threat inside our own house."

"And it wasn't safe for your mother. Not until I flushed out the rat. And then your game happened."

"My game? What does Tergivers have to do with this?"

"I was just trying to show you the ropes. I did not expect what you pulled off. And when you did . . ."

"It provided a secondary opportunity," said his mother coolly. "A game within a game."

"In the straight world, deals get done on golf courses, like you said. In our world, they get done at card tables. People talk, let their hair down. I still have no idea how Tergivers works, but I figured it was close enough. So, I put eyes and ears on it."

"Porks," sneered Tommy. "He was your mole."

"Chongo fed information to Turdo. Porks fed intel to me. He's easy to underestimate, but it's unwise to do so."

"He is repugnant," said Vittoria, "but useful."

"Well, he's down one club."

Vittoria looked to her husband for explanation.

"Tommy firebombed the Fuzzy Navel."

"Adulthood is a process," said Tommy.

Don Fugue's jaw flared again, but Vittoria glanced at him, made the slightest pat of the air with her hand. *Let it go.*

Whatever Don Fugue wanted to say, he swallowed it. Instead, he said, "Chongo confessed to everything. All of it. Years of plotting, trying to take me down. Trying to steal my wife like she's some prize. Putting her in harm's way. Forcing her underground. Those offenses merited days of torture. But I did not kill him."

"That," said Vittoria to Tommy, "was *your* honor."

"My honor?" he said. "Are you even listening to yourselves? Are you both insane?"

Vittoria rushed to her son, held his face in her hands.

"They split up our family for a year. A year! No other New York outfit, no Delgado, no enemy has *ever* wounded the Fugue Family more. It was betrayal of the highest order. Your father was not punishing you that night, he was giving you the privilege to avenge our family. A righteous kill."

"I told you," said his father. "One day you would understand."

"But I'm back now, honey. No one is ever going to hurt us again. We are going to reveal everything to Don Coniglio today."

Don Fugue snorted. "I don't think Turdo's gonna make his return flight."

"The Old Man will be so stunned by our audacity, so humbled by our sacrifice, we will become the Sixth Family."

Tommy stared into his mother's face, saw her cold determination. He had long been accustomed to being afraid of his father, but never his mother.

“He keeps saying *your* plan,” said Tommy. “This was all your idea, wasn’t it?”

She said nothing. His father spoke up in her defense.

“It’s funny, son. Your mother is so beautiful, no one ever sees her coming.”

58

The long-lost queen of Tommy's imagination was pure, a victim of his father. Not this, not an accomplice. At the look of horror on her son's face, Vittoria moved to him and clutched his shoulders for emphasis. He looked at his mother's hands on him, imagined them covered in blood.

"Tommy," said Vittoria, her face creased with pain. "There's what I wanted, and there's what needed to be done. For my disappearance to look real, it had to *be* real. You had to believe it if anyone else was going to believe it."

"Erratic father," said Don Fugue, jerking a thumb at his chest, then pointing at Tommy, "heartbroken son. Had to look real, kid."

Tommy grabbed his throbbing head. He thought it might rupture and an alien might skitter out.

"Are you fucking serious?" he bellowed.

His mother jerked back. His father stepped forward.

"People's lives are ruined—people are dead! I haven't even gotten to poor Todd. He never made it to Kansas!"

"That was Turdo." Don Fugue touched his heart and closed his eyes in a *Swear to God* gesture.

"Tying up loose ends," said Vittoria. "We would never—"

"It *broke* me when you left Commerce City," he yelled. He flung his arm in Jo's direction. "It broke her too. She took an oath to protect you. She's been drowning herself in booze and getting into fights every night to torture herself."

Vittoria looked at her friend, then down at her expensive shoes. "I never intended for that to happen."

"Oh, and the girl I'm in love with is working with the cops, who want me to help put *him* away for killing *you*. Which I thought *he* actually did—because *you* wanted me to think that. Do you have any idea how fucked up that is? Choosing the Family over *our* family and dragging me into this Godfather horseshit? You're *both* monsters. I wish you'd stayed dead and left me with my memories."

"Watch your mouth, boy," growled Don Fugue, raising a single finger in warning.

"I know this is a lot," said Vittoria, her eyes softening, her mouth fixing itself into a sympathetic smile. "But it was the only way to keep us all safe."

"To keep you both in power, you mean."

"They are one and the same," said Don Fugue.

"The point is," said Vittoria, clasping her son's hands in hers, "we've *won*, Tommy. We can go back to being a family again. A real family with no more secrets. And I'm so very proud of how you've handled everything. You have brains, talent, cunning. And fire—I see it in you. You have it all. You're a true Fugue. But you've only begun to realize your full potential. You just need a little polish, darling. I will complete your training. Join us and we can rule the streets as the Sixth—"

There was a knock at the door.

Don Fugue snapped his fingers. "Chenz, gun."

From the couch, grimacing, SuperChenz leaned to one side and removed a pistol from a holster at his waist.

"They're here for me," said Tommy.

"Don't," said Big Al.

Tommy strode for the door.

Don Fugue grabbed for his son's shoulder, but Tommy ducked it. He threw the door wide open just as his father tackled him from behind.

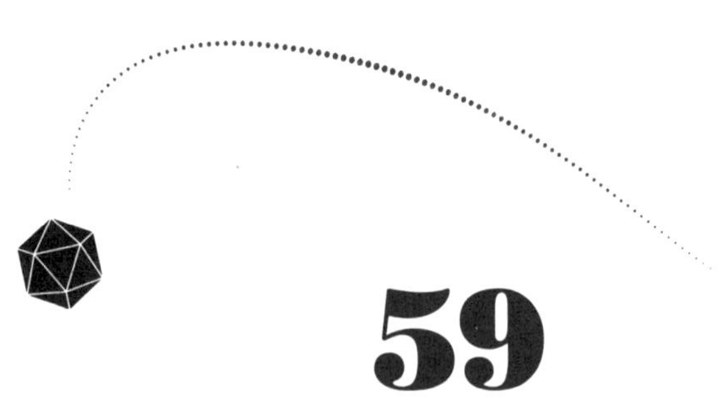

59

Father and son fell in a heap at the feet of their visitor. The first thing Tommy saw was a pair of black suede heeled sandals. From the floor Tommy and Big Al both panned upward, taking in a woman's white dress slacks and a classic navy blazer. They rolled over to look up into her face, framed by a blond bob.

The woman smiled brightly, almost manically, yet she seemed completely unfazed by two grown men wrestling before her. Looking chic and crisp, she appeared both relaxed and ready for business.

"Bad time?"

The question managed to be both curt and cheerful. Without waiting for an answer, she stepped over them and into the room. Tommy pushed off his father, got to his feet, and smoothed his suit jacket. Big Al got up next and stood beside his son.

"Who *the hell* are *you*?" asked Don Fugue.

The woman ignored him, surveying the disarrayed room, pointing a finger first at Jo, then at Nine, then at SuperChenz, who had his pistol resting on the couch. The bodyguard covered it with a pillow.

"No, no, and very no."

She pointed at Vittoria.

"No, but *hello*."

She turned back to father and son. "You must be Tommy."

Tommy smoothed his hair and stepped forward awkwardly, extending his hand.

"I'm Tommy Fugue. Thank you for coming."

"Who are you?" growled Don Fugue.

"Helene Fry of the Fry Agency, where we create boundless opportunities for storytellers, creatives, and trendsetters across all media throughout the known universe forever and ever, amen. In other words, I'm the bitch who will make the One Thousand Blades of Tergivers a household name, so I guess my question is"—she looked Al up and down—"if you're not Tommy Fugue, why are you talking to me?"

The bright smile never left her lips.

Don Fugue blinked.

After a moment of nonreply, Helene turned back to Tommy. "We don't have a lot of time, Tommy, so I'll cut to the chase. Tergivers is creative. Tergivers is innovative. Tergivers is inspiring. I have no idea how it works, but I want to. I know you're meeting with a lot of other agents today, but none will represent you with the tenacity of the Fry Agency."

"You're meeting with managers?" asked Vittoria. "That's what all this is about?"

"*I'm* his manager," said Don Fugue.

"*Not* my manager," said Tommy, leading Helene over to the kitchen area. "Can I get you a drink?"

"The fuck I'm not."

Helene leaned in. "First, it's *agent*. Hence *agency*. Second, I don't do families. Are you or are you not eighteen, Tommy?"

"Nineteen," said Tommy.

"And are you the owner of Tommy Gun Games?"

"I am."

"What?" growled Don Fugue.

"Thank Chongo," muttered Tommy. "Fuck you, by the way."

"Wonderful! As I was saying, from where I'm standing, we are already late. You have some adorable buzz on FunFunder, but if you want to play in the big leagues, we need to start seeding the marketplace *yesterday*. And, if you allow me to represent you and your baby, and we at the Fry Agency see your creations as babies," said Helene, placing her hand on her heart, "we're going to *hyper-expose the shit* out of that baby. I'm talking multimedia, vertical integration, the works."

"What the hell is she saying?" said Don Fugue. He looked around, as if searching for someone who could translate whatever language Helene was speaking. Vittoria placed a hand on his forearm.

"Quiet, darling," she said.

"I'm listening," said Tommy.

Helene walked across the room and took Tommy's hands in hers.

"Look, I'm just a girl, standing in front of a boy, asking him to let her represent him for fifteen percent of all royalties and future earnings across all domains."

"*Fifteen percent!*" exploded Big Al. "Fucking hell, I know loan sharks with a softer touch!"

Helene's manic smile evaporated, revealing steel beneath.

"Industry standard. And spare me the low-level mobster patois. This is New York City, sugar. I'm so not impressed."

Don Fugue balked. "Low-level?"

Vittoria threaded her arm through his. "What my husband means to say is, what does our son get for fifteen percent?"

"Excellent question, Unreasonably Hot Mom. For that you get the head, the tail, the whole damn thing." She put her arm around Tommy's shoulder and spread her other arm as if gesturing to an invisible billboard. "First, we release the game. Next, we get some rando to write a tie-in novel. Then we adapt the novel into a movie, maybe a TV series. Maybe both. Then we're going to *High School Musical: The Musical: The Series* that shit. And just when you think we're done . . . we're going to turn it into a *game*."

Tommy blinked at the invisible billboard.

"It's already a game."

"Second edition."

"Whoa."

"I like her," said Vittoria.

"Who does *Star Wars*?" asked Big Al.

"Disney," said Helene.

"Make her do Disney, son."

"What I do know about Tergivers, Tommy, is that it's special. People discovering the best parts of themselves? Striving to be better? Real hero's journey stuff. It's about *virtue*. And virtue is so hot right now. We should really exploit that."

Tommy didn't know how much of it was Helene's fast talk, the revelation that his mother was still alive, or his father's punches, but his head was spinning. He walked over to a chair and sat down.

"Is there, like, an advance or something?"

Helene laughed good-naturedly. "I want to give you the moon, Tommy. And again, just take a tiny little crescent for myself, but pulling the moon into orbit is going to take a lot of freaking work. I know you have some other agencies lined up today. They'll promise you the moon too. But beware the ones who leave out the bit about the work."

Helene followed Tommy to his chair. "There are no advances and there are no shortcuts. We're going to roll up our sleeves, grind harder than you ever thought possible, and we may even have to get our hands a little dirty."

Tommy stared at his hands. *If you only knew,* he thought.

"That I can do," he said.

"That's good, Tommy. And here's the part of the offer you can't refuse. I never want you to doubt my singular focus and unwavering commitment to two words: *world domination.*"

She rested a hand on his shoulder and looked into his eyes. They were a bright, intense blue. Looking into them, he felt seen. He felt like crying.

"I have a nine thirty," she said. "Kiss whatever frogs you need to this morning, then call me when you're ready to slay some dragons."

She whirled to the rest of the room and her smile snapped back into place. "So lovely to meet everyone."

She marched for the door and in fewer than a dozen steps, she was gone.

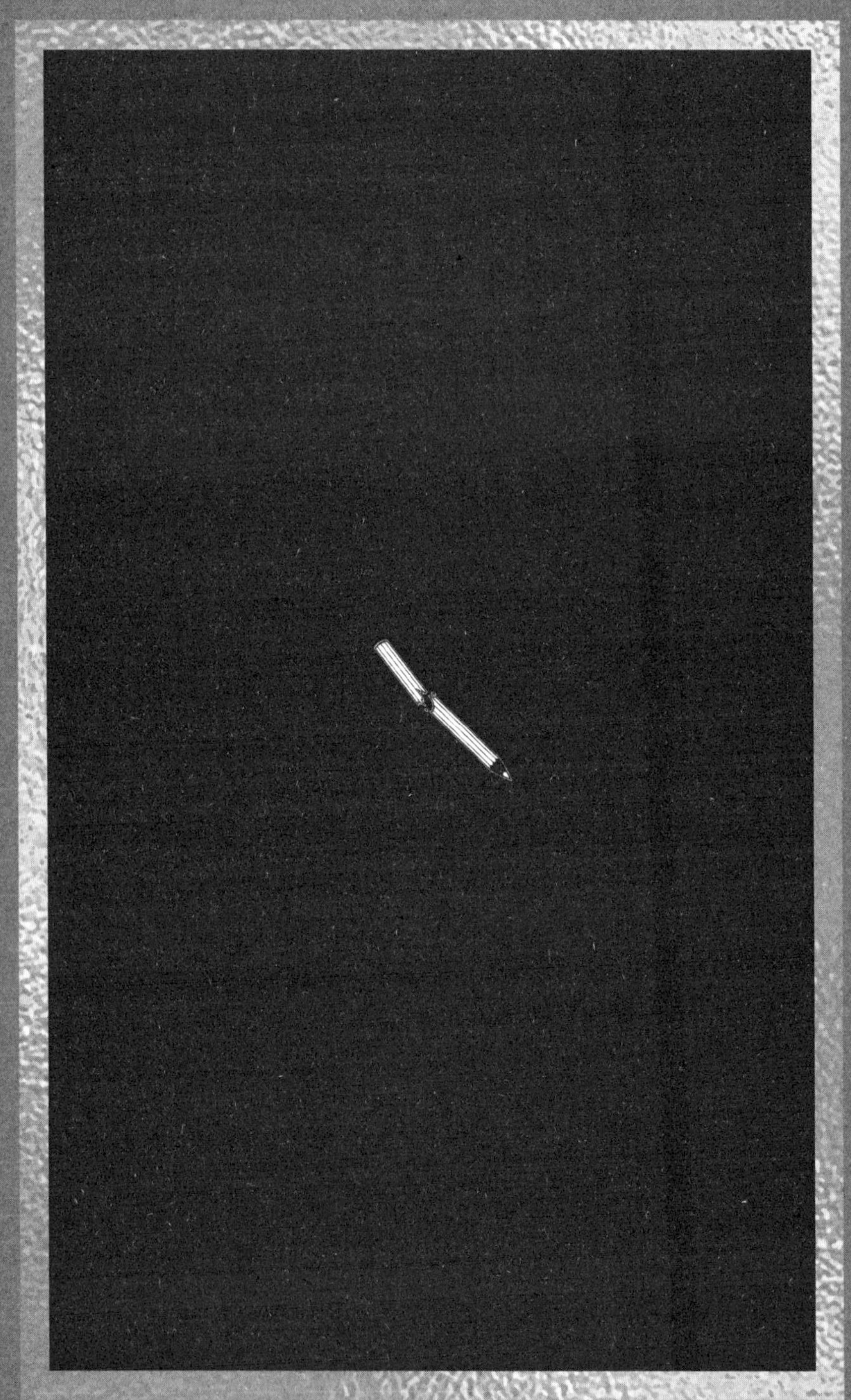

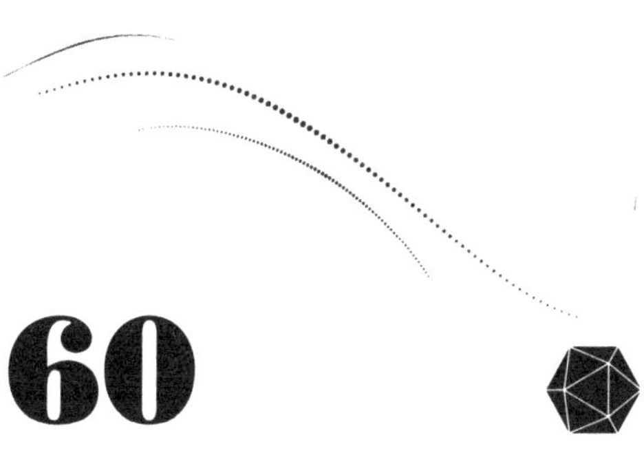

60

It was like the sudden, eerie calm after a tornado had ripped through town. Everyone was quiet, stunned. Tommy could still hear his father's heavy breathing. Out of the corner of his eye, he noticed Jo and Nine and SuperChenz all glancing at each other nervously, waiting on a reaction from the mobster.

"That was your big plan?" said Don Fugue. He snorted. "Some hotshot city bitch sashays in here and you're going to pay her for the privilege of what, exactly? Talk is cheap, son. Let's see what the others have to say."

"You weren't seeing it, Al," Tommy's mom said.

"What?"

Vittoria looked at her son approvingly. For a moment it felt to Tommy like an apex predator sizing up prey. Or worse, a competitor.

"His vision."

"Any jerk-off can have *vision*." His father's disdain practically dripped off the word. "Gimme a guy with grit over a hundred with vision."

"Darling," said Vittoria, "I do believe our son has both."

Nothing about the morning was going how Tommy thought it would go. He needed time to process, to think. It was all getting away from him. Jo and Nine watched him silently.

Then he remembered.

How many times had they, as Bellarmina and Macarro, and yes, even Porks as Bradford—especially Porks as Bradford—thrown him a curveball in gameplay? How many times had he crafted an elaborate scenario only to have one of his players come out of left field with something that sent the campaign spinning off in an entirely different direction? It was maddening, but it was exciting too. Invigorating even. There were always obstacles and challenges and riddles to face. But there was always more than one pathway to achieve the ultimate goal.

All he had to do was roll the dice.

Tommy stood. He brushed off his clothes, smoothed his hair, and smiled.

"I would like you to leave now."

"Bullshit," said Don Fugue.

"Darling, maybe it's best to—"

"Both of you," said Tommy.

"You don't mean that, Tommy," said Vittoria.

"I'm prepared to make a deal, but then I want you to go."

"*I* make the deals and *you* do as you're told, boy," said his father.

Tommy ignored him. "I will give you half . . ."

"You aren't *giving* me anything, kid," said Don Fugue, his voice rising with every word. "I gave you that money to wash—"

"I didn't finish," said Tommy, speaking over the don. "I will give you half of half. The other twenty-five percent covers operating costs, including the salary of my artistic director, Anibal Delgado, per a prearranged agreement."

"Delgado?" said Big Al, his voice barely a whisper, the shock so sudden it was like the wind had been knocked out of him.

"The son of Emiliano Delgado," said Tommy, "who I've found to drive a hard but ultimately reasonable bargain."

"You Judas," seethed Don Fugue. "Over my dead body."

"Thanks to me, that won't be necessary. Anibal is a very talented artist and a valued collaborator. Working with him also has the ancillary benefit of preventing any unnecessary bloodshed. What could possibly be a better show of good faith than the scions of the Fugue and Delgado Families working together? It will usher in a new age of peace on the streets."

Vittoria looked at her husband, fearful for the first time.

"I'll burn it all to the ground first," he said.

"That's zero-sum thinking. While our fathers were locked in a vicious cycle fighting over scraps, Anibal and I increased the size of the pie. Everyone gets a taste, or no one gets a taste. Those are my terms."

Don Fugue bared his teeth. "I wouldn't make so many demands of someone who has a hot piece with your prints on it."

"Don't be stupid, Pop."

"Remember the last time you disrespected me, boy?"

"Yeah, I was the dumb kid who you handed 20K in a paper bag, and now I'm the man who will hand you back 20X on your investment. But sure, have us both thrown in jail. Great plan, Criminal Mastermind."

Don Fugue sneered and reached for his son, but Vittoria raised her hand without even looking in his direction. Don Fugue halted immediately.

"20X?" asked Vittoria. "Is that true?"

"Give or take," mumbled Big Al.

"Real money, Mom. Better yet, *clean* money."

"No such thing," said Don Fugue.

"Come on, you heard Helene. *World domination.* Do you really want to piss away a chance at the big leagues for Commerce City? Over an old gangster grudge? Over your pride?"

"For my pride? For my family?" said Don Fugue. "I would sacrifice anything. Or anyone."

Tommy and his father stared at each other.

"Let me break it down for you one more time. Thanks to Chongo, I am the sole legal owner of Tommy Gun Games. He may have been a lecherous stoner, but he was damn good with a contract. Now, Tommy Gun Games appreciates your seed investment and is prepared to repay your twenty thousand dollars—with two months' worth of interest, or vig if you prefer—buying you out entirely. Or you can remain on, at the aforementioned terms, as an extremely silent partner to ensure your continued cooperation on certain matters."

"I'm not listening to this nonsense any—"

"Such as?" asked Vittoria.

Tommy pointed to Jo and Nine. "They work for me now. Full time. No more gangster bullshit. They're out, free and clear."

Tommy knew Nine Ball was good inside. Jo too. Whatever they had done in their pasts, it was never too late to start over, to roll up a new character.

Still, this was news to them both. Jo narrowed her eyes and watched for everyone's reactions. Nine's head snapped between his don and his friend, then back again. He began to panic.

"Don Fugue, I—I never asked—"

In the end, Don Fugue didn't even look in the direction of the soldier who had idolized him for so long.

"Whatever," said Don Fugue.

In his peripheral vision, Tommy saw Nine's shoulders slump.

Just another piece on the game board, casually tossed aside at the end of a session.

Don Fugue's eyes remained fixed on his son until his glare melted into a sharklike grin. "What else, tough guy?"

Tommy leveled a finger at Don Fugue. "We're done."

"Don't be silly," said Vittoria. "We're finally back together."

Don Fugue's smile vanished again. He looked genuinely hurt. "You'd have nothing if it wasn't for me."

"Trauma, you mean?"

Big Al waved the comment away. "We're a family."

Tommy shook his head. "Not anymore."

His father, Dark Lord of the Denver Streets and prospective head of the elusive Sixth Family, had taken enough indignities. He exploded.

"I will say when we're done!" he roared. "I am Don Alessandro Fugue, the Al Might—"

Tommy flew across the room and stopped inches from his face.

"And I am the fucking game master."

Vittoria thrust herself between them. She pushed Tommy back and pulled her husband into the bedroom suite. Once the door closed, Tommy breathed a sigh of relief. From behind the door, he heard a bitter argument ensue, conducted in harsh whispers.

Tommy looked toward his friends. "You two okay?"

"As long as they don't start doing it," said Jo, leaning dramatically to look toward the bedroom, "I'll live. That took stones, kid."

"Nice work, little guy," said SuperChenz. He gave a wan smile and a thumbs-up from the couch.

"Quiet, you," said Jo.

"Nine?" asked Tommy.

But the young soldier looked a million miles away.

"*Nine*. You good?"

The soldier snapped out of it. He saw Tommy. His eyes welled up, in sorrow or gratitude Tommy couldn't tell, but in the space of a moment, he recovered the effortless cool that Tommy had so aspired to.

"I'm Gucci, boss."

The bedroom door flew open. Don Fugue stormed out. He looked to have downgraded from Category 5 Furious to Category 1 Irritated. Still nothing to play around with, but considerably less deadly. His mother remained the picture of poise, the calm eye in the center of the chaos. Vittoria threaded her arm through Big Al's, effectively pinning him to her.

"Of course your father and I accept your generous offer," she stated. "We are deeply sorry for the pain we've caused you. You must know we did it out of love and for your own protection. That's not an excuse, but an explanation, and I need you to believe it was as deeply painful for us as it was for you. But I just returned, and negotiations will remain open on your definition of 'we're done,' young man."

Her tone at the end was irrefutable and brooked no dissent. She was good, all right. Savvier than her husband. And colder too. It was a perfect marriage. She was the brains; he was the brawn.

How had he never seen it before?

Her face brightened again. "And we're so very proud of the strong young man you've become. Right, darling?"

Big Al said nothing.

She jerked his arm.

"Right?"

Beneath his father's subdued fury, Tommy saw the hurt. The wounded pride.

Big Al opened his mouth to argue, but Vittoria said softly, "Listen to your son, darling. Give him time. Give him some space."

"He wants space, tell him to watch *Star Wars.*"

But Tommy saw his father's sorrowful eyes and heard in his heavy voice that he had truly burned through all his bluster. All that was left was sadness.

"Just let me go, Pop."

"I just get my wife back and now I lose my son?" said Big Al. Tommy heard the man's voice crack, just a hair. "How is that fair?"

Tommy felt his heart crack too, just a hair. He smiled, but not a mean one. "Fare is what you pay to get on a bus, Pop."

Despite himself, Don Fugue chuckled at his own joke repeated back to him. He wiped his eyes roughly, then quickly recovered his machismo.

"Fine. Sow your oats. Be your own man for a while." He freed himself from his wife, and before Tommy could stop it, Big Al cupped his son's neck roughly, but not without affection. He pulled his son's face to his own, until their foreheads touched.

"I don't give a shit what you say. We're family. And family is everything."

His father released him and took a step back. With that, Don Fugue was himself again. Dark and dangerous. He smiled his sharklike grin.

"Because if you're not family, you're just an investment."

He turned to his wife, held out his hand. "Let's not keep Don Coniglio waiting any longer, my love."

A hungry smile spread on her face. "Or our future."

"The Sixth Family," he said, pulling her into an embrace.

She lowered her voice to a husky whisper. "At long last . . ."

Their eyes glazed over. Tommy rolled his. "We're still here," he said. "All of us."

"We'll talk tonight, Tommy," Vittoria said finally. "Just you and I."

Tommy nodded. There was no point arguing with her.

Husband and wife turned toward the door, hand in hand. Vittoria took another look at her son, beamed with pride, then strode out of the room. Don Fugue, holding the door, looked at Jo and Nine Ball.

"You two," he said.

Nine stiffened.

Jo said, "Yes, sir?"

But he turned his cold gaze back to his son.

"Keep my investment safe. Or else."

61

One week later, Tommy and Nine marched side by side, a pair of slick, well-dressed missiles cutting across Larimer Street. Nine wore his usual dark attire, stark in the high noon sunlight, while Tommy favored a light gray suit and eschewed a tie, looking less severe than his friend and bodyguard. Their dress shoes tapped the pavement in perfect cadence.

A van was parked in a line of cars down the street. Nine saw it first.

Without looking or breaking stride, he said, "Three o'clock."

Tommy spied it from behind his designer sunglasses. The van was meant to be nondescript, but its placement on the street was conspicuous and its scuffs and scratches looked too orderly, deliberate. *Practically artisanal,* he thought. "Guess we shouldn't have jaywalked, then."

"Colorado is getting too crowded." It was something Big Al and his cohort had grumbled about all the time.

"I like it. Makes the place feel bigger."

As they stepped onto the sidewalk in front of Crema Coffee House, Tommy looked in the direction of the Rockies, his dream of going west burning more brightly than ever.

1.6 million dollars was a lot of money. More than enough to leave his father and Commerce City behind forever, but that would mean cutting and running on his business and stiffing his patrons. It would mean abandoning Tergivers, not just the game, but the world he had created and the very virtues it was built upon. And it would mean sacrificing his principles and the better, stronger version of himself he had worked so hard to forge.

So, he stayed.

And it turned out 1.6 million dollars was not that much money when you had to pay for an artist, staff, designers, papers and cardboard, printing, coating, gluing and cutting, assembly, packaging, shipping, to say nothing of FunFunder's cut . . .

Tommy sighed. To the west, the Rockies shimmered. Full freedom would have to wait a while longer. The only way out was through.

He looked east too. Where, after a succession of agents had promised him the moon but downplayed the thrust necessary to reach escape velocity, he'd finally signed with Helene. She hadn't tried to sugarcoat it, and now more than ever he needed people he could trust.

In that category already was Nine, who quickstepped ahead to open the door for him. It was an adjustment for them both. Tommy had never intended to be the soldier's new don, just his friend. His soldiering days were over, he told Nine. But old habits die hard.

Tommy hadn't spoken to his father since New York, which wasn't surprising. When Vittoria was in her self-imposed exile, sometimes he would go weeks without speaking to Big Al. But intermittent communication would not fly with Vittoria Rose Fugue. Though Tommy was just as pissed at his mother as he was with his father, she called him every day, dismissing the past year of unpleasantness with a wave of her hand, a mere speed bump on the trip to riches and power.

He had given his conditions in New York—running Tommy Gun Games as he saw fit, finishing school without the constant threat of removal, more freedom in general—but Vittoria had some of her own. She was "allowing" him the rest of the summer to cool off, but once the school year began, she would institute Sunday night dinners. No matter what—rain or shine, war or peace—mother, father, and son would break bread together again.

"I got the idea from Emily Gilmore," she had said.

Vittoria Rose Fugue: Fierce Italian mother and queen of the Sixth Family. And *Gilmore Girls* fan apparently.

Tommy relented, but extracted another promise from her, which brought him to Crema Coffee House.

Crema was Denver at its eclectic best: industrial with funky art inside, and outside a giant yellow mural of a fearsome snake baring its fangs, warning DON'T TREAD ON ME. Upon closer inspection, the snake was coiled in the shape of fallopian tubes.

Tommy smiled. If he was going to be stuck somewhere, there were a hell of a lot worse places than Denver.

As Nine held the door, Tommy removed his sunglasses, rolled his shoulders back, and reached into his pocket. He removed two gunmetal-gray d20 and rolled them between his fingers. Part good luck charm, part calling card, they soothed him like a fidget spinner.

In frightening situations in the past, he had dissociated or pretended he was inside the world of Tergivers.

There would be no such fugue states today.

Nine peeled off to the coffee bar while Tommy scanned the café. He spotted Sanse sitting alone at a table.

She stood awkwardly when she saw him, looking like she wanted to hug him but stopping herself. In truth, he wanted her to hug him. Despite everything, it felt weird not to, but he simply took the seat across from her.

"Thank you for agreeing to meet me," he said.

"I missed you," she said.

Hearing it warmed him. He wanted to believe it. But there was what he wanted and what needed to be done. It was a hard lesson to learn, but he had learned it.

"Is this conversation being recorded?"

Her expression fell. A mixture of disappointment and shame. Her eyes welled up with tears. She blinked them away and shook her head.

He nodded, accepting this. That didn't mean there wasn't surveillance, parabolic mics, a bug under the table. It wasn't like he was going to say anything incriminating, but he wasn't above a little passive-aggressiveness.

"I have to ask." He cocked his head gently to one side, maintaining eye contact. "I'm sure you understand."

Nine approached, placed a latte before him, then resumed his place at the bar. Sanse watched him go.

"Are you still working with law enforcement?" he asked.

"You're really going to make this hard on me."

He sighed. That was as hard as he could go. It was pointless to pretend otherwise.

"You broke my heart, Sanse. You lied to me. But I know what it's like to lose a parent and I wouldn't wish that on anyone. I'm truly sorry about what happened to your father. In all the crazy, I never said that."

Sanse could no longer hold back her tears. She cupped her hands to her face and her shoulders shook. People at other tables looked at him disapprovingly—at the unfeeling, sharply dressed man breaking up with the poor woman in public. He pulled his pocket square from his breast pocket and handed it over.

She wiped her eyes. "I never meant to hurt you, Tommy," she cried. "I just wanted justice. I thought you of all people would understand."

Tommy understood. He was the one who'd pointed the finger at her father. And his father had the man killed, even if he hadn't done it himself.

But it was Turdo who'd set it all in motion.

Turdo, whose treachery—as well as the full scope of the Fugue Family's bold gambit—was revealed before Don Coniglio. The stunned architect of the failed mutiny was last seen being escorted from the meet by the Johnnies. And when the Johnnies had returned, the normally verbose duo had gone stone silent.

"What if I told you justice was served?"

"Sure," she said bitterly. She made a skeptical face. "I've heard that fairy tale before. People telling me ever since I was a little girl that it'll be okay, because God has a plan. . . ."

Tommy looked her in the eye, his natural warmth gone cold.

She looked up from the pocket square.

"The Bad Old Days that took your father are over, and those who started them have seen the error of their ways."

"That's it? I'm just supposed to accept that? Just a big misunderstanding, then, Sanse? Sorry about growing up without a father, but hey, Tommy said it's all good, so it's time to move on, I guess?"

Tommy spread his hands, showed they were empty. He wished he could offer her more. He wished he could tell her sometimes mob justice was better than no justice at all, but he couldn't. Still, he held her gaze.

"You have no idea," she said, "how much I loved my father."

"That sounds nice."

Tommy heard the door to the café jingle behind him and watched Sanse's mouth fall open.

"Tommy," he heard his mother say, *"I had no idea you were going to be here."*

It was part of their deal: His mother would parade herself publicly, in front of Sanse and anyone else who might be watching. He didn't need to turn around to see that she was resplendent. It was in the eyes of every man and woman in the coffee house.

After their double takes, the other patrons fell back into their coffees or conversations or phones. Nine's job was to count the ones who stared long after it was polite. Those were the undercovers, realizing their case had just blown up in their faces. Tommy imagined that if he listened hard enough, he could hear a pair of detectives swear profusely from the van down the street. He stifled a smile.

From behind him, his mother put her hands on his shoulders. She wore a conspicuously fashionable wide-brimmed floppy hat that momentarily blocked his view of Sanse when she bent over to kiss his cheek. In that, she reminded Tommy of Nine's Macarro: Nothing was worth doing if he couldn't look good while doing it.

"Hey, Mom."

Over his other shoulder stood Jolene.

"So nice to see you again," said Jo in an even tone, staring at Sanse. Jo looked good, though, fresh. After New York, she'd started going to meetings. He was proud of her. If Nine was still settling into this new hybrid role of bodyguard and friend, Jo was settling into her role as consigliere and cool aunt, if said cool aunt started barroom brawls and knew how to fillet someone with a switchblade. She was no longer required to serve the Family, but like Tommy, she had some catching up to do with Vittoria.

"We're just out for a girls' lunch," said his mom. "I'm telling her all about my extended shopping trip abroad. I thought I'd get a latte. And here you are."

"Here I am," said Tommy, eyes still fixed on Sanse.

"You must be Sanse," said Vittoria, gushing. She held out her hand, her long nails polished and glowing. Sanse was too stunned not to take it. "I've heard *so* much about you. I've been *dying* to meet you."

Easy does it, Mom, thought Tommy.

"Anyway, I'm back in town for good. Honestly, my boys couldn't survive another day without me. A family needs a woman in charge, don't you agree?"

Sanse nodded, still stupefied.

"You simply must come over for dinner. Now that my trip is over, I plan on spending a lot more time with Tommy. And his friends. And I could *kill* for some girl talk."

Tommy rolled his eyes, then remembered to make it part of the act and added some jokiness to it. "All right, we get it. You can go now."

"Let's *disappear,* Jo. Give these kids their space."

"Mom."

"Love you, Tommy."

"Bye, Mom."

"Remember: Sunday night."

"Yes, Mom."

Tommy watched an astonished Sanse watch his mother glide out of Crema. Only when the front door had closed, with his mother safely on the other side of it and passing the DON'T TREAD ON ME mural, could Sanse pull her gaze back to Tommy.

"She was missing, Tommy. For a *year*."

"Would you believe there was terrible cell reception in Monte Carlo?"

The color began returning to Sanse's face. It painted her as embarrassed, angry.

"You thought she was dead. I know you did. Or was that all just a lie to get me into bed?"

"We never made it that far. There were two detectives in there, remember? And I already told you I wasn't a psychopath sex fiend."

He smiled then. Despite herself, she laughed.

"Look, school is starting soon, and I didn't want there to be any awkwardness," he said. He stood and buttoned his jacket. Across the room, Nine did the same. Tommy waved at the undercovers. "Now all your friends know the score. My mother is alive and well, so they can *fade the fuck out*."

Sanse looked up at him. "So, what, you're like some gangster now?"

"Far from it. But I'm no rat either."

"That sounds an awful lot like 'I'm just a legitimate businessman.'"

"I *am* a legitimate businessman," Tommy said with a grin. Nine joined him at his side. "See you around campus, Sanse."

She called after him. "So that's it, then? We're just going back to school like nothing happened? That's your plan?"

"My plan?"

He paused as Nine held the door for him.

Sanse was right. He had big goals, but a goal without a plan was just a wish. He thought of his upcoming course load, all the work he had to do to get Tergivers to the next level, and now the added headache of weekly dinners with his parents. But he had his friends Nine and Jo by his side. He had a real creative partner in Anibal. And now a dragon-slaying, moon-wrangling agent in Helene.

Despite the bloodshed, his first campaign had been a wild success. His adventurers had each earned their blades, and he had even freed the queen. It was time to set his eyes on Tergivers' next campaign.

He donned his sunglasses and smiled, then stepped back into the fresh Denver air.

"My plan is world domination, baby."

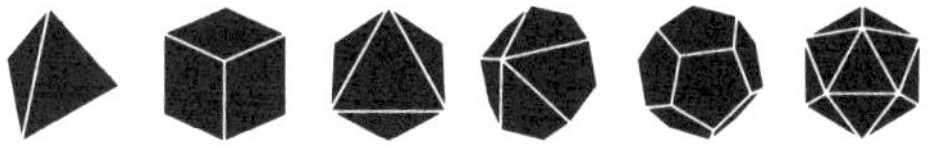

Epilogue

Endings are tricky.

They can be surprising or inevitable, satisfying or leaving one wanting more . . . but mostly endings are tricky because farewells are tricky. Still, a successful campaign needs to know when to say goodbye.

Then again . . . that's campaigns. Friendship *is about knowing when* not *to say goodbye.*

There are always new trails to blaze, strange realms to discover, and more dragons to slay—new campaigns.

Case in point: the Silverback Mammoth Dragon blocking the party's path. There are rolling green fields on either side of the path, so there is no cover and no concealment.

Taller than a castle tower, it looms over Bellarmina, Macarro, Bradford, and their newest companion: the young sorcerer Moebius, whom they met on the Aran trail. Massive silver tusks curve from either side of the beast's fearsome mouth, and when it spreads its leathery wings, they blot out the sun. What light touches its gleaming armored plates makes it look afire.

The Mammoth Dragon issues a mighty roar, shaking the ground.

"I don't suppose it has a thorn stuck in its paw?" asks Macarro.

The only thorn is the proverbial one in its side: namely, the band of adventurers in its path. The Mammoth Dragon stretches its neck and rears back its head, drawing in a mighty breath.

"It's gonna vent," says Bellarmina. "Behind me."

Bellarmina plants her feet as the Mammoth Dragon snaps its long neck forward like a mighty whip and throws open its fanged jaws. The gargantuan beast indeed vents, but rather than fire issuing from its mouth, out comes a massive blast of ice.

"They can do that*?" yells Bellarmina.*

Of course they can.

"Fuck this." Bellarmina stands firm and raises her Blade of Discipline as the dragon spews a concentrated blizzard in the party's direction. Blistering cold, howling winds, daggers of ice . . . all in a single blast.

Bellarmina faces it, her obsidian sword held edge first—and cleaves the wintry assault in two. Sheets of ice pass harmlessly on either side of her.

Breath weapon expelled, the Mammoth Dragon is temporarily weakened. It rears back once more to nourish itself with air and prepare for another volley, and in so doing exposes its underbelly, where the scales are not as dense as the larger plates on its silver back.

Macarro takes the opportunity and vaults across the fresh ice floe. He somersaults in midair toward the dragon, clutching his Blade of Love. He spins so fast, the silver-hilted sword, resplendent with turquoise and bone, flashes like a dazzling pinwheel.

But the Blade of Love glances off the pale scales of the dragon's underbelly.

"Nuts," says Macarro.

The dragon draws itself up to its full height then, looking down at the irritant at its belly. It blinks slowly, registering its opponent.

"No hard feelings?" says the warrior with a shrug.

Jaws agape, rows of teeth bared, each fang the size of a man, the large head dives toward its opponent.

In a flash, Bradford bounds to Macarro's side, shoves the young warrior out of the way.

"I have a plan," says the barbarian. "Mammoth Dragons, thanks to their durable scales, have near-impervious hides . . . from the outside. Barbarian skin is pretty damn tough, so the first step of my plan is to hold the dragon's mouth shut—"

"Um, what?" ask Macarro and Moebius in unison.

Bradford appears to be out of sorts, even more rash than usual, and seemingly heedless of his own safety.

"No," explains Bradford, "if the average strength for most humanoids is like a ten or eleven, barbarians are a solid twenty. So I hold the mouth shut until he swallows that next ice-breath thing, and then I get Big Boy to swallow me *whole. I can survive long enough to cut my way out with the Blade of Wisdom."*

Macarro makes a face and asks, "Does the blade impart *any wisdom to its wielder?"*

Bradford shrugs. But the time for talk is over as the dragon's head—the size of a locomotive, its jaws flung wide—charges down at the barbarian.

"Locomotives aren't actually in Tergivers," says Moebius. "Too modern—"

Okay, the Tergivers-appropriate comp for a locomotive is what comes to everyone's mind.

"A galleon . . . or maybe an airship."

Fine. The Mammoth Dragon's head—the size of a galleon or maybe an airship—charges at the barbarian, its jaws flung wide.

Bradford spreads his arms and turns his face toward the onrushing maw of the Mammoth Dragon, closes his eyes, and smiles beatifically.

"Rolling," says Bradford.

At the last second, the barbarian catches the Mammoth Dragon's head in his strapping arms.

"Ha!" yells Bradford.

With a jerk of its mighty head, the Mammoth Dragon flings the barbarian high into the air. As Bradford somersaults toward his apex, the massive creature unleashes an obliterating ice blast. The icicled barbarian plummets back to the ground, but in a bite as fast as a lightning strike, the beast catches him in its jaws. In fairness, part of Bradford's plan works: The majority of the barbarian passes down the Mammoth Dragon's long gullet; however, the Blade of Wisdom—and the frozen, severed arm that still grasps it—lands at the remainder of the disbelieving party's feet.

"Holy *fuck* . . ." said Nine Ball.

Tommy and the players sat around the deluxe gaming table in silence. A dizzying upgrade from Tommy's scarred, second-hand veneer table, this one—a model called the "Excalibur"—was solid walnut and featured a recessed playing area, a convertible topper, removable velvet and rubber playing surfaces, and a magnetic accessory rail system around the perimeter for cup-holders and trays. Those accoutrements were more than enough to satisfy his needs, but the table also included a Game Master Command Center, LED mood lighting, built-in Bluetooth speakers, and hidden storage cubbies beneath, where Tommy could keep rule books, campaign notes, dice . . . even an actual weapon.

Delivered a week after Tommy's rebellion in New York, the Excalibur came with a card that read: *Every crew needs a table. —Pop*

It was as close to an apology as Don Alessandro Fugue would

ever manage, but Tommy had to admit, it was the most beautiful olive branch he had ever seen. He often caught himself marveling at its design and features mid-game, but now all he and everyone else stared at was the die with the number one face up.

"Are you serious right now?" asked Nine, still stunned by Bradford's sudden fate.

Anibal clamped his hand over his mouth, his shoulders shaking with stifled laughter.

Tommy stared at the mini-fig of Bradford, which almost seemed to stare back at him accusingly. Porks had presented a problem IRL. He had been a mole for Big Al, and Tommy had taken his revenge on his club. When Tommy had returned from New York—even before the Excalibur had arrived—the pimp had shown up at his apartment unannounced. Tommy had braced for war. Still, he'd opened the door, scanning Porks's hands for weapons and his baggy shirt for bulges as he invited the troll in.

Porks hadn't even waited for the door to close behind him to rush Tommy.

But Tommy was ready. If he could throw hands with Big Al, he was confident he could handle a goblin pimp. He brought his fists up, but before Tommy knew it, the pimp went low and wrapped his arms around Tommy's waist.

"I'm so glad you're back!" said Porks.

"Ew, get off!" said Tommy, shoving him aside. "What are you doing?"

Porks dropped to his knees and clasped his hands in front of him. "Don't cast me out, kid, I'm begging you!"

"Why the fuck would I want you anywhere near me or my friends?"

"Because *I'm* your friend too!"

"You're a *pimp* my father saddled me with."

"No!" said Porks, breaking into the smile of a true believer. "Thanks to you, I'm an *ex*-pimp. The Navel was a fucking albatross around my neck. But now? No more yammering girls, no more sweaty johns. No cheap perfume, no shitty music. Don't you understand? You set me free, kid! Thanks to you, I can game full-time now. I'm in a world of pure imagination. It's like Viagra for the soul, Tommy!"

"Keep your soul hard-on in your pants, Porks." Tommy was surprised but not convinced. And yet, Porks didn't smell quite as bad as he usually did, so maybe he *had* changed up a few things. "There's still the matter of you being a mole for my father."

Porks was shaking his head before Tommy could even finish. "I had no choice. But now I'm done. No club, no Porks. I'm out!"

"There is no 'out' with my father. You of all people should know that."

Porks's eyes looked wild, desperate; then they narrowed to clever slits and a smirk spread across his pudgy face. "Yes, I passed information to your father. But at any gaming table, information often flows in multiple directions. . . ."

Tommy was listening. It was interesting, the prospect of a double agent. Tommy considered alignments: There was Lawful Evil, Neutral Evil, and Chaotic Evil. But maybe Porks was something new: Necessary Evil. His own man on the inside, a reverse mole, keeping tabs on his father.

"Why should I trust you?"

"Because the rat is gone and everything is back to normal . . . but whatever. You can trust me because *you* taught this old dog a new trick. You and your game showed me I could be more than who I was. Wasn't that the point of Tergivers—or was it all bullshit?"

The old perv had a point.

But now Bradford was dead.

"He's really gone?" asked Jo.

Tommy gave a somber nod. A hush fell across the Excalibur.

Shortly, the silence was broken by the flushing of a toilet.

"*Who's* gone?" asked Porks, hiking up his pants as he emerged from the bathroom.

"I didn't mean it . . ." said Jo.

"Oh no. You don't mean . . . not Bradford. He was too beautiful for Tergivers," said Porks, suddenly somber. Then he snapped. "What the fuck, Jo? I was gone for two minutes!"

"*Twenty* minutes," said Nine.

"Irregardless! I knew I shouldn't have let you babysit my—" The ex-pimp pointed a stubby finger at her. "Bellarmina *always hated* Bradford!"

"It was an accident," said Jo. "Hand to God."

"It was an overly complicated strategy, almost deliberately so," said Anibal, making a skeptical face. "Practically begging to fail."

"Quiet, Baby Delgado," said Jo.

Porks glared at Tommy. "You're gonna let this stand?"

Tommy did think the whole thing was kind of funny, not that he took pleasure in it. Still, a game's not a game if there are no rules. "She rolled a nat 1. Critical failure, dude. Rules are rules."

"Did I at least go out like a champ?"

Nine and Anibal made uneasy sounds while Jo looked off to the side. Tommy winced.

Porks drew in a long, deep breath, much like the Silverback Mammoth Dragon that had eaten his avatar. They all awaited some—admittedly deserved—tirade from the little man. But instead of spewing a deadly ice blast of his own, he heaved a wistful sigh.

"Eh. I figured something like this would happen. Wisdom, don'tcha know," he said, tapping his temple. "That's why I have *this*. . . ."

Porks reached into his back pocket, removed a crumpled sheet of paper, and smoothed it on the pristine felt surface of the Excalibur. Nine recoiled. Everyone else leaned in.

It was a new character sheet.

"It was time for a fresh start anyway," said Porks.

"Another barbarian . . ." said Tommy, reading. He looked from the sheet to Porks. "And his name is *Bradford . . . son*."

Porks put his hands on his hips and puffed out his chest, striking a hero's pose. "That's because he's the *son* of Bradford."

"I picked that up from the context clues, but thanks, Porks, very helpful."

"How's that a fresh start?" asked Anibal.

"He's younger than Bradford, stronger than Bradford, and wiser than Bradford," Porks said, flashing a grin at Jo. "But Bradfordson is double-hung, just like his old man."

Jo reached beneath the table. Tommy half expected the Stinger's hand to surface with a blade, but instead she lifted a mug from her magnetic cupholder, shook her head, and sipped her peppermint tea.

Once Porks settled down, he resumed his seat and pulled out a second mini-fig that looked suspiciously like Bradford.

Nine lifted a finger to address Tommy. "I have to ask: We have our blades and the queen is free, so like, what's next?"

"Step one," said Anibal, "maybe defeat the Silverback Mammoth Dragon?"

Nine ignored him. "What's the point, Tommy? What are we looking for?"

"I've been giving that some thought," said Tommy. He opened

the Excalibur's secret cubby, grabbed a fistful of flat metal objects, and flung them across the table.

Jo was the first to pick one up. "A key?"

"Keys, plural," said Tommy. "To the kingdom."

"I don't get it," said Porks.

Tommy placed his fists on the table and rose from his seat. "We exposed a hidden spy, defeated an evil lord, and even freed a captive queen, only to discover that nothing has really changed. The realm itself is flawed, corrupt. Rotten. So maybe it's time we stopped roaming Tergivers."

"And do what?"

"And rule it," said Tommy. He looked from player to player, then reached across the Excalibur. "Ourselves."

One by one, the party placed their outstretched hands over their game master's.

Acknowledgments

Like the novel you've just read, these acknowledgments will be a heady brew of fantasy and gangster puns. Proceed at your own risk.

The first person to thank is Adam Wilson, plot master and editor extraordinaire. He was the first to sound the call of adventure and the man who made me an offer I couldn't refuse. I'm so very grateful you brought this project to me, and it's been a joy to build this world with you. I would also like to hoist a flagon of mead to the following alchemists, bards, and warlocks at Hyperion Avenue who—through their arcane sorcery—helped bring this enchanted tome to life and convey it to your waiting hands, dear reader: Amy C. King, Henry Sene Yee, Sylvia Davis, Meredith Jones, Guy Cunningham, Sara Liebling, Crystal McCoy, Raegan Cutrino, Matt Schweitzer, Daneen Goodwin, Greta Shull, Augusta Harris, Lauren Burniac, Holly Rice, Olivia Zavitson, Monique Diman, Vicki Korlishin, Jen Levesque, and Tonya Agurto.

Much gratitude goes to Barbara Poelle, my agent and very own paladin. Charismatic and tireless, she crusades on my behalf. You have my pen.

And hearty cheers to Don Bentley and Nick Petrie, my brothers-in-arms in this writing campaign and weavers of their own magical tales; Rachel Liang, Jeff Liang, and Nino Zambito, who answered my endless questions and showed me the ropes; and the *Major Spoilers* crew of Stephen Schleicher, Rodrigo Lopez, and Matthew Peterson—I first learned by listening to you.

I would also like to raise some Grind to my own consiglieri—Wade Townsend, Greg Ferry, and George Bamford—and to the original gangsters, Linda Schweigart and Jaclin Madarang, and the entire Beech Avenue/Ocean City crew. *Salute!*

And there are not words enough to express my love, gratitude, and devotion to Kate Schweigart, Sidney Schweigart, and Samaira Kale. Thank you for always having my back. Together, we are a perfectly balanced adventuring party, and with you by my side, I can storm any dungeon or slay any dragon.

And finally, the Mighty Bear. He led the way on countless long walks, allowing me to get lost in the stories in my head while always guiding me safely home. Pure of heart, there was no more loyal companion in all the land.